Rom 8/6/23

P9-CBB-214

Serena mentally threw up her hands.

This was hopeless. Why did she even care if something was bothering this boorish man who had come stomping into her house, disrupting everyone without even displaying an iota of remorse that he was doing it? Never mind that her brother had led this invasion into her parents' home. She felt better blaming the detective for this than blaming Finn.

"Never mind," she told Carson, changing topics. "I have to see to my baby—if it's all right with you," she said, a mild touch of sarcasm breaking through.

Rather than say anything in response, Carson just waved her back to her quarters.

Serena's voice was fairly dripping with ice as she said, "Thank you."

With that she turned on her bare heel to walk back into her suite.

"Let's go, Justice," Carson said to the dog, steering the animal toward the stairs.

Keeping a tight hold on the dog's leash, Carson walked out of the house quickly, a man doing his best to outrun memories too painful to coexist with.

UNEXPECTED PROTECTOR

USA TODAY BESTSELLING AUTHOR

MARIE FERRARELLA

& JUSTINE DAVIS

Previously published as *Colton Baby Rescue*
and *Operation Midnight*

If you purchased this book without a cover you should be aware that this book is stolen property. It was reported as "unsold and destroyed" to the publisher, and neither the author nor the publisher has received any payment for this "stripped book."

Recycling programs for this product may not exist in your area.

ISBN-13: 978-1-335-45484-3

Unexpected Protector

Copyright © 2020 by Harlequin Books S.A.

Colton Baby Rescue
First published in 2018. This edition published in 2020.
Copyright © 2018 by Harlequin Books S.A.

Special thanks and acknowledgment are given to
Marie Ferrarella for her contribution to The Coltons of Red Ridge
miniseries.

Operation Midnight
First published in 2012. This edition published in 2020.
Copyright © 2012 by Janice Davis Smith

All rights reserved. No part of this book may be used or reproduced in any manner whatsoever without written permission except in the case of brief quotations embodied in critical articles and reviews.

This is a work of fiction. Names, characters, places and incidents are either the product of the author's imagination or are used fictitiously. Any resemblance to actual persons, living or dead, businesses, companies, events or locales is entirely coincidental.

This edition published by arrangement with Harlequin Books S.A.

For questions and comments about the quality of this book,
please contact us at CustomerService@Harlequin.com.

Harlequin Enterprises ULC
22 Adelaide St. West, 40th Floor
Toronto, Ontario M5H 4E3, Canada
www.Harlequin.com

Printed in U.S.A.

CONTENTS

USA TODAY bestselling and RITA® Award–winning author **Marie Ferrarella** has written more than two hundred and fifty books for Harlequin, some under the name Marie Nicole. Her romances are beloved by fans worldwide. Visit her website, marieferrarella.com.

Books by Marie Ferrarella

Harlequin Romantic Suspense

The Coltons of Mustang Valley

Colton Baby Conspiracy

Cavanaugh Justice

Cavanaugh's Bodyguard
Cavanaugh Fortune
How to Seduce a Cavanaugh
Cavanaugh or Death
Cavanaugh Cold Case
Cavanaugh in the Rough
Cavanaugh on Call
Cavanaugh Encounter
Cavanaugh Vanguard
Cavanaugh Cowboy
Cavanaugh's Missing Person

Visit the Author Profile page
at Harlequin.com for more titles.

COLTON BABY RESCUE

Marie Ferrarella

To
Nancy Parodi Neubert
And
The Successful Return
Of
Happiness

Chapter 1

He *really* did not have time for this.

Detective Carson Gage frowned as he drove down the darkened streets to The Pour House. He had more important things to do than attend his older brother Bo's bachelor party at a second-rate dive bar in the sketchy part of town.

Hell, he would have rather stayed home and spent the evening talking to his K-9 unit partner, Justice. Granted it would have only been a one-way conversation, but the German shepherd was probably more intelligent than half the people who were going to be at the bachelor party anyway.

This whole thing was a joke, the Red Ridge police detective thought. Bo shouldn't be getting married anyway, not to a woman who he'd only known for a total of three months. This was way too sudden.

The whole thing seemed rather strange to him, not to

mention ironic. Bo's bachelor party was being thrown at The Pour House, which just happened to be owned by Rusty Colton, who was the father of Bo's last girlfriend, Demi—the woman Bo had been engaged to for one month, then dumped when he took up with Hayley Patton, his current bride-to-be.

More than likely, Carson thought dourly, given who was being invited to this party, the evening was going to end up in a huge brawl—which was why he intended to stay for just one drink, then get the hell out of there.

Besides, he had work to do. His burning obsession was to find some piece of irrefutable evidence he could use to finally put away the Larson brothers, the cold-blooded twins who fancied themselves up-and-coming crime lords intent on building up a vast criminal empire and destroying everything and everyone in their path.

The Larsons were behind at least two murders that he knew of and they were at the center of a rash of drug busts, but because the thugs who worked for the brothers were more afraid of them than they were of the police, he hadn't been able to find anyone willing to testify against the twins.

But he would. Come hell or high water, he would, Carson swore, his hands tightening on his car's steering wheel. All he needed was to find that one elusive piece of evidence that would start the process of nailing the Larson brothers' coffins shut.

Carson picked his way through the streets, driving slowly. The area seemed even more unsavory at this time of night than it was during the day.

"If you *have* to marry this one, why couldn't you just run off and elope like a normal guy?" Carson asked out loud, addressing the brother who wasn't there. "Why all this need for fanfare and hoopla?"

It almost seemed, what with having the bachelor party at The Pour House, like Bo was deliberately rubbing Demi's nose in his wedding.

Yup, fireworks were definitely going to be on the agenda tonight, Carson thought. One beer and he was out of there, he promised himself again. He had no burning desire to break up a bunch of drunken men who should know better, doing their damnedest to knock each other's heads off. Bo had said he was inviting both Coltons and Gages to this party. Gasoline and fire, Carson thought.

He swore under his breath. No, he definitely didn't need this.

With a sigh, he pulled into The Pour House's parking lot. Because he wanted to be able to drive off the lot with a minimum of maneuvering—*and* make sure that his car didn't get dented by some celebrant who had overindulged in liquid courage, Carson decided to park all the way in the back of the lot. It would be a bit of a trek to the bar's front door, but it was between that and his peace of mind, and his peace of mind definitely made it worth it.

So he guided his vehicle all the way to the last row of the lot. The lot happened to back up against a grassy embankment.

Pulling up the hand brake, he sat there for a while, trying to get into the right frame of mind.

It wasn't happening.

With a sigh, the police detective got out of his car and locked it. Carson was about to start walking toward the entrance of the bar when he thought he saw someone lying facedown at the very far edge of the lot.

Carson paused, squinting. That part of the parking

lot was pretty dark. What streetlights there were didn't reach that far.

"Looks like someone's already been partying too much," he muttered under his breath.

Some people just couldn't pace themselves accordingly and this guy obviously couldn't hold his liquor, Carson thought. With a resigned sigh, he changed course and headed toward the drunk instead of the bar. If he didn't wake the guy up and get him out of the way, Carson had no doubt that during the course of the evening, someone was liable to run the drunk over.

The lot wasn't all that full yet, he observed. This guy must have got a *really* early start. From what he could make out, the man was half on the edge of the lot, half on the grass at the very perimeter of the parking lot.

Drawing nearer, Carson saw that the man, whose face was obscured because it was turned toward the grass, had one arm stretched out with his index finger raised, like he was trying to draw attention to something.

That's odd.

And then, despite the fact that it was pretty dark there, Carson saw that there was writing on the ground just above the man's head. It looked as if he had written something—

In blood?

Taking his phone out, he hit the flashlight app, then squatted down. Using the light from his phone, Carson looked at the ground just above the man's head more closely.

"It looks like you wrote *Demi C*," Carson murmured, half to himself. The last letter was barely finished.

Demi C? Demi Colton?

Carson's eyes widened. What was this guy doing,

writing the name of his brother's former girlfriend on the parking lot asphalt? And where had the blood come from? Had the guy hit his head?

"Hey, fella, wake up. The parking lot's no place to take a nap." He shook the man's shoulder but couldn't seem to rouse him.

Blowing out a breath, Carson rose to his feet and circled the man's body so he could get a look at the drunk's face.

"C'mon, fella, you can't sleep it off here. You've gotta get—"

The rest of the sentence froze on Carson's lips.

The man he was trying to wake up was his brother. Bo's eyes were wide-open and unseeing.

There was a black cummerbund stuffed into his mouth. And he wasn't breathing.

Chapter 2

Detective Carson Gage's hands were shaking as he urgently turned his brother over onto his back. Any hope of trying to revive Bo disappeared the moment he saw the bullet wound.

His brother had been shot right through the heart.

Irrationally, Carson felt for a pulse anyway. There was none. Swallowing a curse, he sat back on his heels. His brother's skin was already cold to the touch. This was January in Red Ridge, South Dakota, but death brought a different sort of cold with it and there was no mistaking it for a simple reaction to the weather.

"Damn it, Bo, I *told* you playing fast and loose with women would be the death of you someday. Why d'you have to prove me right?" Carson demanded angrily.

He curbed his impulse to straighten Bo's clothing. Bo always took pride in his appearance and death had left him looking disheveled. But the crime scene investigators were going to need to see everything just the way he had found it.

Shaken to the core, Carson got back up to his feet and opened up his cell phone again. He needed to call this in.

It took him a minute to center his thoughts. He was a trained police detective, Carson silently upbraided himself. He couldn't afford the luxury of coming apart like some hysterical civilian who had just unexpectedly witnessed death up close and personal—even if this *was* his half brother.

Taking a deep breath and then exhaling, he put in a call to his chief, Finn Colton. As he waited for Finn to pick up, he looked again at the name his brother had written in his own blood.

Demi C.

Demi Colton. Carson shook his head. When this got out, it was going to throw all of Red Ridge into one hell of an uproar, he thought. As if the feud between the Coltons and the Gages needed more fuel.

The next moment, he heard Finn's deep voice as the chief answered his phone. "Hey, Gage, aren't you supposed to be at your brother's bachelor party right now, getting drunk and toasting Bo's last few hours of freedom? What are you doing calling me?"

Carson enunciated the words carefully, afraid that if he spoke any faster, his voice was going to break. He and Bo weren't close, but they were still family. "There's been a murder, Chief."

"Damn," Finn cursed. Instantly, the voice on the other end became serious. "Whose?"

Carson paused before answering. "Bo's."

"This your idea of a joke, Gage?" Finn demanded impatiently. "'Cause if it is, it's not funny."

"I only wish it was, Chief," Carson answered.

"You're serious," Finn responded, stunned. When no contradiction came, Finn asked, "Where and when?"

Carson looked down at his brother's body. The whole scene seemed utterly surreal to him. "I just found him two minutes ago, lying facedown at the edge of The Pour House's parking lot."

"The Pour House," Finn repeated. "Isn't that where his bachelor party is supposed to be taking place tonight?"

"One and the same," Carson answered his superior numbly. He realized he was leaving the most important part out. "And, Chief?"

"Yeah?"

"Looks like Bo wrote a name in his own blood. Maybe his killer's name."

Carson heard a noise on the other end as the other man said something unintelligible before going on to ask, "Whose name did he write?"

"Demi C."

This time there was total silence on the other end for approximately thirty seconds as the information sank in.

The city of thirty-five thousand citizens had more than its share of Coltons. There were three branches in total, as different from one another as the seasons were. The chief liked to say that he belonged to the middle branch, the one that was neither rich nor poor and rough around the edges.

But whatever section he gravitated to, the chief was still a Colton and Carson couldn't help wondering how Finn Colton would deal with having to bring in one of his own as a suspect for first-degree murder.

Finally, the chief broke the silence and asked, "You think Bo wrote that?"

"It's in his own blood, Chief," Carson answered. Then, in case there was any further question as to whether or not Bo was the one who wrote the name, he added, "There's blood underneath Bo's fingernail. Looks like he wrote it."

Finn sighed as if the weight of the world had suddenly been dropped on his shoulders.

"Good enough for me," he replied. "I'll have Demi brought in for questioning. Meanwhile, I'll send some of the team to bring in your brother's body." His voice softened, as if he was feeling sympathetic about what Carson was going through. "You can give your statement in the morning if you need some time, Gage."

Finn was cutting him some slack, Carson thought. He didn't want any slack, he wanted to get his brother's killer.

Now.

"I don't need any time, Chief." Somewhere in the distance, a coyote howled. Carson would have been hard-pressed to name a lonelier sound. "I'll stay here with Bo until the detail gets here," he told his boss. "And then I'm coming down to the station. I want to be there when you interrogate Demi."

"Gage, you can't—"

Carson felt the walls going up. He cut Finn off before the chief could officially exclude him. "I *need* to be there when you question her, Finn. You owe this to me, Chief."

There was silence again. An annoyed silence if he was any judge, Carson thought. He fully expected the chief to argue with him, but he wasn't about to back down.

However, Finn surprised him by saying, "All right,

you can be there, but I'll be the one handling the interrogation. I don't want to hear a word out of you, understood?"

Even though Finn couldn't see him, Carson nodded his head grimly. "Understood."

Terminating the call, Carson put his phone into his pocket. Silence enshrouded him although the distant sound of music and raised voices coming from the bar sliced through the air, disrupting the night.

"Sounds like your bachelor party's getting underway without you," Carson said to the prone figure near his feet. "Not exactly the way you expected the night to go, is it?" he asked ironically. He squared his shoulders. No, he and Bo hadn't been close, but Bo was still his brother and he didn't deserve this. "Don't worry, Bo. If Demi did this, she'll pay. I don't know what happened, but I promise she'll pay. I'll see to it."

It was getting colder. Carson pulled his sheepskin jacket tighter around him and turned up the collar. But he remained where he was, a guard at his post. He wasn't about to go anywhere until the unit came to pick up Bo's body.

"I know my rights. I'm a bounty hunter, damn it, and I know my rights better than you do," twenty-seven-year-old Demetria Colton shouted angrily at the two police officers who brought her into the small, windowless room within the Red Ridge police station. "Why am I here?" she wanted to know.

But neither of the two police officers, one young, one old, answered her, other than one of them telling her, "The chief'll be here shortly."

"The 'chief'?" Demi repeated in a mocking tone.

"You mean Cousin *Finn*? Is he still pretending to be in charge?"

The two officers left the small eight-by-ten room without answering her. An angry, guttural noise escaped the redhead's lips. Frustrated, she would have thrown something if she'd had something to throw.

"Why am I here?" she demanded again, more loudly this time. Furious, she began to pound on the locked door. "I know you're out there! I demand to be released. You can't hold me here like this, you hear me?" she cried. "I haven't *done* anything, damn it! You let me out of here! Now!"

When the door suddenly opened just as she was about to start pounding on it again, Demi was caught off guard and stumbled backward. Had the table not been right there behind her to block her fall, she would have unceremoniously landed on the floor.

"You're here," her cousin calmly told her as he and Carson walked into the room, acting as if they were about to have a run-of-the-mill, normal conversation, "to answer some questions."

Demi tossed her head, her red hair flying over her shoulder.

"What kind of questions?" she asked defiantly, her dark brown gaze pinning him down.

"Like where were you tonight?" Finn wanted to know, gesturing toward the lone chair on the opposite side of the table and indicating that she should sit.

"Home," Demi bit off, grudgingly sitting down. "I was in my home—since 5:00 p.m." she added for good measure.

Finn gave no indication whether or not the answer satisfied him. He waited until Carson sat down next to him, then asked, "Alone?"

"Yes," she bit off, then followed that up with a question of her own. "Why?" she demanded. Squaring her shoulders, she drew herself up and raised her chin, always ready to do battle with the world—and her cousin. "Is that a crime now?"

Hearing Carson's chair scrape along the floor as he started to rise, Finn shot him a warning look before answering Demi's question. "No, but murder is."

"Murder," the redhead repeated, growing more furious by the second. She made the only logical conclusion. "You think I *murdered* someone?" she cried, stunned. "And just who is it I was supposed to have murdered?" When Finn didn't answer her immediately, she pounced on him. "C'mon, you can't just throw something like that out and then leave me hanging in suspense, Finn. Just who was it that you think I murdered?"

Unable to remain silent any longer, his hands fisted at his sides, Carson pinned her with a damning look as he answered her question. "Bo. You murdered Bo and then you stuffed a cummerbund into his mouth."

"Bo," she repeated in noncomprehension. And then, for a moment, Demi turned very pale. Her eyes flicked from Bo's brother to her cousin. "Bo's dead?" she asked hoarsely.

It was half a question, half a statement uttered in total disbelief.

Then, not waiting for an answer, what had become known in the county as Demi's famous temper flared, and she jumped up to her feet, her fists banging down on the tabletop.

"You think I killed Bo?" she demanded incredulously, fury flashing in her eyes. "Sure," she said mockingly. "Makes perfect sense to me. The man's dead so let's blame it on the woman he dumped—EXCEPT I

DIDN'T DO IT!" she yelled, her angry gaze sweeping over her cousin and her former fiancé's brother.

"Sit down, Demi," Finn ordered sternly. "And calm down."

Instead of listening to her cousin and taking her seat again, Demi Colton remained standing, a firecracker very close to going off in a flash of fireworks.

"*No*, I will *not* calm down," she cried. "And unless you have some kind of concrete evidence against me—" she said, staring straight at her cousin.

"How about Bo writing your name on the asphalt in his own blood?" Finn said. "Demi C."

Demi paled for a moment. "The killer is framing me?"

Finn raised an eyebrow.

Demi gave him a smug look. "Just as I thought. You *don't* have any sort of actual evidence against me. Okay, I'm out of here," Demi declared.

"You'll leave when I tell you to leave," Finn told her sternly. Rising from his chair on the opposite side of the table, he loomed over her.

"*Do* you have any evidence against me, other than my name written in Bo's blood and the fact that I had the bad judgment to have been engaged to the jerk for a month?" she asked, looking from her cousin to the other man in the room.

Though it obviously killed him, Finn was forced to say, "No, but—"

Triumph filled her eyes. "There is no 'but' here," Demi retorted. "You have *nothing* to hold me on, that means I'm free to go. So I'm going." Her eyes swept over her cousin and Carson. "Gentlemen, it has definitely *not* been a pleasure."

And with that, she swept past them to the interrogation room door like a queen taking leave of a pair of disloyal subjects.

Finn shook his head as his cousin stormed out. "Hell of a lot of nerve," he muttered under his breath.

"As I recall, Demi was never the sweet, retiring type. If she was, she would have never become a bounty hunter," Carson told him.

Finn blew out a breath. "You have a point." He walked out of the interrogation room with Carson directly behind him. "Well, check out her alibi, talk to anyone who might have seen her," the chief said, addressing the victim's brother. "I'm open to any further suggestions."

Carson looked at his boss in mild surprise. "I thought you made it clear that I wasn't allowed to work on my brother's case." Although, he thought, since Finn could work on the case in which his cousin was a suspect, he should be allowed to investigate his brother's murder.

"Technically, you're not," Finn said as they walked out into the main squad room. "But I'm not an idiot, Gage. You're going to work this whether I give you my blessing or not." He stopped just before his office. "So you have any ideas where to start?"

He'd been thinking about this ever since he'd found Bo's body. The fact that Bo had written Demi's name seemed pretty damning to him, but he didn't want to discount the slim possibility that someone else had killed his brother.

It didn't warm his heart to have to admit this, but in all fairness, he had to. "Well, it's common knowledge that Demi wasn't the only woman Bo romanced and then dumped. I'd say that there were a whole lot of women who'd love to have seen Bo get what was coming to him. And that includes a number of disgruntled husbands and boyfriends, as well. Why don't we start talking to them?"

That Bo was a playboy wasn't exactly news to anyone. Finn frowned. "But would any of them actually resort to murder?"

Carson shrugged. Nothing jumped out at him, but this needed closer examination. "Only one way to find out," he told his boss.

"I agree," Finn responded. "Make up a list. Meanwhile, I'm going to have some of the boys go over the crime scene with a fine-tooth comb, see if someone missed anything just in case. Although the ground's undoubtedly been trampled on," he commented.

Carson nodded grimly. "Nobody ever said that solving crimes was easy. I can swing by my place, pick up Justice," he said, referring to his K-9 partner. "See if maybe he can pick up a scent."

"*After* you put that list together," Finn told the detective.

Carson headed over to his desk. Given the hour, the squad room was practically empty. "Will do," he told the chief.

"Oh, and, Gage?" Finn called after him.

Carson turned around, expecting further orders. "Yeah, Chief?"

"I'm really sorry for your loss."

The words were standard-issue, said over and over again in so many instances that they sounded numbingly routine, yet he felt that Finn really meant them.

"Yeah, me, too," Carson answered stoically, then added, "Thanks."

Carson had just finished making a preliminary list of all the women he could remember Bo having had any romantic encounters with over the last several years when J.D. Edwards, one of the crime scene investigators, came into the squad room. J.D. looked excited.

Temporarily forgetting about the list he'd just compiled, Carson crossed over to the man. J.D., in turn, had just cornered Finn.

"You're going to want to hear this," the investigator was saying to Finn.

The chief, seeing Carson, nodded at him, indicating that he join them. Carson was all ears.

"What have you got?" Finn asked.

"Lots," J.D. answered. "First off, I found this under a wheel near where the body was found." He held up a sealed plastic evidence bag. The bag contained a necklace with a gold heart charm.

Finn squinted as he looked at the necklace. "That looks familiar."

"It should be," the investigator said. "It belongs to—"

"Demi," Carson said, recognizing the gold heart. "That's her necklace."

"And that's not all," J.D. informed them. The investigator paused for effect before announcing, "We've got a witness who says he saw Demi Colton running in the shadows around 6:45 p.m. near The Pour House."

"Six forty-five," Carson repeated. He looked at Finn. "I found Bo's body at seven."

J.D. looked rather smug as he said, "Exactly."

"Who's the witness?" Finn wanted to know.

"Paulie Gains," J.D. answered.

Carson frowned. He would have preferred having someone a little more reliable. "Gains is a small-time drug dealer."

"Doesn't mean he couldn't have seen her," Finn

pointed out. He looked at J.D. "How did he know it was Demi? It's dark at that hour."

J.D. laughed. "Not that many people around here have her color hair, Chief."

Finn nodded. J.D. was right. "Okay, that puts her at the scene. Looks like we've got that evidence Demi kept going on about," he told Carson, adding, "Time for that bounty hunter to do some heavy-duty explaining if she intends to walk out of here a second time. Let's go wrestle up an arrest warrant."

Carson didn't have to be told twice. He led the way out the door.

Chapter 3

It took a little time, but Carson and his boss finally found a judge who was willing to issue an arrest warrant at that time of night.

"Do me a favor, lose my number," Judge David Winkler told Finn, closing his front door and going back to his poker game.

Tucking the warrant into his pocket, the chief turned toward Carson. "Let's go. We're not waiting until morning," Finn told the detective as he got back into his vehicle.

Armed with the warrant, for the second time in less than five hours police detectives hurried back to Demi Colton's small ranch house on the outskirts of town, this time to arrest her.

The house was dark when they arrived.

"I've got a bad feeling about this," Carson murmured as he and Finn approached.

Carson knocked on the door. When there was no response, he knocked again, harder this time. Rather than knock a third time, he tried the doorknob. He was surprised to find that the door was unlocked.

Guns drawn, they entered and conducted a quick room-to-room search of the one-story dwelling. There was no one home.

"Damn it." Finn fumed. "My gut told me to keep her in a holding cell and not let her just walk out of the police station like that."

"Looks like some of her clothes are gone," Carson called out to the chief, looking at a cluster of empty hangers in the bounty hunter's bedroom closet.

"Yeah, well, so is she," Finn answered from the kitchen. When Carson joined him, Finn held up the note he'd found on the kitchen table.

"What's that, a confession?" Carson asked, coming around to look at the piece of notepaper.

"Just the opposite," Finn told him in disgust. "It says 'I'm innocent.'"

Carson said what he assumed they were both thinking. "Innocent people don't run."

The chief surprised him when Finn said, "They might if they think the deck is stacked against them."

"Is that what you think? That she's innocent?" Carson questioned, frowning. He supposed that there was a small outside chance that the chief might be right, but as far as he was concerned, he was going to need a lot of convincing.

"I think I want to talk to her again and find out just how her necklace wound up under the wheel of that car," Finn answered.

In order to talk to the woman again they were going

to have to find her. Carson blew out a long breath, thinking.

"Maybe her father knows where she is," he said, speculating. "Won't hurt to talk to him. Man might be able to tell us something."

Although, from what Bo had told him about Demi's contentious relationship with her father, Carson highly doubted that Rusty Colton would be able to give them any viable insight into his daughter's whereabouts.

But, Carson speculated, the old man might know something he didn't know he knew. They had nothing to lose by questioning Rusty Colton.

At least they would be no worse off than they were now, Carson reasoned as they drove over to The Pour House.

The bar's door was closed when they got there, but the lights were still on. Carson banged on it with his fist until Rusty Colton came to unlock it. The tall, skinny man had his ever-present mug of beer in his hand as he opened the door.

Bleary brown eyes quickly assessed the situation from beneath unruly reddish-brown hair.

"Sorry, boys, I'm just about to close up for the night," Rusty said just before Carson pushed his way in. Taking a step back, the bar owner regrouped. "Okay then, I'll have to limit you to just one round—although I just might see my way clear to staying open a little longer if you two boys are willing to pay extra."

Small, beady eyes shifted from the chief to the detective. Rusty waited in anticipation to have his palm greased.

He waited in vain.

"We're not here to drink, Mr. Colton," Carson told the man coldly.

He'd never cared for the owner of The Pour House. There was something palatably unsavory about Rusty Colton. Carson had no doubt that the man would sell his own mother if he needed the money.

Annoyed, Rusty gestured toward the door. "Well then, 'gentlemen,' I need to get back to closing up my establishment," he told them.

Neither of the men moved toward the door.

"We were wondering if you could tell us where your daughter is, Rusty," Finn asked in a voice that said he wasn't about to be trifled with. "Demi."

Rusty snorted. "She's a grown woman, Finn. She comes and goes as she pleases. Ungrateful whelp never did mind me," he said, banging down his empty mug on the counter. "I can't be expected to keep track of her."

Carson moved in a little closer to the man. He wasn't that much taller than Rusty, but he was a great deal more muscular and therefore more intimidating. "You keep track of everything when it suits you. Now, let's try this again," he said evenly. "Where's Demi?"

"Well, if you must know," Rusty said, smugly drawing out each word, "she's gone. Long gone. I think you two apes probably scared her and she hightailed it out of here."

That wasn't good enough for him. "What makes you so sure?" Carson wanted to know. "Did she tell you?"

"Didn't have to," Rusty answered, pushing together several glasses on the counter in a half-hearted attempt to clean up. "I stopped by her place during my evening break—I leave Amos in charge then. He's dumb, but nobody's going to try to skip out on paying that big ox," he informed the two men at the bar proudly.

"Get back to the point," Finn ordered. "You stopped by Demi's place and then what?"

"Well, she wasn't home so I decided to dip into that big wad of cash she keeps under her mattress like I do every now and then—only when I need a little something to get me through to the end of the month," Rusty admitted without a drop of embarrassment.

"Except that I couldn't this time," he complained. "It was gone. Guess the little witch must have taken it and hightailed it out of here." He looked quite put out by his youngest daughter's action. "Didn't even think to leave me any, my own daughter," he complained.

Carson exchanged looks with his boss. They weren't going to get anything more out of Rusty.

"Let us know if she comes back," Finn told the man as he walked out.

Rusty grunted something in response, but it was unintelligible and they'd already lost too much time, Carson reasoned, following the chief out.

"Warrant's not going to do us any good right now," Carson bit out, handing the paper back to Finn.

"I'll put out an APB on her," Finn said, striding back to his vehicle. "Maybe we'll get lucky. In the meantime, have the team look into those people whose names you wrote down."

Frustrated, Carson nodded as he got into the car. For now, at least it was a place to start.

Early the following morning, Carson stood by as the chief called a staff meeting of all the K-9 cops and gave them instructions. Articles of Demi's clothing, got from her house, were handed out in order to give the dogs a scent to track.

Others on the force got busy looking into Bo's past.

The latter included interviewing women Bo had seen, exploring the various gambling debts he ran up and, since Bo had been an in-demand dog breeder who'd trained and sold dogs to people and organizations besides the police department, Carson started conducting a second background check on those people. Maybe there was a disgruntled client out for revenge and the situation had got out of hand for some reason.

It was time-consuming and grueling and it all ultimately led nowhere.

Serena Colton absolutely refused to buy into all the lurid hype surrounding her cousin Demi.

Here, tucked away in her private wing of her parents' vast, prosperous Double C Ranch, the story of Bo Gage's murder and how *Demi C* was found written in Gage's own blood beside his body sounded like the fanciful imaginings of a second-rate scriptwriter. Except that Bo Gage *was* found murdered and Demi's name *did* appear to be written next to his body.

"I don't believe it," Serena said to her three-month-old daughter, who was dozing in her arms. "There's *got* to be another explanation for this, Lora. Sure, Demi has her shortcomings," she readily admitted, "but she's not a murderer."

Serena sighed, gently rocking her daughter as she restlessly paced around the very large bedroom. "You take all the time in the world growing up, Lora, you hear me? Stay little for as long as you can. And I'll do my part. I won't let anything like this ever touch you," she whispered to the sleeping child. "I'll keep you safe, little one. I promise."

As if to challenge the promise she had just made to

her daughter, the sound of approaching sirens pierced the night air.

The sirens grew progressively louder, coming closer.

Worried, Serena moved to the window facing the front of the house and looked out. She was just in time to see the headlights from two police vehicles approaching the house—mansion, really—where she lived with her parents and younger sister, Valeria.

"What could the police possibly want here, and at this hour?" Serena murmured under her breath. Her brother Finn was the police chief and he wouldn't be coming here like this unless there was something very, very wrong—would he? She couldn't help wondering.

As if in response, Lora stirred in her arms. But mercifully, the baby went on sleeping. Although how she didn't wake up with all this noise was a complete mystery to Serena. The sirens had gone silent, but in their wake came the loud, urgent pounding of a fist against the front door.

Her heart was instantly in her throat. The next second, she heard her parents and Valeria all rushing down the stairs to answer the door.

Still holding her daughter in her arms, Serena left her room and went to the landing, hoping to find what was going on from the shelter of the second floor.

She was just in time to see her father throw open the front door. Not surprisingly, Judson Colton looked furious. The tall, strapping ranch owner wasn't accustomed to being treated in this sort of manner.

"Just what is the meaning of all this noise?" Judson Colton demanded even before he had the door opened all the way. When he saw that his own son was responsible for all this uproar, he only became angrier. "Finn! How dare you come pounding on our door in the middle of the night and wake us up like this?" he shouted. "You're not only disturbing me, you're disturbing your stepmother and your sisters as well, not to mention that you're doing the unforgivable and spooking the horses!"

Lightning all but flashed from the man's eyes as he glared at his son and the three men Finn had brought with him. Especially since one of them was holding on to a large German shepherd.

Judson eyed the dog warily. "We raised you better than this, boy," he snapped at Finn indignantly.

"I'm sorry if you're offended," Finn told his father formally. "But this is police business. Murder isn't polite," he added grimly. He and his men had been at this all day. It was nighttime now and he was too tired to treat his father and stepmother with kid gloves.

"Murder?" Joanelle Colton cried, pressing her well-manicured hand against her chest as if trying to hold a heart attack at bay. "This isn't about that man who was found dead outside of that horrid bar, is it?" Finn's stepmother looked from him to Carson. "What does *any* of that awful business have to do with us, Finn?"

"That's what we're here to find out," Finn answered patiently.

Serena had a feeling she knew exactly why they were here.

Carson glanced at the chief. Because this was Finn's family, he needed to absent himself from the immediate search of the house. If there was anything—or anyone—to be found, the chief wouldn't want that to be compromised in a court of law.

"Dan, Jack and I'll search the property," Finn told his father and stepmother. "Detective Gage is going to search the house." He nodded at Carson.

"Search the house?" Joanelle echoed in stunned disbelief. "Search the house for what?" she added indignantly.

But Finn and the two officers he had brought with him had already left the house to start their search.

Taking his cue, Carson, warrant in hand, quickly hurried up the stairs with Justice leading the way.

"Search the house for what?" Judson repeated more forcefully as he followed Carson and his K-9.

"Demi Colton or any sign of her, sir," Carson answered just as he and Justice came to the landing.

He stopped dead when he saw Serena standing there, holding her baby in her arms. At that moment, totally against his will, he was transported to another time and place in his life. He was back in the hospital hallway where a solemn-faced doctor was telling him that he had done everything he could to save her, but Lisa, his girlfriend, had just died giving birth to their daughter. A daughter who wound up dying the following day.

Carson felt an ache form in the pit of his stomach, threatening to consume him even as it undid him.

He struggled to bury the memory again and regain control over himself, just as he had done when his loss had occurred. He'd learned that 99 percent of surviving was just remembering to breathe and put one foot in front of the other.

His voice was gruff and cold as he told the woman standing there, "If you're hiding Demi Colton, now is the time for you to speak up."

On the stairs behind him, Judson cried, "Demi Colton?" He almost laughed out loud at the detective who worked for his son. "You're looking for Demi *here*? Hell, you look all you want, but I can tell you that you're wasting your time. You won't find that woman here."

"If you don't mind, sir," Carson answered stiffly, "I'd like to check for myself."

"Then go ahead and do it, but do it quickly," Finn's father warned. "And see that you don't disturb my daughters any more than you already have. Do I make myself clear, boy?"

"I'd prefer 'Detective,'" Carson replied. Judson Colton merely glared, then turned and went back downstairs.

Finn's stepmother had another sort of complaint to register with him. "Must you bring that mangy creature into my house?" She looked disdainfully at Justice. The canine was straining at his leash.

"Justice is part of the police department, ma'am, same as the rest of us," Carson informed the woman without missing a step.

Rather than cringing or stepping aside, he saw a slight smile grace Serena Colton's lips as she looked down at Justice.

"My father's right, you know. You're wasting your time," Serena told him. "I haven't seen her since yesterday. Demi's not here."

"I need to verify that for myself," Carson told her shortly. "Why don't you go downstairs and wait with the rest of your family?" he suggested.

Carson could feel Judson Colton watching his every move.

"I'd rather stay up here, thank you," Serena answered. "She didn't do it, you know," she told Carson. "Demi's not capable of killing anyone."

Serena was entitled to her opinion, he thought, even though it was naive. "You'd be surprised what people are capable of if they're pushed hard enough," Carson told her.

"There is a limit," Serena insisted.

"If you say so," he replied, complete disinterest in his voice.

His attention was focused on Justice who was moving around Serena's room with growing agitation. Suddenly, Justice became alert and ran up to the walk-in closet. He began pawing at the door.

Carson looked over his shoulder at Serena, disappointment clearly registering on his face. "Not here, huh?"

"No, she's not," Serena insisted, crossing the room to her closet.

Carson waved her back. Taking out his weapon, he pointed it at the closet door and then threw it open. Justice ran in and immediately nosed the hot-pink sweater on the closet floor. The German shepherd moved the sweater over toward his master.

Picking it up, Carson held the sweater aloft and looked accusingly at Serena.

"I said I saw her yesterday," Serena pointed out. "Demi must have dropped her sweater here when I wasn't paying attention. I never said she wasn't here *yesterday*, only that she's not here now—and she isn't," Serena insisted.

Drawn by all the commotion and the headlights from the police vehicles when they drove to the house, Serena's brother Anders, who lived in a cabin on the property and worked as the Double C foreman, came into his sister's bedroom.

"Serena's right. Demi was here at the house yesterday afternoon, but she left and she hasn't been back since. Trust me, I can't abide that little bounty hunter, and I'd tell you if she was here. But she's not," Anders said with finality.

"And neither one of you would know where she went or might consider going if she was running from the police?" Carson pressed.

Serena and her brother answered his question in unison.

"No."

Chapter 4

"Here." Carson shoved the hot-pink sweater over to Anders. "Take this and put it somewhere, will you? The scent is throwing my dog off."

Anders frowned at the sweater Carson had just shoved into his hand. "Sorry. Hot pink's not my color."

Carson wasn't amused by the foreman's dry wit, not when he was trying to find his brother's killer.

"Just get rid of it for now. As long as that's around, Justice can't home in on anything else Demi might have left behind that could wind up proving useful."

Muttering something about not being an errand boy under his breath and looking none too happy about having Carson on the premises, Anders took the sweater and marched out of Serena's suite. Wadding the sweater up, he tossed it into the linen closet that was down the hall and shut the door.

Carson looked back at his dog. Now that the offending piece of clothing was gone, Justice became totally docile.

"C'mon, boy, keep on looking," he urged his German shepherd partner. "Seek!"

Responding to the command, Justice quickly covered the remainder of the upper floor, moving from one area to another, but nothing seemed to spark a reaction from the dog. Nothing caused him to behave as if he had detected any telltale scent that indicated that the woman he was hunting was hiding somewhere on the floor or had even left anything else behind.

Serena kept her distance but still followed the detective, shadowing him step for step. For now, Lora was cooperating and went on dozing.

Coming back through the adjacent nursery, Carson made his way into Serena's oversize bedroom. His eyes met hers.

"See, I told you she wasn't here," Serena told him. When his face remained totally impassive, she heard herself insisting. "You're looking for the wrong person, Detective. Demi didn't kill Bo. There's got to be some kind of mistake."

About to leave her suite and go back downstairs, Carson stopped abruptly. Justice skidded to a stop next to him.

"My brother's dead. He wrote Demi's name in his own blood on the asphalt right above his head. Her necklace was found at the crime scene, and there's a witness who said he saw Demi running away from the area some fifteen minutes before Bo's body was found in the parking lot. From what I can see, the only mistake here was made by Demi," he informed Serena curtly, doing his best to hold his anger in check.

Part of the anger he was experiencing was because

of the crime itself and part of it was due to the fact that having seen Serena holding her baby like that when he'd first entered had stirred up painful memories for him, memories he wanted to leave buried.

Serena shook her head, refusing to buy into the scenario that Demi had killed her ex-boyfriend in some sort of a fit of misguided jealousy. That was not the Demi she had come to know.

"Look," she began, trying to talk some sense into the detective, "I admit that it looks bad right now—"

Carson barely managed to keep a dismissive oath from escaping his lips.

Serena didn't seem to notice as she forged on. "There's no way that the Demi Colton I know is a killer. Yes, she has a temper, but she wouldn't kill anyone, *especially* not her ex-boyfriend."

Carson looked at her sharply. What wasn't she telling him?

"Why?" he questioned.

Did Demi's cousin know something that he didn't know, or was she just being protective of the other woman? Was it simply a matter of solidarity between women, or whatever it was called, or was there something more to Serena's certainty, because she did look pretty certain?

Serena began to say something else, then stopped herself at the last moment, saying only, "Because she just wouldn't, that's all."

Carson looked at the chief's sister closely. She knew something. Something she wasn't telling him, he thought. His gut was telling him that he was right. But he couldn't exactly browbeat her into admitting what she was trying to hide.

He was just going to have to keep an eye on the chief's sister, he decided.

Just then, the baby began to fuss.

"Shh." Serena soothed her daughter. She started rocking the child, doing her best to lull Lora back to sleep.

But Lora wouldn't settle down. The fussing became louder.

Glancing up, Serena was going to excuse herself when she saw the strange look on the detective's face. In her estimation he looked to be in some sort of pain or distress. Sympathy instantly stirred within her. She hated seeing pain of any kind.

She had to be losing her mind, feeling sympathy for a man who seemed so bent on arresting her cousin. It was obvious that he had already convicted Demi without a trial and looked more than willing to drag Demi to jail.

However, despite all this, for some strange reason, she was moved by the underlying distress she saw in his eyes.

"Is something wrong, Detective Gage?" She waited for him to respond, but he didn't seem to hear her despite their close proximity. "Detective Gage?" she said more loudly.

Suddenly realizing that she was talking to him, Carson looked at the chief's sister. She seemed to be waiting for him to respond to something she'd obviously said.

"What?" he all but snapped.

The man was in no danger of winning a congeniality award, Serena thought. "I asked you if something was wrong."

Damn it, Carson upbraided himself, he was going to have to work on his poker face. "You mean other than the obvious?"

Serena mentally threw up her hands. This was hopeless. Why did she even care if something was bothering this boorish man who had come stomping into her house, disrupting everyone without displaying so much as an iota of remorse that he was doing it. Never mind that her brother had led this invasion into her parents' home, she felt better blaming the detective for this than blaming Finn.

"Never mind," she told Carson, changing topics. "I have to see to my baby, if it's all right with you," she said, a mild touch of sarcasm breaking through.

Rather than say anything in response, Carson just waved her back to her quarters.

Serena's voice was fairly dripping with ice as she said, "Thank you."

With that she turned on her bare heel to walk back into her suite.

"Let's go, Justice," Carson said to the dog, steering the animal toward the stairs.

Keeping a tight hold on the dog's leash, Carson walked out of the house quickly, a man doing his best to outrun memories he found far too painful to coexist with.

Once outside, he saw the other members of the K-9 team. Not wanting to be faced with unnecessary questions, he forced himself to relax just a little.

"Anything?" Carson asked the man closest to him, Jim Kline.

Jim, paired with a jet-black German shepherd whimsically named Snow, shook his head. "If that woman's anywhere on the property, she's crawled down into a gopher hole and pulled the hole down after her," the man answered him.

Finn came over to join them. Carson noticed that the chief looked as disappointed as he felt.

"Okay, men, everybody back to the station. We're calling it a night and getting a fresh start in the morning." The chief glanced over in his direction. "You, too, Gage," he ordered, obviously expecting an argument from Carson.

And he got it. "I'm not tired, Chief," Carson protested, ready to keep going.

"Good for you," Finn said sarcastically. "Maybe when you get a chance, you can tell the rest of us what kind of vitamins you're on. But for now, I'm still the chief, and I still call the shots. We're going back to the station, end of discussion," Finn repeated, this time more forcefully. He left absolutely no room for even so much as a sliver of an argument.

Resigned, Carson crossed over to his vehicle and opened the rear door to let Justice in. Shutting the door again, he opened the driver's side and got into the car himself.

He felt all wound up. Talking to Serena Colton while she was wearing that frilly, flimsy nightgown beneath a robe that wouldn't stay closed hadn't exactly helped his state of mind, either.

Carson shut the image out. It only got in the way of his thoughts. And despite being dragged through the wringer physically and emotionally, he sincerely doubted he was going to get any sleep tonight.

Biting off an oath, Carson started up his car and headed toward the police station.

Serena could tell that the rest of her family was still up. From the sound of the raised, angry voices wafting up the stairs, they were going on about this sudden, unexpected turn of events and how furious her father and mother were that Finn hadn't seen his way to leaving them out of this investigation strictly on the strength of the fact that they were his family.

Instead, Finn had actually treated them like he would anyone else, rousing them out of their beds just because he felt it was his duty to go over the entire grounds, looking for a woman her parents felt had no business being on the family ranch in the first place.

Serena let them go on venting, having absolutely no desire to get involved by sticking up for Finn. Her parents were going to carry on like this no matter what she said.

Besides, right now her main duty was to her daughter. The ongoing commotion had eventually agitated Lora, and she wanted to get the baby to fall back to sleep.

The corners of her mouth curved in an ironic smile as she looked down at the infant in her arms. Funny how a little being who hadn't even existed a short three months ago had so quickly become the very center of her universe. The very center of her heart.

Since the very first moment Lora had drawn breath, Serena felt obliged to protect the baby and care for her, doing everything in her power to make the world around Lora as safe and inviting for the infant as was humanly possible.

These last few months, her focus had been strictly and entirely on Lora. She had long since divorced her mind from any and all thoughts that even remotely had anything to do with Lora's conception or the man who had so cavalierly—and unwittingly—fathered her.

It had all been one huge mistake.

She had met Mark, whose last name she never

learned, at a horse auction. The atmosphere at the auction had been fast paced and extremely charged thanks to all the large amounts of money that were changing hands.

Representing the Double C Ranch and caught up in the excitement, Serena had broken all her own rules that day—and that night. She had allowed the devastatingly handsome, charming stranger bidding next to her to wine and dine her and somewhere amid the champagne-filled evening, they had wound up going back to her sinfully overpriced hotel room where they had made extremely passionate love. Exhausted from the activity and the alcohol, she had fallen asleep after that.

She had woken up suddenly in the middle of the night. When she did, Serena found herself alone, a broken condom on the floor bearing testimony to her drastically out-of-character misstep. Managing to pull herself together and taking stock of the situation, she discovered that the money in her wallet as well as her credit cards were gone, along with her lover.

Canceling the cards immediately, she still wasn't fast enough to get ahead of the damage. Her one-night stand had cost her several thousand dollars, racked up in the space of what she found out was an hour. The man worked fast.

It was a very bitter pill for her to swallow, but she felt that there was an upside to it. She'd learned a valuable lesson from that one night and swore never to put herself in that sort of stupid situation again. Never to blindly trust *anyone* again.

Moreover, she made herself a promise that she was through with men and that she was going to devote herself strictly to raising horses, something she was good at and understood.

That was what she planned.

Life, however, she discovered, had other plans for her. Her first and only one-night stand had yielded a completely unplanned by-product.

She'd got pregnant.

That had thrown her entire world out of kilter. It took Serena a while to gather her courage together to break the news to her parents. That turned out to be one of the worst experiences of her life. They reacted exactly as she had feared that they would. Her father had railed at her, absolutely furious that she had got herself in this sort of "situation," while her mother, an incredible snob from the day she was born, carried on about the shame she had brought on the family.

Joanelle accused her of being no better than her trashy relatives who hailed from the two lesser branches of the family. The only ones in the family who were there for her and gave her their support were her brothers, Finn and Anders.

She also received support from a very unlikely quarter. Her cousin Demi Colton. She and Demi had never been really friendly, given the branches of the family they came from. But Demi had done her a favor involving one of the ranch hands about a year ago. That had earned her cousin a soft spot in Serena's heart.

And then, when she found herself pregnant, with her parents pushing for her to "eliminate" her "shame," it was Demi, surprisingly enough, who had come out on her side. Demi told her that she should do whatever *she* felt she should as long as that decision ultimately meant that she was being true to herself.

At that point, Serena did some very deep soul-searching. Ultimately, she had decided to have her baby. Seeing that her mind was made up, her brothers gave her their full support. However, it was Demi she found herself turning toward and talking with when times got rough.

She wasn't ordinarily the type who needed constant bolstering and reinforcement, but having Demi to talk to, however sporadically, wound up making a world of difference to her. Serena truly believed that it was what had kept her sane during the low points of this new experience she found herself going through.

Because Demi had been good to her when she didn't need to be, Serena wasn't about to turn her back on her cousin just because a tall, good-looking detective wanted to play judge, jury and executioner when it came to her cousin. Demi had obviously fled the area without ever coming to her, but if she had, if Demi had come to her and asked for money or a place to hide, she would have never hesitated in either case.

She believed that Demi was entitled to a fair shake. Most of all, she believed in Demi.

"I wish you would have come to me," she whispered into the darkness. "I wish you would have let me help you. You shouldn't be alone like this. Not now. Especially with the police department after you."

Serena sighed, feeling helpless and desperately wanting to do something to negate that.

Lora began making a noise, her little lips suddenly moving against her shoulder. She was clearly hunting for something.

Three months "on the job" as a mother had taught Serena exactly what her daughter was after.

"You want to eat, don't you?" she said.

Walking over to the rocking chair that Anders had made for her with his own hands, she sat down. Holding Lora against her with one arm, she shrugged out of the top of her nightclothes and pressed the infant to her breast. Lora began feeding instantly.

"Last time, little one," Serena promised, stroking the infant's silky hair. "I'm starting you on a bottle first thing tomorrow morning. Mama's got to get back to doing her job, sweetheart. Nobody's going to do it for her," she told the little person in her arms.

Rocking slowly, Serena smiled to herself. She was looking forward to tomorrow, to getting back to feeling productive. But for now, she savored this very possibly last intimate moment of bonding with her infant daughter.

Chapter 5

As he'd predicted, Carson didn't get very much sleep that night. His brain was too wired, too consumed with reviewing all the details surrounding his brother's murder. There was more than a little bit of guilt involved, as well. He hadn't wanted to go to Bo's bachelor party to begin with, but he still couldn't shake the feeling that if he had only got to it a little earlier, he might have been there in time to prevent his brother's murder from ever happening.

Carson finally wound up dozing off somewhere between two thirty and three in the morning. At least he assumed he'd dozed off because the next thing he knew, he felt hot air on his face. The sensation blended in with a fragment of a dream he was having, something to do with walking through the desert, trying to make his way home with the hot sun beating down on him. Except that he'd lost his way and didn't know just where home actually was.

Waking up with a start, he found Justice looming right over him. The hot wind turned out to be the dog's hot breath. Justice's face was just inches away from his.

Scrambling up into a sitting position, Carson dragged a hand through the unruly thatch of dark hair that was falling into his eyes.

"What is it, boy?" he asked groggily. "Did you solve the crime and couldn't wait to let me know?" Blinking, he looked at the clock on his nightstand. It was a little past six in the morning. How had that happened? "Or are you hungry, and you're trying to wake me up to get you breakfast?"

In response, the four-footed black-and-tan active member of the K-9 police department nudged him with his nose.

"I guessed it, huh?" Carson asked, swinging his legs off his rumpled double bed.

Except for the fact that he had pulled off his boots last night, he was still dressed in the same clothes he'd had on yesterday. He really hadn't thought he was going to be able to fall asleep at all so in his estimation there had been no point in changing out of them and getting ready for bed.

Carson didn't remember collapsing, facedown, on his bed. He supposed the nonstop pace of the last two days, ever since he'd come across Bo's body in The Pour House parking lot had finally caught up with him.

He blinked several times to get the sleep out of his eyes and focus as he made his way through the condo into his utilitarian kitchen.

"I know what you're thinking," Carson said to the

furry shadow behind him. "This whole place could fit into a corner of Serena Colton's suite."

Now, why had that even come up in his haze-filled mind, he asked himself.

Just then another piece of his fragmented dream came back to him. He realized that he'd been trying to cross that desert in order to get back home to Serena.

Home to Serena?

Where the hell had that come from?

He hardly knew the woman. What was his subconscious trying to tell him? It wasn't as if he was in the habit of dreaming about women. When he came right down to it, he hardly ever dreamed at all.

He came to the conclusion that something had to be bothering him about his less than successful interview with Serena last night. At the moment, he just couldn't put his finger on what.

Forget about it for now, he ordered himself. He had something more immediate demanding his attention—and it weighed a little over eighty pounds.

"Okay, Justice. What'll it be? Filet mignon? Lobster? Dog food?" Carson asked, holding the pantry doors open and peering inside at the items on the shelves. "Dog food, it is," he agreed, mentally answering for the dog beside him.

As he took out a large can, Justice came to attention. The canine was watching closely where the can's contents would wind up.

"Don't worry, I'm not going to poach your breakfast," Carson told the dog. "I'm not that hungry."

To be honest, he wasn't hungry at all. But given his present state, he desperately needed a cup of coffee. His brain felt as if it had been wrapped up in cotton and he needed that jolt that his first cup of coffee in the morning brought in order to launch him into his day.

Emptying the dog food into Justice's oversize dish, Carson stepped out of the dog's way as his K-9 partner immediately began to inhale his food. Carson tossed the empty can into the garbage pail in the cabinet beneath his sink and turned his attention to the coffee maker.

He bit off a few choice words. He'd forgotten to program the coffee maker to have coffee waiting for him this morning. Moving over to the refrigerator, he took out the half-empty can of ground coffee and proceeded to make his usual cup of coffee. The end product, thick and rich, was always something that could have easily doubled for the material that was used to repave asphalt. It was just the way he liked it.

Time seemed to move at an incredibly lethargic pace as Carson waited for the coffee to brew and the coffee maker to give off the three high-pitched beeps, signaling that the job was done.

The timer barely finished sounding off before he poured the incredibly thick, sludge-like liquid into his mug. Holding the mug with two hands like a child who had just learned how to drink out of a cup for the first time, Carson quickly consumed the product of his efforts. He drank nonstop until he had managed to drain the mug of its very last drop.

Putting the mug down, Carson sighed as he sat back in his chair. He could almost feel the coffee working its way through his veins, waking up every single blood vessel it passed through with a start.

The fuzziness was definitely gone.

Getting up to his feet, he looked in Justice's direction. The German shepherd had inhaled every last bit of what he'd put into the dog's dish. Carson credited the dog with having the same frame of mind that he did. Justice had needed something to jump-start his day.

"Okay, give me five minutes to shower and change so we can hit the road and get started," he told his furry partner.

As if concurring with what Carson had just said, Justice barked.

Once.

True to his word, Carson was in and out of the shower in less time than it took to think about it. Going to his closet, he found Justice lying on the bedroom floor, waiting for him.

"Don't start nagging me," he told the dog. "I'm almost ready." When the dog barked at him a couple of times in response, Carson said, "Yeah, yeah, I know. I didn't shave." As if in acknowledgement, he ran his hand over what was now beyond a dark five-o'clock shadow. It could have doubled as the inside of an abyss at midnight. "I'll do it tomorrow. There's nobody I'm trying to impress anyway," he added, pulling on a pair of jeans, followed by his boots.

He paired the jeans with a black pullover then put on his go-to navy sports jacket. As a detective, he was supposed to make an effort to dress in more subdued, businesslike attire. This was his effort, he thought drolly.

Adjusting his weapon in its holster, he said, "Okay, Justice, let's roll."

He stopped by the precinct first to see if any headway had been made in the investigation into his brother's murder. Specifically, if there had been any sightings of Demi Colton overnight.

There hadn't been.

When he walked into the squad room, he found that

Finn was in the process of handing out the names of people he wanted interviewed in connection with Bo's murder. Names from the list he had compiled for the chief, Carson thought.

"Just in time," Finn said when he saw Carson coming in. "I was beginning to think that maybe you'd decided to take a couple of days off like I suggested."

The chief knew him better than that, Carson thought. "Not until we catch Demi."

When he saw the chief shifting, as if he was uncomfortable, it made him wonder what was up.

"Yeah, well, on the outside chance that it turns out Demi *didn't* kill Bo, we do need to look into other possibilities. Like whether there might be anyone else out there with a grudge against your brother strong enough to want to kill him."

The way he saw it, even thought he had compiled the list for Finn, shifting attention away from Demi would be a waste of time and manpower.

"Bo didn't write anyone else's name in his own blood," Carson pointed out in a steely voice. "He wrote Demi's."

Finn threw another theory out there. "Maybe there was something else he was trying to tell us other than the name of his killer."

Carson frowned. Finn was stonewalling. Everyone knew that things between the Colton and Gage families weren't exactly warm and toasty. There was a feud between the two families that went back a long ways, and it flared up often.

Was that why Finn seemed so intent on running down so-called "other" leads rather than going after a member of his own extended family? Finn was a good police chief, but his behavior seemed very suspicious to Carson.

"I know what you're thinking," Finn said in response to the look he saw descending over Carson's face. "You think I'm trying to protect Demi. I'm not. I'm the police chief of this county. I don't put family above the law. Hell, you were there. I roused my own family out of bed to conduct a search for Demi.

"But I'm not about to bend over backward and behave like someone's puppet just to prove to everyone that I won't let my sense of family get in the way of my doing my job. However, just because half the force is out for blood, doesn't mean I'm going to put blinders on and pretend there might *not* be anyone else out there who stood to gain something from your brother's death."

"Like what?" Carson wanted to know.

"Well, we won't know unless we look into it, will we?" Finn answered. "Now, aside from all those girlfriends your brother was always accumulating before he got engaged to Hayley, he was married once before, wasn't he?"

Carson nodded. "Yeah, to Darby Gage," he told the chief, adding, "They've been divorced for over two years."

"Which one of them asked for the divorce?" Finn wanted to know.

He didn't have to try to remember in order to answer. "Darby did."

Finn was all ears. "Why?"

A half, rather mirthless smile curved Carson's mouth. Just because he wanted to find Bo's killer didn't mean that he had approved of his brother's fast-and-loose lifestyle.

"Seems that Darby didn't care for the fact that Bo couldn't stop seeing other women even though they were married." He knew how that had to sound to Finn. "I'm not making any excuses for Bo," Carson told the chief. "He was an alley cat. Always had been. And personally, in the end, I think that Darby was glad to be rid of him."

"Maybe she decided she wanted to be *really* rid of him," Finn countered. "In any case, I want you to go talk to the ex-wife. Find out if she has an alibi for the time your brother was murdered."

He should have seen that coming. "Okay, will do," Carson told him. "You heard the man, Justice," he said to the dog. "Let's go."

Since her divorce from Bo Gage two years ago, Darby Gage had been forced to stitch together a number of part-time jobs just to make ends meet.

Carson found her at the diner where she worked the morning shift as a waitress.

It might have been his imagination, but his ex-sister-in-law seemed to tense up when she saw him coming into the diner.

Putting on a cheerful face, Darby walked up to him with a menu and said, "Take a seat, Detective Gage. We've still got a few empty tables to choose from."

Carson picked a table that was off to one side. Parking Justice there, he sat down.

"What can I get you?" Darby asked.

He could see that the cheerfulness was forced. It probably unnerved her to see him here, he guessed. "Answers," he told his ex-sister-in-law.

Her blue eyes swept over him. In his estimation, she

looked nervous. She gave up all pretense of cheerful-ness. "Is this about Bo?"

His eyes never left her face. His gut told him that she didn't have anything to do with Bo's murder, but he was here so he might as well do his job.

"Yes."

Darby sighed as she shook her head. "I don't know what I can tell you."

"Let me be the judge of that," Carson told her.

He'd found that saying something like that took the reins away from the person he was interviewing and put them back into his hands.

Carson kept one eye on Justice, watching for any sort of a telltale reaction on the dog's part. All the German shepherds on the K-9 force were initially bred and then trained by Bo or one of the trainers employed at Red Ridge K-9 Training Center. That was actually where his brother had met Hayley, who was one of the trainers.

Bo had made his living breeding the dogs for the po-lice department as well as for other clients. Darby had been part of that business until the divorce and even now, one of her part-time jobs was cleaning the ken-nels at the training center.

In Carson's experience, German shepherds were ex-ceedingly sensitive when it came to certain character traits and if Darby had somehow been involved in Bo's murder, maybe the dog would pick up on that.

But Justice's response to his former trainer's ex seemed favorable. So much so that when Darby ab-sently stroked the top of the dog's head, Justice wagged his tail.

Taking that into account, Carson still pushed on. "Where were you around 6:30 p.m. the night Bo was killed?" he asked Darby. Then, realizing the waitress might play dumb about the date, he started to add, "That was on—"

"I know when Bo was killed," Darby said, cutting him off. "I was just leaving the kennels after cleaning up at the training center."

Technically, he already knew that because he had got her schedule by calling the places where she worked. But he wanted to hear what she had to say. "Anyone see you?"

"Other than the dogs?" she asked.

He couldn't tell by Darby's expression if she was being sarcastic or just weary. Given that Bo had put her through the wringer and was the reason why she had to hold down all these various jobs just to keep a roof over her head, for now he let the remark slide.

"Yes, other than the dogs."

She thought for a moment. "I think one of the handlers, Jessop, was still there. He might have seen me. To be honest, I didn't think I'd need an alibi so I didn't make a point of having someone see me leave." And then she suddenly remembered. "There's a time card I punched out. That should be proof enough for you."

He knew that there were ways to manipulate a time card. But since, in his opinion, Darby wasn't the type who could even hurt a fly, he nodded and said, "Yes, it should." Getting up from the table, he dug into his pocket and took out five dollars. He put it down on the table. "Thanks for your time, Darby. I'll get back to you if I have any other questions."

Darby picked up the five dollar bill and held it up for him to take back. "You can't leave a big tip, you didn't buy anything," she pointed out.

Carson made no attempt to take the money from her.
"I took up your time," Carson answered.
With that he and Justice left the diner.

Chapter 6

Bo hadn't done right by Darby.

That was the thought that was preying on Carson's mind as he drove away from the diner.

They might have been brothers, but he was aware of all of Bo's shortcomings. His older brother had always been the typical playboy: self-centered and careless with anyone else's feelings. He was making good money with his German shepherd–breeding service and could have seen to it that Darby had got a better settlement in the divorce—at least enough so that she wasn't forced to take on so many part-time, menial jobs in order to keep a roof over her head.

But Bo's lawyer had been a good deal sharper than the lawyer Darby had been able to afford to represent her, so Bo had wound up keeping almost everything. He got the house, the business and most of the bank accounts, while Darby had clearly got the very short end of the stick.

In his opinion, the ultimate humiliation was when Bo had tossed her that crumb by letting her earn extra money cleaning out the kennels at his breeding operation.

If his brother hadn't written *Demi C* on the pavement with his blood, Carson might have looked a little more closely at Darby as a possible suspect in Bo's murder. He certainly couldn't have blamed her for being bitter about the treatment she'd received at Bo's hands both before and after the divorce.

But Darby hadn't seemed bitter to him, just closed off. And decidedly weary.

She probably wasn't getting enough sleep, given the various conflicting schedules of the jobs she held down, Carson thought.

"What do you think, Justice?" Carson asked the dog riding in the passenger seat beside him. "You think Darby might have got fed up and decided to teach Bo a lesson for treating her so shabbily?"

Justice barked in response to hearing his name and Carson laughed.

"That's what I thought. You like her, don't you, boy? Back to Demi, then," Carson agreed.

About to drive back to the station, Carson abruptly changed his mind as well as his direction.

He was heading back to the Double C Ranch.

Something had been bothering him about Serena Colton's testimony. *Why* was she so convinced that Demi hadn't killed his brother despite what could be considered a deathbed testimony? Why was she so certain that her cousin wasn't capable of killing someone even though everyone knew the bounty hunter had a bad temper.

He'd once seen Demi take down a man at The Pour House who was twice her size and obviously stronger than she was. Thin and wiry, the woman was nonetheless a virtual powerhouse. Ever since that day, he'd regarded Demi as being rather lethal.

Given that and her unpredictable temper, he'd never thought it was a good idea for his brother to have taken up with her. Demi Colton wasn't the type of woman to put up with being treated the way Bo obviously treated women he was no longer interested in seeing exclusively.

Carson couldn't shake the feeling that there was something that Serena had held back last night when he'd questioned her.

He had no idea if that "something" was significant or inconsequential, but he knew it was going to keep eating away at him until he found out exactly what it was that Serena wasn't telling him. He might as well get this out of the way before he followed up on some of Bo's business dealings and talked to the women he'd romanced and discarded.

When he arrived at the Double C mansion, Carson debated leaving Justice in his car when he went in. After all, it was January and if he left the windows partially opened, the dog would be all right. However, he regarded Justice as his partner and under normal circumstances, he wouldn't have left his partner just sitting in the car, twiddling his thumbs while he went in to reinterview someone connected to a case.

"You're on your best behavior, boy," he instructed,

taking the leash as Justice jumped down out of the passenger seat.

Alma, the housekeeper who opened the front door when he rang the bell, looked far from happy to see him. The older woman cast a wary eye in Justice's direction.

"I'm sorry, Detective. Mr. and Mrs. Colton are not in," she informed him formally.

"That's all right," Carson replied politely. "I'm not here to see them. I'm here to talk to Ms. Colton."

The housekeeper raised her chin as she asked defensively, "Which Ms. Colton?"

The woman knew damn well which one, he thought. She just wanted to make things difficult for him. She was being protective of the people she worked for.

"The older one. Serena," he specified.

The housekeeper frowned. "I'm afraid that she's not here, either."

Just as the woman was about to forcibly close the door on him, Serena's voice was heard calling to her from upstairs. "Alma, I'm going to need you to watch Lora for me for a few hours while I'm working with the horses."

Carson's eyes met the housekeeper's. "Looks like she came back. Lucky me," he commented.

"Yes," the older woman responded icily. "Quite lucky. I will go upstairs and tell Miss Serena that you want to see her."

"That's all right," Carson said, moving past the housekeeper and entering the foyer. "Don't trouble yourself. I can go tell her myself. I know my way."

And with that, he and Justice headed toward the winding staircase.

Carson took the stairs two at a time with Justice keeping pace right behind him.

* * *

About to go back into her suite as she waited for the housekeeper to come upstairs, Serena was more than a little surprised to see the detective make his way up to the landing in the housekeeper's place.

Now what? Serena thought impatiently.

"Did you forget something, Detective?" she asked, doing her best to sound polite and not as irritated as she felt.

"No," he answered, reaching the landing, "but you did." He signaled for Justice to sit and the K-9 did.

Her brow furrowed a little as she tried to make sense of what he'd just said. "Excuse me?"

"When we talked last night, I got the feeling that there was something you were holding back, something you weren't saying," he told her. "The more I thought about it, the more certain I was that I was right. I figured I needed to get back to you to find out just what that was." He looked at her expectantly.

Alma had just managed to make her way upstairs. The woman was struggling not to pant. "I'm sorry, Miss Serena. He refused to leave."

"Apparently he's very stubborn," Serena said, looking coldly at the invading detective. She drew herself up, moving away from the bedroom doorway. "Alma, if you don't mind looking after Lora, I'll see if I can't put the detective's mind at rest once and for all, so he can be on his way and we can all go on with our lives."

He waited until the housekeeper picked up the baby from her crib and left with Lora before saying anything to Serena.

"Have I done something to offend you, Ms. Colton?" he asked, referring to her rather abrupt tone.

He had gall, she'd give him that. "You want that alphabetically, chronologically or in order of magnitude?" she asked the detective.

"Tell you what, I'll let you pick," Carson said magnanimously.

He didn't think she was going to say anything, did he, she thought. Well, he was in for a surprise.

Serena launched into him. "You come storm trooping into my house at an ungodly hour—"

"You were up," Carson reminded her.

"That's beside the point," Serena retorted. "I was feeding Lora. But that still didn't give you the right to burst in here—"

"The chief knocked," Carson corrected her. He could see she was getting really frustrated. The fire in her eyes was really rather compelling to watch. "And he is your brother as well as the police chief."

Exasperated, Serena switched to another tactic. "You not only accused a relative of mine of an awful crime but already convicted her in your mind, refusing to even entertain the very real possibility that she wasn't the one responsible for killing your brother."

"I might have 'convicted' her a little too readily," he allowed, "but you absolved her just as quickly despite evidence to the contrary."

"That wasn't actual evidence, it was circumstantial evidence," she insisted.

She was beginning to get to him, not to mention that she was obscuring the real reason why he had returned to the Double C Ranch. "I didn't come here to argue with you."

Serena gave him a knowing look. "You could have fooled me," she retorted.

"I'm not here to do that either," he informed her curtly, just in case she was going to go off on that tangent. "All I want to know is what you're holding back, Ms. Colton."

She could feel herself losing her temper. "I'm not holding anything back," she protested a little too vehemently.

Carson had no intention of dropping this until he had his answer. "Last night, when you told me that you hadn't seen Demi since the day before—"

"I hadn't," Serena reaffirmed in case he was going to go in that direction.

Ignoring her, he pushed on to get to his point. "You were convinced that cousin of yours wasn't capable of murder."

"She's not," Serena insisted. She was prepared to say that as many times as it took to convince the detective—because she believed with all her heart that it was true.

He wished she'd stop interrupting and let him get to the heart of his case. He glared at her and continued talking.

"When I asked you why you were so certain that she hadn't killed Bo Gage, you looked as if you were going to say something, but then you didn't. You just repeated what you'd already said. What is it that you actually *wanted* to say?"

"You're imagining things," Serena told him dismissively.

Carson's eyes met hers. Immovable, he held his ground.

"No, I'm not," he told her. "Now, one more time. What is it that you were going to say?" He saw the stubborn look that came over her face. She was digging in, he thought. He tried another tactic. "Convince me, Ms. Colton. *Why* couldn't Demi kill my brother?"

Serena shook her head. "I don't—"

"Why?" Carson repeated, more forcefully this time. He gave no sign of relenting or backing off until she gave him an answer.

Serena glared at him, but inside, she was beginning to relent.

It wasn't as if, if she remained silent, all of this would eventually just go away. It wouldn't. There was a very viable piece of evidence of Bo's connection with Demi that wasn't about to be erased. It was only going to grow more prominent with time.

She of all people knew that.

Taking a breath, Serena finally gave Carson what he was after, albeit reluctantly. "Because she wouldn't kill the father of her baby."

"Baby?" Carson repeated, completely stunned. He was definitely *not* expecting something like this. Maybe he'd misunderstood. *"What* baby?"

Was he really being this dense, or did he just want her to spell it out for him, Serena wondered, feeling her anger mounting.

"Demi's baby."

He thought of the woman he had seen not that long ago. Demi Colton had no children. Carson shook his head. "Demi doesn't have a baby."

"Not yet," Serena agreed, feeling as if she had just betrayed the other woman, "but she's pregnant."

He continued to stare at Serena. When he saw her, Demi had been as thin as one of those swizzle sticks they used in bars a class above The Pour House. Was the chief's sister jerking him around, trying to win sympathy for her cousin?

Or was she telling him the truth?

"Demi's pregnant?" he finally repeated.

Serena nodded grimly. "Yes."

He felt like someone trying to find his way through a foggy swamp. "And it's Bo's baby?"

"Yes!" she cried, feeling like a game show host who'd painstakingly led a contestant to the right answer after a number of wrong turns.

Although Bo had been a womanizer, he had never actually bragged about his conquests or talked about them in any sort of detailed manner. To his recollection, Bo had never said anything about getting Demi—or any other woman—pregnant. He would have definitely remembered something like that.

"Did my brother know she was pregnant?" he asked Serena.

"She didn't want to tell him." She saw the quizzical look on Carson's face. "Your brother was going to be marrying another woman. Demi wasn't about to say anything about the baby until after she actually gave birth. She felt that saying something now, right before his wedding, when she wasn't even showing yet would make her look desperate and pathetic in his eyes. Like she was just trying to keep him for herself. Demi had way too much pride for that."

All this sounded somewhat far-fetched to him. "You're sure about this?"

Serena didn't hesitate with her answer. "Very."

She was obviously missing what was right in front of her, Carson thought. "Seems to me that your friend had a very good reason to kill my brother. It's called revenge and it's right up there as one of the top two reasons people kill people," he told her.

Didn't he get it? "You're talking in general, I'm being specific." Serena tried again. "Demi wouldn't kill the father of her baby no matter how much she couldn't stand Bo."

Carson moved his head from side to side as if he was trying to clear it. "You realize that you just proved my point with those last few words you said, right?"

"No," she cried. "I proved mine. Demi wouldn't want her baby to someday hate her for killing its father. She wanted her baby to eventually come to know Bo—and make up its own mind about what a lowlife your brother was," she concluded with feeling.

Carson laughed shortly again as he shook his head. "You know," he told her, "that almost makes sense—in a weird sort of way."

"The point is," Serena said, "even though she had a temper, Demi was practical. She wouldn't have killed him—she would have waited until the baby was born and then she would have confronted Bo and made sure that your brother lived up to his responsibilities toward the child." She paused, pressing her lips together. It took effort to keep the bitterness out of her voice. "Men can't just have their fun, sowing their seed and disappearing. Not when there's another life involved."

He thought of the baby he saw her with last night. He was aware of Serena's circumstances. "Is that what you told her?"

But Serena shook her head. She wouldn't presume to give Demi advice. "Nobody tells Demi anything. She marches to her own drummer." Serena paused for a moment, her eyes meeting his. "This is just between the two of us."

He thought of Demi. "Seems like there's more people involved than that."

She blew out an exasperated breath. He knew what she meant. "Demi told me this in confidence the last time I saw her. I don't want this getting out, do you understand? I only told you because I wanted you to understand why Demi wouldn't have killed your brother."

He was far from convinced. "If she didn't kill him, why was his last act before dying to write her name in his own blood?"

"I don't know," she exclaimed. "You're the detective. *You* figure it out. But she didn't kill him," Serena insisted again. "I'd bet my share of the ranch on that."

She looked intense as she said that, and he had to admit that it did rather impress him. "You're that certain?" he questioned.

"I'm that certain," Serena confirmed.

He lifted one shoulder in a half shrug. "I'll keep that in mind. And I'll be getting back to you," he told her just before he walked away.

She didn't win, Serena thought. She hadn't convinced the detective that Demi had nothing to do with Bo's murder. But she could see that she'd created doubt in Carson's mind, which meant that she didn't lose, either. And for now, that was good enough.

Chapter 7

Out for a ride to clear her head a few days later, Serena abruptly reined her horse in.

She stared at the horizon, trying to make out the two riders in the distance, also on horseback.

Ever since Bo Gage's murder, everyone in the area was spooked and on high alert, taking note of anything remotely unusual or out of the ordinary.

Anyone who had business with her father or mother came up the main road to the house, driving a vehicle, not on the back of a horse.

Because she no longer felt as safe these days as she used to, Serena had taken to bringing her rifle with her when she went out for a ride on the range. She felt that it was better to be safe than sorry and she was quite proficient with a gun.

Her hand went to her rifle's hilt now as she watched the two riders. There was something uncomfortably familiar about them even though she couldn't make out their faces at this distance.

And then she saw Anders coming from the opposite direction. Her brother was riding toward the two men. Even so far away, Serena could tell from his body language that the Double C foreman wasn't happy.

Rather than hang back, she kicked her mare's flanks, urging Nighthawk to head over in Anders's direction. She didn't know why, but something in her gut told her that her brother might need a little support.

And then, as she came closer, she realized why. The two riders she had observed, who were now engaged in some sort of a conversation, were Noel and Evan Larson.

She felt an icy chill shimmy up and down her spine.

Twins, the Larsons were businessmen with extensive real estate holdings who used both their good looks and highly developed charm to get people to trust them. Word had it from Finn and some of her other law enforcement relatives that the Larsons were dangerous and building a criminal empire involving drugs, guns, high-stakes theft and money laundering.

But to Serena, Noel and Evan Larson would always be the creepy duo who had duped her in high school. Back then, she had briefly dated Evan—up until the time Noel had decided to switch places with his twin. Posing as Evan, he'd tried to pressure her into going further with him than she was willing to go. Upset, Serena summarily dumped Evan only to be told by him that it was his twin who had tried to get her into bed.

Stunned, Serena was furious that he had so cavalierly passed her off to his twin without her consent and Evan had reciprocated by being angry with her because she hadn't been able to tell the difference between him and his twin immediately. He wound up reviling her and calling her a number of names, including a dumb bitch. It was the last time they ever exchanged any words.

From that time on, Serena steered clear of both the twins, wanting nothing to do with either of them because of the deception and because of the demeaning way they had acted toward her.

In a nutshell, the Larsons scared her. They had scared her then and they scared her now, she realized as she rode up toward her brother. Even so, she felt that Anders needed backup.

She reached her brother just as Evan and Noel rode away.

Just as well, Serena thought. The very thought of being anywhere near the Larsons or having to talk to either one of them, left a really horrible taste in her mouth.

The only thing worse was allowing the duo to roam free on the Double C Ranch. She wanted them gone from the family property.

"What did they want?" she asked Anders the moment she reached her brother.

Anders frowned, intently watching the twins as the duo rode away. "Exactly what I asked them—after I told those two that they were trespassing on private property."

"And what was their answer?" Serena had no idea what to expect when it came to those two.

"Noel, at least that was who he said he was," Anders said, "told me they didn't 'realize' that they were trespassing. According to Noel, they were just out here 'admiring the gorgeous land' and they were thinking of buying a ranch themselves. They wanted to know if there were any ranches for sale in the area and asked a bunch of general questions about ranching. Seemed innocent enough, I suppose."

She didn't believe a word of it. There was something underhanded going on, she just didn't know what it was yet.

"They're not," Serena assured her brother with feeling. "Everything the Larsons do or say has some kind of hidden agenda, some kind of underhanded motive. A hundred and fifty years ago those two would have been snake oil salesmen—or made a living as gun runners to the Native population." She felt her stomach turning every time she thought of the twin brothers. "I wouldn't trust either one of them any farther than I could throw them," she told Anders. "From where I was, it looked like those two were riding around, casing the Double C Ranch."

Anders laughed shortly. "They know better than that."

"No, they don't," Serena maintained. "If you ask me, I think we should be on our guard." But waiting for something to happen would put the ranch's hands on edge, she thought. Something more specific was needed. "I think that we should also call Finn so his people will be on alert."

Anders shrugged. She knew he didn't care for the implication. He didn't like the idea of having to go running to his older brother. "I can take care of the ranch."

She was quick to correct the misunderstanding and set his mind at ease. "Nobody's saying that you can't take care of the ranch, Anders. But these guys *are* dangerous," Serena reminded him. "I get a sick feeling in the pit of my stomach just knowing that they're out there, poking around."

Anders sighed. "Okay, if it makes you feel any better, call Finn and tell him the Larsons were out here, looking like they were getting the lay of the land." He paused, his gaze on his sister. "I don't like the Larson twins any more than you do, Serena, but until they do something wrong that can be proved in a court of law, I don't think there's all that much Finn and his people can do about it."

One step at a time, Serena thought. "We can leave that up to Finn. At least we can get him started by giving him the information. Meanwhile," Serena said, as she leaned over in her saddle, patting the hilt of her rifle, "I'm keeping my rifle loaded—just in case."

Turning her mare around, Serena headed back to the stables. She left Nighthawk with one of the stable hands. It wasn't something she would normally do— she liked looking after and caring for her own horse, and that included unsaddling the mare and grooming her—but right now, she felt this sense of urgency nagging at her. She wanted to call Finn and tell him about finding the Larsons on the family ranch.

The call to the station proved frustrating. The person manning the front desk told her that Finn was out on a call. Before she knew it, she was being switched to someone else.

And then a deep voice was in her ear, saying, "Gage. What can I do for you?"

There were a number of Gages working in the police station. The odds of getting Carson were small. And yet, she just *knew* it was him.

Hoping against hope that she was wrong, she asked, "Carson?"

"Yes," the rumbling voice said gruffly.

Oh great, just the person I wanted to have talk down to me, she thought, annoyed. But she had a feeling that it was Carson or no one and she disliked having the Larson twins casing her ranch more than she disliked talking to the K-9 detective, so she decided to remain on the line.

"Detective Gage," she said, addressing him formally, "this is Serena Colton."

The detective's voice was just as cold as hers was. "Hello, Miss Colton. Did you think of something else you forgot to tell me?"

She almost hung up on him then. His tone of voice annoyed her. He sounded judgmental. But then maybe she was reading something into it, Serena told herself, struggling to remain fair. She decided to give him another chance.

"No," she told Carson, "I didn't forget anything. I just thought you might be interested in knowing that the Larson brothers were just out here, riding around the Double C. I swear they were taking measure of the ranch like a tailor measuring someone for a suit."

Mention of the Larsons had Carson immediately sitting up, alert.

"The Larsons," he repeated, digesting what she'd just said. "Anyone in your family have any reason to have dealings with those two?"

"No one in my family deals with vermin," Serena informed him coldly.

"Just checking," he told her. "I meant no offense," he added, taking her tone of voice into account.

And then she suddenly remembered something that had slipped her mind until just now.

"For the record, you might want to look into the dealings that your brother had with them," she told Carson. "Demi mentioned something about that to me one of the last times I saw her," Serena added.

"My brother? Dorian?" he asked.

Dorian, younger than he was by six years, was a bounty hunter, and this last year, Dorian had been Demi's chief competitor.

"No," Serena answered. She paused for a moment for effect before telling him, "Bo."

"What?" He was certain that he had to have heard her wrong.

Serena gave him all the information she had. "Demi told me that Bo sold the Larsons two of his German shepherds and that the Larsons paid one of the trainers at the K-9 center a lot of money on the down low to cross-train the dogs to attack. They were also trained to protect and detect."

"To detect what?" Carson wanted to know. He wasn't exactly happy about this piece of information. Bo had never said anything about selling two of his dogs to the Larsons.

What had Bo been thinking, doing business with the likes of the Larsons? He had to have known that they were under investigation. The twins' unsavory dealings weren't exactly a secret.

"Sorry," Serena answered. "I have no idea. That's something you're going to have to ask the Larsons."

He fully intended to, Carson thought. It was funny how the investigation into his brother's murder was making him come full circle, back to the investigation he'd been focused on prior to Bo's murder.

Were those two would-be crime kingpins somehow responsible for Bo's death? This case was getting more and more complicated.

"Thanks for bringing this to my attention," he told Serena, feeling that he owed her something, especially after the way he'd talked down to her.

It wasn't his attention she'd been after, Serena thought. "To be honest, I was trying to reach Finn to tell him about this," she said, not wanting any credit she didn't have coming to her.

The woman certainly made it difficult to give her a compliment, Carson thought. "Yeah, well, thanks anyway," he said just before he hung up the landline.

The Larson brothers, Carson thought, getting up from his desk. Maybe he was going to get to nail these bastards in this lifetime after all.

Dozing next to Carson's desk, Justice was instantly alert the second Carson had pushed back his chair. The German shepherd scrambled to his feet, ready to go wherever his two-footed partner went.

"I don't want you taking a bite out of either one of these slime-buckets," Carson warned as he secured the dog's leash onto his collar. "Not until *after* we have the goods on them. We got a deal, Justice?"

The German shepherd barked in response and Carson nodded his head as if they had just struck a bargain. "Deal," he echoed.

Noel and Evan Larson had a suite of impressive, swanky offices located downtown. Initially, the office had housed a real estate business. The story was that their business "grew," necessitating more space until their so-called "holdings" caused them to take over the rest of the building.

Decorated to create envy in the eye of the beholder, Carson found that the suite of offices looked to be pretentious. He himself had always favored clean, simple lines. In his home and in his partner, he thought, glancing over at Justice.

Walking into the Larsons' offices, he didn't bother waiting for the administrative assistant sitting at the front desk to announce him. Instead, he walked right past her into the inner suite and announced himself.

One step behind him, the administrative assistant looked at her bosses in obvious distress. "I'm sorry, sirs. He got away from me."

"That's all right, Bailey Jean," Noel said. "We'll take it from here." He waved the woman back to the front desk.

Carson held up his ID for the two brothers to view. "Detective Gage," he told the duo, although he knew that they were well aware of who he was. "I'd like to have a word with you if I could."

He was sure the look on his face told the two men that this wasn't a request but a flat-out order. Knowing that they liked playing the game, he wasn't expecting any resistance from either one.

"Sure thing, Detective," Evan said, standing next to his twin. "You mind leaving that mutt outside? Like in your car?" he stressed. It was obvious that he felt uncomfortable around the German shepherd.

Carson was not about to leave the dog anywhere but at his side. Having the animal there evened the odds in his opinion.

"This is Justice. My partner," he told the duo. "Justice goes where I go."

"Rather simplistic, don't you think, Detective?" Noel asked with a smirk.

Identical in every way when it came to their appearance, Noel had always been the one everyone regarded as the ringleader, and he had taken the lead now, as was his habit.

"No, I don't," Carson answered flatly. He made it

clear that no matter what their unspoken criminal con-
nections were, he was not intimidated. "Can we get on
with this, gentlemen?"

"We'll answer any question you have, Detective,"
Noel said in a friendly, easygoing manner. He glanced
in his brother's direction. In contrast to Noel, Evan appeared to be as stiff as a board. "Sit, Evan," Noel told
his twin. "You're making the detective's dog nervous."

Evan hadn't taken his eyes off Justice since the dog
had walked into the office. Carson saw that there was
a thin line of perspiration all along the quiet twin's
upper lip.

"The dog's making *me* nervous," Evan retorted.

"Don't mind Evan," Noel told Carson. "My brother
doesn't get along well with dogs. Or, on occasion, people," he added as a snide aside. "Now, what is it that we
can do for you, Detective?"

For now, Carson just wanted a couple of questions
answered. "Did you buy two German shepherds from
my brother?" Carson asked.

"Such a shame what happened to Bo," Noel said as
if talking about the weather. "But to answer your question, as a matter of fact, we did."

"Why?"

Noel smiled at him. "I really don't see how that's any
business of yours, Detective."

"This is a murder investigation," Carson informed
him in an unemotional voice. "*Everything's* my business."

"All right," Noel replied in an accommodating tone.
"We keep a large amount of cash in our safe for instant
sales. We need the dogs to guard the place, keep people
from trying to break in and help themselves to it. The
dogs, Hans and Fisher," he said, making the two sound

more like favored employees rather than guard dogs, "were trained specifically to guard the safe." Noel's grin widened. "I can give you a little demonstration if you'd like."

He had no desire to watch a demonstration, not with Justice at his side. If the other dogs showed any sign of aggression, too much could go wrong.

"No, for now your explanation is good enough for me," he told Noel. Although he couldn't help wondering why the dogs had been purchased, given Evan's obvious fear of German shepherds. Something wasn't adding up.

"Great. Anything else?" Noel asked, making it sound as if he had all the time in the world to spare for the detective.

"Yes." He waited a moment before continuing. "Serena Colton said she saw you riding around on her property earlier. Mind telling me why?"

"Don't mind at all," Noel said. "We're thinking of buying a ranch for ourselves and just wanted to take a look at one of the more successful ranches in the area." Noel flashed two rows of perfect teeth at him.

"And that's it?"

"That's it," Noel told him, "Except I think that we must have spooked her. Didn't mean to, of course. Anything else?" he asked.

"Not right now," Carson answered. Holding firmly on to Justice's leash, he nodded at the two brothers and took his leave.

"Well, if you think of anything, you know where to find us," Noel called after him cheerfully.

I sure as hell do, Carson thought, walking out.

Chapter 8

As he drove back to the police station, Carson went over the interview he had just conducted several times in his mind just in case he'd missed something.

Without a doubt, Noel and Evan Larson had to be the friendliest, seemingly accommodating cold-blooded criminals he'd ever had the misfortune of dealing with—and he didn't believe a single word that had come out of either one of their mouths.

There was something about the so-called charming duo, something he couldn't put his finger on just yet, but if the Larsons swore on a stack of bibles that something was true, he was more than willing to go out of his way to find the evidence that proved that it was false, because as sure as night followed day, it was.

He didn't think the two were capable of telling the truth if their very lives depended on it.

"I suppose that feeling that way doesn't exactly make

me impartial, does it, Justice?" Carson asked, addressing the question to the German shepherd riding beside him. "Maybe the problem is that there're too many people willing to give those two a free pass. Too many people trying to get on their good side because they think that ingratiating themselves to the Larsons might get them to be part of their cushy world."

The real problem in this matter, Carson decided, was that he had no idea if what the Larsons were involved in had anything to do with Bo's death at all or if the two were mutually exclusive of one another. What he did know was that he wanted to find Bo's killer *and* he wanted to put the Larson brothers behind bars.

But that very possibly could be two very separate things.

Focus, he ordered himself. *Focus*.

He needed to find Bo's killer and then he could get back to the business of putting the Larsons behind bars, where they belonged.

One step at a time.

Finding Bo's killer brought him back to trying to find Demi. The woman wasn't exactly a shrinking violet in any sense of the term and she just couldn't have disappeared into thin air.

Someone had to have seen her, talked with her, *something*.

Determined to locate the bounty hunter and confront her with the additional evidence they'd found to see how she explained her way out of that, Carson decided to go back to the beginning and question some of the people Demi had interacted with. That would help him piece together her timeline for the day that Bo was murdered.

He hadn't managed to even get his seat warm at the

station before one of the other K-9 cops held their land-line receiver up in the air, calling out to get his attention.

"Hey, Gage, someone's asking to talk to you. Says it's about that missing redheaded bounty hunter," Joe Walker called out.

He'd already got a few crank calls, as well as a couple from people just looking for information about the investigation. These days, every third person with access to a computer fancied themselves a journalist.

He made no effort to pick up the phone. "Who is it?" Carson wanted to know.

"They won't say," Walker said. "Just want to talk to you. Line three," he prompted, wiggling the receiver.

With a sigh, Carson picked up his receiver and punched Line Three. "Gage," he announced.

"Carson Gage?" the raspy voice on the other end asked.

It was someone trying to disguise their voice and doing a very obvious job of it, Carson thought impatiently. He didn't have time for this. "Yes. Who am I talking to?"

"My name doesn't matter," the voice on the other end said. Carson was about to hang up when he heard the voice say, "All you need to know is that I work at the Double C Ranch and I just saw Demi Colton running from one of the barns. The one where the studio apartments are kept. You know, the ones the ranch hands live in."

He was a born skeptic. Still, he stayed on the line. "You just saw her?" Caron questioned.

"Less than fifteen minutes ago," the voice told him. Then, as if reading his mind, the caller said, "Look, you can believe me or not, but I saw what I saw and I heard you were looking for that Colton woman so I'm calling it in. Do what you want with it."

"What did you say your name was again?" Carson asked, trying to get the caller to slip up.

"I didn't."

The line went dead.

He dropped the receiver into its cradle. The call could have very well just been a hoax, someone trying to get him to chase his tail for the sheer perverse fun of it.

But on the other hand, Carson felt that he couldn't afford to ignore it, either. He needed to check out this latest so-called "tip."

"I'm going back to the Double C Ranch," Carson told the detective sitting closest to him just in case the chief came looking for him.

Immersed in a report he was wading through on his desk, Emilio Sanchez raised an inquisitive eyebrow. "Got something?"

"I sure as hell hope so," was all Carson was willing to share at the moment as he walked out of the squad room. Justice quickly followed him out.

Serena was just coming out of the stables, talking to one of the horse trainers who worked for her when she saw Carson driving up. Her first thought was that the detective was coming back because he had something to tell her about the Larsons.

"I'll talk to you later, Juan," she said to the trainer. With her eyes riveted on Carson's approaching vehicle, she hurried toward it.

She saw that, despite the cold weather, the window on his side was partially down. "I didn't expect you to be back so soon," Serena told him as she walked up to the driver's side.

"That makes two of us," Carson answered. He turned off the ignition.

Was he waiting for her to pry the information out of him? "So? What did you find out?" Serena asked impatiently.

The woman was standing right up against his door, inadvertently preventing him from opening it. Carson indicated the door with his eyes, waiting.

Annoyance creasing her forehead, Serena stepped back, allowing him to open the door and get out. Justice was right behind him and came bounding out of the driver's side.

If she thought he was here to fill her in on how his meeting with the Larsons went, she was in for a big surprise, Carson thought.

"I found out that you weren't being entirely truthful with me," he said, thinking of the call he'd taken about Demi's sighting. The call that was responsible for his being here.

Her eyes narrowed to brown slits as she glared at Carson. "What are you talking about? What did those lying snakes tell you?"

What was she talking about? "Come again?"

She bit back the urge to tell him to keep up. "The Larson brothers. What delusional story did they try to sell you?"

"The Larsons?" he echoed. Why would his saying that she hadn't been entirely truthful make her think of the Larsons? Was there a reason she'd pointed him in their direction?

Was the detective deliberately playing dumb? She

was beginning to think that the German shepherd was the smart one of the pair.

"Yes, the Larsons," she said evenly. "Didn't you come back to tell me how your meeting with them went?"

Well, she obviously thought a lot of herself, Carson thought, irritated. "No. I'm here because someone from the Double C just called the police station to say that they saw Demi, not fifteen minutes ago, running from one of the studio apartments you have for the ranch hands." He pinned her with a very cold look. "You lied to me, Ms. Colton."

Serena's temper flared. "I *didn't* lie to you and see-ing as how you keep insulting my integrity, why don't we just drop the polite 'Ms. Colton' act, shall we?" she snapped.

Maintaining a respectful air came naturally to him, but given the situation, it was apparently lost on this woman.

"Fine by me, *Serena*." He deliberately enunciated her name.

"Well, none of this is 'fine by me,'" Serena retorted. "And doesn't it strike you as odd that someone who has a perfectly reliable vehicle the way, I'm sure you know, that Demi does is always being spotted 'running' around?" She blew out a breath trying to tamp down her temper. "This is all getting very tiresome, Carson," she said, calling him by his first name and saying it through clenched teeth. "Please leave."

He had no intention of doing anything of the sort. "Sorry, I can't do that. Not until I've searched the barns and surrounding area for Demi."

Serena fisted her hands at her waist, ready to go

toe-to-toe with him. "And if I tell you that you can't?" she challenged.

Carson took a folded piece of paper out of his pocket, opened it and held it up for her to look at. "This warrant says I can."

Fuming, Serena unceremoniously took the warrant from him and scanned it.

"Meet with your approval?" he asked when she folded the paper and handed it back to him.

"No," Serena snapped. None of this met with her approval. "But it is a warrant," she conceded. "So I guess I can't stop you. But you're wasting your time," she informed him. "Demi's still not here. Whoever called you is sending you on a wild-goose chase. So—"

Serena stopped talking suddenly, her head whipping around to look over her shoulder toward something she thought she heard.

Justice was straining at his leash. Obviously whatever it was, the dog had heard it, too, so this wasn't just an act on Serena's part, he thought.

"What?" he asked her in a hushed voice.

But she didn't answer him. Instead Serena hurried around the side of what had initially been one of the barns on the original ranch, before the ranch had been renovated and expanded.

He read Serena's body language. Something definitely had the horse breeder going, he thought as he and Justice followed her.

He was fairly certain that she was not attempting to lead them to corner Demi, but there was no arguing that Serena was after someone.

Someone she apparently was keenly interested in confronting.

Carson caught her by the arm before she got away

from him. When she tried to pull free, he just tightened his hold. Serena glared at him.

"Who are you trying to corral?" he wanted to know.

"My sister," she hissed, annoyed that he was intervening and getting in her way.

Serena tried to pull free again with the same results. The only way this ape was going to let go of her was if she answered his question. So, unwillingly, she did.

"I think the Larsons are trying to get their hooks into Valeria." The second he released her, she made her way around the barn and looked into the first window she could. "She's impressionable and flighty and," she continued, moving to the next window, "with your brother!"

Rapping her knuckles against the window to get their attention, she didn't stop until the two people on the bed finally separated and looked her way.

The two had been so completely wrapped around one another that had it not been for the different colors of their clothing, it would have been hard to distinguish where all their separate limbs began and ended.

Trying the door, Serena found it unlocked and stormed in. Carson followed behind her just as Justice got past him and got in between the two younger people.

"Vincent?" Carson cried. The last person he expected to find in this compromising position with a Colton was his youngest brother.

Startled at being discovered as well as suddenly having a German shepherd getting in between them and wagging his tail in a display of friendly recognition, Valeria and Vincent instantly pulled apart and were up on their feet.

The two looked somewhat disheveled, not to mention disoriented and embarrassed. At least Vincent was. The nineteen-year-old mechanic had got a job working part-time on the Double C, fixing not just some of the cars but also other, larger mechanical devices on the ranch.

He was not, Carson thought, supposed to be giving the boss's daughter the same sort of close scrutiny he gave the vehicles he repaired.

Vincent gulped and finally found his tongue. "Carson, what are you doing here?"

"Thinking about spraying water on the two of you," Carson answered, frowning.

Incensed, Valeria immediately spoke up, turning her anger on her sister. "Hey, you have no right to be spying on us. We're both over eighteen and we can do whatever we want," she cried.

Serena didn't see it that way. "Are you out of your mind?" Serena demanded. "You know the way Dad feels about Vincent's father, how he feels about the whole Gage family," she emphasized. "If he catches the two of you going at it like two rabbits in heat, he'll string Vincent up without a second thought."

Valeria raised her chin, ready to protect this precious romance she was involved in. "He'd have to go through me to do it!" she declared defiantly, her eyes blazing.

"Don't think for a minute that he won't," Serena retorted. "Nothing is more important to that man than the ideas of family honor—and Dad puts that 'honor' above all of us."

Valeria became angrier if that was possible. "I don't care what's important to *him*," she insisted. "Vincent is important to me," she said, reaching for his hand.

The youngest of the Gage clan closed his hand around hers.

"And you don't have to worry and carry on about honor," Valeria continued. "Vincent and I are getting married on Christmas Eve." She shared a smile with him before turning back toward her sister and Vincent's big brother. "That happens to be Vincent's birthday and it's mine, too," she told them. "That makes the date doubly special. We'll both be turning twenty that day," she added as if that fact somehow added weight to what they were planning.

Ignoring the man next to her, Serena made a valiant attempt to talk some sense into her sister. "Valeria, you're both too young to make such a life-altering decision at this stage."

"For once," Carson interjected, "I agree with Serena."

Valeria tossed her head and looked at her sister, totally ignoring the detective. This was between her sister and her. "Seems to me that a woman with a baby and no husband shouldn't be lecturing us on what we should or shouldn't do," she said dismissively.

Carson saw the flash of hurt in Serena's eyes. No one was more surprised than he was when he felt something protective stir within him.

"Tossing insults at your sister," he told Valeria coldly, "doesn't change the fact that what you are contemplating doing is foolhardy, and it's opening the two of you up to a real flood of anger—coming at you from both families."

"But, Carson, it's a really stupid feud," Vincent protested.

"I'm not arguing that," Carson granted. "It's beyond stupid. Half the members of both families can't even remember how the whole damn thing got started or what it's even about. Hell, I'm not even sure. Near as I can tell, it was something about land issues that had our grandfathers at each other's throats, or so the story goes according to our father," he said, nodding at Vincent.

"But it doesn't matter how it got started. What matters is that it's still going on and if you two go through with what you're planning, that damn feud is probably going to escalate. So, if I were you two," Carson said, looking from one to the other, "I'd hold off getting married for a while."

"Well, you're not us," Vincent told his brother, putting a protective arm around Valeria as if to signify that it was the two of them against the world if that's what it took for them to get married.

Valeria looked at Carson. "And just how long is 'a while'?" she demanded hotly. She had her hand on her hip, the very picture of a woman who was not about to change her mind no matter what.

"As long as it takes to get our families to come around," Serena answered. She knew that was vague, but there was no way to put a timetable on getting the two families to reconcile.

Valeria shook her head. The answer was unacceptable.

"Sorry, can't wait that long. I'll be an old lady by the time that happens. You want them to change their minds?" Valeria laid down a challenge. "You see if you can do it before Christmas Eve," she told her sister. "But one way or another, Vincent and I are getting married."

Taking Vincent's hand again, she laced her fingers through his and said, "Let's get out of here, Vincent. It's way too stuffy for me."

"Yeah," Vincent agreed. The youngest Gage brother only had eyes for Valeria and gave every indication that he would follow her to the ends of the earth if need be. "Me, too."

Chapter 9

Feeling incensed as she watched her sister and Vincent walk away, most likely to find another place where they could be alone, Serena swung around and directed her anger at the K-9 detective who was still standing next to her.

Her eyes were blazing as she demanded, "Are you just going to let them go like that?"

"Can't arrest them for being in love," Carson told her. He was almost amused by the fiery display he'd just witnessed, but he knew better than to let Serena suspect that. "And no matter what your father or my father think about the other person's family, there are no laws being broken here." He could see that Serena was far from satisfied with his answer. "Just what is it that you want me to do?"

Serena threw her hands up, angry and exasperated.

"I don't know," she cried, walking back around to the front of the building. *"Something!"*

"I am doing something," Carson shot back. "I'm trying to find the person who killed my brother," he reminded Serena.

From what she could see, all he was doing was spinning his wheels, poking around on her ranch. "Well, you're not going to find that person here, and you're not going to find Demi here, either," she told him for what felt like the umpteenth time, knowing that no matter what he said, her cousin was still the person he was looking for.

"If you don't mind, I'd like to check that out for myself," Carson told her.

"Yes, I do mind," she retorted angrily. "I mind this constant invasion of our privacy that you've taken upon yourself to commit by repeatedly coming here and—"

As she was railing at him, out of the corner of his eye he saw Justice suddenly becoming alert. Rather than the canine fixing his attention on Serena and the loud dressing-down she was giving him, the German shepherd seemed to be looking over toward another one of the barns that contained more of the hands' living quarters.

At this time of day, the quarters should have been empty. Even so, he intended to search them on the outside chance that this was where Demi was hiding.

Something had got the highly trained canine's attention. Was it Demi? Had she come here in her desperation only to have one of the hands see her and subsequently put in a call to the station? Was she hiding here somewhere?

"What is it, Justice? What do you—"

He got no further with his question.

The bone-chilling crack of a gun—a rifle by the sound of it—being discharged suddenly shattered the atmosphere. Almost simultaneously, a bullet whizzed by them, so close that he could almost feel it disturb the air.

Instinct took over. Carson threw himself on Serena, covering her with his body as he got her behind what had to be Valeria's car. The one Vincent was supposed to be working on.

Startled, Serena couldn't speak for a moment because the air had been knocked out of her. The next second, she demanded, "What do you think you're doing?"

"Trying to save your life, damn it," Carson snapped.

Justice broke into a run and whizzed by him, heading straight for the barn. The main door was open.

Pulling out his sidearm, Carson ordered Serena, "Stay down," and took off after his K-9 partner.

"The hell I will," Serena retorted.

Scrambling up to her feet, she cursed the fact that it took her a second to steady herself. And then she quickly followed in their wake.

Reaching the barn, Carson began to move from one uniform room to another. Whoever had fired at them had done so from one of the windows facing the other barn. They were also gone.

Cursing under his breath, he kept his gun drawn as he scanned the area.

Justice was barking in what could only be termed a display of frustration. The dog was expressing himself, Carson thought, for both of them.

When he heard a noise behind him, Carson whirled around, his weapon cocked and ready to fire. He could feel his heart slam against his chest when he realized it was Serena and that he had come within a hair's breadth of shooting her.

"Damn it, woman," he said, resetting the trigger, "I told you to stay put. I could have killed you."

Her eyes met his. There was still fire in hers. "The feeling's mutual," she informed him.

The sudden, unexpected feel of his body pressing against hers like that had brought back all sorts of sensations and emotions, which were running rampant through her. She welcomed none of them. Even so, her body refused to stop throbbing and vibrating and it totally unnerved her.

Despite her agitation and the anger it created, Serena immediately recognized the feeling for what it was. She had been aroused.

Was aroused. And damn it, she didn't want to be. The last time she'd felt that way, nine months later she was giving birth to a baby.

Giving birth and vowing that she was never, *ever* going to allow herself to get into this sort of predicament again. And, until just a few minutes ago, she was completely certain that she never would. She'd been positive that she had sworn off men for the rest of her life, dedicating herself to her daughter and to her job on the Double C.

And now, after a year's hiatus, her body was practically begging her to abandon limbo and feel like a woman again. Begging her to revisit that glorious feeling of having every single inch of her body tingle because she was responding to a man's touch.

Carson stared at her in confusion. What the hell was she talking about? "I was talking about you sneaking up on me like that."

"I didn't sneak," Serena declared defensively, desperately trying to regain control over herself. "This is my family's ranch, and I've got a right to know what's going on."

"Of all the harebrain— You want to know what's going on?" he shouted at her. "Someone just shot at you, Serena. *That's* what's going on. And if I hadn't been there just now, they might have killed you!" he exclaimed. "You're welcome!" he yelled at her when she said nothing in response.

He'd knocked her down and almost given her a concussion, the big oaf! Serena was the picture of fury as she retorted, "I didn't say thank you."

"I can't help it if you have no manners," Carson shot back. Fed up, he began to storm away.

She wasn't about to stand for him turning his back on her like this. "Now, you just wait a damn minute!" Serena exclaimed, grabbing hold of his shoulder and attempting to pull Carson around to face her.

His emotions were running at a fever pitch and not just because someone had discharged a rifle, narrowly missing them. If he was being honest with himself, something had been stirred up when he had first seen Serena standing at the top of the landing with her baby in her arms. Seeing her had unearthed something, keenly digging into his mind and soul. Reminding him of what he had lost before he had ever been allowed to have it.

It had given him a reason to shut Serena Colton out.

But for some perverse reason, it had also given him a reason to want this woman. Want this woman the way he hadn't wanted any other, not since he'd lost Lisa. All the while, as he had been involved in the search for his brother's killer, this feeling had been messing with his mind.

Messing with it to such a degree that he'd allowed himself to entertain irrational thoughts.

Like pulling Serena into his arms and sealing his mouth to hers so he could still the needs that insisted on multiplying within him. That insisted on taunting him and giving him no peace.

Carson came perilously close to going with that desire. And he would have if a livid Anders Colton hadn't picked that exact moment to all but burst onto the scene.

"What the hell is going on here?" Anders demanded as he came upon his sister and the detective.

For a split second both Serena and Carson shared a single thought. That Anders's question was about what had come very close to happening between them—Serena had felt the pull, too—and not about the gunshot that had resounded loud enough for anyone close by to hear.

Serena drew in a deep breath, trying valiantly to still her pounding heart and get control over her all but runaway pulse.

"What?" she asked.

"The gunshot," Anders shouted. His expression demanded to know if she had gone deaf. "I just heard a gunshot," the foremen cried angrily. "What the hell is going on here?"

By now, some of ranch hands had also come running over as well, as had Valeria and Vincent.

At the sight of the two younger people, surprise and then anger crossed the Double C foreman's face.

"What are you doing with my sister?" he demanded, glaring at Vincent. He forgot all about the gunshot as the thought of the mechanic's questionable behavior came to the foreground.

"Later," Carson told Serena's brother authoritatively.

"Right now, you've got bigger problems than Romeo and Juliet over there," he said. "Someone just took a shot at Serena." Serena had to be the target, he thought. Had the shooter been after him, there had been plenty of opportunities to shoot at him prior to now.

"Serena?" Dumbfounded, Anders's attention shifted to her. She looked none the worse for wear. Was the detective lying to him? "Why would anyone shoot at Serena?"

"Why does anyone shoot at someone?" Carson countered, exasperated.

Realizing that Carson was telling him the truth, Anders put his hands on Serena's shoulders as he looked his sister over closely. His voice was filled with concern as he asked, "Are you hurt?"

"Just slightly bruised," she answered. "Detective Gage decided he was bulletproof and took it upon himself to act as my human shield."

Anders flushed, torn between being grateful and his natural feelings of resentment when it came to anyone who belonged to the Gage family.

Feeling that he should offer the detective an apology, he began, "Look, if I just came off sounding like an idiot—"

"Save it," Carson said, waving away what sounded as if it was shaping up to be a very awkward apology. "The first order of business until I can find this shooter is to pack up your family and get them off the ranch and someplace safe."

Anders was in total agreement with the detective. "I'll have my parents and sisters move into the hotel in town until this blows over."

"Wouldn't be a bad idea for you to go, too," Carson told him.

But here they had a parting of the ways when it came to agreement. Everyone on the ranch couldn't just leave. The ranch had to continue being productive.

"I'm the ranch foreman," Anders told him. "I'm responsible for the staff on the Double C. I'm not about to leave them, especially not when there's some crazy shooter loose."

Carson sighed. "Look, I can't make you go—" he began.

"No, you can't," Anders agreed, interrupting the detective.

"And that goes for me, too," Serena informed him, speaking up.

Carson whirled around to face her. This was getting out of hand. "You were the one who was just shot at," he reminded her.

"How do you know?" she challenged, surprising him. "Maybe whoever it was that was shooting just now was aiming at you."

That was ridiculous. She was grasping at straws, pulling thin arguments out of the air. "If that's the case, they would have had plenty of opportunity to shoot at me. They didn't have to wait until I came here to the ranch. You were the target," he insisted.

Be that as it may, she was not about to have Carson tell her what to do. "If that's the case, I'm a big girl, and I can decide whether I stay or go." She raised her chin, sticking it out as a way of asserting herself. "And I've decided to stay."

Stubborn woman! All he could do was block any of her senseless moves.

"I can't let you do that."

Who the hell did this man think he was? "You have nothing to say about it," she informed Carson. "Besides, whoever just shot at us," she said, deliberately underscoring the word *us*, "can and *will* come after us, no matter where we are. There's no point in me running," she argued. "The ranch has a couple of safe rooms inside the mansion. As a last resort, if it comes down to that, I can hide in one of them," she said, her tone clearly declaring that it was the end of the debate as far as she was concerned.

Caught completely off guard, Carson looked at the foreman. This was the first time he'd heard that there were safe rooms within the sprawling mansion.

"Is this true?" he asked Anders. "The mansion has safe rooms in it?"

"Of course it's true," Serena retorted, speaking up because she was annoyed that the detective had asked her brother instead of her. "There's no reason for me to lie about that."

"No," Carson agreed. "There isn't." He processed this new piece of information, then turned toward Anders. "I want to see those safe rooms."

"Why?" Serena wanted to know, once again interrupting. "You want to inspect them to see if they live up to your high standards?" she mocked.

She felt as if Carson was determined to block her at every turn. She certainly didn't like him questioning her every move the way he did.

Maybe, if she hadn't reacted to him the way she had when he'd thrown himself over her, she wouldn't feel anywhere nearly as combative as she did. She didn't know, but now was not the time for her to suddenly start questioning and doubting herself.

"No," Carson answered Serena. "I want to see if Demi's in either one of them. If you ask me, it sounds like a really logical place for her to be holed up," he told Serena.

"She doesn't know a thing about them," Serena informed him, annoyed that she had essentially been forced to share this secret with the likes of him. "Nobody does. Only family members do. That means," she told him, clenching her teeth, "that Demi's not *there*. Give it up, Detective."

"You won't mind if I satisfy my curiosity, do you?" he asked sarcastically.

"As a matter of fact, I do," she informed him coldly. "And I'm not taking you to them."

"If you have nothing to hide, there's no reason not to take me to those safe rooms," he said, prepared to go toe-to-toe with her—or have a judge sort it out after she spent a night in lockup.

"The reason is I don't want to," Serena informed him stubbornly.

"Not good enough," he said, taking out the warrant again and holding it up to her.

"That doesn't say you can search the safe rooms," she retorted.

"It says," he answered, emphasizing each word, "I can search the immediate premises—so unless the safe rooms are hovering somewhere above the ranch," his voice dripped with sarcasm, "they're considered to be part of the premises."

Valeria uttered a frustrated, guttural sound as she lost her patience. "Oh, take him to go see them, Serena. We're not going to get rid of him or his dog otherwise," she insisted.

"You're getting rid of him because you're going to be staying at the hotel with Mom and Dad," Serena reminded her sister.

Valeria drew herself up to her full height. "I am *not* going," she protested between clenched teeth.

"You're going, little sister, even if you have to be dragged there kicking and screaming," Anders informed her.

Angry, fuming and utterly frustrated, Valeria looked in Vincent's direction as her brother pulled her after him to the mansion. "I cannot *wait* to get married," she cried plaintively.

"Well, you're *not* married, and right now you're my responsibility," Anders informed her, maintaining a tight grip around her wrist as he continued on his way to the mansion.

Chapter 10

As he watched Valeria being dragged back to the mansion, Vincent turned toward Carson. He looked clearly concerned.

"Do you think she's really in any danger?" he asked his older brother.

Carson gave him his honest opinion without sugarcoating it. "I think all the Coltons here are in danger," he answered. "Which is why," he continued, looking in Serena's direction, "you and your baby should go with your parents and Valeria to stay at the hotel in Red Ridge."

Serena made a disparaging, dismissive noise. "Nice touch, Carson, having your baby brother play straight man for you like that, but I'm still not leaving the Double C."

Carson knew he was getting nowhere, but he still felt that he had to try.

"You're being unreasonable," he told Serena, struggling with his temper. "That shooter missed you last time. He—or she—might not the next time."

"There's not going to be a next time," Serena countered with a huff. "Because you are going to catch him—"

"Or her," Carson interjected pointedly.

She knew what he was doing. He was making it seem as if Demi had been the one who'd pulled the trigger. But that was absolutely ridiculous. There was no reason for the bounty hunter to have tried to shoot her. They had actually become friends, at least to some degree. With that in mind, Serena deliberately ignored the detective's interjection and went on talking.

"—like the county's paying you to do."

Carson shook his head, exasperated. The woman was being brave and damn foolhardy at the same time. "You never did have a lick of sense."

Serena flashed a wide smile at him. "Must be nice for you to be able to count on some things never changing," she told Carson sweetly.

He had a feeling that Serena could go on like this until the proverbial cows came home. But he didn't have time for that.

"I hope your brother's having more luck with your parents than I'm having with you," Carson told her as he headed straight for the mansion.

When he walked into the foyer, he was just in time to hear Serena's mother making her displeasure loudly known to one and all. Somehow, though he hadn't walked into the house until just now, Joanelle Colton was holding him *and* his family accountable for this newest inconvenient series of events in her life.

"You," Joanelle cried, sidestepping her daughter as

if she didn't exist and making her way directly over to the detective. She stopped short abruptly, pulling back as if she wanted no part of her clothing to touch either Carson or his K-9 partner. "Just exactly *what* is the meaning of all this?" she demanded, furious. "Anders says we have to leave the ranch. Are you the one behind this proposed exodus?"

Aware that there were four pairs of Colton eyes fixed on him, Carson didn't rise to the bait.

Carson removed his hat before he spoke to Serena's mother. "I did suggest it, yes, ma'am. And it's for your own safety," he told her politely.

"Since when is a Gage worried about a Colton's safety?" Judson demanded, coming to his wife's side, his deep, booming voice all but echoing through the ground floor.

"Since I swore an oath to protect all the citizens of Red Ridge, Mr. Colton," Carson replied calmly.

He was determined that neither of the older Coltons were going to rattle him. If worse came to worst, he could always turn the matter over to Finn and have *him* deal with his family.

Though she had her own issues with Carson, Serena knew that he was only trying to protect her family. She also knew firsthand how overbearing both her parents could get. Memories of their reactions when she was forced to come to them and tell them she was having a baby were very fresh in her mind. Neither parent had been easy to deal with or sympathetic, thinking only how this baby would ultimately reflect on them.

Angry bears were easier to reason with, she thought. Possibly also friendlier. Which was why, just for now, she threw her lot in with Carson.

"Someone shot at me, Dad," she said emphatically.

"Detective Gage is just trying to get you to stay somewhere safe until he can catch whoever it is that's out there, using us for target practice."

By the look on the patriarch's face, this was the first he was hearing of this. Incensed, Judson turned on Anders.

"Is this true?" he demanded.

"Someone did take a shot in Serena's direction when she was out by one of the barns where the hands have their quarters." Anders relayed the incident as best he could, given he hadn't been there to see it for himself. He had arrived after the fact, only drawn by the sound of gunfire.

Joanelle gasped, her hand flying to her chest. Carson expected the woman to express concern about her daughter's welfare, or at least ask Serena if she was all right. However, Joanelle appeared horrified that this sort of thing had happened on her ranch—to her.

"I knew it! I knew something like this would happen when you allowed that dreadful girl to invade our home. She had no business setting foot on my ranch!" Joanelle cried. "That branch of the family is just poor trash, tainting everything they come in contact with and you can't expect anything better from them. How *could* you, Serena?"

Her mother's histrionics never ceased to amaze her. "This isn't Demi's fault, Mother," Serena insisted, annoyed.

"Huh! Well, it'll take more than you saying that to convince me," Joanelle declared, wrapping her arms around herself and in essence sealing herself off. "What sort of a woman makes her living by being a bounty hunter for heaven's sake?"

Serena was exceedingly tired of her mother's judgmental, condescending attitude. "A resourceful one would be my guess," Serena countered.

Frosty blue eyes glared at Serena. "That's not what *I* call it," Joanelle fired back.

Serena was aware of the expression on Carson's face. He looked as if he felt sorry for her. Her back went up. She wasn't about to put on a show for the detective's entertainment.

"Shouldn't you be packing for the hotel, Mother?" she pointed out.

Joanelle scowled, obviously insulted by the suggestion. "That's what I have the maid for," she answered haughtily.

Wanting her mother to leave the foyer, Serena rephrased the question. "Then shouldn't you be supervising Marion as she packs for you?"

Unable to argue with that, Joanelle regally turned on her heel and made her way up the spiral staircase. "Come, Valeria!"

There was no room for argument or resistance in her voice.

Uttering an unintelligible, guttural cry, a furious Valeria stomped up the stairs behind her mother.

Judson looked at Serena. "I'd expect Anders to stay and run the ranch, but you should come with us," he told her in a voice that was only mildly less authoritative than his wife's.

"The household staff is staying," Serena began but her father cut in before she could finish.

"Don't worry." He looked at his son. "Anders will make sure that they don't take anything in our absence," Judson told her.

Serena instantly took offense for the staff. She liked the hardworking people, and they were definitely a lot nicer and kinder than her parents were. How like her father to think that the staff was only interested in stealing from him.

"I'm sure they won't," she immediately replied. "Because they're honest, not because someone is watching them. However, I have work to do with the horses. Anders can't see to that as well as to everything else. Don't worry, Dad, I'll be fine, but you need to take Mother and Valeria out of here," she insisted in case her father was having second thoughts about going to the hotel.

Although she felt she could handle any danger to herself, she did want her family to be safe. "Mother's high-strung. If she stays here, she'll see a gun aimed at her behind every post and tree and make your life a living hell, you know that," she stressed.

The expression on her father's face told Serena that Judson Colton was well aware of what his wife was capable of.

As the elder Colton appeared to be mulling over the situation, Carson spoke up. "I'll stay on the ranch to make sure nothing happens to your daughter or your granddaughter, sir," he volunteered.

Unable to bring himself to actually express his thanks to a Gage, Judson merely nodded curtly.

"I have to pack," he said, more to himself than to the detective or his daughter. With that, he went upstairs.

The second her father left the immediate area, Serena swung around to confront Carson. "You'll do no such thing!"

She caught him off guard. "What is it that I won't do?" he wanted to know.

"Stay here. I don't need you playing bodyguard," she informed him.

Unfazed by her rejection, Carson told her, "Just think of it as your tax dollars at work."

This wasn't funny. "I don't want—"

He'd held his tongue long enough. Serena would try an angel's patience, and he was far from an angel. "What you want, or need, is of no concern to me, Serena," he informed her. "Someone took a shot at you. I aim to find out who it was and to keep it from happening again," Carson told her fiercely. "Now, if you don't mind, I need to see those safe rooms you mentioned earlier."

Serena blew out an angry breath. She'd just assumed that he'd forgotten about the rooms. "I thought we were past that."

"No," he answered, "we're not." Just like Justice when he was hot on a scent, Carson was not about to get distracted. "And the only way we're ever getting 'past that' is if I can find Demi and question her about how her necklace wound up under the tire of that car that was near my brother's body."

Feeling as if she was the only one in Demi's corner, Serena tried to come up with some sort of an explanation for the evidence.

"Maybe someone's trying to frame her." The moment she said it out loud, it sounded right to her. "Did you ever think of that?" Serena challenged.

"No, gosh, I never did. What an unusual thought," Carson said sarcastically. And then he changed his tone, becoming serious as he told her, "Of course I thought of that, but until I can talk to Demi again and get some facts straightened out, I'm not going to waste time investigating that theory. Not when everything else clearly points to her killing my brother. Am I making myself clear?" he all but growled at her.

Serena's eyes narrowed, shooting daggers at him as she struggled to hold on to her temper. "As transparent as glass."

"Good," he retorted with finality. "Now, then, just where are those safe rooms that you said were in your house?"

She was sorely tempted to tell him to go look for the safe rooms himself, but she didn't want to give Carson an excuse to go wandering around the mansion, possibly tearing things up on his own. Although she found that being around him really unsettled her, especially after Carson had thrown his body over her like that, Serena thought it best if she just showed him the two safe rooms herself.

"They're this way," she said, sweeping past Carson.

Her attention was riveted to the top of the stairs. The less she looked at him, Serena felt, the better. Carson was too damn good-looking and she knew all about good-looking men. They were as shallow as a puddle and only interested in their own self-satisfaction.

Been there, done that, she thought as she went up the stairs.

Finding himself unaccountably more amused than irritated, Carson walked behind her. He maintained a light grip on Justice's leash as he led the canine up with him.

Bringing the detective and his four-footed partner to the second floor, Serena made her way into her suite.

When she entered, she saw that the housekeeper was there, changing Lora. The woman appeared surprised to see her—and even more surprised to see the detective and Justice.

"Are you back, Miss Serena?" the woman asked, one

hand on Lora to keep the baby from kicking. Lora's diaper was only half-on.

"Just passing through, Alma," Serena answered. "Detective Gage wants to take a look at something," she explained vaguely.

Carson scanned the area. He'd already been to her suite the other night. There'd been no sign of Demi at the time, except for that discarded sweater.

"Where's the room?" he wanted to know. She had just brought him over to her walk-in closet, but that certainly didn't qualify as a safe room, he thought. Was she trying to pull something on him?

"Right here," Serena answered.

Reaching in, she pressed a button just inside the closet entrance. As she did so, the back wall with all her neatly arranged shoes parted and moved aside, exposing another door. There was a keypad on the wall right next to it.

Serena positioned herself in front of the keypad so that he wasn't able to see which of the keys she pressed. When she finished, the door opened, exposing a room that was nothing short of huge. Carson judged that it took up the entire length of the floor.

In it was a king-size bed, a state-of-the-art kitchenette and all sorts of things that would make having to take refuge here anything but a hardship.

Carson looked around slowly, taking it all in. It was impressive. "My first place was one-third this size," he commented.

Serena didn't doubt it. "My father tends to go overboard," she answered. "And he thought that if it came to us having to actually use a safe room, we might all have to stay in here."

Carson nodded. "It certainly is big enough. Go for

it, Justice," he told the dog as he released the animal. "Seek!"

But rather than take off, the German shepherd moved around the huge area slowly. Nothing had caught his attention.

The safe room was actually more than just a single room. There were a couple of smaller "rooms" attached to it. Justice went from one end of the space to another, but unlike when he had uncovered her sweater, he found no trace of Demi.

In the end, the dog came trotting back to him.

"Satisfied?" Serena asked the detective.

Instead of answering her questions, he said, "You said safe *rooms*."

Serena sighed. "So I did."

Resigned, she turned around and led the way out of that safe room and then her suite. She wordlessly proceeded to lead Carson to another wing of the mansion.

"How do you not get lost here?" Carson asked her as they went to the wing that faced the rear of the property.

"I use bread crumbs," she answered drolly, then immediately regretted it.

The sound of his laughter was way too sexy.

This safe room, like the other, turned out to be a room within a room. This one was hidden behind a floor-to-ceiling bookcase that housed a wealth of books as well as expensive knickknacks and memorabilia.

"It's here," she told him, entering another code on the keypad beside *that* door.

In Carson's estimation, the second room looked like a carbon copy of the first one, containing the same supplies, the same well-furnished distractions.

She stood off to one side, silently telling him he was free to search this room the way he had the other. She felt that the sooner this was out of the way, the sooner Carson would leave and she could stop feeling as if she was having trouble breathing.

"Okay, Justice," Carson said, removing the canine's leash for a second time. "Go for it. Seek!"

Again the German shepherd moved about the large room and its connecting rooms as if there was a heavy dose of glue deposited in his veins.

Nothing seemed to pique the canine's interest, but the dog dutifully went around the entire area, sniffing, nudging items and in general taking a very close account of the room. Again there was no sign that Justice detected Demi anywhere within the very large area.

Finished scouting around the second safe room, Justice returned to Carson's side.

He looked up at his partner's face, waiting for further instructions, or the command that allowed him to lie down on the door and rest.

"Are these the only two safe rooms?" Carson asked her.

She laughed drily. "My father believes in overkill, but even he has his limits, so yes, these are the only two safe rooms in the mansion." She looked at Carson pointedly, expecting him to finally take his leave and go away. "Are you satisfied now?"

"Not by a long shot."

Chapter 11

Serena stared at the detective. He'd asked to see the safe rooms and she'd shown him the safe rooms—why wasn't the man leaving?

"What is that supposed to mean?" she wanted to know.

"It means," Carson said patiently, "I'm still looking for Demi."

"Even your dog doesn't think she's here," Serena pointed out. She petted Justice's head despite the canine's partner annoying the hell out of her. "You're welcome to continue turning over rocks on the property and looking for Demi, but I guarantee that no matter how long you spend here, you're going to have the same results," she told him, straightening up. "You're beating a dead horse, Detective. And where I'm from, that's offensive in too many ways to count."

"It's not my intention to offend you," Carson said as they left that wing.

"Good." She gave it another shot, hoping that this time she could induce him to leave. "Then go back to the police station or home or wherever it is you go after you clock out."

"Funny thing about police work," he told Serena. "You really don't get to 'clock out.' It's a twenty-four-hour-a-day, seven-days-a-week calling." His eyes met hers. "I can't go 'home.'"

She made her way to her wing of the mansion. "Sure you can. All you have to do is just get in that car of yours and drive away."

Maybe she forgot the exchange he'd had with her father when Judson had tried to get Serena to go with her family to the hotel. "I told your father that I'd look after you and your daughter."

Did he actually believe that was a compelling argument? "I'm sure he didn't take it to heart. You're a Gage. Not believing a word you say comes naturally to him."

"And living up to my word comes naturally to me," he countered. Maybe the idea of having him stay here made her uncomfortable. He could understand that. He didn't want to make her uncomfortable. "Don't worry, Justice and I will just sack out in one of the empty rooms upstairs. We won't get in your way."

Her eyes met his pointedly. He had got in her way from the first minute he'd stormed into the house that night, waving a warrant.

"Too late," she said.

Blowing out a breath, she tried to tell herself that he wasn't trying to annoy her. That he was just doing his job as a member of the police department. But if he had to be here, she didn't want him underfoot.

"There's food in the refrigerator in the kitchen. Why don't you go help yourself? I've got work in the stable," she said. Maybe keeping him informed of her work schedule would buy her a little good grace and some leeway.

When Carson followed her down the stairs with Justice, she didn't think anything of it. But when the two continued walking behind her as she headed for the front door, Serena stopped dead.

Pointing behind him, she said, "The kitchen's in the other direction."

"I know where the kitchen is," he answered matter-of-factly.

"So why aren't you headed there?" she wanted to know. "It might sound unusual to you, but that's where we keep the refrigerator."

"I'm not interested in the refrigerator," he told her in a no-nonsense voice. "I'm interested in keeping you alive."

Serena rolled her eyes. "Now you're just being melodramatic," she insisted.

And she was in denial, he thought. "You felt that bullet whiz by just like I did. That's not being melodramatic. That's just using the common sense that the good Lord gave each of us. Now, do yourself a favor and stop arguing with me."

"I don't need you hovering over me. I'll be fine," Serena insisted, pushing past him.

Not about to be shrugged off, Carson followed her outside.

Serena took exactly five steps then swung around to face him. How did she get through to this man? "Look, Detective, you're beginning to really annoy me."

"I'm not trying to do that, Ms. Colton," he said, reverting back to addressing her formally. "But someone killed my brother and now someone's taken a shot at you." His voice became deadly serious. "I don't intend to have you added to the body count on my watch."

Serena gave up. Trying to reason with the man was just a frustrating waste of time and she had things she wanted to do before nightfall, which came early this time of year. Besides, she thought, there was a small chance that he was right. She could take care of herself, but there was Lora's safety to think of. Better safe than sorry, she decided.

"Suit yourself," Serena told him as she continued on her way to the stables.

"I intend to," Carson murmured under his breath. Sparing a quick glance at Justice as they followed in Serena's wake, Carson said, "She's a regular spitfire, isn't she, boy?"

The dog made no sound, but Carson still took it as tacit agreement on the canine's part.

Carson had learned how to take in his surroundings and be vigilant without calling any attention to himself or what he was doing—and without missing a thing.

As daylight began to wane, he took note of Anders watching him in the distance, saw the handful of ranch hands the Double C foreman had working with him to reinforce a length of fence just beyond the corral. And all the while, he continued to look for something out of the ordinary, for that one thing that didn't mesh with everything else.

"Don't your eyes get tired, staring like that?" Serena finally asked him after she'd taken in the horse she'd been working with and brought out another from the stable.

Carson slid his gaze down the length of her, taking in every curve, every soft nuance her body had to offer. "Depends," he answered.

The man was as communicative as a rock, Serena thought, waiting for him to say something more. When Carson didn't, she finally asked impatiently, "Depends on *what*?"

There was just possibly the smallest hint of a smile on his lips when he answered, "On what I'm staring at."

Serena knew he meant her but there was no way she could say anything about that without sounding full of herself or, at the very least, without borrowing trouble. All she could do was say something as enigmatic as what he'd just said.

"Careful your eyes don't get tread worn."

She saw the corners of his mouth curve just a tiny bit more as he answered, "I'll do my best."

Serena continued to feel like she was under a microscope, even when she looked up to see that Carson was scanning the horizon and not looking at her. Somehow, she thought, he was managing to do both.

Serena did her best to concentrate on the stallion she was working with and not on the man who had somehow done the impossible—he made her feel warm despite the cold temperature.

An hour later, exhausted, Serena decided to wrap it up and call it a day. The sun had gone down and it was really cold now. It was time to go in. Anders and his men had already gone to their quarters.

Bringing the stallion back into the stable, she brushed the horse down, the way she had the others and then walked out. Before she headed toward the mansion, she made sure to lock up the stable. In her present state of mind, the last thing she needed was for something to spook the horses and cause them to get out of the stable. She had no desire to spend hours tracking them down and rounding them up.

"You do this all the time?" Carson asked, picking up his pace as he and Justice fell into step beside her.

For just a moment, she'd forgotten he was there. It took all she had not to react as if the sound of his deep voice had startled her.

"Yes, when I'm not taking care of my daughter or going to horse auctions," she answered.

"You look like you're really good at it," Carson observed.

The detective was actually complimenting her, she realized. Serena hadn't expected that.

"I am," she answered. She wasn't boasting, she was just stating what she knew to be true.

"Must be nice to do something you're good at," Carson commented.

"It is." She'd enjoyed working with horses for as far back as she could remember. His comment piqued her curiosity about the man, who refused to go away. "How about you? Do you like what you do?"

His answer was vague, leaving it up to her to interpret. "I like keeping order," Carson replied.

Was that his way of avoiding telling her the truth? She decided to prod him a little. "I thought you like ordering people around."

Carson actually seemed to consider her question for a moment before giving her an answer. "That's part of it sometimes."

They'd reached the house and she, for one, was grateful. The walk from the stables to the mansion wasn't technically long enough to warm her. However it turned out to be long enough to make her aware of just how warm talking to him actually made her.

Opening the front door, the first thing that hit Serena was how quiet it all was. Her parents and sister made more noise than she'd realized. Shaking herself free of that thought, Serena proceeded to shrug out of her sheepskin jacket.

Hanging the jacket up in the hall closet, she turned toward Carson and asked, "Are you hungry now?"

Hunger had never governed his eating habits. He'd learned how to deal with perilous conditions and how to ignore a rumbling stomach. Ignoring it became a habit.

"I don't get hungry," he told her. "I eat to keep going."

"You sound like you have a lot in common with my horses," she commented. Feedings were carried out at regimented intervals.

The term "magnificent animal" suddenly flashed across her mind out of nowhere, catching her completely off guard and stunning her. The moment she thought of it, Serena realized that it just seemed to fit.

She found herself staring at Carson almost against her will.

"If you're trying to insult me, you haven't," he told her.

"I'm not insulting you," she said crisply. "But maybe I shouldn't have compared you to a horse. I find horses to be very noble animals."

He surprised her by laughing, but it wasn't at her. Her comment just seemed to tickle him.

"They are," he agreed. "And if you're interested, I don't fancy myself as being noble, just hardworking." He paused for a long moment, just looking at her. "Sometimes I just have to work harder than other times."

She struggled not to shiver. There was just something about the way he looked at her that caused her self-confidence to disintegrate into little tiny flakes that blew away in the wind.

"Why don't you go into the kitchen and have Sally whip up something for you?" she told him, referring to the cook. "I'm just going to go upstairs for a minute and check on Lora."

Carson never hesitated. He just started to walk upstairs with her. "I'll go with you."

Serena sighed. "You really are determined to be my shadow, aren't you?"

The detective said neither yes nor no. Instead, he told her, "Just doing whatever it takes to make sure that you and your daughter are safe."

Serena surrendered. She didn't even bother trying to argue with that.

The housekeeper was on her feet the moment Serena walked into her suite. The woman placed her finger to her lips, warning them not to raise their voices.

Crossing over to Serena, the housekeeper told her, "She just now fell asleep."

Serena lowered her voice to a whisper. "Did she give you any trouble?"

Alma shook her head, beaming. "No, she was a little darling. But she doesn't really sleep all that much for a three-month-old," she observed. "I was trying to keep her up so she'd sleep through the night for you, but just when I didn't want her to, she dozed off."

"Don't worry about it, Alma. I'm not planning on getting much sleep tonight anyway," Serena told the housekeeper.

Alma's eyes darted toward the man standing

behind Serena. Understanding suddenly blossomed on the woman's round face. "Oh."

At that instant, it suddenly dawned on Serena what the housekeeper had to be thinking. She was about to protest and set the woman straight. But then she caught herself. She knew that if she protested, that would only convince the housekeeper that she was right in thinking there was something going on between her and the detective.

So, hard as it was, Serena pressed her lips together and kept silent about the misunderstanding.

Instead, she told the housekeeper, "I'm going to go downstairs and get some dinner. After I finish, I'll be back for the night. You'll be free to go on with your evening after that."

Stealing another long look at the detective, Alma said, "Take your time, Miss Serena. I don't mind staying here with your daughter. She's a little angel. Reminds me of my own when they were little."

As she and the detective walked out of the suite, Serena was positive the housekeeper was watching every step they took. The woman, she knew, was a great fan of romances, both on the screen and within the pages of a book. She had no doubt that Alma was probably fabricating a story about her and the brooding detective at this very moment.

The less said, the better, Serena decided.

Sally, the cook who was currently in her parents' employ—they had gone through an even dozen in as many years—was just cleaning up the kitchen when she and Carson walked in.

Immediately coming to attention when she saw them, Sally, a pleasant-faced woman in her early fifties, asked her, "What can I prepare for you and your guest, Miss Serena?"

"He's not my guest. He's a police detective, part of the K-9 division," Serena added before Sally could ask about the dog. She didn't want the cook to think that she was willingly entertaining Carson.

"What can I prepare for you and the police detective?" Sally asked, amending her initial question.

But Serena shook her head. "That's all right, Sally. You can take the rest of the evening off. I'll make something for myself. For us," she corrected, remembering to include the silent shadow beside her. Given what he'd said earlier, Carson probably ate nails or something of that nature.

Sally looked at her hesitantly. "Are you sure, Miss Serena?"

"My parents and sister have gone to stay in a hotel in town," she said by way of an answer, indicating that this was going to be an informal meal. "I'm sure."

"There are some leftovers on the two top shelves," the woman began, still not leaving.

"I'm good at scrounging, Sally. Go. You deserve some time off," Serena said, smiling as she waved the woman out.

Sally's smile was as wide as her face. "Thank you, miss!" she cried before she hurried off.

Turning back to the refrigerator, Serena found that the detective was already there.

"Can I help you find anything?" she asked him a little stiffly. It was a large kitchen, but somehow, it felt smaller to her because of his presence.

"No," Carson answered simply. Then, because she continued to stand there next to the refrigerator, he told her, "I'm good at scrounging, too."

Giving him space, Serena looked down at Justice. The dog was never more than a few paces away from his partner. "I don't have any dog food."

Carson didn't seem fazed. "That's okay. He adjusts. Same as me."

She wasn't sure exactly what that comment meant when it came to Carson, but she had an uneasy feeling that maybe this was the detective's way of putting her on some sort of notice.

As if she wasn't tense enough already.

Chapter 12

After watching Carson stand there, looking into the refrigerator without taking anything out, it was obvious to Serena that the detective either couldn't make up his mind, or he really didn't feel right about helping himself to something from the giant, industrial-size refrigerator.

Serena decided to take matters into her own hands. "Sit down, Gage," she said, elbowing Carson out of the way.

"Excuse me?" Carson made no move to do what she'd just very crisply ordered him to do, at least not until he knew what she was up to.

Okay, maybe she'd been a little too abrupt, Serena silently conceded. She decided to word her request a little better. "Well, you've taken it upon yourself to be my and my daughter's bodyguard so the least I can do is get you something to eat."

He didn't want her to feel she needed to wait on him.

"I'm perfectly capable of getting something to eat for myself."

Serena rolled her eyes as she suppressed a sigh. "Does *everything* have to be an argument with you?" she asked. "Just sit!" she ordered.

Justice dropped down where he was standing, his big brown eyes trained on Serena. She laughed. "At least one of you doesn't have trouble following instructions."

"Hey," Carson pretended to protest. The protest was directed toward the German shepherd. "You're only supposed to listen to me, remember?" he told the canine.

"Too bad your dog can't teach you a few tricks," Serena quipped. Because the refrigerator was rather full and she had no idea what Carson would prefer eating, she asked, "Do you want a sandwich or a full meal?"

Carson had always leaned toward expediency. "A sandwich'll do fine."

There were sandwiches, and then there were *sandwiches*. "Okay, what do you want in your sandwich?"

Wide, muscular shoulders rose and fell in a dismissive, disinterested shrug. "Whatever you've got that's handy. I'm easy."

"Ha! Not hardly," Serena observed. His eyes met hers as if to contest her statement. However, Serena was not about to back down. "You, Detective Carson Gage, might be many things, but easy isn't one of them."

"And just what are some of those 'many things'?" Carson wanted to know, his eyes pinning her in place. He was ready for another argument.

There it was again, Serena thought. That flash of heat when he looked at her a certain way.

Stubbornly, Serena shut out her reaction, telling herself that she was smarter than that. There was no reason in the world for her to react like that to this rough-around-the-edges man or regard him as anything beyond a necessary evil.

Finished putting slices of freshly baked hickory-smoked ham on the extra thick bread that Sally baked for the family every other morning, she topped the sandwich off with slices of baby Swiss cheese. Serena put the whole thing on a plate with some lettuce and tomato slices on the side and pushed the plate over to him on the table.

"I see you finally sat down," she commented as she took out a bottle of ketchup and jars of mayonnaise and mustard. Serena paused over the last item. "Spicy or mild?"

Carson's mouth curved as he looked at her. "I like spicy."

There was that flash again, Serena thought in exasperation. She was just going to have to stop making eye contact with the man. But if she did that, he'd probably think she was avoiding him for some reason that she'd wind up finding insulting when he voiced it.

She took the jar of spicy mustard out of the refrigerator and placed it next to the other condiments. "Spicy, it is."

Eyes as dark as storm clouds on the horizon took measure of her as he reached for the mustard. He nodded toward the mayonnaise and the ketchup. "I don't need the others," he told her.

There was absolutely no reason for her heart to have sped up, Serena told herself. For pity's sake, it was just a conversation about some stupid mustard, nothing else. But she could feel her neck growing warmer, her palms getting damp and her knees felt as if they were getting ready to dissolve any minute now.

It was just the tension of recent events that were

getting to her, Serena silently argued. A panic attack after the fact. Once everything got back to normal, so would she.

Carson took a bite of the large sandwich that now also included lettuce as well as a healthy slice of tomato.

"The ham's good," he pronounced.

Serena smiled. "I'll tell Sally you said so. She doesn't get any positive feedback from my family. My mother usually berates her over things that she found lacking, things that poor Sally usually has no control over. Mother demands perfection—as well as mind reading— which would explain why we've been through a dozen cooks in the last twelve years," Serena commented, placing several slices of ham on a plate and then putting the plate in front of Justice.

The plate was cleaned before Carson had finished half his sandwich.

Done, Justice looked up at her, clearly waiting for more. When she made no attempt to move toward the refrigerator to give him more ham, Justice nudged her with his nose as if he was trying to get her to go back to "the magic box" that contained the meat.

"Justice, sit," Carson ordered sternly.

The canine instantly obeyed, looking rather dejected about it in Serena's opinion. Feeling sorry for the canine, Serena pulled a slice of ham out of the sandwich she had just fixed for herself.

She was about to give it to Justice when she heard Carson gruffly tell her, "Don't."

Startled, she looked in Carson's direction. Her eyes narrowed. "Are you ordering me around?"

Rather than answer her question, Carson felt it would be wiser to explain why he'd stopped her.

"Like the rest of the K-9s, Justice was painstakingly

trained. If I give him a command and you do something that negates what I'm trying to convey to him, he's getting mixed signals that are bound to confuse him. There are times when my life depends on his reaction, and I'd rather that Justice wasn't confused."

Serena frowned. "I really doubt that he's going to have to defend you from being assaulted by a slice of ham," she told him sarcastically.

"The point I'm trying to get across is that disobedience just breeds more of the same," Carson informed her matter-of-factly. "And as I said, all the dogs that are part of the K-9 unit were very specifically trained."

"I know," she said, trying not to sound impatient, "by your brother."

But Carson shook his head. "Bo just raised the dogs," he told her. "He did some early work with them, but then the K-9 Training Center selected professional dog trainers for their program. Professional trainers like Hayley," he said, thinking of the woman Bo had been engaged to, "who worked with the dogs to train them for a number of diverse fields within the K-9 department. My brother definitely wasn't disciplined enough in his private life to train a goldfish, much less a German shepherd.

"Hell, Bo couldn't even discipline himself. Part of me," he admitted seriously, "is rather surprised that a jealous boyfriend didn't take him out long ago. Bo was always playing fast and loose, seeing one girl behind another one's back, jumping out of bedroom windows to avoid being on the wrong end of a jealous boyfriend's or enraged husband's gun."

Serena suddenly felt her opinion validated. "So you do have other people to investigate instead of just Demi," she cried.

"Yes and no," Carson said. "Bo actually settled down once he took up with Hayley," Carson said. Of course, he added silently, that had been for only the last three months, but it was a new pattern. "He didn't cheat on her, so jealous husbands and boyfriends were no longer prominently in the picture." He couldn't help thinking of what a terrible waste it all was. "I thought that maybe he finally grew up."

"Grew up?" Serena repeated, surprised. She thought about how Lora's father disappeared on her, taking her money and her credit cards with him. She'd been abandoned, humiliated *and* robbed, a veritable trifecta. "I thought that most men felt that this was the kind of lifestyle they aspired to—juggling women, enjoying them, then disappearing once it got too serious."

"I wouldn't know," Carson told her. "I never took a survey."

She decided the detective wasn't going to squirm out of giving her a straight answer. "How about you?" she pressed. "Did you look up to Bo? Did you want to be like him?"

Carson looked at her as if she had lost her mind. "Why the hell would I want to be like Bo? I'm already looking over my shoulder to make sure that there aren't any bad guys trying to take me out as it is. I wouldn't want to add disgruntled husbands and angry ex-girlfriends to that number."

He almost sounded as if he meant it. Serena caught herself wanting to believe him, but her experience with Lora's father had tainted her.

"So then you're monogamous?" she asked.

"What I am," Carson told her with a finality that said he wanted to be done with this conversation, "is focused on my job. That takes up all of my time. Right, Justice?" he asked, looking at the dog.

Justice barked, then looked at Serena. The German shepherd began to drool, clearly eyeing the remainder of her sandwich.

Serena, in turn, looked at Carson. "Here," she said, pushing her plate and what was left of her sandwich toward him. "You give it to Justice. I wouldn't want to interfere with the connection you two have."

"Justice," Carson said sternly. The dog immediately became alert, looking at Carson and waiting for his next command. "At ease."

With that, the canine relaxed, almost flopping down on the floor.

"Okay, now you can give that to him," he told Serena, nodding at what was left of her sandwich.

She could only stare at him, stunned. "'At ease'? You're kidding."

"No," he answered. "Training is training. Trust me, this is for everyone's own good. Justice has to know who to listen to. If I tell him 'at ease,' he knows it's okay with me if he goes with his instincts."

"All that with 'at ease'?" she said, marveled but somewhat skeptical nonetheless.

"There's a little more to it than that," Carson admitted. Now, however, wasn't the time to get into it. It was getting late. "But yeah."

She shook her head, then held out her sandwich to Justice. The dog quickly consumed every last bite, carefully eating it out of her hand.

His teeth never once even came close to nipping her skin.

When the sandwich was gone, Serena brushed off

her hands against one another, still marveling at how gentle Justice had been.

"You're right," she told Carson. "Your dog is very well trained."

"He's not my dog," Carson corrected her. "He's my partner. Best partner I ever had," he said, affectionately petting the animal and ruffling Justice's black-and-tan fur. "He doesn't mouth off, doesn't give me any grief and always has my back."

"Sounds like a match made in heaven," Serena commented.

"It pretty much is," Carson agreed.

He got up and carried his empty plate to the sink. She expected the detective to leave his plate there and was surprised to see him wash the plate and place it in the rack to dry.

Turning around to see that she was watching him, Carson made an assumption as to what she was probably thinking.

"I wasn't raised in a barn," he told her.

"I didn't think you were," she assured him quickly. "It's just that nobody does that around here," she explained. "I mean, I do sometimes, but Anders doesn't take his meals here and my parents and sister just assume that's what the housekeeper is for. In their opinion, it's all just part of 'keeping the house.'"

She'd managed to arouse his curiosity again. "What makes you so different from them?" he asked.

She hadn't given it much thought. It was just something that had always been that way. Since he asked, Serena thought for a moment before answering.

"I think for myself. And I like working with the horses." She thought of the way Joanelle turned her nose up at things. "My mother wouldn't be caught dead near the corral unless the rest of the ranch was on fire. Maybe not even then," she amended with a whimsical smile.

Serena realized that the detective had grown quiet and was just studying her. She'd said too much, she admonished herself.

Clearing her throat, she picked up her own plate and glass and made her way over to the sink, where she washed them.

"I'd better be getting back up to Lora," she told him, paving the way for her retreat. "She's probably waking up about now. Poor Alma's practically put in a full day taking care of her. It might not look it, but taking care of a baby is exhausting. Alma doesn't complain, but I know she'd welcome having the rest of the evening to herself. With the rest of the family gone, there won't be any sudden 'emergencies' cropping up."

When Carson began to follow her out of the kitchen, she was quick to try to divert him.

"You don't have to come up right away. There's a big-screen TV in the entertainment room if you want to watch anything." She gestured toward the large room as she passed it on her way to the staircase.

"I'm not here to watch TV," he told her. "I'm here to watch you."

"I didn't think you meant that literally," she protested. At the very most, she'd thought he'd just be somewhere on the premises, not really with her. Not for the night.

Carson could almost read her mind. "I don't intend to hover over you, if that's what you're afraid of, Serena. But I do intend to be close by."

Serena made her way up the stairs, then paused and turned around. She was two steps above Carson. Just enough to bring them eye to eye, literally rather than figuratively.

"Define 'close by.'"

"A room near your suite," he answered. "Or I can just bed down in front of your door if need be."

What she needed, Serena thought, attempting to reconcile herself to this turn of events, was to get her life back.

She blew out a breath. "You really intend to go through with this."

"I said I would and I always live up to my word."

"Why couldn't you be a liar like every other man?" she murmured under her breath as she turned around and started to go up the stairs again.

He couldn't make out what she'd said, only that Serena had said something. "What?"

Serena merely sighed and continued walking up the stairs. There was no point in repeating what she'd said. "Never mind."

Chapter 13

The housekeeper was on her feet the moment that Serena walked into the suite.

Serena could see by the look on Alma's face that the woman seemed very interested in the fact that Carson still hadn't left the Double C.

Not only hadn't the detective left it, but he gave no indication that he was going anywhere this evening.

Normally, Serena prided herself as being a private person who didn't go out of her way to justify her actions. What people thought about her was their own business and she was not in the habit of making any excuses. But she liked Alma. The woman had been exceptionally helpful and kind to her, especially when she'd been pregnant with Lora.

Right now, she could see that Alma was dying to ask questions, but her mother had been very specific when it came to what her "place" was as a housekeeper for

Judson Colton and his family. Consequently, the woman would explode before asking anything concerning why the detective was still here.

"Justice and I are going to take a look around the second floor," the detective told Serena, walking out of her room. "We're going to make sure that there's nobody up here, present company excepted."

Serena waited until Carson was out of earshot. "Alma," she began. "I'm going to need you to bring some bedding into the spare bedroom that's next to my suite. Detective Gage is spending the night," she added, watching the housekeeper.

Alma's expression remained impassive. She nodded dutifully. "Very good, Miss Serena."

"No, it isn't," Serena corrected, knowing exactly what was going through the other woman's head. "But it is what it is and we're just going to have to deal with it for the night." That didn't come out right, Serena thought. She tried again. "It's the detective's intention to stand guard over us to make sure that Lora and I stay safe."

This time she saw Alma smile, sanctioning what the detective was doing. "Very good, Miss Serena."

"Then you approve?" Serena asked, trying to find out just what the woman thought of the whole setup. As for herself, she hadn't reconciled herself to the idea of having Carson hovering around like a brooding guardian angel.

"It's not my place to approve or disapprove, Miss Serena. I'm only supposed to follow orders," Alma replied quietly.

"But you must have an opinion," Serena pressed.

"I am not being paid to have an opinion, Miss Serena. Only to make things as comfortable as possible for you and your family." When Serena gave her a look that clearly said she wanted the woman to give voice to something a little more personal than that, Alma gave every indication that her lips were sealed.

And then the housekeeper leaned in a little closer to the young woman, who, unlike her parents and younger sister, always treated her with kindness and respect.

Lowering her voice, Alma said, "It's a good thing to have someone so capable and good-looking watching over you."

Serena bit back a laugh despite herself. Obviously Carson's looks had won the housekeeper over. "I didn't know you noticed things like that, Alma."

"I'm not dead, miss," the woman replied just as Carson and his four-footed partner returned to the suite.

Carson looked from the housekeeper to Serena. Judging from the housekeeper's expression and the sudden onset of silence as he walked in, he guessed that something was up. "Did I miss something?" he asked after the other woman left the room.

Serena looked at him with wide-eyed innocence. "I thought you never missed anything," she told him. "Isn't that why you're here?"

She was clearly baiting him. He deliberately ignored it. Instead, he merely gave her his report. "Justice and I swept through your floor. Everything looks to be in order."

She couldn't explain why, but Carson's solemn expression just made her want to laugh. "Nobody's hiding in the closet?"

His eyes went flat. "This isn't a joke, Serena," he said gruffly. "Someone took a shot at you today."

She was not about to allow herself to be paralyzed by

fear. "I'm really not worried about someone who can't hit the broadside of a barn," Serena told him.

He didn't like the fact that she was taking all this so lightly. Didn't she realize the very real danger she could be in?

"Maybe they can and they're just toying with you first," Carson pointed out. "Are you willing to bet your daughter's life that you're right?" he demanded, struggling to keep his voice down so as not to wake up the sleeping baby.

Serena frowned, glancing over her shoulder toward the crib. "You really do know how to get to a person, don't you?"

Carson definitely didn't see it that way. "If I did," he told Serena, "you and your daughter would be in town by now, staying in the hotel with the rest of your family."

This wasn't going anywhere, and she was not about to just stand here, listening to him go over what he viewed as her shortcomings.

"My housekeeper put fresh linens in the guest room for you," she told the detective. "It's this way." Crossing to the doorway of her bedroom, she found Carson blocking her exit. She could see that he wasn't about to go anywhere. She glared at the man. "I can't walk through you," she said pointedly.

He had no desire to be down the hall from her. If something went wrong, seconds would count. "That's okay. Justice and I'll just bunk down outside your door. It's closer that way," he emphasized.

Enough was enough. "Aren't you carrying this whole thing a little too far?" she asked, irritated. "If this person is dumb enough to show up here, we're dealing with someone with an ax to grind, not a professional cat burglar who's light on their feet."

And then Serena decided to attempt to use another tactic.

"Alma made the bed up for you," she reminded him. "If you don't use it, the woman's feelings will be hurt and heaven knows my family's done enough of a number on her. To be honest, I have no idea why Alma puts up with it and stays."

Carson laughed shortly and shook his head at her in wonder. "And that's supposed to get me to use the guest room?"

"No," she corrected, "common sense is supposed to do that. Besides, you're probably the type who sleeps with one eye and both ears open, so if anyone does try to break in and shoot me, you'll hear them before they get off a shot."

Carson knew she was mocking him. But he also knew that he wasn't about to get anywhere arguing with her. Justice was with him; he was confident that the German shepherd would alert him if anyone who didn't belong on the premises entered the house.

So, because it was getting late, and in the interest of peace, Carson gave in. "Okay, you win. If you need me, I'll be in the guest room."

Serena looked at him in surprise. She'd expected him to put up more of a fight than this. Was he up to something?

"You're being reasonable?" she asked, looking at him uncertainly.

The expression on her face was worth the capitulation. "It's been known to happen."

She decided it was best to call it a night before Carson decided to change his mind and resurrect the argument.

"Good, then if you don't mind, I'm going to try to get some sleep while my daughter's still napping." She gestured to the open door down the hall. "That's your room. I'll see you in the morning, Detective."

"Yes," he assured her, standing there a moment longer and looking at her, "you will."

Why did such a simple sentence cause her to suddenly feel hot ripples going up and down her skin? He wasn't saying anything out of the ordinary. The detective was agreeing with her, for pity's sake.

So why did she feel as if he'd just set up some sort of a secret rendezvous between them?

He hadn't done anything of the sort, Serena silently insisted, firmly closing her bedroom door behind her. All he'd said was that he'd see her in the morning, which right now seemed like an inevitable fact of life. But by no means was he making some sort of an earthshaking revelation.

Was he?

She was getting punchy, Serena told herself with a sigh. Punchy. That was why she wasn't thinking straight and coming up with all these strange thoughts and reactions.

She supposed that, in all honesty, the missed shot really had unnerved her.

What if it *had* been someone out to shoot her?

But why? Why would anyone want to shoot *her*? She just didn't understand. No one had come out and threatened her and she certainly wasn't a threat to anyone. It all had to be some kind of a gross misunderstanding, and the sooner it was cleared up, the sooner she would be able to get back to her old life.

Her relatively uneventful, humdrum life, she thought as she sat pulling a hairbrush through her hair, something she had done religiously ever since she'd been old enough to hold her own hairbrush.

Feeling exceptionally tired all of a sudden, Serena gave up brushing her hair and laid the brush aside.

She slipped into the nursery, checking on her daughter. The crib had just been moved there from her own room yesterday. Lingering, she watched Lora sleep for a minute or two, then crossed back to her bedroom. Mechanically turning off the lamp, Serena crawled into bed, bone weary beyond words.

She was asleep within less than five minutes.

It was the dream that woke her. A dream that a tall slender person had slipped into her room and was now running off with her daughter.

A scream rose in her throat, but try as she might, Serena just couldn't make herself release it, couldn't scream to alert Carson so that he could come and rescue her daughter.

Oh, why hadn't she allowed him to spend the night on the floor right outside her suite the way he'd wanted to? The kidnapper would have never got in to steal her baby if Carson had been standing guard right by her door.

Frightened, she tried to scream again, but nothing came out. It was as if her throat had been sealed shut.

Just like her eyes. They were shut, too, she realized. Shut and practically glued together.

Was that it? Were they glued shut?

Why couldn't she open her eyes? She needed to be able to see the person who had broken into her suite. The person who had just made off with her baby.

How could she give Carson a description of the fiend when she couldn't see him?

A hot wave of desperation washed over Serena as she tried to scream again. To make some kind of a noise, any kind of a noise, in order to scare away the intruder.

No sounds came.

She felt absolutely powerless.

Carson wasn't in the habit of falling asleep while on duty. It had never happened to him before. He prided himself on being able to get by with next to no sleep for several days on end.

But he'd been going nonstop for more than a few days now and though he really hated to admit it, hated what it ultimately said about his stamina, it had finally caught up to him.

Carson didn't remember his eyes shutting. But they must have because the next thing he knew, they were flying open, pried open by a sound.

A sound that had seeped into his consciousness.

The sound of Justice's nails along the marble floor as he suddenly scrambled up, completely alert.

Carson was still groggy and half-asleep, but he knew that his K-9 partner had been awakened by something.

Or someone.

Suddenly as alert as his dog, Carson immediately scanned the darkened room, searching for movement, for some minute indication that something was out of place.

Everything was just the way it had been when he'd settled back on the bed.

But he knew he'd heard something.

And from the way Justice had gained his feet, so had the German shepherd.

Opening the door ever so carefully, Carson slipped out into the hall. Nothing was moving, nothing was out of place.

Maybe he'd been dreaming after all.

But glancing at Justice told him that it wasn't a dream. Something was definitely up.

Exercising the same stealth movements, Carson opened the door leading into Serena's suite. He knew he ran the risk of having her think he was taking advantage of the situation, but that really didn't matter in this case. His gut was telling him to push on.

Something was up.

Moving in almost painfully slow motion, Carson opened Serena's door. With his fingertips against the highly polished door, he eased it back until he was able to look into the room.

It was cold, unusually cold.

The door between the bedroom and the nursery was open.

A movement in the nursery caught his eye.

As his vision acclimated to the darkness, Carson saw a tall slender figure dressed completely in black leaning over the baby's crib.

Reaching in.

Carson had his gun in his hand, but he couldn't risk taking a shot. The dark figure was too close to Lora.

"Freeze!" he ordered in a loud, menacing voice.

Startled, the figure bolted toward the open balcony doors on the other side of Serena's bedroom.

Serena had jackknifed upright in bed and screamed when she realized that someone was in her room. Instinctively, she knew that her daughter's life was in danger.

She hadn't been dreaming; this was very real!

Justice and then Carson whizzed by her bed, running toward the balcony. There was a new moon out so there was nothing to illuminate her room and help her see what was happening.

She sensed rather than saw that someone was in her suite. It was possibly more than just one person.

Serena quickly turned on the lamp next to her bed. Light flooded the room at the same time that she reached into the nightstand drawer. She pulled out the handgun she always kept there.

Carson and Justice had reached the balcony, but they were too late to stop the fleeing potential kidnapper. All Carson saw was a dark figure who had managed to get down to the ground unhurt and was now sprinting away from the mansion.

The darkness quickly swallowed the would-be kidnapper up.

"Damn it," Carson cursed under his breath. His weapon was still drawn, but he wasn't about to shoot at what he couldn't really see.

Turning back toward the suite, he went in and was about to close the door—by now the suite was absolutely freezing—when he saw Serena. She was pointing a handgun at him.

"Whoa, whoa, whoa," he cautioned, raising one hand while the other still held his weapon. "Put that thing down. I'm one of the good guys, remember?"

But Serena kept her weapon trained on him. She wasn't about to lower it until he answered some questions to her satisfaction. She was breathing hard and her heart was racing like crazy.

It took her a second to catch her breath. "What just happened?" she wanted to know.

Turning his back on her, Carson secured the balcony

doors and then turned around to face her. "As near as I can figure it, Justice and I just stopped someone from kidnapping your baby."

Serena's arms sagged. The handgun she was holding suddenly felt as if it weighed a ton.

With concentrated effort, she put it back in the open drawer. All she could do was stare at the detective, dumbfounded.

Her throat almost closed up as she cried, "Kidnapping?"

Chapter 14

"That's what I said," Carson confirmed quietly with just the slightest nod of his head as he looked at her. "Kidnapping."

If anything, the idea of someone shooting at her ultimately made Serena angry. She could deal with that, find a way to fight back and defend herself. It was in her nature to fight back.

But the thought of someone kidnapping her child, that was an entirely different matter. That was scary.

She could feel a cold chill not only running up and down her spine, but gripping her heart and squeezing it so hard that she could barely breathe.

She moved over to the crib in the nursery. Somehow, Lora had slept through all the commotion. Serena felt a very real desire to stand here forever and just watch her daughter sleep. The scene was such a contrast to what *could* have happened.

"Who would want to kidnap Lora?" Serena wanted to know, her voice quavering as she tried to come to terms with the frightening thought.

Carson shrugged. He moved a little closer to Serena but still managed to maintain a safe distance. He didn't want her to feel that he was crowding her. He just wanted her to realize that he was there for her. For her daughter and her.

"Maybe Demi was looking for some leverage to use to get the police off her back."

"Demi again," Serena cried, stunned. She moved away from the crib, taking their conversation to the threshold between her bedroom and the nursery. "You think that Demi Colton is behind this, too," she said incredulously, then demanded, "Are you kidding me?"

Carson's expression was deadly serious. "That shadowy figure could have easily matched a description of Demi's body type."

At another time, she might have been rendered speechless, but this was about her daughter as well and she needed Carson to find whoever was behind this threat—and it *wasn't* Demi.

"Good Lord, by the time you're done, Demi Colton is going to be behind every crime committed in the county, maybe even in this part of the state." Did he see how ludicrous what he'd just said sounded? "Demi's smart, I'll give you that. But she isn't some kind of criminal mastermind," Serena cried.

"What is this obsession you have with her?" she wanted to know. And then, as if hearing the exasperation in her own voice, Serena took a breath and backed off. "Look, I'm sorry. You saved my baby, and I am very grateful to you. I didn't mean to go off on you like that." She dragged her hand through her hair. "I guess

I'm just on edge. But I think I got a better look at whoever was in my room than you did—"

Carson was immediately alert. "You saw the kidnapper's face?"

She only wished she had. "No, the kidnapper had on a ski mask. But whoever it was that ran by was too tall to be Demi."

Carson wasn't so sure. "Demi's about five foot nine, five foot ten and slim. The kidnapper was under six feet and on the thin side."

But Serena just shook her head. "No, it's not her," she said with conviction. "She doesn't need to steal *my* baby."

There was something in Serena's voice that he couldn't quite put his finger on. Maybe she was just being overly protective of the other woman.

Carson pressed on. "Maybe she wants to hold your daughter for ransom. She knows you'll pay whatever she asks and a big payoff will go a long way in setting her up in a new life somewhere else." And then he stopped, thinking. If the kidnapper had tried once, maybe Demi, or whoever it was, would try again. "Maybe you should reconsider staying at the hotel with your family until this blows over."

But that was definitely the wrong thing to say to her. "No. I'm not going to let whoever's doing this run me off my own land," Serena said fiercely.

There was bravery—and then there was such a thing as being *too* brave without considering the consequences. "Even if it means putting your daughter in danger?" Carson wanted to know.

"I have you to protect her, don't I?" Serena responded. She could feel anger bubbling up inside of her. "And just what kind of a mother would I be, teaching my daughter that it's all right to run at the first sign of trouble?"

Serena had leaped out of her bed when he and Justice had raced into the room. Confronted with the possibility of her daughter being stolen, she hadn't thought to put on a robe.

She still hadn't, and now he found himself wishing that she would. It wasn't his place to say anything. The nightgown she was wearing wasn't exactly transparent, but it did cause his imagination to wreak havoc.

Carson forced himself to focus on what had almost just happened and not on the tantalizing way her breasts rose and fell.

"Your daughter is three months old. I don't think she'll know the difference if you dig in or leave," he told her sternly.

Serena's eyes flashed. Did he think that she was going to hide behind the fact that her daughter was an infant? "Maybe she won't," she agreed. "But I'll know."

There were several choice words he wanted to say to her about taking risks and being foolhardy, words that were hovering on the tip of his tongue. With steely resolve, Carson managed to refrain from uttering any of them.

Instead, he merely grunted in response to the sentiment she'd expressed. He was learning that arguing with the woman was just an exercise in futility.

"Justice and I are going to have another look around the place, make sure your night caller didn't get it into his head to double back and try again." He crossed to the balcony, checking to make sure that the doors leading out were still locked. "When I leave, I want you to lock your doors. Don't open them to anyone."

"Except for you," she amended, certain he had omitted that part of the instruction.

"You don't have to concern yourself with me," he told her. He nodded toward her bed. "Just try to get some sleep before morning."

Right. Sleep. Easy for you to say, Serena thought as she closed her bedroom doors behind Carson and then locked them.

She went to the balcony doors and checked them even though she had seen Carson lock them earlier and just check them before he left.

She crossed back into the nursery. It amazed her again that Lora had not only slept through the kidnapping threat but had slept through the raised voices, as well. As for her, she knew that there was no way she was going to get back to sleep, not in her present frame of mind. Every sound that she would hear—or *thought* she heard—was going to be magnified to twice its volume, if not more.

Resigned, Serena didn't even bother lying down. Instead, she decided just to sit and keep vigil in the oversize rocker-recliner that Anders had got her as a gift when Lora was born.

Wanting to be fully prepared for whatever might happen, Serena took her handgun out of the nightstand drawer and put it on the small table next to the rocker-recliner.

Sitting down, she proceeded to wait for the intruder to return or for dawn to break, whatever would happen first.

Serena was still in the recliner when daybreak finally came. It seemed like an eternity later to her and she felt somewhat stiff after spending what was left of the night in an upright sitting position.

But she'd had no intention of being caught off guard again if the intruder returned. An aching body was more than a fair trade-off to knowing her daughter was safe.

As it was, the only "intruder" she had to deal with was Lora, who woke up twice in the last few hours, once because she was wet, once because she was hungry. Taking care of both needs as they arose, Serena returned her daughter to her crib and each time Lora obligingly went back to sleep.

Feeling achy and stiff, Serena really wanted to take a shower, but she wanted to make sure that nothing else had gone down during the past night. She'd half expected Carson to check in on her. When he hadn't, she just assumed that he and his German shepherd had gone back to the guest room.

However the more time that passed, the more uneasy she became. So finally, pausing only to throw on some clothes, Serena opened her bedroom door, ready to go and knock on the guest room door in order to wake Carson up.

She didn't have to.

Carson was right there, sitting cross-legged on the floor in front of her door. The second she opened the door, the detective was up on his feet—and Justice was right there beside him.

Startled, she was quick to silence the gasp that rose to her lips. She did her best to look unfazed about finding him even though the exact opposite was true. Bending down to pet Justice—the canine appeared to have taken a liking to her—she was able to effectively mask her surprise.

"I thought you were going to spend the night in the guest room," she said, straightening up.

"Never said that," Carson reminded her. He was relieved that she'd got dressed before coming out, although there was a part of him that had to admit he'd liked the previous view.

"You spent the whole night on the floor outside my bedroom?" Serena questioned. Who did that when there was a comfortable bed only yards away?

"There wasn't a whole night left after the kidnapper ran off," he corrected.

Serena sighed. Her surprised observation wasn't meant to be the opening line for a debate.

"Isn't *anything* a simple yes or no with you?" she asked, frustrated that there wasn't such a thing as a simple conversation when it came to this man.

"No," he answered honestly.

The maddening impossibility of the whole situation suddenly hit her and Serena started to laugh.

Her laughter was infectious and after a minute, Carson's laughter blended with hers. The laughter continued for more than a couple of minutes and managed to purge some of the ongoing tension that was shimmering between them.

It also managed to draw the housekeeper, who was already up and dressed, to Serena's suite.

The woman made a quick assessment of her own about the state of affairs. Alma looked from Serena to the detective, then smiled. "Apparently, from the sound of it, the night went well."

Serena decided to wait to tell the woman about the aborted kidnapping after she had a chance to get some coffee into her system.

So all she said in response now was, "Well, we're still here."

Alma nodded, looking pleased. "Yes, so I see. There's a pot of fresh coffee downstairs," she told Serena.

"Music to my ears, Alma," Serena responded.

Obviously thinking that the two were about to go downstairs to the kitchen, the housekeeper offered, "If you give me a moment, I'll get Sally up to make you breakfast."

But Serena waved away the suggestion. "No, don't bother. Let Sally sleep in for once. I can handle breakfast for the detective and myself," Serena told the housekeeper.

"Are you sure, Miss Serena?" Alma asked.

"I'm sure," she told the housekeeper. "As long as you watch Lora for me."

"Consider it done," Alma answered with pleased enthusiasm.

"Should I be worried?" Carson asked Serena as they went downstairs.

Reaching the landing, Serena went on to the kitchen. The house seemed almost eerily quiet to her. She was accustomed to hearing her mother's voice raised in displeasure, ordering someone around.

"Only if you get me angry when I have a frying pan in my hand," Serena replied. "But if you're referring to my cooking, I haven't poisoned anyone yet."

It was hard for him to believe that a pampered Colton was serious about making breakfast. "I didn't know you cooked."

"Lots of things about me you don't know," she answered. Opening one of the refrigerator doors, she took out four eggs. "I don't like being waited on," she went on, "so I learned how to cook."

Putting the eggs on the counter, she paused as she reached for some bread. And then it occurred to her that she had just assumed what he wanted for breakfast without asking.

Turning toward Carson now, she remedied the situation. "I didn't ask you. Eggs and toast okay, or do you want something else? I can make pancakes or waffles, or—"

"Eggs and toast will be fine," he answered before she could go through an entire litany of all the different things that came under the heading of breakfast.

"Eggs and toast, it is," Serena agreed. "How do you want your eggs?"

He'd already told her last night that he was generally indifferent to food. "Any way but raw."

Serena laughed in response.

He wasn't aware that he'd said anything amusing. "What's so funny?"

She shook her head. She supposed that the man just didn't see it. "Anyone who didn't know you would say you were easy."

So far, he still didn't see what was so amusing to Serena. "I *am* easy."

She put four slices into the toaster, adjusting the lever for medium.

"You keep telling yourself that, Carson."

"I *am* easy," Carson stressed. "I have few requirements." Serena handed him a cup of black coffee. He accepted it automatically. "One of which is that I don't like being lied to."

She stopped pouring coffee into her mug and turned to look at him. Was he deliberately being enigmatic, or was he just fishing for a response from her? "Are you saying I did?"

Carson raised one eyebrow, his gaze pinning hers. "Did you?"

Serena never flinched or looked away. Instead, she raised her chin defiantly and told him, "No."

Carson decided to believe her—unless she gave him reason not to. "Then we should keep it that way," he told her.

"No problem here." She took a long sip of her coffee, then turned her attention to preparing the rest of the breakfast. "By the way, does that go both ways?"

"Are you asking me if I lied to you?" Carson wanted to know.

Two could play at this vague game of his. "I am."

His voice was dead serious as he answered her. "I didn't."

Maybe she was just being naively foolish, but she believed him. Or maybe she just wanted to feel that there was someone on her side. "Looks like everything's just coming up roses between us then," she responded. And then she saw him grin. "What?"

"That strange, ungodly sound that you're hearing are dead Coltons and Gages, collectively rolling over in their graves," he said.

Buttering the slices of toast that had just popped up, she laughed. "They would, wouldn't they? You know, I kind of like that idea, doing something to cause past generations of Coltons and Gages to roll over in their graves.

"I always thought the idea of a family feud was the stupidest waste of time imaginable," she continued. "That sort of thing belongs to the Hatfields and the McCoys, not to people who live in the twenty-first century," Serena said as she scrambled the four eggs together in a large frying pan. Looking at the pan, she grinned. "My mother would be horrified if she saw me making a Gage breakfast in our kitchen. Hell, she'd be horrified if she saw me making breakfast, period, but especially for a Gage," she told him.

"I said you didn't have to," he reminded her.

Detective or not, the man could be very dense, Serena thought. "You're missing the point," she told him.

"I guess I am," he was willing to admit. "Educate me. What is the point?"

She lowered the temperature under the frying pan. "That two intelligent families feuding over something that happened between two people decades ago is stupid and anyone with half a brain should definitely not allow themselves to be pulled into this feud."

"Do I qualify as someone with half a brain?" he wanted to know, amused by her description.

Still scrambling the eggs, Serena looked at him. "At least half," she deadpanned.

"Thanks."

"Don't mention it," she managed to say before the grin won out, curving her mouth. "Get a couple of plates from the cupboard, will you?"

There was no shortage of cupboards and cabinets in the large kitchen. He could be opening and closing doors for several minutes.

"You want to point me in the right direction?" he asked.

Responding, Serena moved the frying pan off the active burner. "Typical male," she commented with amusement. Hands on his shoulders, she literally pointed Carson toward the cupboard that held the everyday dishes. "That one," she told him.

He knew it was his imagination, but he could swear that he felt the warmth from her hands coming through his shirt, seeping into his shoulders. The warmth found its way into his system, spreading out through all of him.

He hadn't been with a woman since Lisa had died, and for some reason, he was acutely aware of that lack right at this moment. Aware of the fact that it had been eating away at him, bit by bit, from the first time he had laid eyes on her.

"Are you all right?" Serena asked when he made no move toward the cupboard.

"Yeah." Carson forced himself to shake off the feeling that was taking hold of him and got the plates she'd requested. He placed them on the counter. "Just wondering why anyone would need this many cabinets, that's all."

"That's an easy one to answer," she told him, dividing the eggs between the two plates. The mansion belonged to her mother when her father had married her and Joanelle was responsible for every part of its decor. "For show."

Chapter 15

"For show?" Carson repeated as Serena took her seat at the table.

He thought he understood what she was saying, but he wanted to make sure he wasn't assuming too much, so he waited for a little clarification.

And Serena had no problem giving it. "It is my mother's life ambition to make every other living person be in total awe and envy of her—and she won't rest until that happens." As far as she was concerned, her mother's attitude was deplorable, but she wasn't about to say it out loud.

Joanelle Colton's shallowness was nothing new as far as Carson was concerned. He shrugged, paying far more attention to his bracing cup of coffee than to the conversation.

After taking a long sip, he quipped, "I guess everyone should have a goal in life."

"Well, the baby and I definitely put a crimp in her goal," she commented more to herself than to Carson as she quickly consumed her breakfast. She had a full day ahead of her and she needed to get to it.

Carson, however, seemed to have other ideas. Serena was about to get up when he asked her another question.

"Earlier, you said that Demi didn't need to kidnap your daughter. What did you mean by that?" The way she had phrased it—as well as her tone of voice—had been preying on his mind.

That had been a slip on her part, Serena thought. She shouldn't have said anything.

She shrugged now, trying to dismiss the whole thing. "Oh, you know. The usual."

"No," he answered, not about to let the matter go so easily. "I don't know. Enlighten me." As he looked at her across the table, Carson once again had the distinct feeling that there was something she wasn't telling him. "Serena, if you're holding something back, I need to know. What is it you're not telling me?" he pressed. "You used the word *need* before. Was that just you talking a mile a minute, trying to find a way to make me stop looking at Demi as a suspect, or was there something more to this? I know that she took a lot of cash with her, but that doesn't mean she has enough to fund being on the run."

When Serena made no answer, it just reinforced the idea that he was on to something. "*Why* did you say she didn't *need* to kidnap your baby? Oh wait—you mean because she's pregnant herself."

He was crowding her and Serena lost her temper. "Exactly. She's going to have one of her own," she snapped. "That's all I meant. The idea of her kidnapping Lora for ransom is ludicrous and never would have occurred to me."

Serena stared up at the kitchen's vaulted ceiling, searching for strength.

"As I already asked, please don't say anything to anyone," she implored, looking into his eyes, trying to make contact with his soul—if he had one. "Demi didn't want anyone else to know. She only told me because she thought that I'd understand since I'd just gone through the same thing myself."

Carson looked at her, debating whether or not he was buying this. He hadn't told Finn, despite the pregnancy speaking to motive, no matter what Serena had said in opposition about how Demi wouldn't kill her child's father. Maybe because he wasn't sure yet if Demi was really pregnant at all. For reasons of her own, Serena might have made up the pregnancy to get him to feel sorry for Demi or go easier on her cousin.

For the moment, he decided to go along with Serena's story. "And she was sure that Bo was the father?"

Serena nodded. "Yes."

He waited, but Serena didn't say anything further. Instead, she reached over and gathered his empty plate, then stacked it on top of hers.

Carson put his hand over hers, stopping her from getting up with the plates.

"You said he didn't know about the baby."

"Right. Demi didn't want to tell him yet. He was marrying someone else. She didn't want to look as if she was trying to get him to call off the wedding and marry her instead. She didn't *want* him to marry her. Demi told me she had finally come to her senses and realized that Bo was loathsome—no offense."

"None taken." Serena wasn't giving voice to anything that hadn't crossed his mind about his brother more than once.

Serena went on to tell the detective, "Demi told me that she wouldn't marry Bo if he was dipped in gold and covered with diamonds."

He wondered if Demi had laid it on a little thick to cover her tracks. "Pretty harsh words for the father of her baby," Carson observed.

"Demi had caught him cheating on her more than once and, don't forget, they'd broken up," Serena reminded him. "Bo being the baby's father was just an unforeseen accident."

He saw the pregnancy in a slightly different light. "Certainly gives her motive to kill Bo."

He was back to that again? Serena rolled her eyes in exasperation. "Only if she'd wanted something from him, which she *didn't*. All Demi wanted before Bo went and got himself killed was just to have her baby and make a life for the two of them."

"Well, the simplest thing for Demi to do would be just to—"

Serena knew what he was going to say. He was going to say that Demi should do what her mother had told her to do when she had to tell her parents that she was pregnant. She cut Carson short before he was able to finish his sentence.

"No, that's not the 'simplest thing' for some women," she informed Carson, annoyed that he'd even think to suggest it. "For some women, that would be the worst course of action to take. Besides," she passionately maintained, "it's a baby, not a mistake."

Taking a breath, she forced herself to calm down. "But all that aside, you can see why she wouldn't want to kidnap my baby. She's already got one on the way to worry about."

"Yes, but a sizable ransom would go a long way to helping her raise that baby," Carson reminded her again.

"Except for one thing," Serena countered.

"What's that?"

"I already offered to *give* Demi money to see her through this, and she turned me down," she told the detective. "She wouldn't just turn around and then kidnap my baby."

He really did want to believe this scenario she'd just told him. "All right, let's just say that for now, you've convinced me—"

"Let's," Serena agreed, a semblance of a relieved smile curving her mouth.

There were other avenues to explore regarding the foiled kidnapping. For now, he went that route. "Do you have any enemies who would want to get back at you by kidnapping Lora?"

"I'm sorry to disappoint you but I don't have any enemies, period," she told him. "At least," she qualified, "none that I'm aware of."

Given her personality, he tended to believe that was true. He tried something else. "How about the baby's father?"

The smile vanished and her face sobered, darkening like a sky just before a winter storm rolled in. "What about him?"

"Would he kidnap Lora?" he asked. "You know, because he wants full custody of her?" He was familiar with cases like that and they left a bad taste in his mouth, but that didn't change the fact that they existed. "If you give me his name and where I can find him, I'll go question him, see if we can rule him out."

"I'll give you his name," she willingly agreed, "At least the one he gave me, but it's an alias," she told him. "And I have no idea where you can find him. Besides, even if you *could* find him, you'd be wasting your time asking him if he tried to kidnap Lora."

"And why is that?" Before she answered him, Carson read between the lines. "You're telling me he doesn't want to be a father?"

Serena's laugh was totally without a drop of humor. "I don't know what he wants to be, other than a full-time thief." She took the dishes over to the sink and began rinsing them.

Carson came up behind her. "You know you're going to have to give me more details than that," he told her.

She didn't look at Carson at first. She just braced her hands against the sink, desperately trying to center herself. "You're not going to be satisfied until you make me wind up spilling my insides to you, are you?"

His tone softened just a little. "I have no interest in your private life, Serena, but there's more at stake here than just your pride," he told her.

Serena closed her eyes for a moment, trying to separate herself from the words she was about to say. And then she turned around to tell Carson what he was waiting to hear.

"I was out of town at one of the region's bigger horse auctions. We were both bidding on the same horses. When I outbid him, he asked if he could buy me a beer to celebrate. A number of beers and whiskeys later, we were in my room, discussing the finer points of a horse's flanks," she said wryly.

"The next morning, I woke up to find that he was gone, along with all the cash in my wallet and my credit cards." She tried her best to keep the edge of bitterness out of her voice, but some of it came through. "I thought that was the worst of it—until three months later when I found that I was pregnant. And, like I said, the name he gave me was an alias so there was no way I could get in touch with him and tell him that he was about to become a father. He probably still doesn't know—and that's fine with me."

Offering comfort had never been something he was good at. Right now, Carson found himself wishing that it was. "I'm sorry."

She raised her eyes to his. "For asking?"

"No," he said honestly, "for what you went through."

That caused her to instantly rally—and grow slightly defensive. "Don't be. Lora's the most important person in my life and if I hadn't gone through all that, she wouldn't be here. She's my silver lining."

He took his cue from that. "I'm sure she is. And I'm going to keep you both safe." He said it matter-of-factly, but it was a promise, one that he intended to stand by.

"Thank you for that," she told him, her voice growing a little raspy. "If I ever lost her, I don't know what I'd do or how I'd ever recover from that."

The very thought of that happening caused tears to form in her eyes. Serena was immediately embarrassed about being so vulnerable in front of someone, especially in front of the detective.

"Sorry, you don't need to have me carrying on like a hysterical female. Go about doing whatever you're supposed to be doing," she told him, turning away so Carson wouldn't see the tears that she couldn't seem to stop from falling.

He stood there for a moment, watching her shoulders as they moved ever so slightly. He knew she was crying, and he hated that he had inadvertently caused that. He was torn between pretending he didn't notice and trying, ineptly, to comfort her.

But he was afraid that if he took her into his arms, strictly to comfort her, something of an entirely different nature might result.

However, he couldn't bring himself to just callously walk out, either. So he plucked a napkin from the napkin holder on the table and handed it to her.

"Thought you might need this," he murmured as he and Justice left the room.

Carson and his canine partner made the rounds on the ranch, covering the perimeter outside the mansion first. Urging Justice over to where the would-be kidnapper had jumped from Serena's balcony, he had the canine carefully survey the entire area, looking for a scent that would lead the dog to find whoever had made the inept attempt.

Justice suddenly became alert, finding a scent and eagerly following it for approximately a quarter of a mile where the scent, from the K-9's reaction, began to fade. Right next to a set of tire tracks.

Carson cursed under his breath, frustrated. Whoever the kidnapper was, he'd apparently made his escape via some sort of vehicle. Most likely a Jeep from the looks of them, he guessed.

The Jeep had driven onto a gravel road several yards away and that was where both the tire tracks and the scent abruptly ended.

Justice moved around in circles, looking as frustrated as he felt, Carson thought.

"You did your best, Justice," he told the dog. "But if the guy's stupid enough to come back, we'll be ready for him and he can kiss his sorry butt goodbye."

It occurred to Carson as he continued covering the grounds, looking for another lead or clue, that he was no longer referring to the person who had invaded Serena's home as "she."

"How about that?" he muttered to himself.

He supposed that Serena had finally won him over. Despite the necklace and the name written beside his brother's body, he was beginning to consider that Demi Colton was not behind any of this. Maybe Serena was right.

Maybe someone *was* trying to frame her.

With Demi out of the running—for now, he qualified—that brought him back to square one and a world full of possible suspects.

Carson dug in.

He spent the rest of the day questioning ranch hands to see if any of them had heard or seen anything last night that could help him identify who the potential kidnapper was.

As he'd expected, none of the hands had anything in the way of positive information to offer. The one thing he came away with was that they all sounded as if they were eager to help. They all seemed to like Serena.

"Hell, she doesn't treat us like we're dirt under her fingernails, like her mama does," one of the hands, Jake Rowan, confided when he was out of Anders's earshot.

"She's fine with working right alongside of us," Ramon Del Campo, another hand, told Carson. "You need anything to help find whoever took that shot at her, you let us know."

Carson nodded. For the most part, he'd found that when civilian volunteers got involved, things became more dangerous, not less. But wanting to foster this display of goodwill, he made a point of thanking each of the ranch hands before moving on.

During the course of the day, while conducting the interviews, Carson also checked in a number of times on Serena. She was working with the horses in the stable and the corral under the watchful eyes of several ranch hands at any one time. It put his mind somewhat at ease about her welfare.

Carson also stopped at the house to make sure that Lora was safe. Alma seemed capable enough, but the housekeeper, although quite sturdy, wouldn't be a match for anyone who chose to overpower her. Carson directed a couple of the ranch hands to keep watch outside the house, both front and back. They had instructions to fire off a round to get his attention in case someone they didn't know tried to get into the house.

Dusk was just setting in and he was bone tired as he walked into the mansion. Serena was in the living room, sitting on the sofa with Lora on her lap.

"So how are you?" Carson asked, crossing over to her.

"Tired. Why?" Serena asked warily. It was obvious that she thought he was about to spring something on her.

Carson shrugged, thinking that maybe he shouldn't have said anything. But he had had enough of isolating himself the way he'd been doing these last few years. A man shouldn't have to live like that, he silently argued.

He forced himself to continue. "It's just that when I left this morning, you seemed kind of upset. I just want you to know that I wasn't trying to pry."

He definitely wasn't the kind to pry, Serena thought.

If anything, he was the kind to encourage building up barricades. Barricades kept him safe from making any personal contact.

"I know that," she said.

Carson forced himself to go on. "I just wanted to rule out the possibility of Lora's father kidnapping her, either for the ransom or because he just wanted custody of the baby."

"I know that, too," she replied quietly. She didn't want to talk about what amounted to a one-night stand. "Could we change the subject?"

He wasn't finished yet. "In a minute."

Annoyed, she asked, "What else do you want to ask me?"

"Right now, nothing," he answered. "I just felt that since I burrowed into your life, making you uncomfortable, I should tell you something about mine so we're on equal footing."

She didn't quite understand where this was going, but she felt she had to tell him that, "I have no desire to make you feel uncomfortable."

"Yeah, well, then, maybe I feel that I owe this to you," he said. This was hard for him, but he felt he needed to share this with someone and if anyone would understand what he'd gone through, it would be Serena. "Just listen, okay?"

"Okay," she agreed, hoping he wasn't about to tell her something that she was going to regret hearing. "Talk."

Chapter 16

Carson thought of sitting down before he spoke, then decided that he would rather be on his feet when he told Serena what he had been keeping to himself for such a long time.

For some inexplicable reason, standing made him feel less vulnerable and more in control of a situation.

The silence began to deepen.

It is now or never, he told himself.

"I was in a relationship—" he began slowly.

"'Was' or 'are'?" Serena wanted to know.

Despite the fact that she was having feelings for him, it occurred to her that she had no idea about Carson's actual personal life, knew nothing about him at all outside of the fact that he worked for her brother. If Carson had someone in his life, she needed to know now, before anything went any further.

Before her feelings went any deeper.

She'd been blindsided by a good-looking man before and she didn't intend for that to ever happen to her again. Carson might be here at the mansion for the sole purpose of keeping her and Lora safe, which was quite admirable of him, but that still didn't mean that the man wasn't out to further his own personal agenda.

"Was," Carson told her, stressing the word. "Her name was Lisa," he added, knowing that Serena, like most women, would want to know that. "We were starting to get really serious when she told me that she was pregnant."

Haunted by her own memories, Serena's back automatically went up. "Let me guess, you dropped her like a hot potato."

"No," Carson replied, then further surprised her by saying, "I asked her to marry me, but she wouldn't. Said she needed time so that she could work some things out."

"And?" Serena asked, fully expecting Carson to tell her that he then had his own second thoughts and used the time to make his getaway.

"She took a *really* long time thinking," he continued stoically, "and while she was doing all this thinking, the baby decided to come early. Lisa went into premature labor." There was a great deal of emotion brimming in his voice as he told her, even though he was doing his best to keep that emotion at bay. "I didn't find out until after the fact."

Serena grew very quiet, waiting for him to finish his story. At this point, she no longer knew what to think or where this was going. All she knew was that he sounded extremely sad.

Carson avoided looking at her. "I got to the hospital just before Lisa died," he said quietly.

"I'm so sorry." Moved, Serena reached over and covered his hand with hers in an effort to offer comfort. "And the baby?"

"It was a girl." His eyes met hers. "She died the next day."

Serena felt her heart twisting in her chest. For a moment, she couldn't even breathe. "Carson—"

He shrugged away her pity and whatever condolences she was trying to convey.

"These things happen," he told her gruffly. "I didn't tell you this to get your pity. Since you felt I was digging into your life, I wanted to tell you something about mine so that you didn't feel like you were the only one who was exposed." He nodded toward the baby. "I think you'd better get her up to her room," he told her. "She's asleep."

"In a moment," Serena answered.

She rose to her feet and placed Lora in the cradle by the sofa, then walked over to Carson. She had sworn to herself that she had absolutely no time for any meaningless dalliances with men. As far as she was concerned, her life was full just the way it was, with her daughter and her work. Good-looking men were nothing but trouble.

But there was something in Carson Gage's eyes that not only moved her, it spoke to her.

As he was telling her about his unsuccessful relationship and the newborn who had died, even though he'd tried to turn away, she'd seen indescribable pain in his eyes. That was something that couldn't be faked.

She found herself pushing aside her own situation, her own barriers, and wanting to comfort him. At least that was what she told herself.

Before she could think it through, she'd moved closer

to Carson and in the next heartbeat, she found herself raising her face up to his and kissing him.

Everything became blurry.

She wasn't even sure if Carson met her halfway or if he had just stood very, very still and allowed her to make the final move.

All she knew was one moment her heart was reaching out to him, the next her mouth was sealed to his.

But while she might have started the kiss, Carson certainly completed it.

His arms went around her, drawing her even closer to him as the kiss deepened to the point that she felt as if she was falling headlong down into a wide, bottomless abyss.

She caught herself clinging to him, trying to keep the room from spinning so fast that she lost her balance. So fast that she lost all perspective.

Carson was the one who ended the kiss, drawing back from her.

She looked at him in dazed surprise.

His pulse was racing faster than the car he'd once taken for a joyride years ago. Part of him, the part that belonged to the reckless teen he'd once been, wanted to take her right here and make love to her. Wanted her so badly, he physically ached.

But he wasn't that reckless teenager anymore, he was a police detective with responsibilities. That meant that he couldn't allow his desires, no matter how strong they were, to dictate his behavior.

Taking hold of Serena's shoulders, he looked into her eyes. "You don't want to do this," he told her.

Serena's heart was hammering so hard, she found that she could hardly breathe. With slow, measured words, she told Carson, "I'm only going to say this once. I'm going to go upstairs to put the baby to bed. After that, I'm going to my room. If you want me, you know where to find me."

She wasn't sure exactly how she managed to walk over to the cradle. It almost felt like she was having an out-of-body experience. She could see herself doing it. Her legs felt so wobbly, she was certain she'd collapse on the floor before she got to the baby.

But she didn't collapse. She made it to the baby's cradle.

Digging deep for strength, Serena picked Lora up in her arms.

With the sleeping baby cradled in her arms and operating on what amounted to automatic pilot, she went to the staircase and slowly made her way up the stairs. All the while, Serena kept praying for two things: that the baby would go on sleeping and that Carson would come upstairs.

Reaching the nursery, she went in and very gently placed her daughter down in the crib. She stood there for a moment, watching Lora sleep. Then, leaving the door between the two rooms opened just a crack, she tiptoed out again and went into her own bedroom.

Her hands were actually shaking as she shed her clothes and then slipped on a nightgown. It was her favorite nightgown, a soft, light blue garment that looked and felt as if it had been spun out of gossamer angel wings.

She looked down at the nightgown. *That's it, Serena. Play hard to get. You're going to wind up with gooseflesh, waiting for a man who isn't going to show up.*

Her heart stopped the very moment she heard the light rap on her door. The roof of her mouth felt so dry, she could barely get the two words out.

"Come in."

The next moment, the door slowly opened and then Carson slipped into the room. He closed the door behind him but made no move to come closer.

Instead, he remained where he was, as if second thoughts had immobilized him.

But he wasn't having second thoughts. He was looking at Serena. His gaze washed slowly over her. She looked like a vision.

Serena was standing next to her bed. The light she'd left on shone right through her nightgown, leaving very little to the imagination.

His imagination took flight anyway.

Carson had no idea how he didn't wind up swallowing his own tongue.

"It's cold tonight. You're going to wind up freezing to death," he told her in a voice that was so low, it was hardly audible.

"Not if I find a way to keep warm," Serena answered him.

Was he going to turn away? Had she made a terrible mistake? She refused to allow her mind to go there.

Her eyes never left Carson's face, waiting for him to make a move. Praying it was the right one.

And then, because he could resist her for only so long, because he needed what Serena was offering him, needed it not just physically but emotionally as well, he cut the distance between them and swept her up in his arms.

This was wrong and he knew it, but he just couldn't help himself. "I should have my head examined," he whispered.

"Later," she said just before she brought her mouth up to his.

His last ounce of resistance disappeared, evaporating in the heat that had just flared up between them as her body pressed up against his.

Any last efforts he might have put forth to talk her out of what they were about to do vanished, burned away to a crisp as one kiss mushroomed into another.

And another.

It was hard for him to say which of them was more eager for this to happen. Up until now, he'd thought of himself as a tower of restraint. But faced with her eager mouth trailing along his face, his neck, his throat, restraint shattered into more pieces than he could ever possibly count.

When Lisa had died, followed by the death of their daughter, Carson had felt like a man who had been literally gutted. He became merely a shell of a man who was just going through the motions of pretending to still be alive. He walked, he talked, he got things done, but he simply didn't feel.

Not a single thing.

But now, tonight, with Serena in his arms like this, he felt as if he had suddenly been brought back from the dead.

And it felt incredibly wonderful to realize that he was alive.

Carson couldn't remember stripping off his clothes. There was a vague awareness that Serena had helped, but he couldn't say that for sure. All he knew was that the clothes had been in his way and he'd got free of them as quickly as possible.

The diaphanous web that Serena'd had on was discarded as well, becoming a shimmering, barely blue heap on the floor next to his clothes.

Then there was nothing left between them except for unresolved passion.

Pulling her against him, Carson exulted in the intoxicating feel of Serena's bare skin heating against his.

His hands traveled along the length of her body, caressing, stroking, glorying in the softness that had him all but drunk with desire.

He made love to her a hundred different ways, his lips trailing along the curves and swells of her supple form, lingering over her breasts, her hips, working his way slowly down to the very core of her.

When she suddenly gasped and reared, grabbing hold of the comforter beneath her and all but shredding it, Carson lingered longer. He used his tongue, his lips and his very breath to bring her up and over into a climax that had her biting her lip to keep from crying out his name and waking up the baby.

When he moved up along her body again, Serena was all but numb for a moment.

And then, as if suddenly infused by a bolt of sheer energy crafted out of her ecstasy, Serena reversed their positions, straddling him. Working magic she hadn't known that, until this very moment, she was capable of.

With carefully calculated movements, she teased his body until she managed to bring him close to the brink of fulfillment.

Carson caught her hand, stilling it. Then, with his eyes on hers, he switched their positions again until he was over her.

His eyes holding her prisoner, he parted her legs and entered.

But where she expected an overpowering thrust, Carson delivered a gentle, determined one instead. The thrusts became magnified and increased with every movement thereafter until they were both moving so fast, she found herself as breathless as he was.

They raced up the steep incline together, silently focused on mutual satisfaction.

She clung tightly to him and then it happened. The final plunge that sent them into a star-filled euphoria that exploded, then embraced them as the stars showered down around them.

Her heart was pounding so incredibly hard, Serena didn't think she was going to be able to ever catch her breath again, to ever have her heart slow down to a decent rate.

It didn't matter. At that moment, it didn't matter. If this was the way she was going to exit the world, so be it.

And then, slowly, the world came back into focus. The room took on form and dimensions, and just like that, she was back in her bed again.

Back in her bed but not alone.

Serena knew she should say something, but she didn't want to.

Not yet.

Right now, all she wanted to do was lie there and feel the heat of his body mingling with hers, feel his heart hammering as hard as hers.

Listen to the sound of his ragged breathing as it echoed hers.

Later there would be time for all the other things. For words and for the inevitable regrets that were bound to follow in their wake.

But right now, at this very moment, she wanted to pretend that she lived in a perfect world and that every glorious thing that had happened just now would continue to happen.

Given enough time.

As his euphoria slowly dissolved, he realized that Serena was being extremely quiet. Had he hurt her? Had she gone into some kind of shock over what had just happened between them?

Or was that fear that had immobilized both her tongue and her body this way?

Carson wanted to reassure her. To say something to make her feel better about what had just transpired between them—something that he thought was wonderful—but for the life of him, he didn't know how.

So for now, he chose to take the easy out.

He remained silent, just listening to her breathe.

And wishing that there was a way to make this moment last if not forever, then at least for a long, long time.

Chapter 17

She was alone.

Serena could sense it even before she opened her eyes to verify if that the sinking feeling in the pit of her stomach was true.

Carson had gone.

After a night of what she felt was the most incredible lovemaking she had ever experienced, Carson had slipped out of her bed while she was asleep, disappearing from her room without a word.

Exactly the way that the man who had fathered Lora had done.

Disappointment raked long, sharp fingernails across Serena's soul, scarring her. Making her want to throw things.

Making her want to cry.

She rubbed the heel of her hand against her eyes, wiping away tears before they had a chance to fall. How could she have been so stupid, so wrong about someone? Yet here she was, alone in bed, so there was no other conclusion left for her to draw except that Carson was just like every other male on the face of the earth: self-centered.

He had seen his opportunity and he'd taken it without a single qualm.

Serves you right for being such a blind idiot, Serena upbraided herself. *Now, just stop feeling sorry for yourself and get over it!* she silently ordered. *You've got a baby depending on you, that's the only thing that matters here.*

The second she thought of her daughter, Serena realized that Lora had been unusually quiet during the night. Was there something wrong? Or had the housekeeper got up early and gone to the nursery to look after the baby?

She's a better mother than I am, Serena thought, feeling ashamed of herself. She should have been thinking about Lora, not about her own long-suppressed needs and desires.

What was wrong with her? she silently demanded, annoyed with herself.

Kicking aside her covers, Serena suddenly realized that she still had nothing on. Swearing softly, she grabbed a robe in lieu of a nightgown and quickly made her way to the nursery.

Softly opening the door so as not to wake her daughter on the outside chance that Lora actually *was* asleep, Serena looked into the room.

And stopped dead.

Carson was sitting in the rocking chair with Lora in his arms, quietly rocking her. Not only that, but he was feeding the baby a bottle. He'd obviously found one of

the formula bottles that were kept in the miniature refrigerator for just these sort of midnight feedings. She'd
put them there so that there'd be no need to go all the
way down to the kitchen while she was half-asleep. A
bottle warmer stood on the counter and she could see
that it had been pressed into use, as well.

Justice lay on the floor right in front of Carson's feet.
The German shepherd had raised his head the moment
she walked in, alerting Carson to her presence.

When he looked at her over his shoulder, Serena
asked, "What are you doing?"

It absolutely stunned her at how very right this incredibly domestic scene seemed.

"Lora was hungry. I didn't want her to wake you up,
so I got a bottle to feed her," Carson answered simply.

If he knew Lora was hungry, she must have been crying. Guilt took a bite out of her. She should have been
up at the first whimper.

"How did I not hear her crying?" she asked, puzzled.

"I think probably because you were pretty exhausted
at the time," Carson told her, his voice low, soothing.

She knew he didn't mean it this way, but she felt pa-
tronized. "And you weren't?" she challenged.

Was Carson saying that even though he'd worn her
out, he was still full of energy and ready to go? In either case it seemed that of the two of them, he made a
better mother than she did.

"I'm used to sleeping with one eye and one ear open,
remember?" he reminded her. "I heard Lora stirring and
making noises, so I figured it was just a matter of time
before she'd start crying. I thought you might appreciate
sleeping in for a change. My guess is that you haven't
had a decent night's sleep in a while now."

He talked as if he knew what new mothers went

through. Pretty insightful for a man who had never been married, she thought.

"I haven't," she admitted, staring at him as if he had just suddenly acquired a halo.

This, to her, was almost better than the night they had just spent together. That had been wondrous, but this spoke of a type of kindness that she knew wasn't all that common. It touched her heart in ways that their lovemaking hadn't.

Serena roused herself before she melted completely. "I'd better change her," she said, moving closer to take Lora from him.

He rose but not to turn the baby over to her. Lora had fallen asleep midfeeding, and he wanted to place her in her crib.

"Already taken care of," he said.

He was telling her that he had actually changed Lora's diaper. She stared at Carson again, stunned speechless.

Finding her tongue, she said, "I don't believe you."

"The old diaper's in the covered pail," he told her, nodding to the container next to the changing table. "You can check if you want to."

Serena was almost tempted to do just that. Pressing her lips together, she could only shake her head in wonder. "How did you—"

He grinned. "It's not exactly rocket science, and despite what you might think, I'm not an idiot. Disposable diapers, wipes, lotion, a secured place to do the changing and voilà," Carson rattled off in a low whisper. "No big mystery."

He placed the sleeping baby back into her crib and quietly withdrew from the nursery.

Leaving the door open just a crack as he entered

Serena's suite, he turned toward her. "When I was with Lora just now, I had a chance to do some thinking."

He was about to tell her what had occurred to him while he'd been rocking and feeding Lora, but he never got the chance. Because the moment he'd turned toward her, Serena threw her arms around him and sealed her mouth to his in an expression of utter gratitude.

Whatever he was going to say was lost for the next hour as they once again became reacquainted with just how very in sync they were with one another.

Lovemaking begot lovemaking.

Finally, tottering on the edge of exhaustion, they lay next to one another, wrapped in the last fragments of soul-comforting euphoria. Carson drew her a little closer to him.

He was in total awe of how she seemed to be able to unlock all these feelings within him, feelings that had him wanting to protect her and her baby, not just as a member of the police department, but as a man. A man who hadn't realized just how very lonely and alone he'd been until last night.

So, with one arm tightly around her, he stroked Serena's hair, content to remain that way for as long as humanly possible.

That was exactly the moment that Serena chose to raise her head from his chest and look up into his eyes. "You said something about you thinking of something while you were feeding Lora. What was it?"

It took him a moment to recreate that moment. Making love with Serena had a way of clouding his brain and making everything else vanish.

And then he remembered. "A while back you mentioned something about seeing the Larson brothers riding around on your ranch."

She recalled the incident perfectly, as well as the cold shiver that had gone down her spine. "They were. They told Anders that they were thinking about getting their own place and just wanted to take a look around ours."

"Did you believe them?" He thought he knew the answer to that, given her tone of voice, but he just wanted to be sure.

"No," she retorted with feeling. Rising above the last of the intoxicating feeling that making love with Carson had created, she was now focused on telling him about how she'd felt seeing the Larsons skulking around her ranch. "I couldn't shake the feeling that they were somehow casing the Double C Ranch. You know, getting the lay of the land, things like that."

Carson filled in what she wasn't saying. "So a kidnapper would know what he was up against and which way he needed to go to make a quick getaway once he had the baby."

The very thought filled her with horror. Serena was fully alert now and sitting up. She put into words what he hadn't said yet. "Do you think one of them tried to kidnap Lora?"

He'd already discarded that idea—in part. "Probably too risky for one of them to make the actual attempt. They don't like putting themselves on the line like that. But that doesn't mean they wouldn't send someone else to do it."

He saw Serena's eyes widen and he wished he didn't have to be the one to tell her this. But he knew she wasn't the type who wanted to be kept in the dark. Serena was better off being made aware of all the possibilities.

"Your father's a powerful man around here, Serena, not to mention wealthy. Kidnapping Judson Colton's grandchild would mean a fast payoff for the Larsons." He could see that he'd struck a nerve and he was quick to reassure her. "Don't worry, I'm not going to let anything happen to you or to Lora."

She wanted him to focus on Lora, not her. "I can take care of myself, Carson," she told him. "But you can't be everywhere, and Lora's just a baby."

"How do you feel about protective custody?" he wanted to know. "I can have one of the K-9 officers take her to an undisclosed location and watch over her."

"And Alma," Serena added. "I want Alma to go with Lora."

"You would be the more logical choice to go with Lora," Carson pointed out.

"I know," she admitted, but she just couldn't indulge herself that way. She had responsibilities here, as well. Responsibilities to the ranch. "But Anders can't watch over everything on the ranch on his own. Besides, I can't just abandon the horses. As much as I hate to think about this, there's no telling just how long it'll take you to find this would-be kidnapper," she said. And then she added hopefully, "Maybe you scared him off and he's long gone by now."

He shook his head. "We can't count on that. I'll call Finn and tell him that you've agreed to protective custody—for Lora," he added quickly when he saw the protest rise to her lips. "He'll have one of the detectives come out to the ranch and pick up Lora and your housekeeper," he said. "Meanwhile, I suggest you go tell Alma that she's in for a change of scenery for the time being."

Serena was already up and slipping her robe back on. She quickly crossed back to the nursery in order to get together some things for Lora to use for her protective custody stay.

"Alma loves the baby," she told Carson just as she was about to leave the room. "She'll go anywhere if it means keeping Lora safe."

When he made no answer, she turned around to look at Carson, but he had already left her suite.

"Man moves like smoke," she murmured, shaking her head.

She focused on packing a suitcase for Lora.

Carson admitted to himself that he was operating purely on a hunch. The other day he'd searched only some of the ranch hands' studio apartments, the ones that had been opened to him. But there were other living quarters that he hadn't looked into. At the time, he had been strictly searching for some sign of Demi.

But now, since he believed that perhaps the Larson brothers were somehow involved in this unsavory business, he needed to look through all the ranch hands' quarters, looking for anything that might connect the brothers to the botched kidnapping attempt and/or the equally unsuccessful attempt on Serena's life.

He was keenly aware of the fact that he had a myriad of questions and so far, no answers, but he had nothing to lose by pushing ahead with this search.

Because the ranch hands were working on the ranch that belonged to Judson Colton, they had no right to an expectation of privacy. They had all signed contracts to that effect when they came to work on the Double C; the thinking being that if any of the ranch hands decided to take it into their heads to steal something—anything at all—from the ranch, a search of their living quarters would be conducted at any time to find it.

So, after telling Anders what he was about to do and with Justice beside him, Carson went from studio apartment to studio apartment, meticulously searching through everything. It was a case of "I'll know it when I see it" since he had no idea just what he was looking for. He just knew that he needed *something* that would help him connect one of the ranch hands to the Larsons.

For the most part, the search wound up being an uneventful parade of one small messy studio apartment after another. They all looked depressingly alike to him, yielding nothing.

He was close to giving up when Justice suddenly came to life in the next to last studio apartment they entered. The canine barked several times and began trying to dig his way under the ranch hand's bed.

Carson got down on his belly and, snaking his way under the bed, he found nothing but dust bunnies for his trouble.

"Nothing here, boy," he said, getting back up again and dusting off his knees.

But Justice kept barking.

"Really wish you could talk, Justice," Carson said. "It would make my life a lot easier."

On a hunch, since Justice continued barking at the bed, Carson lifted the mattress up off the box springs. There were a number of large sealed plastic packets tucked between the two pieces that made up the twin bed.

"Well, what do you know? Sorry I doubted you, boy," he said, gathering up all the packets from their so-called hiding place.

"Hey, what do you think you're doing?" Pete Murphy, a tall, skinny cowboy demanded as he came into the studio apartment behind Carson. "That's my stuff!"

By now there were seven large packets on the floor and Justice was circling the lot, growing more and more agitated.

Carson squatted down to examine one of the packets more closely. "Are you dealing drugs, Pete?" he asked the cowboy.

"Am I— What? Dealing drugs?" he repeated, his voice cracking in the middle. "No, those are mine. For me," he emphasized.

Carson held up the packet he'd been examining. "Are you trying to tell me that you take these for 'recreational' purposes?"

"Yeah, right. Recreational purposes, that's it. Now, give them back!" he demanded, trying to take possession of the packets that were closest to him.

Rising, Carson looked into the ranch hand's eyes, pinning him in place. "You're selling these for the Larsons, aren't you? How much are they cutting you in for?"

"I don't know what you're talking about," the cowboy denied. "They're not cutting me in for anything."

Which meant that the brothers probably had something on the cowboy that they were holding over his head, Carson thought. "You tried to kidnap Serena Colton's baby, didn't you?"

"Kidnap the baby?" Murphy stuttered, growing visibly frightened. "No, I wouldn't do something like that!"

Carson continued to press, "You certainly match the description of the kidnapper who broke into Serena Colton's suite, trying to steal her baby."

Murphy was sweating now. "You're out of your mind! Okay, maybe I do a little business on the side for the Larsons, but it's strictly the drugs—working out here is hard, damn it, and a man can't be faulted for wanting to take the edge off once in a while. But kidnapping? Hell, no way!"

The cowboy suddenly turned and ran, leaving behind the drugs and everything else in his quarters.

For a split second, Carson debated giving chase, but the cowboy was moving pretty fast. Carson decided that it wasn't worth working up a sweat. Instead, he looked down at Justice. The canine was so well trained, he refrained from running after the cowboy until told to do so.

Carson gave his partner the go-ahead.

"Justice, fetch!" was all he had to say. It was the key phrase he used to train the K-9 to stop someone from fleeing the scene.

Murphy got approximately ten feet beyond his studio apartment before the German shepherd caught hold of his boot and brought him down. Justice pinned the cowboy to the ground with the force of his weight.

"Justice, off!" Carson ordered as he calmly walked up to the fallen cowboy. Murphy began to scramble up to his feet, most likely intending to run again. "I wouldn't do that if I were you," Carson advised quietly.

Murphy froze, fearfully eyeing Justice. To anyone watching, it appeared that the German shepherd was eyeing him in return.

Carson took out his handcuffs.

Chapter 18

"Then it's over," Serena said, breathing a sigh of relief.

It felt as if a huge weight had been taken off her shoulders. Carson had sought her out in the stables after he had returned from town, specifically from the police station where he had taken Pete Murphy. The cowboy had been placed under arrest for possession of cocaine with the intent to sell.

Serena was overjoyed when Carson told her about the arrest. "This means that I can bring Lora back to the ranch."

It had only been less than a day since she'd handed her daughter over to the police detective who had taken the baby into protective custody, but it felt as if it had been weeks.

Carson frowned. He hated doing this to Serena, but in all good conscience, he had to. Lora couldn't be allowed to be brought home yet.

"Not so fast," he warned.

She was ready to have Carson take her to wherever her daughter was being held. Her heart sank when he just stood there.

"Why not?" she wanted to know. "You got the guy, right?"

"I'm not so sure about that."

"But those drugs you found in his room tie Murphy to the Larsons," Serena cried. "They're drug dealers. He's working for them."

Carson shook his head. He'd spent two hours interrogating the cowboy, but he'd got nowhere and it frustrated him.

"Murphy claims that he's not working for anyone, that he just bought those drugs from a dealer to sell on his own. He swears he's not working for the Larsons and that he doesn't know anything about a kidnapping."

"But he's lying, right?" Serena cried desperately. "You told me that the Larsons' thugs are afraid of testifying against them. This could just be another example of that."

He felt for her. He knew exactly what she was going through, but that still didn't change anything. "They are, and I've got no doubt that Murphy is selling drugs for the two brothers. I also wouldn't put it past the Larsons to try to steal a wealthy family's baby just to ransom it back to them—"

Serena didn't let him finish. "So I can't bring Lora home yet."

"Not until I get some proof of that," he continued, determined to get his point across even though it really aggravated him to be the bearer of bad news. "I can't charge Murphy with kidnapping, and as much as

I would like to, I can't charge the Larsons with conspiracy to kidnap or anything of the kind."

Disappointment spread out all through Serena. She felt as if she was caught up in a nightmare. She wanted to keep Lora safe, but she missed her daughter more than she thought possible.

"So you're telling me that it's *not* over," she concluded, exasperated beyond words.

"Not yet. But soon," he added quickly. "I promise, soon. Until then, Lora's safe and I'm going to keep you safe, as well. And to make sure nothing happens to you, I'm going to have Detective Saunders stay with you," he told her, mentioning another member of the K-9 team. "I'm leaving Justice here with you, too."

Serena had an uneasy feeling he was telling her that he wasn't going to be around. She looked at him suspiciously. "Why? Where are you going?"

"I just got a call from Bo's lawyer, Jonathan Witherspoon," Carson answered. "He told me that he's going to be reading Bo's will to his heirs this afternoon, and I feel I need to be there."

"Out of respect, or because you think he left you something?" Serena wanted to know.

He laughed shortly. He'd long since lost all respect for Bo, and he knew without being told that he wasn't in his brother's will. He had a different reason for attending the reading.

"Neither," he answered. "I want to see who else turns up at the reading and if there are any 'surprises' in the will. Maybe that'll give me some kind of a lead as to who might have actually killed my brother."

She looked at Carson, taking solace where she could find it. "So you don't think it's Demi anymore," she assumed.

He knew how much that meant to Serena and if he was being perfectly honest with himself, he was beginning to have suspicions that someone actually *had* tried to frame Serena's cousin.

"Let's just say I'm more open to other possibilities," he answered.

Serena nodded. She didn't care how he phrased it just as long as he stopped obsessing that Demi was the one who had killed his brother. "Good. What time's the reading of the will?"

"Two o'clock." Carson looked at her, his curiosity aroused. "Why?"

She was already stripping her leather gloves off. "Give me half an hour, and I'll get ready," she said, already halfway out of the stable.

Carson still didn't understand. "Why?" he asked again.

"Because I'm going with you," she answered Carson simply.

Maybe she'd misunderstood him. "There's no need for you to go—" he began.

Carson had been the one to discover his brother's body and since then, she knew that Carson had gone through a lot, even though he kept it all bottled up. She didn't want Carson sitting through the reading of the will by himself. Who knew what emotions he'd wind up dealing with? She wanted to be there for him, to let him know, even silently, that he wasn't alone.

However, she knew that if she began to explain any of this, he would just balk at her reasons. Most likely he'd just tell her to stay here.

Knowing that the detective appreciated minimalism, she merely told him, "Yes, there is," and hoped he'd leave it at that.

Carson was about to argue with her, to insist that there was no reason for him to drag her to the reading. He wouldn't be going himself if Bo had died in his sleep at some ripe old age. There'd be no reason to go then. It was Bo's murder that was forcing him to attend this reading like some undercover voyeur.

Given that, he reconsidered and grudgingly admitted that he needed to have her with him. So he sighed and echoed, "Half an hour," as if putting her on notice that he would wait half an hour and no more. He wanted her to believe that if she took longer, he'd just leave without her—even though he knew he'd wind up waiting for her anyway.

As it turned out, he didn't have to wait.

"Five minutes to spare," Serena told him proudly, sliding into the passenger seat of his car. She looked in the rear of the vehicle and saw that Justice was already in the car. They had *both* been waiting for her to come out. "Is he going to the reading, as well?" she asked. The question was asked only partially tongue in cheek.

"I'm on duty," he told her. "I don't go anywhere without Justice."

Leaning back, she put her hand out for the dog to sniff, then petted his head. "Does the lawyer know you're bringing a 'friend'?"

"I don't think Witherspoon'll mind my bringing you," Carson said, starting up his vehicle.

He didn't fool her, she thought. He knew perfectly well that she was referring to the K-9. But she said it anyway.

"I was referring to Justice. This is a will reading. Mr. Witherspoon might not be prepared to have a German shepherd 'attend' the reading."

"Justice goes wherever I go," he told her matter-of-factly. "We're a team."

"I know that," she said, petting the dog again, "but some people might not be comfortable having a big German shepherd so close to them."

Carson met her observation with a shrug. "Well, that's their problem, not mine," he told her. "Besides, if they don't have anything to hide, everything'll be all right."

Serena settled back into her seat. "This should be interesting," she said, bracing herself for what the next hour or so held.

Jonathan Witherspoon looked as if he had been born wearing a three-piece suit with a matching shirt and tie. The two or three times that Carson had crossed paths with the lawyer, he got the impression that the word *casual* had no meaning for the tall, angular man who looked at the world through thick, rimless glasses. Sporting prematurely gray hair since he had turned thirty-five, the lawyer was only now approaching the age where his gray hair finally suited him, even though it had begun to thin considerably.

When Carson arrived with Serena for the reading of the will, the folding chairs that Witherspoon had his administrative assistant set up in his office were almost all taken. There were only a few remaining empty seats.

Carson guided Serena in first and took a chair on the aisle so that he could easily hold on to Justice. Specifically, he wanted to see if Justice would react to anyone at the reading. He'd always felt, right from the beginning, that Justice seemed to be able to actually *sense* evil. Carson took himself to task for not having brought the dog with him to the bachelor party, despite being off duty. He might have been able to find the killer right then and there and there would be no need for this elaborate game of hide-and-seek.

Witherspoon drew his shallow cheeks in even more than he usually did when he saw the dog sitting beside Carson. The lawyer looked none too pleased about the four-footed attendee, but apparently knew better than to say anything to Carson. He only scowled.

Looking around, Carson noted that Bo's ex-wife, Darby, was seated all the way in the back. Hayley, Bo's fiancée was front and center, just as he had expected her to be. As he watched, she turned around twice to shoot dirty looks at Darby.

This, he thought, was really shaping up to be a very interesting afternoon.

Leaning in closer to Serena, he whispered, "You sure you want to be here?"

"You're here, so I'm here," she told him. "Besides," she added, keeping her voice low, "this makes me realize why I like working with horses so much more than working with people."

Carson suppressed a laugh.

The next moment, Witherspoon cleared his throat rather loudly, indicating that they should all stop talking and pay attention to what he was about to say.

"All right, it looks like we're all here," the lanky lawyer said. He sat down behind his desk as he looked around at the various people who had gathered here in hopes of getting at least a piece of the considerable amount of money that Bo had accrued or, if not that, then a part of his breeding business. "Let's get started, shall we?"

In a monotonous, droning voice that seemed incredibly suited to the lawyer's face and demeanor, Witherspoon read the will in its entirety, stating every single detail that the law required in order for the will to be deemed a binding legal document.

When the lawyer came to the part that everyone had been waiting for—the distribution of Bo's possessions—the reading went far more quickly than anyone had actually anticipated.

"And I leave the entirety of my dog breeding business, as well as my ranch, both located at—" Witherspoon paused to read the address that everyone was well acquainted with, unintentionally stretching out the drama.

Almost everyone in the room had leaned forward. No one wanted to miss a single syllable of this part.

"—to my ex-wife, Darby Gage. I hope that this will make up for some of the things that I put you through, Darby."

"No!" Hayley screamed, all but going into shock. She jumped to her feet, knocking over the folding chair she'd been sitting in and discarding any and all pretense of grief. "There's got to be some kind of a mistake," she cried glaring accusingly at Witherspoon.

Witherspoon maintained his composure. It was obvious to Serena that the lawyer had to have been the target of angry heirs before Hayley's vitriolic display.

"I assure you that there's no mistake. I was there when Bo signed this." Holding up the last page of the document he'd been reading from, he displayed a seal. "It's been notarized."

"I don't care if it was signed by all the saints in heaven and half of Congress. That piece of paper's a fake! Bo would never have done something like this to me! He wouldn't have given that little scheming witch everything!"

Practically choking on her fury, Hayley gave every indication that she was going to lunge at Darby. Her hands went up and her freshly lacquered nails were outstretched, ready to rake over the ex-wife's face. Carson was immediately on his feet and got between his brother's fiancée and his ex-wife.

Justice growled at the woman, ready to take Hayley down on command. Serena had got to her feet as well, waiting to help Carson if he needed it. Since she was a woman, she felt she could restrain Hayley in ways that Carson couldn't.

But he caught Hayley's hands before she could do any damage.

"Settle down, Hayley," he ordered sternly.

"Settle down?" she shrieked, trying to pull free. "Didn't you just hear what Witherspoon just read? Everything's hers! That miserable liar didn't leave me *anything*!"

The more Hayley struggled, the tighter his grip on her hands grew. "You can get a lawyer and contest the will if you feel this strongly about it," he told her, his voice unnervingly calm.

"I'm not getting a damn lawyer," she spit, then retorted, "There are other ways to resolve this injustice!"

Carson immediately cut her short. "Don't say anything you're going to regret," he warned.

"What I regret is wasting my time with that back-stabbing, worthless brother of yours," Hayley cried.

Still watching her carefully, Carson released the woman.

Swinging around, Hayley glared at Witherspoon. "You haven't heard the last of this!" she declared.

With that, she stormed out of the lawyer's office,

pausing only long enough to spit on the floor right in front of Darby.

For her part, Darby didn't react. She appeared to be absolutely stunned.

The people sitting near her, many of whom had either been bequeathed a nominal sum of money or had learned that they would be receiving nothing at all, murmured among themselves. They filed out of the lawyer's office one by one, many in a state of disbelief.

In the end, only Carson, Serena and Darby were left with Witherspoon.

"Are you all right?" Carson asked his ex-sister-in-law.

He couldn't quite read the expression on Darby's face. It was a cross between what he took to be utter shock and something like subdued joy. He had the feeling that Darby wasn't quite sure exactly where she was right now.

"Fine," she finally managed to reply. And then, as if coming to, she turned to look at Witherspoon. "Did you just say that Bo left *everything* to me?" she asked in total disbelief.

"Why don't you come over here closer to my desk so I don't have to shout?" the lawyer told her, not that he appeared to be capable of shouting.

Rising from the last row, Darby made her way forward, moving in slow motion like someone who wasn't sure if they were awake or caught up in some sort of a dream.

Still looking dazed, she sat down in the single chair that Witherspoon had facing his desk.

The lawyer raised his tufted gray eyebrows and looked over expectantly toward Carson and the woman who was beside him. "I'm going to have to ask the two of you to leave now. I have several details to discuss with Ms. Gage."

Carson nodded. Bo had managed to drop a bomb-shell, even in death.

Chapter 19

"Well, certainly didn't see that one coming," Carson commented to Serena.

He was driving them away from Witherspoon's office. For all intents and purposes, Justice appeared to have fallen asleep in the back seat the moment they'd taken off.

"Then Bo and his ex-wife weren't on friendly terms?" Serena asked.

She was totally in the dark about Carson's older brother in general beyond the fact that Bo Gage owned a breeding business and supplied the K-9 unit with German shepherds.

"Bo wasn't the type to worry about being on good terms with any of his exes, including his ex-wife," Carson told her. "I think it's fair to say that he was always only looking out for himself." As far as brothers went, he and Bo were as different as night and day. "Once Bo got what he wanted, he moved on. When he decided that Darby was cramping his style, he shed her like a snake sheds its skin, without so much as a backward glance. When the marriage ended, he only tossed a couple of crumbs her way and by crumbs, I mean literal *crumbs*. Bo gave her a part-time job cleaning kennels at the breeding business they *both* had once owned."

Serena viewed that as pretty callous, but she did always like to think the best of people. "Maybe it was like Bo said in his will. He felt guilty about the way he'd treated her and this was his way of making it up to Darby."

"Maybe," Carson answered, but he was highly skeptical. Bo wasn't nearly that noble. There had to be some other reason for what he had done.

Serena glanced at him. Carson didn't sound convinced. "You think the will was a forgery?"

Carson thought of the lawyer. "No, the will's real all right. Witherspoon's so conscientious, he would have known if there'd been a substitution or switch. No, I'm thinking something else."

He'd mounted his cell phone on the dashboard when he'd got into the car and he now pressed a button that connected him to his boss's cell. When he heard the deep voice answer, Carson started talking.

"Chief, it's Gage. I think we just might have ourselves another suspect in my brother's murder," Carson told Serena's brother.

"Make this quick, Gage. I'm in the middle of something right now," Finn prompted. "And this better be something more than just an off-the-wall theory."

There was noise on the other end of the line and Carson couldn't quite make it out, but he knew better than to ask. The chief would tell him what was going on if Finn wanted him to know.

"I was just at the reading of Bo's will," he told Finn. "And?"

He knew he had to cut to the chase, but he felt certain that this would give the chief pause. "You're never going guess who my brother left his ranch and dog breeding business to."

"Well, it's not you because you would have led with giving me your notice," Finn said impatiently. "And I take it that it's not his fiancée because that was what everyone was expecting. Okay, I'll bite. Who did Bo leave his ranch and business to?"

"Darby Gage, his ex-wife."

For a moment, there was nothing but silence on the other end, as if Finn was trying to make heads or tails out of what he'd just been told.

"You're putting me on," he finally cried. From the sound of his voice, Carson surmised that the chief was as stunned as everyone else at the reading had been. "Seriously?"

"Seriously," Carson confirmed. "You realize what this means, don't you?"

"Yeah, I realize," Finn answered with a heavy sigh. "You're right. We just got ourselves another suspect." He had a question for Carson. "You think your ex-sister-in-law knew she was getting everything?"

Carson told the chief what he'd observed upon coming into the office. "I don't think she even knew she was in the will. From what I gathered, she was only there because Witherspoon told her to be there."

"Well, what do you know," Finn murmured more to himself than to Carson. "This certainly expands our playing field, doesn't it?"

"That's what I was thinking," Carson replied, glad he and Finn were on the same page.

Listening in on Carson's part of the conversation, Serena couldn't hold her tongue any longer.

Raising her voice so that her brother could hear, she said, "Maybe Darby found out about the will and she decided to kill Bo to get her hands on the business—and to pay him back for the way he'd treated her. To cover her tracks, she could have framed Demi for the murder out of spite. You know, as gruesome as it sounds, dipping Bo's finger in his own blood and guiding it to write Demi's name. That way you'd find the blood under his fingernail."

Carson nodded in agreement. That sounded about right to him. "Did you hear that?" he asked, addressing Finn on the cell.

"Is that my sister?" Finn wanted to know. There was a note of confusion in his voice.

"Yeah, she's right here in the car," Carson answered. Knowing Finn wanted more detail, he added, "She insisted on coming to the reading of the will with me."

He heard Finn laugh shortly.

"That's pretty good. Maybe she should be working at the police department instead of with the horses," Finn said.

"No, thank you," Serena said, speaking up. "Horses don't have agendas."

"You want me to bring Darby in for questioning?" Carson asked him.

"No, she's your ex-sister-in-law. You're too close to this," Finn answered. "Let's keep this all above reproach. I'll have Galloway bring her in."

"While you're at it, maybe you should have another go at the 'eyewitness,'" Carson suggested. "It's entirely possible that someone looking to frame Demi paid Paulie Gains off to say that he saw Demi fleeing from the area just before Bo's murder."

"For that matter, if we're considering possibilities, Darby could have put on a red wig and pretended to be Demi as she ran from the crime scene," Serena chimed in.

"Yeah, maybe," Finn agreed. "Anything else happen at the reading, Gage?"

"Yeah, I think you might want to consider putting Darby into protective custody. Bo's fiancée looked like she could have killed Darby with her bare hands once she heard that Darby was inheriting practically everything. Unless you've got any objections, I think I'm going to go and have a word with Hayley, see if she had any clue that this was coming. She looked surprised, but you never know."

"Sure. Go talk to her and get back to me on that," Finn told him.

"Right." As he was about to end the call, a thought occurred to Carson. "Oh, any word on Demi?" he asked.

"There've been a few so-called Demi-sightings in the area, but nothing that panned out. The rest of the team's still out there, looking for her. But now that you've told me about the will, I'm thinking we're going to be changing the focus of our search. At least for the time being. Get back to me if you find out anything," Finn told him again, then terminated the call.

"So we're going to see Hayley?" Serena asked as soon as she heard her brother end the call.

"*I'm* going to see Hayley," Carson corrected. "*After* I take you back to the Double C."

But Serena had other ideas. Now that she'd finally got out, she wanted to help Carson. The sooner all this was resolved, the sooner she could get her daughter back and life could return to normal.

"I think I should come with you," she told him, sounding a lot more confident than he'd anticipated. "Hayley looked like she wanted to kill someone. She won't kill you if there's a witness."

"Or she could kill the witness, too," he pointed out, momentarily indulging in some black humor.

"There's safety in numbers," Serena reminded him. "Besides, I'm not as fragile as I look."

A smile curved his mouth. He thought of the other night. Delicate, yes, but definitely not fragile. Still, out loud he told her, "Good to know."

She got the feeling that he wasn't talking about anything that had to do with Hayley.

They found Bo's former fiancée at home. As they approached her house, they heard the sound of breaking glass and crockery and Hayley yelling at the top of her lungs.

Carson decided to leave Justice in the car for everyone's safety. He didn't want to get the dog unnecessarily agitated. There might be unforeseen consequences of that.

He cracked the windows before turning his attention to the screamfest in Hayley's house.

Still apparently grappling with the huge disappointment she'd just experienced, Hayley Patton was calling Bo every name in the book. And with each name, she hurled another breakable object against the wall.

Carson hesitated and looked at Serena. "Maybe you should stay outside," he told her.

"The hell I will," she countered. "She can't hit both of us at once."

"That's not exactly a consolation," Carson informed her.

The incensed, newly spurned dog trainer's door was unlocked. Carson pushed it open slowly in order not to attract Hayley's attention. He still just narrowly avoided getting hit by a brightly painted vase that smashed into smithereens after a fatal encounter with the wall just beside the door frame.

"Hey!" Carson cried sternly, pushing Serena behind him so she wouldn't get hurt with any flying debris.

Caught up in her rampage, Hayley swung around to face him and glared. "What the hell do you two want?" she demanded angrily, looking as if she was going to hurl the next object at them.

Since Carson was Bo's brother and possibly a target for Hayley's rage, Serena was quick to take the lead and answer the woman's question. "We just came by to see if you're all right."

"All right?" Hayley echoed incredulously. "Of course I'm not all right! I'm the laughingstock of Red Ridge. That no-good, womanizing jackass made me look like a fool in front of everyone I know." Angry tears came to her eyes. "We were supposed to get married, damn it! Everything was supposed to be mine, not hers! Mine! How could he just give it away to her like that? Like I didn't matter?" Hayley shrieked.

Serena tried to sound as understanding and sympathetic as possible when she asked, "Did Bo ever do or say anything to make you think that he was going to leave it all to Darby?"

Hayley looked at her as if she was crazy. "You think I would have stayed with him if he so much as *hinted* that he was going to do that?" she demanded. "Looks and charm wear pretty thin pretty fast, even Bo's," she told them. "I was in it for the long haul because I thought I'd be taken care of."

Her face darkened as another wave of fury took hold. "Well, he took care of me all right, that dirty, rotten son of a bitch," she cried, picking up another glass and throwing it against the wall.

Carson and Serena moved out of the way as shattered glass flew everywhere.

Carson stayed a few minutes longer, asking Hayley several more questions in between her tirade and the ongoing cavalcade of objects being hurled against the wall and meeting their untimely demise.

It became very clear that as far as knowing that Bo was about to leave the breeding business and his ranch to another woman, Hayley hadn't had a clue.

When Carson told her he had to make one more stop before they went back to her ranch, Serena thought he wanted to talk to another possible suspect. Either that or he wanted to talk to her brother about Hayley's meltdown in person.

She didn't know what to think when Carson stopped his car in front of a toy store.

"What are we doing here?" she asked as she followed him inside.

The only thing that occurred to her was that he wanted to buy her daughter a toy, but she sincerely doubted that. At three months of age, Lora's favorite playthings were still her fingers and toes. The baby could spend hours just moving them in front of her face, fascinated by the sight.

The answer he gave her caught her off guard. "I want to buy a doll."

Lora was too young for a doll at this point. "Excuse me?"

"I'm buying a doll," he repeated. Caught up in his plan, Carson realized that there was no way Serena could know what he had in mind, so he explained. "I'm looking for one of those lifelike dolls. You know, the ones that look like a real baby." And then he qualified what he meant. "I'm sure this store doesn't carry one of those really specialized ones that I saw advertised in a catalog, the ones that look and feel like a real baby. Some of them even move when you touch them," he said, recalling the description. "I just want one that's about the size of a three-month-old and lifelike enough to fool a kidnapper."

She felt as if her throat was closing up again. There was only one reason he would be doing this. "You think he's coming back, don't you?"

He hated bringing fear back into her life, but she had to understand that there was still a very real danger of her daughter being kidnapped.

"I'm counting on it," he told her. "Because we're going to set a trap for him so that he stops being a threat to you and Lora." He looked at her and saw that she had grown a little pale. He stopped looking up and down the aisles and put his hands on her shoulders, in essence creating a "safe space" for her. "It's the only way, Serena."

"I know," she answered in a hoarse voice.

Pulling herself together, she joined the search for the perfect doll to use as a decoy. Carson was right. Until the would-be kidnapper was caught, she would continue to live in fear for her daughter—and that really wasn't living at all.

* * *

"I didn't realize that they could look *this* lifelike," Carson said. They were back in her room at the Double C and he was looking at the doll that had taken them close to an hour to find and cost a great deal more than he'd expected. "Too bad we couldn't have just rented the damn thing," he commented. He thought of the receipt in his wallet. "These dolls are expensive."

"That's because a lot goes into making one of them. Touch its face," Serena urged.

"Once was enough, thanks." He'd already done that in the store. That was how he'd decided which doll to pick. When he'd picked up the doll from its display, he found that the doll's actual weight felt as if he had a real baby in his arms. It was damn eerie, he thought.

She couldn't tell if it was the doll's lifelike quality or its expensive price tag that made him more uncomfortable.

"Once this is over, maybe you can take the doll back to the store and get them to refund your money," she suggested.

He glanced at the doll again. "I've got a better idea."

She had no idea where he was going with this. "Oh?"

"Yeah, once this is over, I'll give you the doll for Lora. When she gets bigger, she can pretend it's her baby sister, or whatever it is that little girls pretend when they're playing with baby dolls."

She was both touched and impressed. "That's very generous of you," Serena told him.

Carson shrugged. Praise of any sort always left him feeling uncomfortable, like finding out he'd put on two different boots.

"Beats the hassle of trying to get my money back from a salesclerk," he told her.

He was just making excuses. "You're not fooling me, Detective Carson Gage. You might have everyone else thinking that you're this big, hulking tough guy with a heart of steel, but I know better."

For the time being, the doll and its purpose was forgotten. "Oh, do you, now?"

"Yes, I do. Underneath that scowl of yours is a heart made out of pure marshmallow."

"Marshmallow?" he echoed, amused. "Well, that doesn't sound very manly now, does it?"

"Oh, you're plenty manly," she assured him. "But you're also kindhearted and generous, and that's even more important than being manly."

He found himself getting all caught up in this woman that fate had brought into his life. "That all depends if you're staring down the barrel of a gun—or looking into the deep brown eyes of a woman with the kind of wicked mouth you've spent your whole life dreaming about."

She could feel that excitement generating in her veins, the excitement that he could create just by touching her face.

"Oh? And do I have the kind of wicked mouth you've spent your whole life dreaming about?" she asked him, lacing her arms around the back of his neck.

Carson pulled her to him, fitting her body against his. "What do you think?"

His grin was so sexy, she could hardly stand it. "I think you should stop talking and show me."

"I thought you'd never ask," he said, and the next moment, he did.

Chapter 20

Lying there in the dark beside Serena, Carson was beginning to think that the kidnapper had lost his nerve and wasn't going to make a second attempt to abduct the baby.

Two nights had gone by since the first attempt. It was the third night and still nothing.

Carson had to admit that it was getting harder and harder for him to stay awake, allowing himself to take only ten-minute catnaps every few hours as he waited for the kidnapper to make a reappearance.

Maybe it had been strictly a one-shot deal, he thought. Maybe—

Despite the darkness in the bedroom, he saw Justice suddenly sit up. The canine's entire body looked to be rigid and alert. In addition, Justice's ears were moving so that they were directed toward something he heard coming from Lora's nursery.

Tense now, Carson did his best to noiselessly slip out of bed, but Serena still woke up.

Her eyes were wide as she looked in his direction. "Did you hear something?" she asked in what amounted to a stage whisper.

Carson nodded. "Stay here," he mouthed. There was no mistaking that it was an order.

But Serena slipped out on her side anyway. "You might need help," she told him, her voice so low it was all but inaudible.

"Damn," Carson muttered under his breath, but with no less feeling than if the word had been shouted. He didn't have time to argue with her. This could all go south in the blink of an eye and his window to capture the kidnapper was small.

Aware that there was no way he could get Serena to remain in her room, he waved for her to stay behind him, then made his way into the nursery, his weapon drawn and ready in his hand.

Moving just ahead of his partner, Justice saw the intruder first.

The thin, shadowy figure dressed in black had found a way into the nursery. Carson had wanted to make the nursery accessible but not so accessible that the kidnapper smelled a trap.

The intruder was just leaning over the crib and about to scoop up what he believed to be the baby. At that moment Justice flew across the nursery, grabbing the kidnapper's arm.

Startled, there was a guttural screech from the man, whether out of pain or surprise was unclear.

Somehow managing to pull free from the canine, the kidnapper tried to barrel out of the room. Moving deftly, Carson was quick to block the man's exit.

In doing so, he managed to pull off the intruder's ski mask, exposing his face.

"Mark!"

The cry of recognition came from behind him.

Surprised, Carson looked over his shoulder at Serena. It was just enough to throw his timing off, causing Carson to lose the upper hand. The kidnapper immediately took advantage of the opportunity, grabbing Serena's arm and pulling her against him like a human shield. Out of nowhere, a handgun materialized. The unmasked kidnapper held the muzzle against her temple.

Afraid that the canine would jostle the kidnapper and possibly cause the gun to go off, Carson caught hold of Justice's collar, pulling him back to keep the canine still.

"If you don't want her pretty brains splattered all over the room, you'll put your gun down, cop," the man holding Serena hostage snarled.

"Take it easy," Carson told the intruder, speaking in a tranquil, sedate tone and doing his best to harness both his anger and his fear. He shifted his eyes toward Serena. Wanting to keep her calm, he told her, "It's going to be all right."

"Only if you put your gun down and keep holding on to that dog of yours," the man Serena had called Mark snapped. "Now!"

Still holding on to Justice's collar with one hand, Carson raised the weapon in his other hand, pointing the muzzle toward the ceiling.

"I'm putting it down. Don't do anything you'll wind up regretting," he warned the intruder.

"Same goes for you," the man growled. He cocked the trigger.

"I'm putting it down," Carson repeated more urgently, making an elaborate show of laying the hand-gun down on the floor beside his foot.

The second that Carson's gun was on the floor, the intruder shoved Serena into him. With a startled cry, she stumbled against Carson and Justice.

Carson caught her before she could land on the floor. "You okay?"

She nodded. "I'm fine. Go, get him," she cried urgently.

Carson ran after the man, but as fast as he was, the foiled kidnapper turned out to be faster. The man fairly flew down the stairs and out the back way. Carson kept going until he reached the nearby creek that ran through the property.

That was where Justice lost the would-be kidnapper's scent.

Carson kept searching the area for another twenty minutes, hoping that Justice would pick up the scent again. But after twenty minutes, he was finally forced to give up.

"It's okay, Justice," he said, calling the dog off. "You did your best. We'll get him next time. Let's go back, boy."

When he returned to mansion and went up to Serena's suite, Carson found that she had got dressed. It was still the middle of the night, but it was obvious that she'd given up all hope of going back to sleep.

The second he entered the room, she ran up to Carson. "Did he get away?" she asked.

Despite the fact that she'd asked that, Serena was nursing the outside hope that he'd caught the man and that he was sitting handcuffed in Carson's car, waiting to be transported to jail.

But one look at Carson's face told her that wasn't the case. Mark had indeed got away from him. The nightmare was to continue.

"Yeah," Carson answered darkly. "He ran through the creek and Justice lost his scent."

"You'll get him, Carson," she said with such conviction, it was obvious that she firmly believed that there was no other way for this scenario to play out.

Carson sat down on her bed. Serena dropped down beside him, her courage flagging.

"Who is he, Serena?" Carson asked. "You called him by his name."

"I called him by *a* name," she corrected. She wasn't sure just what to expect or how Carson would handle being told about her connection to the man. "The one he told me when we met."

Carson shook his head. "Still doesn't answer my question. Who is he—to you?" he specified.

"Someone I thought I'd never see again," she told him.

Serena paused, pressing her lips together. It took her a moment to gather her courage together. What she and Carson had was all still very brand-new and fragile. She didn't want to jeopardize it by throwing this other man into the mix.

But she had no choice.

She took a deep breath and told him, "He's Lora's father."

"Oh."

It was one thing to know that Serena had lost her head one night and got involved in what amounted to a one-night stand. It was another to actually meet the other person who had been involved in that evening.

It took Carson a moment to come to grips with the

situation, to deal with what he was feeling—a strong flare-up of jealousy. With effort, he tamped it down and forced himself to put it all into proper perspective.

He blew out a long breath. "Well, it's obvious that he's not looking for a happy reunion between himself and his daughter."

Serena felt relieved and threatened at the same time. Relieved because Carson was taking her side in this. She knew that there were men who would have taken the situation and turned it into an opportunity to revile her for foolishly getting intimately involved with a stranger. The fact that Carson didn't, that he didn't lash out at her or upbraid her, making this all her fault, made her feel incredibly relieved and grateful.

"I know it's no excuse," Serena began, "but I'd had too much to drink and—"

"Stop," Carson said sternly. When she did, looking at him quizzically, wondering if she was wrong about him after all, Carson told her, "You don't owe me an explanation, Serena. Whatever happened between you and that man is in the past. What matters is now. We have to move forward from here—and we've got to get that bastard. Do you have any idea where he lives? Is he local or from out of state?"

"Not a clue," she admitted, embarrassed at her helplessness in this matter.

There were other ways to find things out, Carson thought. "I'll get in contact with the county's forensics team, and they can at least dust your suite for any fingerprints that don't belong. Maybe we'll get lucky and Lora's father is in the system."

Serena nodded. Although she was doing her best to get herself under control, she could feel the tears forming. That just made things worse. She didn't want to cry in front of Carson. Crying was something a helpless female would do, and she refused to see herself as helpless.

But despite her resolve, she couldn't find a way to just blink back her tears.

She could feel her eyes welling up so she turned her head away from him. She cleared her throat and said, "Um, maybe I should go down and make breakfast for us."

Rather than let her leave the room, Carson circled around until he was in front of her, blocking her way out. Taking her face in his hand, he tilted it toward him. Looking at her, his suspicions were confirmed. He wasn't about to ask her if she was crying until he knew for certain.

However now that he saw for himself that she was, he wasn't about to fall into that old cliché and tell her not to cry. He just silently took her into his arms and held her.

"We'll get this SOB and find out what his game is. I promise," he told her.

She pressed her lips together, burying her face against Carson's shoulder.

"I'm not going to cry," she told him, her voice breaking.

"Nobody asked you to," he answered matter-of-factly, trying to lighten the moment for her.

"I just want my life back," she told him.

"I know, and you'll get it back," he said, stroking her hair, wishing there was some way he could really reassure her.

Her sigh created a warmth that penetrated right through his shoulder, causing his stomach to tighten. He was prepared to go on holding her for as long as she needed him to.

But the shrill sound of the landline ringing shattered the moment.

He felt Serena instantly stiffen against him, as if the phone call couldn't be anything positive despite the fact that there could be a whole host of reasons why someone might be calling.

He looked over toward the phone on the white antique desk. "You want me to get that?" he offered.

"No, it's my house," she told him, grateful for his offer but refusing to hide behind it. She wasn't going to allow what was happening to diminish her in any way. She'd always been strong and she intended to remain that way. "I should be the one answering my own phone."

Moving away from the shelter of Carson's arms, she crossed over to the antique desk and picked the telephone receiver. "Double C Ranch."

"I know the name of the freaking ranch," the voice on the other end snarled.

It was him, the kidnapper. She would have recognized the man's voice anywhere. Serena instantly made eye contact with Carson, urging him over.

He was at her side immediately, gesturing for her to tilt the receiver so that he could hear what the caller was saying.

Holding the receiver with both hands, she asked, "What do you want?"

Instead of answering her question, Mark said, "I'm calling to find out what you want."

Still looking at Carson, she shook her head, mystified. "I don't understand."

"All right, I'll spell it out for you," Mark said, irritated. "I'm guessing that you want me to disappear and never bother you and that cute little girl, our daughter, again."

Serena cringed. She wanted to shout at the man and tell him that he had no claim to Lora. That Lora *wasn't* his little girl and never would be, that it took more than a genetic donation to make a father.

But she knew she had to remain calm. If she didn't, then Mark would get the upper hand. So she took a deep breath, and as Carson silently urged her on, she told Mark, "Yes, I do." Taking a shaky breath as she desperately tried to steady her nerves, she asked, "How do I make that happen?"

"Easy." His voice sounded almost slimy, she thought. "All you have to do is bring me a million dollars."

She hadn't been expecting for him to demand that much. "A million dollars?" she repeated, stunned.

As if sensing her reaction, Mark went on the defensive immediately. "Hey, that's not too much for your peace of mind—and your brat. Not to someone like you. Hell, that's practically like petty cash for your family. A million dollars and I'll go away."

She clutched at that phrase. "For good?" she asked.

"Yeah, sure. For good," he told her. "That sound good?"

"Yes." It also sounded like a lie, she thought. "I don't have that kind of cash readily accessible. I need time to gather it together."

"How much time?" he asked angrily.

Her mind scrambled as she tried to come up with a reasonable answer. "At least a couple of days."

"Too much time," he snapped. "You've got nine hours."

"I can't get that much money in nine hours," she cried, thinking of the logistics that were involved.

"*Find* a way," he retorted. "Unless you want to deal with the consequences."

Her eyes met Carson's. He nodded, mouthing instructions and encouraging her to tell Mark that she'd meet him with the money.

Serena let out a shaky breath. "All right. Where and when?"

"Atta girl, now you're playing the game. I want you to meet me in front of that fancy restaurant in town. The one that just opened up. The Barbecue Barn. Be there at three o'clock. Just you and our daughter," he instructed with a mocking laugh. "Bring the million in unmarked bills in a backpack, the kind that schoolkids use. And make sure you come alone. I see anyone else there, if I see anything out of the ordinary, I promise I'll make you very, very sorry—and our kid'll be playing a harp. Understand, princess?"

He was making her skin crawl, as well as making fear skewer her heart. "I understand. If I get you that money, I don't ever want to see you near my daughter or me again," she said with feeling.

"Why, Serena, after everything we've meant to one another? I'm hurt," Mark said sarcastically. And then his voice became deadly serious. "You bring that money, then yeah, you'll never see me again and you and that cop you got guarding your body can go on playing house to your hearts' content.

"Remember, tomorrow, three o'clock. Unmarked bills in a backpack. You can put the backpack in the kid's stroller so nobody'll get suspicious," he added. "You got that?"

"I've got it." Sensing he was about to hang up, she said, "Wait a minute. How do I know you'll keep your word and disappear after you get your money?"

She heard him laugh on the other end. The sound caused another cold chill to slither up and down her spine.

"Well, honey, you're just going to have to trust me on that," he told her.

"Trust you," Serena repeated. What she wanted to do was rip his heart out and feed it to him, but she forced herself to sound docile.

"Yeah, trust me," he said.

Carson was silently telling her to stay calm. But Lord, she was finding it hard to stay civil. "Okay. I'll hold you to that."

He laughed again, the sound slicing through her this time. "You do that, honey. You just do that."

Chapter 21

Serena didn't remember hanging up the phone. She didn't remember crossing to her bed. She *was* aware of her legs giving out from beneath her so that she wound up collapsing onto it.

The next moment, she felt Carson's arm encircling her shoulders. "By this time tomorrow, it'll all be over," he promised.

His words echoed in her head. In the meantime, she thought, she had all this terrible blackmail to deal with. Had to see that disgusting excuse for a human being again for the handoff.

She just wanted this to be over with. "Maybe I should just pay him off," she told Carson.

He looked at her in surprise. "What are you saying? No, don't even think about doing that," Carson told her sternly. He realized that this was her fear talking, but paying this bastard off was not the way to go, she had to know that.

Serena felt as if she was in between the proverbial rock and hard place. "But if paying him off means getting rid of him—" she began.

He stopped her right there. "But that's just it, Serena. You won't. You won't get rid of him. He'll keep coming back, always asking for more money. Blackmailers never stop blackmailing, Serena. They just keep getting greedier." Carson took hold of her shoulders, looking into her eyes and trying to cut through her fear. He had to get her to understand. "You're going to the bank and taking out just enough to fill the top portion of that backpack he wants you to bring. The rest of it will be filled with cut-up newspapers."

"He also said to bring Lora," she reminded Carson.

"You'll be bringing her stand-in instead," he told Serena, nodding toward the crib in the other room where he'd put the decoy doll. "Don't worry," he said, "I'm going to be with you every step of the way."

Much as she wanted him there, she felt she couldn't risk it. "You heard that bastard. He said if he saw anyone with me—"

"He won't," Carson cut in. "Don't worry. I'm very good at my job," he assured her without any bravado. "And after today, he's never going to bother you again." Very gently, he raised her chin so that her eyes met his. "You believe me, don't you?"

"I believe you," Serena answered, although her voice sounded a little hoarse.

"It'd be better with a little more enthusiasm," Carson said, "but I'll accept that."

He kissed her on the forehead in an attempt to comfort her. His lips migrated down to her cheek, then to her other cheek. Before she knew it, the small act of comfort mushroomed into something much more than that.

For the next hour, Serena found solace in his arms as well as sanctuary from some very real fears that existed just beyond the boundaries of her suite.

"That is one hell of a stroller," Carson commented as he helped her load it into her car later that afternoon.

Because they really weren't sure, despite the fact that the blackmailer said he would meet her in front of the restaurant, exactly where Mark might be hidden, Carson didn't want to take a chance on the blackmailer seeing them come into Red Ridge together. So he was driving his own car to town while Serena was going to Red Ridge in hers.

"How much did you say it cost?" he asked her, still looking at the stroller.

Serena flushed, knowing that the pink stroller was exceedingly ostentatious. It had been a gift from her mother. Joanelle Colton always needed to make a big show out of everything, even something as simple as a stroller. Ordinarily Serena wouldn't have accepted it, except that after what her mother had put her through, she felt the woman did owe her something. The stroller was her mother's way of apologizing. Throwing money at something had always been preferable for her mother than admitting to a mistake.

She'd seen the price tag. There was no doubt in her mind that her mother had left it there on purpose. "A thousand dollars."

Carson let out a low whistle. "For something Lora's going to outgrow in a year? Does your mother always throw money around like that?"

"Always," Serena answered without hesitation, then

added as she shook her head, "She thinks it puts people in awe of her."

Carson held his tongue, thinking it best not to say what he thought of that. Instead, he handed the decoy, dressed in Lora's clothes, to Serena.

"Don't forget to put this in the car seat and buckle it up. You don't want this Mark creep to suspect something's wrong," Carson cautioned.

Taking the doll, Serena had to marvel about it again. "This is just *too* lifelike," she told Carson. Not to mention that it felt a little eerie, handling the doll and pretending it was her daughter.

Carson went to the heart of the matter. "Just as long as that doll does the trick and fools Mark, that's all that counts."

She had her doubts about that. "Anyone stopping to look at 'my daughter' will see that it's not Lora—or a real baby."

He had a solution for that. "Then just pull that little cotton blanket down over 'her.' Tell people she's coming down with a cold, and you don't want to take a chance on it getting worse because people are touching her and breathing on her."

Serena got in behind the wheel. "Shouldn't I have left her at home if she's coming down with something?" she asked.

Carson shook his head. "You're overthinking this thing. Just tell them what I said and people will be sympathetic—and they'll leave 'Lora' alone." Standing next to the open driver's-side window, he bent down and put his hand on hers. "Okay, remember to do what we rehearsed. You go to the bank, make that withdrawal, then put the money into the backpack and tuck the backpack into that carry section at the back of the stroller."

Serena was doing her best not to allow her nerves to get the better of her. There was a great deal riding on this. She wasn't worried about getting hurt, she was afraid that Mark would get away again.

She ran her tongue along her very dry lips. "And where will you be again?"

"Out of sight," he told her. "My team and I will be watching you. The second that guy turns up and grabs the money, it'll be all over for him." Carson squeezed her hand. "Trust me."

"I do," she told him. And she did. With her life *and* her daughter's.

Just to reassure her, Carson added, "I won't let him hurt you."

She could see the concern in his eyes. He was worried that *she* was worried. It touched her heart. "I know that."

Even so, Serena was still nervous as she drove from the ranch.

Serena parked away from the bank. She wanted to be able to walk slowly back to her car once she had made her withdrawal from the bank. She reasoned that the longer the walk, the more opportunity Mark would have to steal the backpack from her. What she *didn't* want was to be close enough to her car to have Mark push his way into it, stealing both the backpack *and* her.

The thought galvanized her and made her more determined than ever that the only place Mark was going after today was prison.

"This is rather a large amount of money you're withdrawing, Ms. Colton. Is everything all right?" Edward Abernathy, the bank manager asked.

When she'd initially handed the teller the withdrawal slip, taking the sizable amount from her savings account, the teller had mumbled something about needing to get approval for such a large sum and then went to get the bank manager.

The portly man had greeted her with a profusion of banal small talk ranging from the weather to the state of her family's health. Then he looked at the withdrawal slip as if he hadn't already seen it when the teller had brought it to him.

The bank manager eyed her now, waiting for her answer to his question.

"Everything's fine, Mr. Abernathy," Serena told him with a broad, easy smile. "It's just that I'm dealing with a seller who insists on being paid in cash. I think he's paranoid about having checks bounce on him. It's happened before," she added for good measure.

"That must be some horse you're acquiring," Abernathy marveled. After a beat, he signed his approval for the transaction.

"Oh, it is," Serena assured the man, wishing he would hurry up. It was a quarter to three and she felt that she was cutting it very close. "It's a beautiful palomino. I have to act quickly. There are two other buyers who are interested in the stallion."

"I quite understand," Abernathy said sympathetically. "I'll be back in a moment. Wait right here, please," he told her just before he went into the vault.

He returned a few minutes later.

"Well, there you go," Abernathy said, counting out a number of banded stacks of hundred-dollar bills before tucking all of them neatly into a sack for her. "I see you brought your daughter in with you. Never too young to start them on a sound financial footing. We could open an account for your little darling today if you're interested," the bank manager told her.

"Some other time, Mr. Abernathy," Serena said, then reminded him, "I have that appointment with the seller to keep."

"Of course, of course," the manager answered, watching her tuck the sack into her backpack. He angled his head, as if trying to get a look beneath the screen cover draped across the front of the stroller. "That certainly is one well-behaved baby you have there. I don't believe I heard a single peep out of her this whole time."

"She's a heavy sleeper," Serena replied.

Abernathy chuckled. "Both of mine were screamers. Or so my wife said. I had to work of course, so I missed all that."

"You were lucky," Serena told him, knowing the man was expecting some sort of a comment.

Turning away from the bank manager, she quickly began to make her way to the bank's double doors, anxious to leave the bank before Abernathy could ask any more questions or, worse, ask if he could sneak in one peek at her "baby."

Serena could feel her heart hammering hard as she approached the exit doors.

The bank guard moved toward them at the same time, then obligingly held one of the doors open for her. He tipped the brim of his cap. "Nice seeing you again, Ms. Colton."

"You, too, Eli," she murmured, forcing a smile to her lips.

She had less than five minutes to make it to the rendezvous point.

Focused on getting back to her car in order to make it to the restaurant in time, Serena didn't see him until it was too late. One second, she was walking quickly, pushing the stroller in front of her; the next, she felt a jolt coming from the left and going through her whole body.

It sent her flying to the ground.

Mark had darted out of the alley next to the bank and lunged at her, catching her completely off balance.

Rather than grab the backpack, he grabbed the whole stroller and made a mad dash for the parking lot that was across the street. Obviously intent on upping his game, he was running to his truck with both the money and what he presumed was the baby. The latter was to be his collateral, assuring him of a safe escape.

But he never reached the truck. Instead, he howled in pain as Justice came out of nowhere and caught his arm, dragging him down to the ground.

The second the canine caught him, Mark let go of the stroller. It hurtled toward the street and would have been smashed by an oncoming truck if Finn hadn't managed to grab it just before it went careening off curb.

Several of the K-9 team closed ranks around Mark, although the latter wasn't really necessary. The moment Mark had lunged out of the alley and grabbed the stroller, Carson had transformed from an elderly man dozing on a bench to a K-9 detective and sprinted over toward the blackmailer. Justice had brought the man down, but Carson had been less than half a second behind the German shepherd.

Grabbing Mark by the back of his collar, he shoved him in Finn's direction. "Here's the guy who wanted to steal your niece. I'll be in to do the paperwork as soon as I make sure that your sister is all right and bring her home," Carson told the chief.

"You're making a mistake," Mark cried, appealing

to Finn. "The stroller was about to go into the street and I was just trying to catch it before the baby had a terrible accident."

Carson snorted. "You're the one making the mistake if you think any of us are actually buying that lame story," he told the blackmailer.

The next moment, he turned away, not giving the brazen blackmailer another thought. Right now, all his thoughts were centered on Serena. He swiftly checked her out, his eyes sweeping over every inch of her. She'd got back up to her feet, but Carson wanted to see for himself that she was unharmed.

"Are you all right?" he asked her anxiously.

She didn't bother answering that. Instead, she had an important question of her own. "Is Mark going to be going to jail?"

"Yes. For a long, long time if your brother and I have anything to say about it," Carson answered.

"Then I'm fine," she said, answering his question as she breathed a huge sigh of relief. Turning toward Carson, she looked up at him and very plaintively asked, "Can I please go get my daughter now?"

He grinned. "I'll take you there myself," Carson said.

She remembered what he'd just told her brother. "But what about the paperwork you said you were going to write up?"

"It's not going anywhere," he assured Serena. He glanced over toward the blackmailer. One of the officers was pushing the man's head down and getting him into the back of a squad car. "And neither is Mark." Giving her his full attention, Carson asked, "You ready for that reunion now?" he wanted to know.

"Oh, so ready."

He grinned, expecting nothing less. "Then let's go

see that little girl of yours." Carson let out a piercing whistle. "Justice, come!"

The German shepherd was instantly at his side, ready to follow him wherever he went.

As it turned out, Lora wasn't sequestered all that far away.

Will Taggert, the detective—and father of three—who Finn had entrusted with the baby's safety, had taken her as well as the Colton housekeeper to stay at his family's small ranch.

The second they walked into the room where she and the baby were staying, Alma made no secret of the fact that she was overjoyed to see Serena *and* Carson.

"Did you catch that hateful scoundrel?" the house-keeper asked, excitement and hope clearly written all over her face.

Carson smiled at the woman and nodded his head. "We did. He won't be threatening anyone anymore," he told Alma.

"Oh, thank you!" Alma cried.

Carson murmured something in response, however his attention was focused on Serena. When they had entered the bedroom where Alma and Lora were stay-ing, Serena had instantly rushed over to the cradle and scooped her daughter up in her arms.

"Oh, I have missed you," she told her daughter, press-ing the baby against her breast. Serena took in a deep breath. "You smell so good," she said with enthusiasm.

"You're lucky you didn't get here ten minutes ear-lier, Miss," Alma said with a laugh. "You might not have said that then."

Serena raised her eyes to look at the housekeeper. "Oh, yes I would have. I missed everything about Lora, even changing her diapers." Turning toward Carson, she said, "I don't know how to thank you."

He smiled in response. He had a few ideas on that subject, but nothing he could say right now, not in front of the housekeeper or in front of Taggert, who had just walked into the room. So instead, he said, "Just all part of the job. Right, Justice?" he asked, looking down at the German shepherd.

As if knowing that he was being asked a question, the canine barked in response.

Carson looked over at the housekeeper. "How long will it take you get pack up and get ready to leave?" he asked.

"Is five minutes too long?" she asked.

Carson laughed. "You can have half an hour if you'd like."

"No, Miss Lora and I are all ready," Alma assured him. "No offense," she said to Taggert, "But I never bothered unpacking when we got here."

"None taken," Taggert assured the woman with a laugh.

"Well, if you're all ready," Carson began.

"Then let's go home," Serena said, concluding his sentence.

Carson grinned as he took the suitcase that Alma had produced out of the closet from the woman. His heart swelled as he joined Serena and her daughter.

"Let's go home," he echoed.

Epilogue

Order, to some extent, had been restored.

Serena's daughter as well as the family housekeeper were back at the Double C, as they should be. The rest of Serena's family—her parents and younger sister, Valeria—would be coming back in the morning, Finn had told his sister. Returning on such short notice was "inconvenient" for the older Coltons according to Joanelle. Carson imagined that packing up alone, even though someone else would undoubtedly be given that task, would take some time.

Carson had to admit that he wasn't exactly overly thrilled anticipating Judson and Joanelle's return to the ranch. They had both made no secret of the fact that they looked down on him, as well as down at his family, but in the grand scheme of things, he viewed that as just a minor problem.

Besides, he still had tonight with Serena and tonight, if all went according to his plan, was all he needed.

"You're thinking about your brother, aren't you?" Serena asked, putting her own interpretation to the pensive expression on Carson's face.

It was evening and they were back in her suite at the ranch. For now, Lora was dozing in the other room in her crib.

"No, actually I'm thinking about finding his killer," Carson said. Now that the threat to Serena was over, finding Bo's killer had become his main focus again. "And finding Demi Colton."

She immediately focused on his phrasing. "So now those are finally two separate concerns—aren't they?" she asked hopefully.

Carson smiled. The woman's loyalty was incredible. "If you're asking me if I still think that Demi killed my brother, no, I don't. We're following up on other leads and looking at other suspects." He tucked his arm around her as they lay on her bed. "But that doesn't change the fact that Demi is still out there somewhere, missing—*and* pregnant with my brother's baby. I need to find her," he said seriously, "and bring her in—for her own safety."

Sitting up, Serena shifted so she could look down at him. "Really?" she asked.

"Really," he replied with sincerity. "She shouldn't be alone at a time like this."

Would wonders never cease? "Who *are* you and what have you done with Carson Gage?" she asked playfully.

"I'm right here," he answered, slowly running his hand along the swell of her curves and relishing every sensation that contact created within him. "You're responsible for this, you know, for changing me and making me see things I'd never noticed before."

He watched the warm smile blossom in her eyes before spreading to her lips. That, too, gave him an immense amount of pleasure.

"Then I guess I did a good thing," Serena said.

He laughed, toying with the ends of her hair. "That all depends on whether or not you like the new me."

Crossing her arms on his chest, she leaned her chin against them as she gazed into his eyes. "Oh, I like him. I like the 'new you' a great deal," Serena told him and she pressed a kiss to his lips to show Carson just how much.

"Good, because that makes this a lot easier."

And just like that, Serena could feel herself starting to grow uneasy. Things had been going too well. They'd caught Mark and she'd been reunited with her daughter. That meant that she was due for something to go wrong.

Trying not to sound as nervous as she felt, Serena asked, "Makes what a lot easier?"

Carson took a deep breath. He'd never found himself lacking courage before, but this was an area he'd never ventured into until now. The whole idea of marriage and family was all new to him and there was a part of him that worried it might all be one-sided.

He backtracked. "On second thought, maybe it doesn't."

"Doesn't what?" Serena wanted to know. "What are you talking about—or *not* talking about?"

Because he was accustomed to always having an escape route for himself, he edged his way into what he was about to say slowly.

"I know that your parents don't much care for anyone who's part of the Gage family—"

"I am not my parents' daughter," she was quick to assure him. "And I don't think the way they do. Now, will you *please* tell me what you're trying to say before *my* daughter wakes up and I have to tend to her—instead of you?" she urged.

As if on cue, Lora began to cry.

"Too late." Serena sighed. She tossed off the covers and began to get out of bed. "I'd better go get her."

Carson caught her by the wrist, holding Serena in place.

"She only gets louder," she told Carson.

He wasn't thinking about the baby right now. "Will you marry me?"

The four words stopped her cold. Did she just imagine that? "What did you say?"

This wasn't the way he wanted to propose. "I didn't want to blurt it out that way, but I was afraid I'd lose my nerve if you—"

She shook her head. She didn't want an explanation. She wanted the words. "Again, please," she requested.

"You want me to ask you again?" he asked, not quite sure this was what she was telling him.

Serena bobbed her head emphatically up and down. "Yes, please."

"I know that your parents don't much care for—"

"Not that part," she told him. "The *good* part."

And then he knew what she was asking him to say. "Will you marry me?"

"Yes!" she cried, throwing her arms around his neck. Then, in case there was *any* lingering doubt, she repeated, "Yes!" And then her eyes suddenly widened. "Listen."

She'd lost him again. He cocked his head, doing as she'd asked. "What am I listening for?"

Her grin all but split her face. "Lora stopped crying. You really do have a magic touch," she told him with unabashed approval.

"Then let me give you a real demonstration of that," he said, bringing his mouth down to hers.

"Yes, please," she said one more time before she lost herself in the wondrous world that only Carson could create for her.

For them.

* * * * *

Justine Davis lives on Puget Sound in Washington State, watching big ships and the occasional submarine go by and sharing the neighborhood with assorted wildlife, including a pair of bald eagles, deer, a bear or two, and a tailless raccoon. In the few hours when she's not planning, plotting or writing her next book, her favorite things are photography, knitting her way through a huge yarn stash and driving her restored 1967 Corvette roadster—top down, of course.

Connect with Justine on her website, justinedavis.com, at Twitter.com/justine_d_davis or on Facebook at Facebook.com/justinedaredavis.

Books by Justine Davis

Harlequin Romantic Suspense

Cutter's Code

Operation Power Play
Operation Homecoming
Operation Soldier Next Door
Operation Alpha
Operation Notorious
Operation Hero's Watch
Operation Second Chance

The Coltons of Red Ridge

Colton's Twin Secrets

The Coltons of Texas

Colton Family Rescue

Visit the Author Profile page
at Harlequin.com for more titles.

OPERATION MIDNIGHT

Justine Davis

For Nikki, the first, when I was too young
to understand.

For Whisper, who taught me so much, and
deserved better than I and life gave her at the end.

For Murphy,
because without him there might not have been
a Decoy (and now his sister Bailey, too).

And for Chase,
who proves that boys can be sweet, too.

To all the sweet, funny, smart, wonderful dogs I've
known. But most of all for The Decoy Dawg who,
against all odds and predictions, at this moment has
seen another summer. I love you, my sweet girl.
I won't give up until you do. And when you do,
I'll try to let go with the grace you've taught me.

Chapter 1

"Cutter!"

Hayley Cole shouted once more, then decided to save her breath for running. It wasn't that the dog was ignoring her. Sometimes he just got so intent on something, the rest of the world ceased to exist.

Serves you right, she told herself, *for spoiling him. Treating him like a human just because half the time he acts like one.*

That he'd shown up on her doorstep when she most needed him, that she now couldn't imagine life without the uncannily clever Cutter didn't help at the moment, as she was traipsing after him through midnight-dark trees. If she hadn't known these woods from childhood she might be nervous, but it was the wrong time of year for bears, and she wasn't afraid of much else. But a sassy dog could get into trouble; just last night she'd heard coyotes. And a cornered raccoon could be nasty. While she had faith in the clever dog's ability to come out on top, she didn't want him hurt in the process.

At least out here, if you heard a sound in the night, your worry wasn't who, but what. Well, maybe except for that blessed helicopter that had buzzed the house a while ago, setting Cutter into the frenzy that started this whole chase. They weren't uncommon in the Pacific Northwest, what with the navy and coast guard coming and going. Normally they didn't ruffle the dog, but this smaller one had been frighteningly low and had set him off like a rocket.

She dodged around the big cedar tree on the north side of the trail that could barely be found in full daylight. She should have grabbed her heavy, hooded parka with the flashlight in the pocket, but while fall was in the air it was still merely cool at night, not cold. Besides, she hadn't realized this was going to be a lengthy expedition.

She was on her neighbor's property now, and she doubted the reclusive older man would welcome either her or her four-legged mischief maker, so she forged onward.

"Like some stupid character in a bad horror movie," she muttered under her breath, rethinking sharing the last of the beef stew she'd made with the carrot-loving dog.

She rounded a large maple and nearly tripped over Cutter, who had stopped dead.

"Whoa," she said, recovering. "What—?"

The dog's tail gave an acknowledging wag, but his attention never wavered. He was staring through the trees at something. A little wary—it *was* too early for bears, wasn't it?—she moved up beside the dog to look. For a moment it didn't register, it seemed so unlikely.

In the darkness it was almost indistinguishable, in fact would be invisible if not for the faint light from the house. That light slipped over polished, gleaming black, so that the shape she saw was a series of faint reflections, curved and straight, rather than the object itself.

But she still knew what it was, instantly.

The helicopter that had rattled her windows fifteen minutes ago was sitting in her reclusive neighbor's yard.

Something about the thing sitting there, glimmering faintly in the dark, unsettled her. The fact that it had no apparent markings unsettled her even more. Weren't they like planes? Didn't they have to have numbers on them?

Maybe it's a prototype, her logical mind said. Hasn't been registered yet. Lots of aircraft industry up here in the Pacific Northwest. Maybe her neighbor was a designer or something. She had no idea what he really did, nor did any of the others in this semirural, forested little community. Being mostly kind, they didn't call him antisocial, at least not yet. The speculation ranged from eccentric hoarder to grief-stricken widower, depending on the mind-set of the speculator. Hayley, who herself valued her privacy and the quiet of this wooded setting, preferred to simply leave him alone if that's what he chose.

Being right next door, she'd seen him more often than anyone, which meant exactly twice. And both times he'd retreated immediately inside, as if he feared she might actually approach him.

But now she was wondering if a little more curiosity might have been wise. Scenarios from mad scientist to terrorists foreign and domestic raced through her mind. Her mother would have laughed at the very idea of such things in quiet little Redwood Cove, but her mother had been unaware of many dark things in the world in the last years of her life. Not by choice, but because she was focused on the battle to extend that life as long as possible, a battle Hayley had fought beside her for three years, until it was lost eight months ago.

She heard a sliding door opening, and in the next instant a bright light on the side of the house came on. Instinctively she jerked back, even though the apparently motion-sensing floodlight didn't reach this far. Cutter, on the other hand, took a half step forward as two men stepped out onto the deck. His nose lifted, twitching rapidly as he drew in the scents the faint breeze wafted his way.

The light threw the helicopter back into the realm of, if not ordinary, at least no longer sinister—at least it did until she realized she could now see that indeed, there wasn't a single marking to identify the craft.

The light also made the silver in her neighbor's neatly trimmed beard gleam. The second man, much younger, with a buzz cut and a leather jacket, was a total stranger. He seemed to be helping the older man as they went down the steps, gripping his arm in support.

Her breath caught as, coming down the steps into the yard where the helicopter waited, the leather jacket parted and she saw a holstered handgun on his hip.

She grabbed Cutter's collar; all her silly notions about men in black and their black helicopters suddenly didn't seem so silly anymore. Were they the good guys, if any still existed, and was her neighbor being arrested? Was the reason for his reclusiveness something worse than she'd ever imagined?

She shivered, wishing more than ever for her parka. And then another thought followed rapidly: What if he was the good guy? What if these men in the black helicopter were the bad guys, and her neighbor was being snatched by them? That it could be some twisted combination of both also occurred to her; these days it was harder than ever to tell bad guys from good.

The two men got into the helicopter, the younger one again helping the older, with every evidence of solicitousness. Moments later, the helicopter came alive, engine humming, running lights blinking on.

Her mind was racing. Two men, one of them armed, get on the helicopter, and it starts up. So obviously, unless her neighbor was the pilot, which seemed unlikely, the other man was. Which had to mean her neighbor was going willingly, didn't it? Otherwise, wouldn't he run while the other man was occupied with…well, whatever you did to fire up a helicopter? Unless he couldn't. Perhaps he wasn't well enough? Or was simply too frightened to try to escape?

Or…could there have been a third man, waiting aboard the craft all this time?

Cutter made an odd, uncharacteristic, whining sort of sound just as a movement on the deck caught her eye. And she realized there was at least a third man, because he was coming out of the house now. Tall, lean, with hair as dark as the sky. He had a large duffel bag slung over his left shoulder. He started down the deck steps, and two things happened simultaneously. The sound of the engine got louder. And Cutter let out a sudden, sharp bark.

Before she could react, the dog had twisted free of her loose grip on his collar. And to her dismay he bolted, straight toward the third man. Tail up, head down, he raced out of the trees and across the open yard. Cutter was never vicious, but the man he was charging didn't know that, and she took off after him.

So much for a silent retreat, she thought as the man, obviously having heard the dog's bark, dropped the duffel bag to the ground.

"Cutter!"

The dog ignored her, intent on his target. But he was running happily, joyously, as he did when he greeted her if she'd been away and left him home. Some part of her mind wondered if perhaps he knew the man. She'd never seen him before; now that he'd turned in their direction she knew she wasn't likely to forget a guy who looked like this one.

She had a split second to wonder if the mystery of Cutter's appearance in her life, at the time when she'd needed the distraction most, was about to be solved.

The man turned to face the dog's onslaught.

And pulled a gun. Aimed it at Cutter.

"No!"

Panic lifted her shout to a scream. He didn't shoot. It should have been reassuring. Except that he instantly turned his attention—and his weapon—on her. She kept going. He hadn't shot Cutter, and he had to be a lot more threatening than she was.

Then again, maybe not, she thought, her pace slowing as the dog reached his goal. And while she'd never expected him to launch into an attack, she certainly hadn't expected what he did next; the dog sat politely at the man's feet, then looked over a furry shoulder at her with an expression of utter delight. His tongue lolled happily, his ears were up and alert and he looked just as he did when he found the exact toy he'd been searching for.

He looked, for all the world, as if he were saying, "Look, I found him!"

The man lowered the lethal-looking black handgun but did not, she noticed, put it away.

She grabbed Cutter's collar, firmly this time.

"I'm sorry. He got away from me, but he's harmless, really. He doesn't usually… I mean, he's usually a bit slow to warm up to strangers. He doesn't generally charge up to them…"

She was babbling, she realized, and made herself stop.

"I'm sorry," she repeated. "We didn't mean to trespass." She glanced at the waiting helicopter, gave an embarrassed smile, hoping her neighbor could read her expression since he doubtless couldn't hear her inside and over the noise of the engine.

"Damn."

Her gaze shot back to the man who had just muttered the curse. The light was behind him, silhouetting his rangy frame, making him seem even taller, looming over her. Her gut told her the quicker she got them out of here, the better. She tugged on Cutter's collar, but the dog was reluctant and reacted with uncharacteristic resistance.

Everything the darn dog had done since that helicopter had buzzed the house had been uncharacteristic, she thought, tugging again.

The door of the helicopter opened. The first armed man she'd seen leaned out.

"Time, Quinn," he shouted over the noise of the engine and the growing wind of the main rotor.

"I know."

Hayley heard the exchange and registered that the man her suddenly recalcitrant dog seemed so attracted to was apparently named Quinn, but she was mainly focused on getting them both out of here. Normally she was able, barely, to lift Cutter if she had to. But dragging him when he was actively resisting was something else.

She turned, intending to walk away, hoping the dog would just follow; normally he always did, not liking her too far away from him. Not that he was behaving normally just now, but—

She gasped as the man called Quinn suddenly appeared in front of her, blocking her path. She hadn't even heard him move. And in that instant the entire scenario went from ominous and unsettling to threatening. Because clearly this man was not going to let her just walk away.

"I'm sorry," the man said.

Then he grabbed her, so swiftly she had no time to react. He ran his hands over her, so obviously searching that any thought that it was some personal assault never really formed.

She elbowed him. "What do you think you're doing?"

It was a rhetorical question, and it got the answer it probably deserved: nothing. She tried to pull away again but he held her in place with ease, warning her without a word that he was much stronger than she.

And then he lifted her off the ground. She fought, clawing, kicking, landing at least one solid blow. She barely had time to scream before she was physically tossed aboard the helicopter. She twisted, trying to get out before the man called Quinn got aboard. Cutter, she noticed through her panic, did nothing but whine in obvious concern. Somehow she'd always assumed the dog would defend her, would attack, bite—

She was pushed down into a seat. She scrambled to get to her feet, but Quinn leaned over and grabbed Cutter, tossing the fifty-pound dog into her lap as if he weighed no more than the duffel bag that followed. And then he was aboard himself, and the door slammed shut behind him with grim finality.

She sat in the seat he'd shoved her into, her heart hammering, her hands shaking as she clung to Cutter, fighting to wrap her mind around one simple fact.

They were being kidnapped.

Chapter 2

"You were no help at all," Hayley muttered to the dog overwhelming her lap. Yet despite her surprise at that—a tiny emotion next to the fear that was growing every second—she clung to the furry bundle. The dog didn't seemed bothered at all by what was happening, just as he hadn't protested by even a yelp when this total stranger had grabbed him, never mind her.

She, on the other hand, was terrified. If she hadn't had the dog to hang on to, to focus on, she was sure she'd be shrieking. And then the rotors began to turn, and she did let out a little gasp.

"Thanks for the help, Teague," Quinn snapped at the other armed man. Even though he was practically yelling to be heard over the engine and growing rotor noise, the sarcasm came through.

The other man laughed. And grinned, a boyish, crooked grin she would have found charming under other circumstances. Now it just added to her growing fears.

"The day you can't handle a woman and a dog is the day I quit this gig," the man called Teague shouted back.

"I let you fly, so get us out of here."

Teague's grin flashed again, but then he was all business, turning his attention completely to controls that, Hayley noted, seemed to take not only his hands and eyes, but feet, as well. Flying a helicopter was apparently a complicated affair.

"Belt up," Quinn instructed her.

Hayley didn't react, still watching the pilot as she tried to analyze the easy, friendly banter between the two men. Did that bode well, or worse? She didn't know, and—

"Let go of the damn dog and put your seat belt on." He was yelling again now as the sound of the engine and rotors increased again.

There was too much dog to just let go of and get her hands on the belt she could see at her sides. And then the man realized that, grabbed Cutter and again lifted him as easily as if the animal didn't weigh almost half what she did. To her annoyance, the dog didn't even growl at the usually unwanted liberty taken by a stranger. But she kept her mouth shut. She didn't want to anger the man while he had the dog in his arms.

He seemed to realize that. "You want him back, do it."

She reached for the belt ends, then glanced back at her traitorous dog. Just in time to see him swipe a pink tongue over the set jaw of their captor.

"Talk about fraternizing with the enemy," she muttered as she fastened the harness-style belt, figuring she was safe enough saying it aloud, it was so noisy in here.

The only saving grace was the expression on Quinn's face; utterly startled. She wasn't sure how she knew it was not an expression he wore often, but she did. He plopped the dog back into her lap.

"Must you?"

The barely audible question came out of the darkness beside her, and Hayley realized it had come from her neighbor, the first time she'd ever heard him speak. His voice was a bit raspy, probably, she thought wryly, from disuse. And she thought it might hold a bit of an accent, although it was hard to tell from two words called out over the noise of a helicopter.

"Sorry, Vicente," Quinn said, sparking another spurt of annoyance in her; if anybody should get an apology, it should be her, shouldn't it?

Teague yelled something Hayley couldn't hear well enough to understand, but Quinn must have, because he turned his head to answer. Then he reached out and picked something up from the empty front seat. If she had any guts, now would have been a chance, while he was turned away. She could lunge for the door, get away. Problem was, she didn't think she could undo the belt, hang on to Cutter and get the door open fast enough. She—

Quinn turned back, and the moment was lost. To her surprise, he jammed himself onto the floor at her feet, although he was tall enough to make it a tight fit. It took her a moment to realize he was staying to keep an eye on them, rather than strapping himself into the vacant seat beside the pilot. That must have been, she thought, what that exchange she hadn't heard was about. And what he'd picked up was some kind of headset, perhaps something that enabled him to talk to the pilot, or at least muffled the noise that made normal conversation impossible.

And then she felt the undeniable shift as they went airborne into the midnight sky, and it was too late to do anything but try not to shiver under the force of the sheer terror that was rocketing around inside her. Why on earth had he done this? She'd done nothing, had been more than willing to vanish back into the woods and let them go. All she'd wanted was her dog....

She clung to her furry companion, his thick, soft coat warming her hands. If there were lights inside this thing they weren't on, but she didn't need them to visualize the dog's striking coloring, the near-black face, head and shoulders, fading to a rich, reddish brown from there back. The vet said he looked like a purebred Belgian breed, but since—despite being the smartest dog anyone she knew had ever seen—he hadn't shown up with papers, she didn't know for sure.

And as comforting as the dog's presence was—even if he did seem inordinately fond of their kidnapper—she regretted it now. The dog was indeed clever, sometimes to the point of seeming unnaturally so. More than once since the day he'd appeared and proceeded to fill the void in her life, she had wondered if he was really just a dog. He seemed to sense, to understand, to *know* things that no ordinary dog did or could. And because of that, he would be safer on the ground, able to survive on his own. At least for a while.

She didn't want to think about the possibility that it might be longer than a while. Much longer. That it might be forever, if these men had lethal intent.

She hugged the dog so tightly that he squirmed a little. What had her bundle of energy and fur gotten them into? The dog didn't seem at all bothered by the fact that he was airborne. He seemed to be treating it as if it were merely a more exciting version of the car rides he so loved.

She ducked her head, pressing her cheek to Cutter's fur. In the process she stole a glance sideways, to where her neighbor was seated, carefully strapped in. She still couldn't see much of him, just the gleam of the silver-gray beard, and a faint reflection from his eyes. He'd said nothing else through this, in fact after his query had seemed to shrink back against the side of the noisy craft, as if he were wishing he could vanish as he had on the two occasions she'd come across him outside his house. She wondered what he was thinking about her sudden intrusion into his affairs, inadvertent though it was.

But at least he'd made a token protest. She supposed that counted for something.

Vicente. She'd never known his name. And from the way he'd asked the question, hesitantly, it seemed clear he wasn't in charge of this operation, whatever it was. Was he rich, was that what this was all about? A kidnapping for ransom? But if so, why was he so cooperative? Not that guns didn't engender cooperation, but he'd seemed awfully willing.

Besides, why would somebody who could afford an aircraft like this one need money so badly they'd commit a crime like kidnapping? Unless of course that was *how* they afforded it.

Maybe they were drug dealers, she thought, barely resisting the urge to look around and see if there were drugs piled in the small space behind her. Did helicopters have separate cargo spaces? She had no idea. She pushed the media-inspired image of wrapped white packages of cocaine out of her mind.

There were other possibilities, of course. Terrorists, for instance. They didn't look it, but what did she know? Maybe Vicente was some sort of master bomb maker, maybe they—

The helicopter seemed to lean sharply, cutting off her careening thoughts. *Just as well,* she told herself, *you were getting silly.*

At least, she hoped she was getting silly. But what simple explanation could there be for being scooped up in the middle of the night by strange men, along with her possibly stranger neighbor?

She lifted her head, realized Quinn was staring at her from his spot on the floor. She had no idea what he might be hearing in that headset, but there was no doubt about what he was looking at. As with Vicente, all she could see was the reflection of what dim lights there were in his eyes, and a different sort of gleam on the dark, thick hair.

Since talking and asking the myriad of questions she had was impossible, her mind was free to race to turn over every rock looking for possibilities. This was not necessarily a good thing, she realized. She'd never thought of herself as particularly imaginative, but the things that tumbled through her mind now could be called nothing less. In the light of day, anyway.

Quinn seemed focused on her, as if he wasn't worried about Vicente at all. And if that were true, that confirmed her neighbor was part of this, in some way. It made her shiver anew to think what the man might have been up to just a couple of hundred yards away from her home. That he might have had very good reason to stay hidden.

Cutter returned the scrutiny, keeping his eyes on the man on the floor, occasionally stretching out toward him with his nose, apparently still in love at first scent. It really was strange, the way the dog had reacted to this man. Under other, normal circumstances, she might be inclined to trust the dog's judgment; more than once he'd been wary of someone she'd later learned was worthy of the distrust. And if he liked someone…well, at the moment the jury was out on that.

And it finally occurred to her to wonder why the man had brought the dog along. He'd only hesitated a fraction of a second before picking him up and putting him in the helicopter after her. Had he assessed that quickly that she'd do what she had to to protect the animal? Including cooperate with him?

The more she thought about that, the more it frightened her. That he had realized, that quickly, that Cutter could be the key to her cooperation told her more than she wanted to know. Clearly whoever and whatever he was, he would use any tool that presented itself.

She stared back at the man, her mind providing an image of what she couldn't see in the darkness, filling in details she'd glimpsed in the deck light. The strong jaw, the stern mouth, the dark brows with the slightly satanic arch—

Okay, that's enough of that, she ordered herself, and looked away. At least his image would be clear enough to tell someone what he looked like, she thought.

Someone? Like the police?

Her breath jammed up in her throat, unable to get past the sudden tightness as the obvious belatedly hit her. She'd seen them. All of them. But why hadn't they just killed her on the spot, then? Had they been in too much of a hurry to get away? Or had they just not decided her fate yet?

More likely, she thought grimly, they had a place

where they disposed of bodies, and it was easier to wait until they got there.

And all her imaginings suddenly didn't measure up to the horror of the reality, and even the darkness couldn't make it any worse.

They flew on and on, until her half-crazed mind would have sworn it had been days if it weren't for the fact that they were still and ever in darkness.

And underlying it all was the grimmest imagining of all, that she might never see the light of day again.

Chapter 3

"Coming up on the airport in about ten."

Teague Johnson's voice came through loud and clear over the headset, with none of the crackle or hiss the old headsets had been prone to. Worth the price, Quinn Foxworth thought as he lifted the flap on his watch that kept the dial's glow from being seen. 0315 hours. Not bad, well within the parameters they'd set despite the... complications.

"Fuel?" he asked.

Normally it wouldn't be an issue, they planned carefully, but they were carrying an extra passenger. And a half, he added with a grimace. That dog....

"It made a difference," Teague answered. "It'll be close, but we'll make it."

"Copy."

He went back to his study of their unplanned-for passenger, while that half-passenger continued to study him. The dog's dark eyes never left him, and he didn't have to be able to see in the dark to know it, although his night vision was remarkably good.

He knew little about the workings of the canine brain. And had no idea why the dog seemed so...taken with him. It would be amusing if it wasn't so puzzling.

His owner, on the other hand, wasn't taken with him at all, Quinn noted wryly. Too bad. She wasn't bad-looking. At least, from what he'd seen. And felt, during his cursory pat down and when he'd put a hand on a curved, tight backside to shove her aboard. It had startled him, that sudden shock of interest; there'd been little time for women in his life for...a very long time.

And there was no time now, he told himself. They'd be on the ground soon, and vulnerable for the few minutes it would take to refuel. And it had better be only a few minutes; they'd paid enough extra to guarantee it. They could have avoided this by using a plane, with longer range, but in this semirural area it would have meant transporting Vicente by ground to an airstrip, and then from an airstrip to the location on the other end. And that would have made them even more vulnerable.

The unexpected intrusion of woman and dog hadn't delayed them much, since he hadn't wasted any time dithering about what to do. But it was costing them more fuel; even though she looked to weigh maybe one-twenty at most, the dog added another forty-five or fifty pounds—five of that fur, he thought—and together that was the equivalent of another passenger about Vicente's size. On an aircraft this small it mattered, not so much in space as in fuel efficiency. But their timetable, and getting Vicente out of there, had been the most important thing.

And secrecy. The man was a valuable commodity,

and they couldn't risk leaving behind somebody who could tell anyone anything.

He felt the shift in angle of the chopper, knew they were approaching the small airfield where they would refuel. He saw the woman's head come up a moment later, as she apparently realized it, too. Her gaze shifted to the port window, then, obviously able to see nothing but night sky, shifted forward, as if she were trying to read the controls for a clue.

Could she? Did she know something about helicopters, or aircraft gauges? She didn't seem to be affected by the flight, no sign of air sickness or dizziness when they had made any quick changes. Unlike Vicente, who had required a serious dose of motion sickness medication to tolerate the flight. Quinn had been glad to give it to him; drowsiness was a side effect, and that was fine with him.

He'd thought about making the woman take some, too, under the guise of not wanting her to throw up in his helicopter. But there hadn't been time, and getting it down her would have been too much hassle. Besides, he wanted a chance to assess her under controlled circumstances. And there weren't many more controlled circumstances than strapped into a helicopter seat at ten thousand feet and a hundred and thirty-five knots.

So far, she hadn't been trouble, but he wasn't about to turn his back on a woman who rushed a man with a drawn weapon. And even when her face had been hidden as she clung to that damned dog, he couldn't escape the feeling that she was thinking like mad, and that didn't bode well for keeping things simple.

As they dropped lower she became more alert. He smothered a sigh; as if he could hear her thoughts, he knew she was trying to figure out a way to escape. He reached out and slid down the built-in shade on the porthole she'd been looking out; the more ignorant they could keep her of the surroundings, the better.

He flicked a glance at Vicente, who seemed to be sound asleep, propped in his corner. He was a tough old bird, he'd give him that. He'd barely turned a hair when they'd shown up in the middle of the night and taken over. But given his history, that wasn't surprising.

But this young bird, this wary, watchful female of the species, he didn't know. So he had to assume the worst.

"It's all yours when we touch down," he said into the headset.

"Problem?"

"The old man's asleep. Our uninvited guest is plotting."

"What'd she say?"

"Nothing. And how do you know I didn't mean the dog?"

He heard the short laugh. "The dog clearly thinks you're some kind of dog-god. The woman, not so much."

"Figures," Quinn muttered.

Another laugh, and as if in punctuation they dropped rather sharply.

"Got the signal light," Teague said.

Moments later he set the craft down with the gentlest of thumps, barely perceptible, nearly as soft as he himself could have managed. He'd have to let the guy fly more often, Quinn thought.

The noise lessened as the rotors slowed. The fuel truck was already there and waiting, as planned, a good sign. He would have preferred to keep her running, but the crew here wasn't trained for a hot refuel so they had to shut down. They didn't want the kind of attention flouting the local rules would bring. The anonymity of the small field was worth it, they'd decided.

Teague waited until the rotors had stopped, then opened his door and stepped down to the tarmac. There was a floodlight on the side of the hangar they were closest to, and it brightened the interior of the helicopter. Quinn glanced at Vicente, making sure he was truly sleeping; he hadn't seemed to stir at all, even when they'd landed. The old man better not be getting sick on them. But his eyes were closed and Quinn could hear, in the new silence, the soft sound of snoring. Maybe the guy just was particularly susceptible to those meds, he thought.

The quiet seemed deafening, nothing but the brief exchange between Teague and the fueler and the sounds of the process audible in this dead time between night and morning. He'd read somewhere that more people in hospitals died at 3:00 a.m. than any other time, that it just seemed to be the time people gave up.

Not sure why that had occurred to him just now, he wondered if he could just leave the headphones on and stave off whatever she had in mind. But the moment it was quiet enough to be heard, she dove in.

"I need a bathroom."

Ah. So there it was, her first approach, he thought. Short, to the point, grounded in reality, and hard to deny. But deny he would; they couldn't risk it. For what it told him about her, he filed it away in his mind in the section he'd labeled "uninvited guest."

"Hold it," he said, brusquely, taking the headphones off. He stood up, even though he had to hunch over; he needed to stretch his legs after the hours of being cramped on the floor.

"I can't."

He nodded toward the dog. "If he can, you can."

She drew back slightly. When she spoke, her tone was that of teacher on the edge of her patience to an unwilling-to-learn child. "He's a dog, in case you hadn't noticed."

Definitely got a mouth on her, Quinn thought.

"I noticed," he said drily. And now that he could see her better, could see that his earlier impression had fallen short of the reality, he silently added, *and I noticed you certainly are not.*

He felt another inner jolt, a flash of heat and interest, more intense than the first time, fired further by thoughts of that mouth. He clamped down on it harder, angry at himself; he never let anything interfere on a job. It was why jobs kept coming.

"Then you should know he can hold it longer. How do you think they wait all night inside a house?"

"I never thought about it," he said, although now that she'd said it, it sparked his curiosity. "Why can they?"

She seemed startled by the question. But she answered reasonably. "My guess is it's because when they were wild, they had to, to hide from predators. Now will you please find me a bathroom?"

"Hold it," he repeated.

"I'm a human, not a wild animal," she snapped.

"You think humans weren't wild once?"

"Some," she said pointedly, "still are."

He ignored the jab. "So hold it," he said a third time, trusting his instincts and her body language that this was just a ruse to get out of the helicopter and onto the ground, where she likely figured she could make a run for it. Not a bad plan, and just about the only one possible given her circumstances.

"Humans haven't needed that talent since we hit the top of the food chain," she said.

Oh, yeah, a mouth. And a quick wit. If he wasn't otherwise occupied, he'd like to find out just what else went on in that mind of hers.

And he interrupted his own thoughts before they could slide back to that mouth.

Teague was back then, announcing they were all fueled up. As he started to climb back into the pilot's seat, the woman turned her plea on him. The younger man looked startled, then disconcerted, and Quinn had to admire the way she switched to the younger, possibly more vulnerable target.

"Bathroom?" Teague echoed. He flicked a glance at Quinn.

"She can wait."

"How would you know?" There was the faintest change in her voice. Her snappishness had an undertone now, just a slight flicker. But he recognized it; he'd heard it too often not to.

Fear.

Now that he thought about it, it was somewhat amazing that it hadn't been there before. Something he should remember, he told himself. She doesn't scare easy, or she hides it very well.

"You'll wait."

"Want a mess in your pretty helicopter if we're in the air when I can't?"

"Then I'll push you out." She drew back, eyes widening. He pressed the point. "Or maybe the dog."

She gasped, as if that thought horrified her even more. *And there's my lever,* he thought, as her reaction confirmed what he had suspected from the moment he'd seen her racing across that stretch of open yard after the animal. She'd risk herself, but not the dog. She'd protect him, no matter what.

He pounded the point home.

"He won't save as much gas as you would, but maybe some."

She stared at him, saying nothing, but he could almost hear her mind racing, trying to analyze and assess if he really meant what he'd just said.

"Get us out of here, Teague," he said, and reached for the headphones. He put them on before they were really necessary, and pretended not to hear her call him an epithet he'd last heard from the lips of his ex-wife. Except she'd said it sadly, ruefully, whereas there was nothing but venom in this woman's low, husky voice.

Still fighting, he thought, but not stupidly. She didn't try anything she was doomed to lose, like getting past him, or striking at him.

He filed the knowledge away in his head as he settled into his cramped spot on the floor, shifting once to avoid pressure on the spot on his left leg where she had kicked him. She'd fought hard. He was lucky she hadn't gotten his knee—or worse—with that blow, or he'd be gimping around for two or three days. As it was, he was going to be feeling it for at least that long.

And if looks could kill, he'd already be dead.

Chapter 4

This wasn't the first time Hayley wished she had a better sense of direction. Without the little compass reading in her car's rearview mirror, she'd never know which way she was going, unless she was headed into a rising or setting sun.

She wasn't sure a good sense on the ground would translate to a good one in the air, however. And while she was sure this beast must have a compass, it was situated where she couldn't see it from back here, so she had no idea which way they were headed. They'd changed direction more than once, and she was completely lost now.

Her sense of time passing was pretty good, though, and she guessed they'd been airborne this second time over a couple of hours. Almost as long as the first leg, which she had pegged at around three hours. So they were better than five hours away from Vicente's front yard, and her own little house among the trees. A long time in cramped quarters; even Quinn had shifted so he could stretch out his long legs on the floor of the craft.

I hope your butt's numb by now, she thought uncharitably. *Even if it is a very nice one.*

She quashed the traitorous thought; not every bad guy was a troll, after all. The world would be in much better shape if they were, of course, but life was never that simple. If they were the good guys, surely they would have pulled out a badge and shown it to her by now, to ensure her cooperation?

She tried to puzzle out at least how far they'd come, but she had no idea how fast they were flying, and without that crucial factor of the equation, what she did know was useless.

The only thing she knew for sure was that her dog was about at the end of his considerable patience. He'd begun to squirm again about a half hour after they'd taken off the second time, clearly wanting down off her lap. Since it was awkward, overheating and by this time generally uncomfortable to hold the animal, who seemed to get heavier with every passing moment, she'd looked for a space to let him down. But there was little, not with Quinn on the floor in front of her.

It occurred to her she should just dump the adoring Cutter in the man's lap. That perhaps she should have done that while they were on the ground, then maybe she could have gotten to the door while he disentangled himself.

But that had never really been an option. The man still had a gun, and he'd already threatened to pitch the dog overboard. That had been when they'd still been on the ground, but she wouldn't put it past the steely-eyed man to do it when they were airborne.

Cutter squirmed again. He gave it extra effort this time, and it worked; his hind end slipped off her knees and she couldn't stop him. He gave a final twist and she had to let go or risk hurting him. And in the next moment, he was exactly where she'd thought of pitching him; in Quinn's lap.

Her heart leaped into her throat. Her common sense told her the man wasn't likely to shoot inside his own helicopter, but she was scared and this was her beloved pet, and logic wasn't her strongest point just now.

"Please, he's just a dog," she said urgently, leaning forward as far as she could belted into her seat, hoping he would hear her over the noise of the flight.

He said something, but so quietly she knew it was meant for the pilot. She held her breath, praying it wasn't an order to open the door so he could toss the animal to his death.

They kept flying. Quinn lifted the fifty-pound dog easily off his lap. And then, to her amazement, he bent his knees and turned slightly, wedging himself into what had to be a much less comfortable position, and put the dog down on the floor beside him.

He'd moved to make room for Cutter.

Hayley closed her eyes, nearly shaking with relief. She didn't know what to think, now. It was such a simple thing, but yet so telling.

Maybe.

Maybe he just didn't want to risk opening the door and tossing the dog out. Or the mess of shooting him. She fought to hang on to the cynical view, knowing it was both the more likely, and safer for her to believe, for Cutter's sake and her own.

Gradually she became aware that she could see a little better. She cautiously looked around, wondering if Quinn would try to stop her from doing even that. From where she was, thanks to the shade he'd pulled down, she could only look forward. It seemed the sky looked lighter along the horizon there, but without the rest of the sky to compare it with, it was hard to be sure. Quinn, down on the floor with Cutter, who was apparently happy now, was still in darkness. But the fact that she could now see Vicente's face where he'd been in stark shadow before told her her guess about time was accurate. Dawn was breaking.

She saw Quinn's head move as he put a hand to the headphones as if listening. She guessed he spoke then to the pilot, or perhaps answered something the pilot had said.

If they'd been headed east there was geography to deal with, and that little problem of the Cascade Mountains. Could a helicopter even go high enough to get over them? Or would it have to fly along the same passes and routes used by men on the ground? She had no idea.

You really don't know much useful, do you? she thought sourly.

But who would have ever thought she'd need to know how high or fast a scary black helicopter could fly? Just the phrase *black helicopter* was so laden with images and ideas from books and film that it made clear thinking almost impossible.

Vicente moved slightly, shifted position. For a moment she wished she'd been able to sleep as well as he seemed to have; her weariness just made rational thought even harder. But sleeping under the circumstances, especially with the lethal Quinn—for she had no doubt he could be just that—barely a foot away, was beyond her, even tired as she was. Fear-induced adrenaline was still coursing through her system, and she was jittery with it.

Vicente moved again, then opened his eyes. With the added light, she was able to see him go from sleepiness to awareness to full wakefulness, and he sat up sharply. And when he looked her way, a parade of expressions crossed his face, first surprise, then recognition as he remembered, and then, somewhat mollifying, regret.

It was at that moment she realized they were dropping in altitude. Another refueling stop? Well, this time asking for the bathroom wasn't going to be a ruse, it was going to be a necessity. And if he didn't believe her this time—

The sharp pivot of the helicopter interrupted her thought. They were definitely landing. This time she recognized the feeling. And as the direction they were facing changed, she saw indeed the first light of dawn on the horizon.

They touched down even more lightly than last time, so lightly she wasn't sure they were actually down until Teague began to flip off switches and the sound of the rotors changed as they began to slow.

And then, as she got her first glimpse of their surroundings in the still-gray light of dawn, she wondered if they were here to refuel at all. Because this certainly was no airfield, not even a small, rural one. And there was no sign of a fuel truck.

What there was, was a big, old, ramshackle barn several yards away across an expanse of dirt dotted with low, scraggly-looking brush. A bit beyond that was what appeared to be an old, falling-down windmill. And coming toward them from the barn was a man, dressed in khaki tan pants and a matching shirt that made him hard to see against the tan of the landscape in the faint light. Hayley thought he might be limping, just slightly, but she couldn't be sure. What she was sure of was the rifle he held. Not a classic, elegant one with a polished wood stock, but an all-black, aggressive thing that looked as if it was out of some alien-invasion movie.

Quinn pulled off the headset, and this time instead of putting it in the empty front seat, hung it on a hook overhead. Did that mean they were here? Wherever "here" was? Was this their destination?

Quinn pulled himself to his feet, dodging the now-alert-and-on-his-paws Cutter. He looked at Vicente, who was now sitting upright, fully awake.

"We'll have you inside shortly, sir," Quinn said.

Sir?

Respect, she noted. While she obviously didn't even rate an acknowledgment, now that they were…wherever they were.

"I really need that bathroom now," she said.

Quinn glanced at her. Seemed to study her for a moment. She didn't know what he saw that was different, but he apparently believed her this time.

"It'll only be a few minutes." Then his glance shifted to the dog. "He can get out now, though."

Hayley didn't quite know how to take that; was it thoughtfulness for the dog, or did Quinn want control of him, so that he could control her?

If that's his thinking, he's in for a surprise, Hayley thought. About the first part, anyway; she didn't think anybody really controlled Cutter.

Quinn got out of the chopper, and she saw him bend and stretch his legs as if they were cramped. They must be, cramming a body she guessed was at least six feet tall into that small space on the floor couldn't have been easy. Not that she felt sorry for him.

But he had made room for Cutter, despite the cramped quarters. And the dog seemed no less enamored of him this morning than he had been from the moment he'd encountered this dark stranger.

But to his credit, he did hesitate when Quinn held the door open for him. He looked back over his shoulder, his dark eyes fastened on her in a silent appeal for permission. She selfishly wanted to tell him no, wanted him to stay with her, but she knew the sometimes-hyperactive dog was probably about to jump out of his fur after being trapped in this small space for so long. Not to mention he probably needed his much more convenient sort of a bathroom as much as she needed one.

"Go ahead," she told him, and with a small, happy woof, he leaped from the helicopter to the ground. He looked up at Quinn expectantly. Quinn seemed puzzled, and made a broad gesture toward the open space they were in, as if to tell the dog it was all his now. It was strange how much smaller Cutter looked standing next to the tall man; to her he seemed like a big dog, next to Quinn, more average.

Cutter briefly checked out the surprised newcomer, but despite the aggressive weapon, and unlike with Quinn, after a moment he seemed to find nothing of particular interest there and quickly moved on at a brisk trot, checking out his new surroundings.

The new man was speaking to Quinn and Teague, in the manner of someone giving a report. Teague was listening carefully, but it was clear the report was directed at Quinn. To Hayley, everything sounded a bit muffled; her ears must be humming a little after the hours of noise, and she could make out only an occasional word; she heard the newcomer say "perimeter" and "secure," but not much else.

"I am very sorry."

Her head snapped around as her fellow passenger spoke into the fresh silence. He did have a slight accent, Hispanic, she thought, and he was looking at her with that same expression she had seen earlier, tinged with more than a little regret.

That she had gotten sucked into this? she wondered.

Or that she wasn't going to get out of it?

At the moment, the latter seemed more likely. And by the time Quinn turned back and gestured her out, she was oddly reluctant; the stealthy black helicopter seemed suddenly safer than whatever she was going to be stepping into out there.

Chapter 5

"We're up and running," Liam Burnett said briskly as he joined sniper Rafer Crawford in reporting in.

Quinn nodded as he stretched gratefully; he'd expected nothing less. His crew was well trained and could think for themselves. They'd have everything ready to roll.

Then Liam spotted their extra half-passenger roaming about, and Quinn could see his detail-oriented mind kick in. And then he noticed the woman still aboard, and that mind revved up even further. Quinn followed the progression of his thoughts as they went from the logistics of an extra person and an animal, to the realization that person was a woman, to the recognition that she was a rather attractive one. Liam always had had the worst poker face of them all. Came with youth, Quinn supposed.

"So," Rafer said, with a sideways glance of his own at the woman still in the chopper, "how'd *she* happen?"

"Unavoidable," Quinn said with a grimace, and gestured with a thumb toward the dog, who was ranging out toward the barn, investigating the grounds with a thoroughness he had to admire. The animal would probably know who and what had been through here for the past six months before he was through.

"The dog's fault?" Rafer sounded even more puzzled.

"It's a long story," Quinn said as he watched Teague open the far door of the helicopter and help Vicente out. The older man moved stiffly, almost gingerly. Rafer quickly went to help; he had some experience with moving through pain.

"We have any painkillers in stock?" Quinn asked Liam. "Seems the old man's got arthritis pretty bad."

"Standard first-aid kit issue, plus Rafer's stash of ibuprofen."

"May have to raid that," Quinn said. "Hope he's not having a bad week."

"Seems okay," Liam said.

Since Liam and Rafer worked together a lot, he should know, Quinn thought. As much as anyone did, anyway; Rafer did a good job of hiding any pain the old injury gave him. If it wasn't for the slight limp, no one who hadn't seen the impressive scar would know there was anything wrong. And he refused to let it slow him down; it had been a long, painful process, but he'd pushed so hard and learned to compensate so well he was as efficient as any of them at anything short of long-distance running.

"Sometime today?"

The words came from inside the helicopter. She was

sounding a bit snappish, Quinn thought, smothering a wry quirk of his mouth.

"If you're lucky," he retorted, not even looking at her.

"What's her name?" Liam asked, lowering his voice.

"No idea."

Liam stared at him for a moment, then shook his head ruefully. "Only you could spend all this time with a woman who looks like that and not even find out her name."

"If you're so interested, you watch her," Quinn said drily. "You might find her more trouble than she's worth."

"I don't know," Liam said, giving her a sideways look, "she looks like she'd be worth a lot."

"I'll get her inside while you secure and refuel the chopper, then she's all yours," Quinn said. He reached over and yanked open the door. "Keep her under control."

From the corner of his eye he saw the woman stiffen, drawing up straight. She'd reacted to his last words much as he'd expected, and he felt a tug of relief as he handed responsibility for her over to the young and earnest Liam. If she was the girl-next-door type her loyalty to the dog suggested, they'd be perfect for each other.

"What about the dog?" Liam asked, keeping his eyes on the woman as she emerged from the helicopter.

"Our other uninvited guest? I'll round him up," Quinn said. "He seems to like me."

"No accounting for taste," the woman muttered, and he saw Liam smother a grin.

"No, there surely isn't," Liam said, no trace of the grin on his face sounding in his faint Texas drawl.

Quinn watched as she stepped down to the ground. It was past dawn now, and he could see what he'd missed before. She was a little taller than he'd first thought, maybe five-five. The curves were definite but not exaggerated. And the hair he'd thought was simply brown in fact was a combination of brown and gold and red that made the chill morning air seem warmer.

I think you've been cooped up too long, he told himself, smothering another grimace.

"She says she needs a bathroom," he said, quickly reducing things back to the basics. He thought he saw her cheeks flush slightly as he announced her needs to all present, but as he'd guessed, it truly was a necessity this time, because she didn't protest.

But then she turned and got her first look at where they were. And her thoughts were clear on her face; he had the feeling that, maybe for the first time in her life she really, truly knew what the phrase "the middle of nowhere" meant.

They were on a slight rise, but as far as the eye could see around them was nothing but empty, nearly flat land, unrelieved by anything but dried-up grasses, scrubby plants and an occasional tree. It wasn't desert, at least not the kind the word summoned up in his mind—sand and wind and dunes—but it was very, very far from the green paradise they had left last night.

He could almost see her hopes of escape plummet; not that he would have let her get away anyway, but she wouldn't be the woman he was beginning to think she was if she hadn't at least been thinking about it. But he saw the realization of the odds that she would make it to any kind of help or even civilization dawn in her eyes as she looked out over the remote emptiness.

"Be careful what you wish for," she said softly, in an almost despairing whisper.

It didn't take a genius to guess what she meant; all

those hours when she'd probably been wishing the interminable helicopter flight would end, and now that it had she wanted nothing more than to get back on the thing and get out of here. Because that seemed the only way to leave this utterly isolated place.

Good, Quinn thought. As long as she realized that, hopefully she wouldn't try anything stupid.

And then she turned around, and saw the cabin.

She really did have an expressive face, Quinn thought. Playing poker with her would be like taking money from a baby, even more than Liam. Not that he really blamed her. The cabin looked as if it was about to fall in on itself. All but a strategically placed couple of windows were boarded over, and the roof sagged and looked as if it would leak like a sieve, if it ever rained in this place. There were loose pieces of siding here and there, and things at odd angles and heavily weathered. The only solid-looking piece of it was the river-rock chimney, standing as a testament to the skill of the long-ago stonemason. The place looked as if it had been abandoned for years.

It looked exactly as it was supposed to look.

"Quinn?"

He turned to look at Liam. "The dog. Are we going to need a run into—"

The words broke off as Quinn gave a warning flick of a glance at the woman. Admittedly the nearest little town, tiny though it was, was not one she'd likely heard of, but he didn't want to give her any ideas.

"Don't worry about feeding the damned dog."

The woman went still. "He has to eat," she said.

Quinn didn't even look at her.

"I'll get everybody inside, and out of sight," he told Liam. "You get with Teague and secure the bird."

Liam nodded.

"He has to eat," she said again.

He turned then. "Shouldn't you be worried about how and whether we're going to feed *you?*"

She never hesitated. "He comes first."

He blinked. "He's a dog."

"I'm responsible for him. He trusts me to take care of him. It's part of the deal."

He thought she might be getting a bit esoteric about it, but he couldn't deny he admired her sense of responsibility. And thankfully, Charlie believed in overkill when it came to stocking up for an indefinite stay.

"He can eat what we eat, for now."

She seemed to relax a little at that, letting out a breath of relief. And she still didn't ask if that *we* included her. He watched the dog for a moment as he sniffed around the barn. And then, as if aware of Quinn's gaze, the dog turned, head up, looking toward them. And unbidden, started toward them at a tail-up trot. He really was a distinctive-looking dog, with alert, upright ears and a dark head and thick ruff that gradually shaded back into a lighter, reddish-brown coat over his body. He looked intense, like the herding dogs he'd seen in Scotland on the many pilgrimages he'd made.

"His name's Cutter?" he asked, almost absently as he watched the animal cross the yard between the ramshackle barn and the even more ramshackle cabin.

"Yes," she said. "And mine is Hayley, not that you bothered to ask."

No, he hadn't asked. Hadn't wanted to know. Had been much happier when she'd just been "the woman," an unexpected annoyance that had to be dealt with.

"Don't tell me," he said. "Tell Liam. He thinks you're a welcome addition to the scenery."

Like you don't? a traitorous little voice in his head spoke up.

But she didn't seem bothered by the implied aspersion. Instead she looked around at the barren landscape before saying with a grimace, "Middle of nowhere, careful what you wish for, and now damning with faint praise. My life's suddenly full of clichés."

Quinn nearly gaped at her for a moment as her first words echoed his exact thoughts of earlier. Any other normal woman he could think of would be in hysterics by now. Or at least too frightened to think straight, let alone come back at him with wit. He was beginning to think she was going to be more than just a fuel-eating inconvenience.

He'd better tell Liam to keep a *really* close eye on her.

Chapter 6

Hayley stopped dead in the cabin doorway, startled. No, beyond startled, she was stunned. After the outside, she'd been expecting thick dust, holes in the walls, broken furniture if any and traces of wildlife.

Instead, she was confronted by a spotless and amazingly whole and modern interior. Most of the main floor was one big room, the upper level an open loft that looked down into the main room. There was new-looking furniture that was surprisingly nice. A sofa in a soft green and tan, and four armchairs in a matching green, seemed to echo the colors outside. Yet where they were drab out there, inside they seemed soothing. There were loose pillows on the sofa for lounging, and a knitted green throw for cozying up in front of a fire in the big stone fireplace. Decidedly—and unexpectedly—homey. Except for the large, utilitarian metal locker that sat between the door and one of the few unblocked windows.

There were even coordinating area rugs on the floor, which was wood burnished to a high sheen, although it was slightly uneven and looked distressed enough to be the original. It fit, she thought. With the big, square coffee table, it was a comfortable and inviting setting. Which shocked her to no end.

"I thought you wanted a bathroom."

Quinn's voice came from right behind her, sounding clearly impatient.

"Judging from the outside, I didn't expect one inside," she snapped.

To her surprise, his mouth quirked at one corner, as if he were about to smile. If so, he efficiently and almost instantly killed the urge.

She stepped inside, looking around even more intently. There was a big table with eight chairs, in the same style as the coffee table, over near a half wall that formed what appeared to be the kitchen. There was a compact stove, a small refrigerator, and even a microwave sat on the counter, so clearly they had power. Which, come to think of it, was puzzling as well, since she hadn't seen any power lines. Not surprising; if they told her they were literally a thousand miles from nowhere, she'd believe it. A generator? She hadn't seen that, either, or heard it. They weren't uncommon where she lived, she had one herself, and she'd never heard a truly quiet one.

Maybe they're environmental fanatics and there are solar panels hidden somewhere, or maybe that windmill wasn't really broken and had been converted to power production instead of pumping water, she thought, not finding the idea particularly comforting. Zealots of any kind made her nervous.

She nearly laughed at herself. Nervous? How about

terrified? Spirited off in the middle of the night by one of those black helicopters that had become a cultural myth....

Something else registered as she studied the kitchen area. Instead of cupboards there were open shelves, and they were clearly well stocked with easily stored food, some canned, some freeze-dried, some packaged. So well stocked, her stomach sank; just how long did they plan on keeping them here?

"In there," Quinn said, pointing toward one end of the room where a narrow hall led off to the right.

The need was rapidly approaching urgent, so she followed his gesture. For a moment she wondered if he was going to follow, to watch, and she frowned inwardly. But, in one of those constant trade-offs of life, dignity lost out to bodily imperative.

To her relief, he let her shut the door. Probably, she thought as she flipped on the light and glanced around, because there was no window in the small bathroom. The sink, with a narrow cabinet, was in the far corner, with the toilet—thankfully—opposite. There was no tub, and the stall shower was tight quarters; she couldn't imagine a man the size of Quinn using it easily.

Oh, good, she thought caustically, *let's start thinking about the man in the shower, naked and wet.*

Although she had to admit, it would be a good way to keep her mind off the fact that he'd kidnapped her and dragged her off to a place that looked, on the outside at least, as if it could belong to some crazed, manifesto-writing bomber or something. Probably about the only thing that could keep her mind off it; for all he'd done, she couldn't deny Quinn—was that his first or last name?—was a fine-looking man.

"The laws of the universe really should include one

requiring bad guys to look like trolls," she muttered as she finished making use of the facility.

Then she turned on the water, quickly washed her hands and dried them on the hand towel politely waiting on a wall hanger. With the outgo problem resolved, she took a quick drink, her dry mouth and throat welcoming the soothing wetness. Then she left the water running while she investigated the cabinet and the small medicine chest.

She found nothing but more towels, and unopened packages of soap, toothpaste, toothbrushes and safety razors. She pocketed one of those, even as she told herself they were called safety razors because you couldn't do any major damage with them. It just made her feel better, and she left it at that.

And then, for the first time, she looked in the mirror over the sink. Bleary, tired eyes stared back at her. And as if they'd been a signal her brain had until now been too revved up to hear, a wave of weariness swept her.

She shouldn't be so tired, she told herself. She'd often pulled all-nighters with her mother in those last, grim days. She'd learned then to nap in small increments when she could, getting just enough sleep to keep going. And that had gone on for months, so one sleepless night, even a stressful one, shouldn't make her feel like this.

Maybe being kidnapped is a different kind of stress, she thought, then nearly laughed aloud at herself, trying to be reasonable and logical when her entire world had gone insane.

"The water supply isn't endless."

The sharp words came from outside, and with a start she quickly shut the water off. When she opened the door, Quinn was leaning against the doorjamb, left thumb hooked in the front pocket of his jeans, his right hand loose at his side. Keeping the gun hand free? she wondered, scenes from a dozen movies coming to mind. Did he really think she was going to attack him or something?

It was all she could do not to reach into her jacket pocket and finger the razor she'd snagged.

"Find anything?"

The question was pointed, in the tone of a man who knew perfectly well there was nothing to find, and was just letting her know he knew she'd looked.

"I'm sure you already know the answer to that. What do you think I'm going to do, sharpen a toothbrush?"

"No, although it's been done. You might want to use one, though."

She instinctively drew back; was he saying her breath needed it?

He's just trying to keep you off balance, she told herself. And succeeding, she amended sourly.

"How kind of you to offer," she said sweetly. "Should I waste the water?"

His mouth quirked again, but he only shrugged. "Just don't be profligate. You're already an extra person. Unless you want the dog to go thirsty."

"He's going to need water," she protested instantly. "In case you hadn't noticed, he's got a pretty heavy coat."

"Not my problem."

"Yes, it is. He didn't ask to be dragged off to the middle of this desert, wherever it is."

"Then you can give him your share."

She would, of course, if it came to that. "I didn't ask for this, either," she reminded him.

For the first time she saw a trace of weariness around

his eyes. Blue eyes, she saw now, in the growing morning light. Very blue.

"I know," he said, that barest hint of weariness echoing in his voice. "But there was no choice."

Was he softening, just slightly? She was torn between wanting to demand answers and a gut-level instinct that she might be better off not knowing the answers.

"I am very sorry, miss."

The quiet words came from her left, and snapped her head around. It was her neighbor, looking at her with troubled dark eyes.

"It is my fault," he began, formally, still apologetically. "I—"

"Enough, Vicente," Quinn cut him off sharply. "Don't talk to her."

Hayley smothered a gasp, as if he'd slapped her. So much for any softening, she thought angrily. Vicente sighed, and retreated to the living room. Then Quinn turned on her.

"You, get upstairs. And stay there. Don't leave except for the bathroom."

She had to fight the urge to scamper up the narrow stairs like a skittish cat. It took every bit of nerve she had to meet his gaze.

"He was just trying to apologize."

"And he did. Go."

"Cutter—"

"We'll round him up later, if he hasn't taken off."

Her mouth quirked this time, at the very idea of the loyal animal deserting her. Even if he was fascinated by their captor.

"Never had a dog, have you?" she asked.

His brow furrowed, as if thinking her words a complete non sequitur. Then, slowly, a distant sort of look crept over his face.

"Not in a very long time," he said, not even looking at her. And Hayley couldn't help wondering what inward image he was seeing.

It lasted only a couple of seconds. Then the cool, commanding Quinn was back. And even she could tell he was out of patience, such as it was.

"You going, or do I have to drag you?"

"Going," she muttered.

Liam was coming in as they came out of the hallway.

"All set," he said. "You guys came in on fumes."

"Extra weight," Quinn said.

Hayley kept her expression even this time; he'd gotten to her with the toothbrush comment, and she wasn't going to let it happen again.

"Not much," Liam said, eying her with male appreciation that was a marked contrast to Quinn's sharp impatience.

"She goes up in the loft. And don't forget the dog," Quinn said with a grimace.

"Who could be very handy," Liam said, shifting his gaze to Quinn. "Warned Rafer off a rattlesnake out there."

Rattlesnake. Wonderful, Hayley thought. Her home was blessedly free of the venomous types, so this was a new one. She had no problem with a nice garter snake, or the helpful kings, but—

"Don't like snakes?" Quinn asked.

Did the man never miss anything? "I'm talking to you, aren't I?" she snapped.

Liam let out a whoop of laughter. Quinn gave him a sour look.

"She's definitely all yours," he muttered, and walked away.

Chapter 7

Quinn wasn't one to believe in omens or premonitions, but as he stood in the doorway of the cabin, he was starting to have a bad feeling about this. Usually one or two, or even more, little things would go wrong on a job. Didn't mean a thing. And this job had gone like clockwork—until they were leaving the target's location.

Then, from the moment that damned dog had blasted out of the woods at him, things had gone to hell.

The dog. Where was he, anyway?

On the thought, the animal trotted around the far end of the barn where, if there were more delays and this turned into a long stay, the helicopter would be stored. With the ease of long discipline he managed not to think of the ramifications of a long stay with a recalcitrant, smart-mouthed woman, one he just knew wasn't going to settle into any easy waiting routine.

The dog's head and tail came up, and he started toward Quinn at a gallop. Quinn shook his head in puzzlement. Why would a dog he didn't even know act like this? He'd never even seen such a dog, with that distinctive coloring. He was a very square, lean animal who moved with a swift grace that Quinn could appreciate.

Teague had apparently been following the dog, and as he came around the barn he gave Quinn the hand signal that meant hold. Quinn had put the order out for silent ops, until they knew they hadn't been seen or followed. And thankfully, he thought as he watched the dog slow to a trot, then came to a halt in front of him, the dog didn't seem to be a barker.

Quinn waited, guessing from the signal Teague had something to report. Almost absently, he reached down and scratched the dog's ears. The blissful sigh the animal let out made one corner of his mouth twitch, and it was all he could do to keep from smiling. He didn't get it, this sudden and inexplicable reaction from a strange dog, but he had to admit it was…enjoyable. Flattering. Something.

Teague slowed to a trot, then a halt, much as the dog had. The man's right arm moved, then stopped, an oddly jerky motion. Teague was the newest member of the squad, and Quinn guessed the movement, if completed, would have been a salute. It would be a while before he got over the automatic response.

"Go," he said with a nod.

"Yes, sir. Perimeter's clear. But he—" he gestured at the dog "—found some big animal tracks in the gully on the north side."

"Animal tracks?"

"Just a couple. I might have missed them, they were

up under the lip, only reason they weren't erased by the wind, I guess."

So, as Liam had said, the dog could end up being useful. Quinn's brow furrowed as he remembered some of the K-9 teams he'd worked with in the past, and he filed away the idea of adding one to the crew.

"Any idea what?" he asked.

"They were blurred, but paws. Big ones. Don't have wolves out here, do they, sir?"

"More likely a mountain lion."

The man blinked. Although well trained and fearless, Quinn knew Teague was a born-and-bred city boy. He knew what he needed to know for survival in the wild, but it wasn't second nature to him as it was with many on the various crews.

He'd come to them through their website, where his long, thoughtful, articulate posts had first drawn the attention of Tyler Hewitt, the webmaster, who sent them to Charlie, who in turn had started sending them to Quinn. Unlike many, Teague had survived the incredibly long and difficult vetting process without faltering, and the first time Quinn had met the young former marine in person, he'd known he'd be a good fit.

That had been just before the flood, the deluge of dissatisfaction that had swept the Corps and the other branches. They could, if they wanted, pick and choose now, from a multitude of skilled, experienced warriors who had had enough, had finally realized just what was happening. Quinn didn't want any of them.

He and Charlie had picked a date, somewhat arbitrarily, but a date that became the marker; aware before that and they still had a shot. Not, and…not. He wanted men like Teague, who had been smart enough, aware enough, and had the brainpower to see the patterns and read the proverbial handwriting on the wall. And see it early, not just when it became so obvious that the lowliest grunt couldn't miss it.

And no one above a certain rank, he'd added. Once you got that high, there was no way you couldn't see what was happening unless you purposely ignored it. It cut them off from a lot of experience, but to Quinn the other was more important.

"Tracks seemed old," Teague was saying. "And he—" again he gestured at the dog "—was very interested but not…frantic."

He ended the sentence hesitantly, as if he wasn't sure the word conveyed what he meant, but Quinn got the image immediately. He nodded in approval.

"Then you're likely right. They're old. But tell the others, we'll keep an eye out just in case."

"And I'm guessing the dog will let us know if it comes back," Teague said.

Quinn looked down at the patient animal at his feet. "Probably," he agreed, "but we can't rely on it. He's not trained and we don't know him well enough."

"You know, it was funny, out there. It almost seemed like…"

Teague trailed off, looking a bit awkward.

"Like what?" Quinn asked, reminding the man with his quiet tone that in this world, his opinion was welcomed, and sometimes even acted upon.

"Like he *was* trained. I mean, I've only worked with K-9s a couple of times, but it was like that, the way he seemed to know why we were out there, the way he tracked, searched almost in a grid."

Quinn's gaze shifted back to the dog, who sat patiently still, looking up at him with a steady gaze. As if waiting for further orders. Was it possible? Did the animal have some training? He looked too young to be a retired police or military dog, and moved too well to have been retired due to injury. Was he a washout of a program, for some other reason? Or was he just darn smart?

The thoughts about the dog brought him back to thinking about the dog's owner. And that brought on the need to move, to do something, anything.

"Good work," he said briskly. "We're in two-man teams. Four hours on. You and Rafer take first watch. Work out who does what between you, but I want that perimeter checked every quarter hour. Liam and I will relieve you at—" he glanced at his watch, the big chronograph that told him more than he needed on this mission "—eleven hundred hours."

"Yes, sir!" Again Teague barely stopped the salute. Quinn gave him a wry smile.

"It takes a while," he told him.

"It's not just that." Teague hesitated, then plunged ahead. "It's being able to salute a boss who deserves it."

And that, Quinn thought sourly, was what happened when you assigned a young, honest, decent, smart kid to work for brass who thought only of their next political move and made every decision based on how it might move their personal agenda forward. If Teague had been in a combat unit, he would have lasted a lot longer.

And he wouldn't be here, which would be their loss, Quinn thought.

"Thank you." He acknowledged the tribute with more than a little sadness. "Now get to it."

The young former marine turned on his heel smartly and headed out to connect with Rafer, who had just emerged from the barn where he'd been checking on the big power generator. He saw Quinn, gave him the

"Okay" signal; Rafer was the mechanical guy on the team, and if he said the generator was okay, they were set for as long as the fuel lasted. The big underground tank held enough to keep them going for a month, if they were a little careful. If this turned out to go longer than that, then refueling would become an issue.

If this turns out to go longer than that, insanity is going to become an issue, Quinn thought. They really were out in the middle of a lot of nowhere.

Middle of nowhere, careful what you wish for, and now damning with faint praise. My life's suddenly full of clichés.

The woman's words—he refused to think of her by name, it would be better if she remained just the woman, the glitch, the impediment, the nuisance—rang in his head. Oh, yes, she definitely had a mouth on her. And the wit and spirit to use it.

And both were things he'd be better off not thinking about.

Chapter 8

Hayley drew back from the banister that topped the three-foot-high wall running along the edge of the loft. Her anger had ebbed slightly now, allowing her to think. Her father had once told her that anger fogged the brain, and she'd never had a clearer demonstration than just now.

It was absurd, after all, to have anger be the thing her brain seized on when Quinn had told her neighbor not to speak to her, as if she were some sort of pariah. Absurd indeed. But anger, her father had added, was still better than despair. At least it was more useful, if channeled properly.

She sat in the single chair in the long but narrow space, realizing she needed clear thinking now more than she ever had in her life. While her mother was ill, she'd gotten used to having to fight through the cloud of exhaustion for every decision, for the steps of every action, had been aware she had to be extra careful simply because of it, careful not to make a mistake she would normally never make if she weren't so tired.

She was tired after the harrowing night without sleep, but that was nothing compared with months on end of sleeping less than four hours at a time. She could do one sleepless night standing on her head, she told herself. So it was time to start thinking hard about the situation and a way out of it, now that she was alone and could concentrate.

Liam had left her there with polite but firm instructions to stay put, that someone would always be downstairs watching. And for all his joking and smiling, Hayley sensed the man meant what he said; there was a steel core beneath the young, affable exterior.

She doubted Quinn would have any other kind of man working for him.

And Quinn was obviously and indisputably the boss. She'd heard enough when he'd been in the doorway, giving orders with precision and decisiveness. Clearly all of the men followed his lead without question or hesitation. He was definitely the leader, and one who commanded respect.

Among other things, she thought. This would all be simpler if he wasn't so damned…impressive. A shiver rippled through her, a reaction she'd not had to any man in a very long time. That she was having it now was nothing short of infuriating.

But Teague's last words, about saluting someone who deserved it, stuck in her head. At first it had made her feel oddly comforted, until she realized it all depended on Teague's frame of reference. If he was a young, honestly idealistic sort, it could mean Quinn was a good guy.

But then it struck her that one of those zealots she'd thought about could use the same words about whatever leader had hit upon the right buttons to push. They could all be deluded, working for Quinn out of some misguided devotion to an idea. Or worse.

She got up, moving as silently as she could around the loft, looking. It was only about ten feet deep, but it ran the width of the entire cabin. Besides the chair, which sat next to a reading lamp, there was a double bed against the other side wall, a nightstand next to it and a low dresser against the back wall.

Under the window.

Her hopes leaped, but the moment she got close enough, she could see that the lack of morning light streaming through the window wasn't, as she'd hoped, simply because there were shutters she could open. It was because the window was solidly, carefully boarded over, just like most of those downstairs.

A quick test of the blockage told her there would be no budging it without some serious tools or a lot more strength than she had. Nor was there anything else in the room that she could use as a weapon.

Not, she thought wryly, that there was anything she could see herself using as a weapon against these obviously well-trained and dangerous men.

She sank down on the edge of the bed. Now that they had stopped moving, there was little left to distract her from the reality of her grim situation.

She wondered where Vicente was. There was room for a bedroom below this loft. Was that where he, as the primary—what? Guest? Prisoner?—was? The man had obviously been sincerely bothered, felt responsible somehow for getting her into this.

Although it was, she had to admit ruefully, mostly

Cutter's fault. If he hadn't burst out of the trees like that, refusing to heed her recall, neither of them would be here. But it was so unlike the dog that she couldn't help thinking there was something else going on. While Cutter was an independent animal, he was also usually obedient, unless what she wanted him to do conflicted with something he knew he had to do.

That might sound odd to some, but she'd seen it too often in the months since he'd landed in her life. Like the time when he absolutely refused to come inside one night, and she'd had to go retrieve him physically from the side of the house. Only then did she notice the distinctive smell of propane, and realize that there was a dangerous leak. Or the time he'd literally dragged her outside into a pouring rain, then up the hill to where she'd found the neighbor who'd been pinned by a fallen tree, hurt and unable to reach his cell phone, and soaked through by the gush of water from the skies.

Water.

Had Quinn really meant he'd withhold water from Cutter? She couldn't believe anybody would do that to an innocent animal, but then she couldn't believe anybody would grab an innocent bystander—two, counting Cutter—and throw them onto a helicopter in the middle of the night and fly them off to who knows where and—

As if her thoughts had made him materialize, she heard the familiar click of toenails on the wood floor downstairs. And after a moment, she heard Quinn's voice.

"Take him upstairs. Tell her to keep him up there, out of the way."

There was another exchange she couldn't hear. Then, a moment later, she heard Teague laugh.

"He's not going anywhere for me, boss."

"So carry him."

"You seen his teeth?"

"Afraid of a pet dog?"

"Nope. Just doing what you've always said. Each man to the job he does best. The dog likes you, ergo, you do it."

There was a pause, then a sound that could have been a half-suppressed snort of laughter, or a not-at-all-suppressed sound of disgust.

She heard footsteps on the stairs. With an effort she stayed seated on the edge of the bed; for some reason it seemed important that he know she wasn't going to jump at his every appearance or command.

Moments later Cutter appeared at the top of the stairs and ran to her with every appearance of his usual delight at seeing her after time apart. Quinn was right behind him, but he stopped—thankfully—at the top of the stairs.

"*Now* you remember me," she muttered to the dog, not really meaning it as she gratefully scratched his ears. Cutter sighed and leaned against her.

She looked over at Quinn then. He was watching her steadily. An old joke flashed through her mind, about how the best way to make yourself feel insignificant was to try to give orders to someone else's dog. Obviously that didn't apply here. Or else Quinn was incapable of feeling insignificant.

Now, that I'd believe, she thought.

"You wouldn't really deny him water," she said, as if stating it as a fact instead of a question would get her the response she wanted.

"Wouldn't I?"

It had been a silly effort, she'd known that even as she'd said it.

Quinn moved farther into the loft, and she was reminded sharply how tall he was. The low roof that was
still a good foot above her head was bare inches above
his.

"Whether he drinks—or eats—is entirely up to you."

She blinked. "Me?"

"You behave, he gets what he needs."

The word "behave" nearly set her off; she didn't care
for being spoken to as if she were a recalcitrant child.
But she had to look out for Cutter now, not herself.

"You'd abuse an innocent animal to manipulate me?"

"I'm not convinced he's all that innocent," Quinn
said, with a hint of something in his voice as he glanced
at the dog—who seemed annoyingly happy at the moment—that sounded almost like amusement. Almost.

She challenged him, hoping he'd think she wasn't
afraid of him. That mattered, for some reason. Never
mind that inside she was practically quaking.

"What makes you think it will work?"

He shrugged. "You saw we were armed and you still
came running after him."

She drew back slightly, looking up at him in genuine
curiosity. "Why would you shoot an innocent woman
chasing an even more innocent dog?"

"I didn't know you were innocent."

Something curled and knotted inside her. What kind
of world did he live in, where the assumption was the
opposite, where you were presumed guilty, or at the
least a threat, until proved otherwise?

*The kind of world that can put that look in someone's
eyes, that coolness, that control, that world-weariness
and distrust,* she thought. His eyes weren't just blue,
they had a tinge of ice.

"For all I knew you'd set him on us," he said.

That was so preposterous words burst from her. "Do you often get attacked by total strangers' dogs?"

He shrugged again. "It's happened."

"Hard to believe, you're so charming," she said, then wondered when she'd developed the habit of speaking before she thought.

But there it was again, that hint of a change in his face that could, if you stretched your imagination a bit, be amusement.

"And you," he added, almost conversationally, "charged armed men. Given the circumstances, the wise thing, the thing most people would have done, was turn tail and get as far away as they could. But you—"

"So I'm an idiot. Fine," she said, bitterly aware it was true.

"You love him." His gaze flicked to Cutter, then back to her. "Enough to charge into figurative hell for him."

"And that makes me easy to manipulate."

"Among other things, yes."

She didn't want to know what those "other things" were. Anybody who'd use a dog, threaten to starve it, wasn't starting out in a good place with her.

Not that it mattered. It would work. She couldn't do anything, risk anything, because he just might be cold enough to do exactly what he'd said. And if she made him angry enough, there was that gun....

Although killing Cutter—she swallowed as the words went through her rattled mind—would lose him his lever.

"You said he could be helpful." Even she heard the undertone of desperation in her voice.

"He already has been," Quinn admitted. "But we've survived this long without a dog on the team, I think we can make it a bit longer."

"What 'team'? Who are you?"

The thought that she was better off not knowing made her regret the question as soon as it was out.

"Right now, we're the ones in charge of you, and your dog. You should remember that."

Another threat? It took every bit of nerve she had left to meet his warning gaze. It seemed important somehow, not to cower in front of this man, even if that was what she felt like doing.

But she couldn't fight them. Couldn't fight him. She had no weapons, not enough strength or knowledge, and even if she could get free, there was that middle-of-nowhere thing to deal with.

No, it was in her and her dog's best interest to... just behave.

And she hated that she was scared enough to decide to do just that.

Chapter 9

"Boss?"

Quinn snapped out of his musings about the woman upstairs and turned to look at Liam. The young man was also their IT guy, or as he jokingly called himself, their propeller head. He had his laptop, a rugged, rubber-bumpered version that was utilized by many military operations, set up on the coffee table in the center of the room.

His skill with computers, matched with a surprising skill with weapons and physical toughness, was a prized combination Quinn had been glad to find, even if it had come with the beginnings of a police record. But Liam had taken to their work with dedication and flair; all he'd needed was a purpose.

"You need to take a look at this."

Quinn looked up from the status report—they had another team on a secondary mission—he'd been reading on his smartphone, aided by the cell tower they themselves had installed, disguising it much as they had the cabin, inside the weathered, broken-looking windmill.

If Liam said he had something worth looking at, he did; the man was a master at tracking, in both the real and cyber worlds. And he also understood what some didn't, that checking your back trail could sometimes be as important as checking the trail ahead.

"What is it?" he asked as he walked over to look at the laptop screen.

"Found this on a local news station out of Seattle."

Quinn leaned in to look at the video embedded beneath a large headline that read "One Feared Dead After Explosion, House Fire."

Back trail it was, Quinn thought as he looked at the video. He read the first paragraph of the story.

"I'm pretty sure—" Liam began.

"It is," Quinn agreed.

"They're saying the explosion could have been propane."

"Logical assumption. There was a tank."

They both knew better.

"It says the explosion was reported just after 0100 hours," Liam said. "We lifted off at 0032 hours, so they were right on our tail. Minus a few minutes for them to set up whatever they blew it with, that's less than a half-hour margin."

"Close."

"Way too close. There's no way they should have been able to pull that off."

"They shouldn't have been able to find him in the first place."

"You think we've been compromised?"

"You think that—" Quinn gestured at the laptop "—is coincidence? That an empty house just happened to blow up within a half hour of us being there?"

"No, sir. I don't believe in coincidence any more than you do."

"Occam's razor, Liam."

"What?"

"If you have to work too hard to make another theory fit, it's probably wrong."

Quinn took his cell phone out again, and keyed in the message he hated having to send.

"We're going dark?"

"We are," Quinn said grimly. It cut them off from all information and help, but he had no choice until they were able to set up secure communications again.

"We have a leak?" Liam sounded disbelieving; Quinn liked his faith in their own people.

"Someone does," Quinn said, and sent the signal that shut them down.

Hayley backed silently away from the edge of the loft and sat on the edge of the bed. Her legs were a little cramped from crouching there so long, peering over the railing down into the living room. Cutter followed, and jumped up on the bed beside her.

She wondered if the men below had heard her. She hadn't been able to hear much of what they'd said, since they had their backs to her. And only when Quinn had moved aside to take out his complicated-looking smartphone had she been able to see the laptop screen.

She'd barely managed to suppress a gasp of shocked horror at what she'd seen. She'd only been able to read the blaring headline on the news site from up here, but the accompanying video had begun by showing the road in front of the location, and then the distinctive peaked roof of her neighbor's house. Engulfed in flames that shot toward a dark sky.

The headline had said one was feared dead, yet she knew her neighbor was here, alive and well. And as far as she knew, he'd lived alone.

As far as she knew.

All sorts of wild scenarios began to race through her head; had there been another person living there? Had the person died in the fire? Or was he or she already dead? Was her quiet, reclusive neighbor really a killer, hiding some poor soul in that house, and—

Cutter let out a small sound and squirmed slightly; she'd tightened her grip on him too much, tugging on his fur.

"Sorry," she whispered to the dog.

In case someone came up to investigate the sound, she lifted her feet up to lie on the bed, where she had been before she'd decided to take a look downstairs. She'd been futilely trying to rest with some idea her mind might sharpen up enough to figure a way out of this if she just got some sleep.

But everything had shifted now. Had they set some kind of bomb, to blow the place up after they'd left? With someone still inside? Quinn had come out a few minutes after Vicente and Teague, so perhaps he'd set it himself. Which would make him…a murderer.

Of course, the headline had said "feared dead." Maybe they just didn't know yet, maybe they were assuming it was her neighbor, since they obviously wouldn't be able to find him.

She wouldn't have thought things could get more ominous than they already were. But somehow the idea that they had destroyed that quirky house that had stood for over half a century, just to cover their tracks, made it worse.

But had they? The only two words she was certain she'd heard from up here were "explosion" and "leak."

Had it been an accident?

In a house that had had propane for years without incident, precisely when all this had happened?

Her own thoughts rang with such sarcasm in her mind that she chastised herself for being fool enough to even consider the idea. She might not live in Quinn's world, whatever it was, but even she couldn't believe in that much coincidence.

On the comfortable bed, her tired body at last succumbed to sleep. But her mind never surrendered, and treated her to a string of nightmare scenarios that made the sleep anything but restful. And on some level, in that strange way of dreams, her mind knew that what it was producing was no more frightening than the reality she was going to wake up to.

Chapter 10

Hayley awoke with a start. And alone; Cutter had vanished. Under the circumstances, it was disconcerting to think the dog had slipped out of her grasp without waking her, jumped off the bed without waking her and apparently gotten down the stairs without waking her.

She sat up, looking around to make sure the dog hadn't simply decamped to the floor. It was still full daylight, but she sensed she must have slept at least a couple of hours, maybe three. It was starting to get a bit warm up here in the loft, which made her think it must be afternoon by now. And that perhaps Cutter had headed down to cooler environs; that dense, double coat of his made him well suited for the cool, rainy Northwest, but not so much for this hotter clime, wherever it was.

She got up and walked as quietly as she could to the edge of the loft and looked over. There was no one in sight. Even the laptop that had displayed the video that had unsettled her sleep was gone.

As was her dog.

She hoped Cutter hadn't irritated the already irascible Quinn. Although he'd seemed much more kindly disposed toward Cutter than her. The dog, he'd admitted, could be useful.

And unless you were utterly stone cold, it was pretty hard to ignore a dog who took a liking to you. She didn't want to know the person who could look at those bright eyes, lolling tongue and happy tail and walk away without even a smile.

But she wasn't sure she liked the idea of her dog being useful to a bunch of armed men of uncertain purpose. That kind of usefulness often didn't end well.

Cutter's instincts about people were almost supernaturally accurate. In fact, she couldn't think of an occasion—until now—that they had failed. It had been the dog who had led her to make overtures to crusty Mr. Elkhart from the library, who, as it turned out, had merely been a lonely old man who had always relied on his late wife to break the ice with people. He was also, she'd found to her awe, a war hero who had come home from Korea with a box of medals and stories that made her marvel at where such men came from. And, even more surprising, he was an artist of no small talent. The quick charcoal sketch he'd done of Cutter hung in a place of honor in her study.

The image of the drawing hit her unexpectedly hard, and it took her a moment to realize she was wondering if she'd ever see it again. What would happen if she never came back? There was no one left in the family except for some cousins in Missouri whom she rarely saw, and of course Walker, her wandering brother. She wasn't even sure where he was just now. She hadn't heard from him in nearly a month. But she knew he wouldn't want the house. She didn't think Walker was ever going to settle in one place. Never had anyone been more appropriately named.

And she was ginning up chaos in her head again, thinking of any and everything but the situation she was in. And that needed to change. Now.

Steeling herself, she crept quietly down the stairs. Surely they didn't expect her to stay up there all the time? Quinn had ordered her to stay except for bathroom runs, but maybe he wasn't here right now. Besides, if they really meant it strictly, wouldn't they have tied her up or something?

She shivered at the idea. Maybe they would, if she poked around too much. That they hadn't, while encouraging, did little to relieve her fears.

When she got to the bottom of the narrow stairs, she saw Liam in the kitchen, drinking from a bottle of water. The young man smiled at her, looking oddly apologetic.

"Hi," he said, as if she were just an ordinary guest. He lifted the bottle. "There's more in the fridge."

Was that an invitation? She walked toward him cautiously.

"I thought water was an issue."

"Just from the well. It's never failed, but it's kind of slow. You can't use a lot at once." The young man smiled again, more normally this time. "No twenty-minute showers, I'm afraid."

"But now there's me. And my dog. Where is he, by the way?"

"We tend to overstock, so we'll be okay, and if we run low, there are options. And your dog is out with

Quinn. He's out on watch. We stagger them. I'm hydrating because I'm his relief in ten minutes."

"He takes a watch?"

Liam shrugged. "He doesn't ask anybody to do what he won't do himself."

"You sound…admiring."

Liam looked puzzled. "Of course. I wouldn't work for him if I didn't admire him. He pulled me off a bad path. He's the best boss I've ever had."

For a guy who looked so young he could have been flipping burgers at a fast-food place not so long ago, Hayley wasn't sure that was saying much.

"Oh, that reminds me. He left some stuff for you in the bathroom."

Hayley blinked. "Stuff?"

"Pair of sweats, a T-shirt, that kind of thing. To wear while those—" he gestured with the water bottle "—are in the wash."

She was so startled it took her a moment to process. "Quinn did that?"

Unlike his boss, Liam's smile broke free. Was it just that he was younger, or that he hadn't been at this—whatever "this" was—as long?

"He's not nearly as bad as he comes across. He's just all business, all the time."

All the time?

She managed to stop the question before it came out, realizing ahead of time—for once—what it might sound like.

"So," she said instead, "is that part of the overstocking, extra clothes? And what wash?"

Liam grinned then, and for the moment looked like any ordinary guy. If it hadn't been for the weapon on his hip.

"Let's just say we have the best logistics person on the planet. Thinks of everything." He pointed toward the bathroom. "And there's a small washer and dryer in the closet opposite the bathroom."

Since he seemed open enough, Hayley decided to risk something she instinctively would never try with Quinn. "What on earth is going on? Who *are* you guys?"

As quickly as that, the easy demeanor was gone, vanished behind the brisk, professional manner.

"You'll have to talk to Quinn about that."

"And I'm sure he'll answer loquaciously," she said drily.

"Quinn," Liam said, with a glint of humor returning to his eyes for a moment, "doesn't do *anything* loquaciously."

"Now there's a surprise."

Hayley was startled at her own snarkiness. She was being held by armed men of unknown intent. She should be thinking of survival, not mouthing off and inviting a smackdown.

She studied Liam a moment, finding it hard to believe that open, boy-next-door face would be involved in something as nefarious as this seemed to be.

"Question is," she murmured, almost to herself, "is his hat black or white?"

"Oh, definitely white. He's the goodest of the good guys," Liam quipped, then snapped his mouth shut, as if he regretted speaking so impulsively. Or perhaps that he'd talked so much at all.

He finished his water quickly, said a goodbye that was just as quick and started to walk away. She wished she felt more reassured than she did by his quick, heartfelt response. But she wasn't a fool. She knew that many people who did crazy, even evil things thought they were in the right. From eco-terrorists to the international variety, from black-swathed anarchists to fist-clenching Marxists, they were all convinced their cause was right.

She heard steps on the porch before Liam got to the door, and realized only then that he must have heard someone coming. Something she hadn't heard at all. Then she realized she should have known; they would never leave her here alone, unguarded, so he would never have started to leave unless he knew someone else was coming.

She'd doubled their workload, she realized. They not only had to watch for whatever outside threat they were worried about, they had to worry about her. If they were somewhere where escape might do her some good, she could use it as a tool, but not out here, where it seemed there was no possible help for miles, miles she couldn't cross without supplies, especially water, if she could at all. She was in decent shape, but she had the feeling an escape would require a lot more than decent.

It would require someone in as good condition as these men were.

On the thought, the primest specimen of the four of them walked in. Quinn spoke briefly to Liam, who nodded and left. She wondered where the other two men were. Staggered shifts, Liam had said. So one person at least was always out there, watching? That would fit; Quinn obviously ran a tight operation.

And then Cutter came through the door, spotted her and dashed across the room with his usual joyous greeting.

"Have you stayed out of trouble?" she asked the dog as she bent to pet him, paying special attention to that spot below his right ear that he loved having scratched long and hard. She couldn't really blame the dog, after all; he was an independent spirit, and why stay cooped up if you didn't have to? Although she still found his sudden attraction to Quinn decidedly unsettling.

Almost as unsettling as her own. Because she couldn't deny the way her pulse leaped every time she saw him, and how her breath caught every time those cool blue eyes focused on her. And it was getting harder and harder to convince herself it was simply out of fear.

"He's a smart dog," Quinn said.

"Usually," she agreed.

If he caught the veiled jab, he didn't respond. "I gather he doesn't usually…react this way to strangers?"

"He usually has better judgment, yes."

This time one corner of his mouth twitched slightly. Hayley remembered her earlier thought about the imprudence of her smart mouth. She mellowed her tone.

"Are you sure he wasn't yours once? Maybe in another life?"

"I'm sure. In either life," Quinn said.

He walked toward the bedroom in back, where, as far as she could tell, her once-neighbor was ensconced with no desire to emerge.

Hayley stood still, trying to figure out what he'd meant by "either life." For that matter, what he meant by anything.

And realizing she could spend all her time trying to figure out the man called Quinn, and never get any closer to the truth.

Chapter 11

Always watch the head of the snake.

She'd heard that, somewhere, some nature show. Or maybe one of the documentaries on a military operation she watched when she needed to believe there were still heroes in the world. Either way, it made sense. So she watched Quinn. And it wasn't as if looking at him was any sort of a hardship. And when he wasn't there, she asked about him. What else was she going to do?

But it was odd, she mused. All four men here, excluding the still-reclusive Vicente, were tough, strong—and handsome, in a hard-jawed sort of way—young men. Yet it was Quinn who still drew her eye.

Hayley shifted the pillow behind her back. She'd managed to convince Teague to let her stay downstairs, promising to restrict herself to the bathroom and the seating area by the fireplace. When Quinn had returned from his patrol outside a few minutes ago—Cutter at his heels—she'd half expected him to order her back upstairs. And he did give Teague a sharp look.

"I showed her the bookshelf. She's been reading the whole time I've been here," the man explained, then hastily retreated to the other side of the room before Quinn could...what? Take his head off? For telling the truth?

Because it was true. She'd been surprised at the eclectic selection of books hidden behind one of the sliding doors in the hallway. The top shelves held nonfiction, biographies and history, and fiction, short stories from Hemmingway to Daoul, and novels from Twain and Austen to today's Roberts and Flynn. There were other volumes in Spanish, French and a couple of other languages she didn't recognize.

They had about every taste covered, she thought, and had suddenly realized that was likely the goal, if they used this place for this sort of thing often. Which they must, or it wouldn't be so well organized and stocked. The realization didn't make her feel any better.

But the thought that they had provided books to read oddly did, a little. Especially given the lack of television or any computer except their own. Security precaution, no doubt; they could follow any news of their doings, but their victims were kept in the dark.

She noticed the lower two shelves were full of young adult and kids' books to cover a wide gamut of budding tastes. She saw at one end the familiar wizard books. Smiling, she reached for the first one and lifted it from the shelf. She wouldn't mind reading it again, or all of them, for that matter. She could use a bit of escapism at the moment.

Yeah, since it's as close to escape as you're going to

get, she thought sourly. *Gee, maybe you'll have time to read them all before you get out of here.*

If she got out of here, she amended silently.

Belatedly, the significance of the presence of kids' books down to the picture book level, on the bottom shelf, hit her. They brought children here?

That thought rattled her almost more than anything else had, and all the time she sat reading the exploits of three smart, nervy and, yes, noble kids, she was wondering about the children who must have passed through here. Were they still alive, or had their lives been cut short, as witnesses it was too dangerous to let live?

Tough as they were, she couldn't picture any of these men cold-bloodedly murdering a child, but she also knew her brain probably couldn't wrap around the idea anyway.

Cutter's leap up into her lap jerked her out of her reverie and back to the present. She had to watch that, she thought as she hugged the dog. It wouldn't do to get so lost in thought, especially around Quinn. She needed her wits about her with him. With all of them, really, but especially with him.

Now, he had disappeared down the hallway toward the bedroom. She heard voices; he was having some sort of conversation with Vicente. She got up, signaling Cutter to wait, not wanting his toenails on the floor to give her away, not that Quinn needed the warning since he seemed to have eyes in the back of his head anyway. She headed for the kitchen, slowly, as quietly as she could manage. She got a bottle of water from the small fridge, taking her time about it.

Listening.

"—will not do it."

"Vicente, listen to me. Do you want these guys to win—"

"I want *you* to do the job you were hired to do. You are the best, correct?"

"We will. We are. But there are no guarantees."

"If I do what you ask, they who want it will have no need of me. No reason to keep me alive."

"That's not true—"

"You are a good man. I respect you. But I will not do it."

Quinn let out an exasperated sound. A split second later Hayley realized the conversation was over, and she darted out of the kitchen, hoping he'd been too focused on what had apparently been a futile attempt at persuasion to either hear or worry about what she was doing in the kitchen. She scurried back to her spot on the couch, making sure her fresh water bottle was visible.

What was it Vicente had refused to do? Whatever it was, Quinn hadn't forced him to do it. In fact, he had deferred to the man's decision. Of course, one thing was clear. They'd been hired to do this, whatever "this" was. Were they simply incredibly well-equipped bodyguards, was that all this was? Was Vicente in some kind of trouble, so big he needed such elaborate protection? Who was it who needed him alive now, but no longer would if he did whatever it was Quinn had asked of him?

She tried hard to keep her mind focused on all of those questions, so that it wouldn't hover over the one statement that had jolted her the most.

You are a good man. I respect you.

Was he? Didn't the perception of what was a good man depend on who was doing the looking? Having the respect of, say, an upstanding citizen was one thing, but having the respect of some street thug was something else entirely.

Quinn came back into the room, stopping for a moment just past the kitchen entryway. She realized he was staring at her, perhaps assessing if he should give that order for her to get back upstairs. She wondered that she had ever thought she'd seen a trace of softening in this man; he was brusque, cool, unemotional and not the least inclined to explain himself or anything else to her. He was utterly focused on his mission, and she a mere—and minor—distraction.

"Interesting choice," he said, looking at her book.

There was no more emotion in his words than if he'd been checking off an item on a list. So if he thought her silly to be reading what was pushed as a book for kids, it certainly didn't show.

"Escape," she said shortly, well aware of the multiple ways he could interpret that answer. And yet again she questioned the wisdom of it, after the fact.

Think before *you speak, that's the way it's supposed to go,* she chided herself.

She turned her gaze back to her book, hoping if she appeared to be simply reading, and not making any trouble, he would let her stay and not banish her to the loft. She nearly laughed inwardly at the idea that he might be courteous enough not to want to disturb someone's reading. Especially one of his captives.

It was hard not to look up at him again. She could feel him studying her. In a way, the intensity, the alertness, the sense of a mission reminded her of Cutter. The dog exhibited the same sort of single-mindedness sometimes, the same sort of prowess at filtering priorities; that squirrel scampering past might be tempting, but he kept his focus on the larger goal, be it Mrs. Kerry's haughty gray cat or some bigger intruder.

Maybe that's why the darn dog was so enamored, she thought. He sensed a kindred spirit. The object of his attention clearly wasn't so sure; Quinn appeared more bemused than anything at the dog's attitude.

At last she heard him move, and a quick glance told her he'd walked over to Teague, and they were conversing quietly, too quietly for her to hear.

After a few moments, despite the gripping story, she gave up on trying to read. It simply wasn't possible with Quinn in the room. The energy he brought with him was as tangible as gravity, and when he walked in, everything shifted.

As did Cutter. He slipped off the sofa and made a beeline for his new idol.

Quinn, listening to Teague now, didn't seem to notice the dog at all, but Hayley suspected he knew exactly when the dog had begun to move. He seemed hyperaware of everything around him. He'd have to be, she supposed, if he did this kind of thing often. She didn't want to think about that, about the others who might have been through here, others who might have been—

Her thoughts were interrupted sharply by a simple, almost absent motion from Quinn. What would be a completely natural action, under normal circumstances. But now, under these circumstances, from this man, it stopped her breath.

Without even looking he reached down and scratched Cutter's right ear.

She stared as the dog wiggled in delight, then leaned against Quinn's leg. Quinn still didn't look at him, but the gentle, affectionate caress continued. And the dog sighed happily.

This couldn't be the first time, unless Quinn had somehow magically guessed that was the exact spot Cutter loved, just behind and below his right ear.

Hayley stared, unable to look away. And telling herself it meant nothing didn't help. She knew it was silly, even foolish, but she felt reassured. Quinn might be cool, efficient and unapproachable, but apparently he wasn't untouchable.

Teague made a gesture in her general direction. Quinn glanced at her, then shook his head.

The chill that swept her washed away the tiny bit of reassurance she'd felt at his kindly gesture toward the dog. Obviously, she had become a topic of discussion, and the realization made her very nervous.

It was foolish, really. She'd read too much into that one gesture. Even evil men in history had had dogs they apparently cared for, hadn't they? It was people they didn't give a damn about, and while she could list several reasons why animals might be preferable, it was still a very unsettling thought.

She realized with a little jolt that she was staring at him, transfixed. And as if he felt it, he looked at her again. This time it was more than just a glance. It was a steady gaze, and she felt her heart start to thud heavily in her chest.

She made herself look back at her book, more than a little frightened at how hard it was.

Telling herself it was all part of observing him, of learning about him for her own safety, was one thing.

Believing it was, apparently, something else altogether.

Chapter 12

This had the potential, Quinn thought, to degenerate into a complete FUBAR.

Hell, it already is beyond all recognition, he muttered inwardly as the dog trotted happily at his side. That sure as hell was never in the plan.

Cutter came to a halt suddenly, and half turned. Instinctively Quinn stopped as well, wondering what had drawn the dog's attention.

"Hey, boss."

Rafer's voice came softly out of the darkness from behind him, making Quinn feel both satisfied and worried. Satisfied because he'd never heard Rafer's approach; the man was good. Worried because he'd never heard Rafer's approach; he himself was obviously a screwup.

Or far too distracted.

"All clear?" he asked.

"Yes, sir. All quiet. Teague's on the southern perimeter, he says the same." Rafer glanced at the dog. "He sure makes it hard to sneak up on anybody."

Except me, apparently, Quinn thought. "Noted. He's handy. Go on and get some rest. I'll take it now."

"You're not due for forty-five minutes yet."

"And yet here I am," Quinn muttered. "Go." *Somebody might as well get some rest, and it obviously isn't going to be me.*

"Yes, sir."

Quinn started walking again, and the dog immediately took up the same position at his side.

Maybe it's a damned good thing the mutt is here, he thought, *since you've got your head so far up—*

Cutter made a low, whuffing kind of sound, quartered to the right and picked up the pace. Quinn realized in that moment the very slight breeze had shifted, and wondered if the change had brought the dog some new scent.

Then he saw a movement far off to his right. Teague, he guessed, in the second before the man flashed the all-clear arm signal. Quinn returned it. The dog halted, as if he had understood the signal, that it meant all was well. The animal trotted back and took up his position at Quinn's side.

Maybe it *was* a good thing, having a dog around. Especially one as smart as this one seemed to be. He'd worked with K-9 units before, and while they'd always amazed him, he'd never thought about adding one to their staff. But this dog, who he'd first assumed was all beauty and little brain, was rapidly proving him wrong. For a dog with no military or law enforcement training, he either had incredible instincts, or was learning so fast it was uncanny.

That is, assuming he hadn't had any of that training. He had never actually asked that question of the dog's owner.

...Hayley, not that you bothered to ask.

He had the feeling she wouldn't have stayed anonymous for long anyway. He'd had to deal with other types of women in these situations before, and many of them became nearly nonfunctional. Certainly few had ever held on to the nerve to get up in his grill the way this one did. He had to grant her that, she wasn't lacking nerve.

Nor, he thought wryly, several other attributes the other men hadn't failed to notice. And with the intuition that was part of the reason they were working for him, they all unerringly seemed to realize that this woman was somehow getting under his skin.

The jokes hadn't degenerated into crude masculine teasing. They often dealt with a more fragile sort of woman who might be genuinely hurt by such jesting. Or worse, one who would take serious offense and probably spread the word at the first opportunity; that kind of notoriety was not helpful. So it was easier to never do it, than to remember not to when they were within earshot of said females.

Or just stay away from them. That was always good.

And so here he was. And he wasn't happy about that, either. Had he, Quinn Foxworthy, really passed up on the opportunity for enough sleep to continue to function at his preferred level, just to get out and away from that smart-mouthed, too-clever woman with the eyes the color of a grassy meadow?

And when the hell did you start thinking in similes?

He swore at himself sharply. If he kept this up, he was going to make some stupid, rookie mistake, simply because he was too damned distracted to keep his head in the game. So things had gone a bit awry, but hadn't he always preached flexibility? Hadn't he lectured time and again on the fluid nature of their work, how you had to be ready without warning to respond to rapidly changing conditions? So why the hell wasn't he taking his own advice? Why was he so rattled over this?

It was her own fault. That's what you got when you wandered around in isolated woods at midnight. She should have stayed home and let the dog find his own way back. Obviously he was smart enough to do so.

More than smart enough; whatever annoyance his owner might bring, the dog was proving anything but a hindrance. Quinn could see coming to trust the animal's much more powerful ears and nose. It wouldn't take much, he guessed, to turn him into a top-notch service dog.

He wondered if she'd sell him.

He nearly chuckled aloud at the image that flashed through his head at his own question. Judging by the way she looked at him, she'd probably figured he'd just appropriate the dog. He hadn't missed the moments, usually right after she'd come back at him with some smart remark, when fear had flashed through her eyes. The moments when, too late, her common sense must have kicked in and reminded her it might be wiser to stay quiet.

He should be grateful for that fear, he told himself. If she stayed quiet, maybe he could keep her out of his mind. He had the discipline, hard-won. He just had to apply it, that's all.

But the memory of that look of fear in her eyes stayed with him. Bothered him. It pushed at him, prodded, until he almost sent the dog back to her just to get rid of the reminder.

He wondered if the animal would go if he told him to. He seemed to make a lot of his own decisions, and while he vanished regularly to check on her, he always returned, as if he'd decided this, too, was his job.

"You should be riding herd on her, not me," he muttered to the dog. Eerily, as if he truly had understood, the dog looked at the cabin, and then back at him. If he'd spoken the words he couldn't have said more clearly "She's safe inside."

"You're almost spooky, you know that?"

Cutter watched him intently, those dark eyes again putting him in mind of a herding dog who controlled his animals by sheer force of the will pouring out of those eyes.

The dog walked forward a few steps, then turned back, clearly waiting for him to continue. After a moment he did, shaking his head wryly, wondering who was really running this duty shift.

FUBAR, he thought again. Making rounds with a dog had never been in the plan.

Nor had having to fight to keep his mind off that dog's person. He didn't want her scared, he thought. He just wanted her gone. Wanted her never to have shown up last night.

And that kind of hopeless, helpless wishing was something that he'd thought had been blasted out of him by real life decades ago.

Yes, things were definitely FUBAR.

The only question was, did it apply to the plan, or just to him?

Chapter 13

Hayley woke up with a start. For a moment the dream lingered, so vivid and real that she actually turned to look at the wall beside the bed. In the dream she'd begun tracking the days in that old, clichéd way, by making hash marks on the wall. She'd been using the handle of the razor she'd snagged from the bathroom, which had so far in reality proved as useless as she'd feared.

But that wasn't what made her shiver now. It was the image in her mind from the dream, so clear and sharp she was almost surprised the wall she was staring at was untouched.

She sat up slowly, wrapping her arms around herself, feeling as if the room were much colder than it probably was. She didn't know where they were, but it was warm during the day, and downright chilly at night. Someone started a fire in the fireplace every evening, with what Teague had told her were energy logs, made of sawdust and wood chips compressed into solid, round logs that burned hotter, cleaner and longer than any natural log. It kept it nicely warm up here where the heat collected.

When she'd asked Teague why not use the also-efficient furnace, he'd explained this saved propane from the big tank in the barn for other operations—cooking, heating water and, most important, generating electricity.

He'd seemed so willing to talk she'd risked asking how long they were going to be here. And he'd instantly clammed up, excusing himself abruptly. He hadn't even explained that he couldn't talk about it. He simply ignored her question and left.

The image from her dream shot through her mind again.

Four sets of five hash marks, followed by the one she'd been making in the dream. Twenty-one days.

Twenty-one days. Three weeks.

The thought that she might still be sitting here in three weeks—or even longer—was horrible to contemplate. Three days had been bad enough.

The alternative, however, was worse.

She kept telling herself that. As the hours crept by and she was still alive, she found herself thinking maybe they weren't going to kill her. After all, if they were going to, why not do it now and avoid the hassle of feeding and sharing water with her? As Quinn had so pointedly observed, Cutter was at least useful. She was just...

What? A nuisance? An annoyance?

She shook her head sharply. She was nothing so mild, and she'd better remember that. She was a witness, an unwanted witness to a kidnapping. And then a victim of abduction herself. And none of that added up to her simply walking away and going home unscathed when this was over.

Yet her mind kept trying to convince itself that was possible. Teague seemed like a nice guy, with a bright sense of humor that surprised her. Liam seemed so young and innocent she couldn't figure out why he was doing this. Rafer was quiet, almost withdrawn, with shadows in his eyes that she didn't think were totally due to what must have been a serious injury to his left leg; she'd been right about the limp, but it didn't seem to slow him down much.

As for her neighbor, he might as well be a ghost for all she'd seen of him. He had apparently taken Quinn's order to heart, since he'd made no effort to speak to her. And when they had happened to meet in the hallway near the bathroom last night, he had scuttled away as if she were somehow scarier than the men holding them.

Or as if he knew better than she the price for dis-obeying one of Quinn's orders.

Yeah, there was always that to be considered.

Not that the man had given her any orders beyond staying put. Good thing she wasn't prone to cabin fever, although she was starting to chafe at never being allowed outside. He didn't seem to be in the house much at all. He was always outside. Overseeing. Ordering.

And overachieving, no doubt. He seemed the type.

That was the downside to the relief of thinking they weren't going to kill her after all, at least not right away. Of course, they might just fly off and leave her here, out in the middle of a nowhere that for her truly was no-where, since she had no idea where that nowhere was.

She groaned at her own tangled thoughts. That's all she seemed capable of lately, a confused bunch of ideas that seemed to chase each other's tails faster than Cutter could chase an unwary squirrel.

Light was growing in the loft. She had no clock, but obviously it was after dawn. That surprised her; she'd slept better than she expected, under the circumstances.

She heard the familiar sound of canine nails on the stairs. Cutter had been there last night when she went to bed, but had been gone once when she'd awoken in the night. She'd assumed, since it had become as much of a pattern as anything could in thirty-six hours, that he was with Quinn. The dog would accompany the other men if asked, but with Quinn, it was always so obviously the dog's decision that the other men laughed aloud. And he let them get away with it, giving only a wry quirk of his mouth in response.

The dog hopped up on the bed and presented her with a good-morning kiss.

"I wish you could talk," she said, hardly for the first time since the clever animal had dropped into her life. "I'd love to hear your explanation for this. Was he your person in another life? When he was maybe just a regular guy, an engineer or a software geek?"

"I prefer to think I was Sun Tzu."

She smothered a gasp; how did a man of his size manage to come up those stairs so quietly? And now that he was there, at the top of the stairs, looking at her, the last words she'd said echoed in her mind with a resounding silliness. This man, a software geek? Never happen. Too indoor. An engineer? Only if he was designing lethal weapons, she thought.

Sun Tzu, ancient warrior and author of *The Art of War?* Oh, yeah, she could see that.

For a long moment he just stood there, watching

her. In fact, the few times he was inside when she was awake, he seemed to be doing just that, watching her.

Only to be expected, she told herself. After all, she watched him every second she could, and she knew he knew it. The man missed nothing. But she continued. The more she knew, the more chance she had of surviving this, right?

At least, that's how it had started out.

She remembered too clearly the moment yesterday when she'd realized something had changed. When she'd risked that Liam was engrossed enough in whatever information he was gleaning from that industrial-strength laptop not to notice her going over to peer out the one unboarded window at the front of the cabin, next to the intimidatingly large gun locker.

The scene that had met her eyes outside was as disconcerting as it was unexpected. Cutter, gleefully engaged in one of his favorite things in life, a serious game of fetch. Chasing a stick thrown again and again and again by an apparently equally tireless Quinn.

For an instant she had just stood there, staring, not at the dog but at the man. The man who moved so easily, so powerfully, with such tightly wound grace and strength. He threw that stick farther than she could ever have managed, and Cutter was loving it. It was a tableau that had made her chest tighten in a new, strange way that had nothing to do with fear and everything to do with the simple fact that Quinn was a very attractive man.

Now she began to move, intending to get to her feet, not liking the disadvantage of being in bed while he towered over her. But just in time she remembered she was clad only in the oversize T-shirt he'd found for her. It was all she could do not to grab the blanket and pull it up in front of her like the heroine of some old melodrama.

He'd still tower over you anyway, she muttered to herself, staying put.

"What do you want?" she snapped, her tone an effort to hide her agitation.

For an instant, the barest flash of a moment, Hayley thought she saw something flare in his eyes, something hot and tempting. But it was gone so instantly she would have thought she'd imagined it, if not for the sheer force of her own physical reaction; she nearly shivered.

"Supply run," he said simply. He shifted his gaze to the dog. "What does he need?"

"Going to helicopter to the nearest Walmart?"

"You might want to rethink the smart mouth when I'm asking what you might need."

"You asked what he needed."

"I like him."

"Because he doesn't ask questions?"

"Nor is he sarcastic."

She couldn't stop a rueful chuckle. "Oh, he can be, if he feels the need."

"Sarcastic? A dog?"

He was looking at her as she imagined he would one of those people who anthropomorphized their pets to extremes, attributing to them human thoughts and motivations as if the canine brain and the human brain were the same. She'd never been one of them, but Cutter...well, he was different. She supposed those other pet owners felt the same way, but Cutter really was.

"What would you call it when he howls whenever our frustrated-opera-singer mail carrier arrives?"

Quinn blinked. "What?"

"She's always singing, not very well. Flat at the top

of her lungs, as it were. So Cutter took to announcing the mail delivery with a howl that sounds frighteningly like her. Complete with vibrato."

She was babbling about inanities now, but she supposed it was better than that sarcasm and making him angry at her. And he looked more bemused than angry as he looked at the dog sitting beside her on the bed. But then, he seemed bemused most of the time around the dog. And now, as Cutter looked back at him with that tongue-lolling, doggy grin, Hayley could swear she saw the corners of Quinn's mouth twitch as if he were fighting a return grin.

She wondered what he would look like if he ever cut loose that grin. He was devastating enough already, if he really opened up he'd be—

He'd still be the guy who kidnapped you.

She interrupted her own thoughts rather sternly. *You're supposed to be watching him to learn how to deal with him, to keep yourself alive, not noticing that he was annoyingly long, lean, dark and sexy.*

Although how she was supposed to overlook that she wasn't quite sure.

So don't overlook it, she ordered herself. *Just don't turn into a cliché here, the victim who falls for her kidnapper. Especially since you're just a sidelight here.*

"Why didn't you send Liam to ask, as usual?"

"He's sleeping. He had the late shift."

He said it negligibly, as if they were working in a factory or something, just ordinary men going about ordinary jobs. But there was nothing ordinary about what they were doing. And nothing ordinary about these men.

Especially the one standing in front of her, arms folded across his broad chest as he leaned against the loft railing.

She'd wondered who his boss was. Not just because he was so clearly the boss here, but also because she had a hard time picturing him taking orders from anybody. He took suggestions from his men, she'd seen that, and sometimes even acted on them, but orders from a superior? Even in her imagination, she just couldn't make it happen.

Her too-vivid imagination. The imagination that had her half convinced that every time he looked at her something turned over inside her. The imagination that fancied that something was growing larger, more consuming, with each passing hour.

Worst of all, the imagination that insisted there was some sort of answering heat in those intense eyes when he looked at her.

Oh, yeah, a walking cliché, that was her. And a fool.

And if she wasn't careful, she'd be a dead fool.

Chapter 14

"She's just scared," Teague said.

Quinn stopped in the act of pouring coffee into a heavy mug and turned his head to look at the former marine. "Scared?"

Teague shrugged. "My sister was like that. When she got scared, she turned into a smart-ass. Lots of wisecracks, in your face, that kind of thing. I think it was her way to keep from getting hysterical."

His eyes went suddenly distant, as if looking at a scene far away. Quinn knew, too well, what vision had formed in the young man's mind. But he didn't comment; they'd had that discussion once before, and Quinn knew if Teague had his way, they never would again.

"She's asking a lot of questions," Teague said now. "Maybe we should tell her."

Quinn lifted a brow.

"I mean, she seems…pretty sane, and smart, maybe she'd understand," he said.

"Smart enough to pick you as the one to question," Quinn said, making Teague grimace. "Don't," Quinn said at the expression.

"That's me, the nice guy on the team," Teague said wryly.

"One of the reasons you're here," Quinn pointed out. "And you know smart doesn't equal common sense."

Teague shrugged. "I know. Most of my college profs proved that. It's why I joined the marines."

Quinn's mouth quirked. Teague definitely had a good helping of both smart and common sense, not always the best recipe for academic survival these days.

"We can't take the chance, Teague. Too much depends on keeping this operation secret."

The man didn't argue, just nodded. That common sense kicking in, Quinn thought. He just wished their extra guest had enough to keep her mouth shut.

"Uh…boss?"

Something had shifted in Teague's tone, and an extra wariness changed his posture.

"Yeah, I know," Quinn said. "She's eavesdropping."

He heard the tiny gasp from behind him, just outside the kitchen entryway. Teague glanced that way, then back at Quinn's face.

"I'm going to go see what Vicente needs before I head out," he said quickly, and vanished.

Quinn was a little surprised when, instead of retreating after being caught out, their eavesdropper pressed forward. Whether Teague's assessment was right or not, she certainly wasn't lacking in nerve.

He watched as she took a mug from the rack, poured her own cup of coffee. Then she turned to face him, only the slightest ripple in the surface of the dark liquid hinting that she wasn't quite as cool as she seemed on the outside.

"What did you expect?" she asked.

She had, he conceded, a point. He just hadn't expected her to confront him with it, or so openly admit what she'd been doing.

"Knowledge is power," he said in acknowledgment.

"You'd do the same, if you were in my position. Not," she added, a note more wry than bitter coming into her voice, "that you would have allowed yourself to be kidnapped in the first place."

He studied her for a moment. "Although I dispute the word 'kidnap,' you didn't have much choice in the matter."

"What," she said, her tone turning sour, "would you call it?"

"A strategic decision."

She studied him in turn. And again, if he was judging strictly from the steady way she held his gaze, he would have said she wasn't scared at all. Only her protective body language, with the mug of hot coffee held as if it were a weapon, and the slight tremors that sent ripples through the dark liquid, gave her away.

"Well, your *strategic decision* sure looked and felt like a kidnapping from here."

"I'm sure it did."

Her brows lowered. "Don't patronize me, on top of everything else."

"Patronize?"

"Don't agree with me just to shut me up."

"I was agreeing with you because what you said was true. I'm sure it did seem like that to you."

She was looking at him as if she didn't trust a word

he was saying. And he couldn't really blame her for that, either.

He began to gather things; skillet, eggs, bacon.

"Who are you guys?"

He hadn't expected that, either, a blunt, straightforward question. Maybe she wasn't as scared as Teague thought. Or maybe she just had enough grit and nerve to get past it.

"Right now," he said, "we're the guys who control things."

"You mean your guns control things."

"Just balance them."

"Balance?" Her voice went up a little, the first vocal betrayal of her nerves.

"'God made man, Sam Colt made them equal,' is how the saying goes, I believe."

She grimaced. "That was a different time," she said, and with a glance at his holstered sidearm added, "and that is not a Colt."

He didn't react to her unexpected knowledge, but he filed away the fact that she recognized the weapon; his handgun of choice was generally an H&K unless the job called for something else.

"A different time, yes," he agreed as he got out a bowl. "But people, they haven't changed much, not under the surface veneer of civilization."

"If that's supposed to be reassuring, it's not."

"It should be," he said. "We need tough people for tough times."

"If we need thugs and kidnappers, we're in more trouble than we can get out of," she retorted.

Quinn couldn't help it, he chuckled. He caught himself and kept it inward, but he realized with a little jolt that he liked the way she got in his face, came back at him despite her fear.

He started breaking eggs into the bowl. When he passed six, her brow furrowed. "Good thing they found out eggs aren't as bad for you as they thought."

He glanced at her. "Worried about my health?"

"Aren't you?"

"No, since this isn't just for me."

She blinked. "You're cooking breakfast for everybody?"

"Everybody takes their turn."

"Even you?"

He lifted a brow. "You'd rather I assigned it to you?"

"Depends. Any rat poison around?"

This time he didn't manage to keep the chuckle suppressed. "Sorry. Wanna come after me with this?" He lifted the large, heavy cast-iron skillet.

"Please, not another cliché," she muttered.

A third chuckle threatened. Which in itself amazed him. He couldn't remember the last time he'd felt this close to laughing, even once, let alone three times. But between her and her dog, he was grinning—albeit inwardly—a lot. That was disconcerting. He put the large skillet on a burner, and while it was heating he turned his focus to scrambling the eggs in the bowl and adding some seasonings.

"People will be looking for me by now. Probably him, too," she said as she gestured toward the bedroom where their prize prisoner seemed content to hide for the duration, coming out only for meals and the bathroom.

"Oh, people are looking for him, all right. You? Maybe. But you haven't exactly been a social butterfly since your mother passed away."

He flicked a glance at her in time to see her jaw drop. She stared at him, clearly stunned by his knowledge.

"How did you know about my mother?"

"We do our homework."

"And who the hell is 'we'?" she demanded. "Who are you people?"

He ignored that. Not that it stopped her.

"I've been thinking. You're either some huge criminal operation, or you must be the government in some way."

"Some," he said as he added some salt and pepper to the eggs, "would say there's not much difference."

"Government, I think," she said, as if he hadn't spoken. "They're the only ones who'd think you can swoop in and snatch people off their own property."

"Technically," he said mildly, "you were on somebody else's property."

She rolled her eyes. "Should have taken the skillet," she muttered.

And again he had to smother a chuckle. And she wasn't done yet.

"So what alphabet soup agency is it? CIA? DEA? DHS? Who spent my tax dollars for you to show up and treat me like a common criminal?"

"Rather better than, I think," he said, another little jolt hitting him as he realized he was actually *enjoying* this. He quashed the feeling as he laid the bacon into the now-hot skillet.

"Fine," she snapped. "So we're at Camp Cupcake. That's still not an answer."

"We're not government."

He was a little surprised he'd made the admission. Not that it wouldn't have a desired effect; if they were government, she might be more inclined to just cooperate. Then again, she didn't seem overly appreciative of the "alphabet soup," as she'd put it, that gurgled out of Washington, D.C. Maybe not knowing would keep her scared, and thus more cooperative. But he didn't like the idea of trying to keep her scared, effective though it might be.

As the tempting smell of sizzling bacon began to wake up his stomach—and hers, too, judging by the way she tilted her head and sniffed—he made a decision. He turned to face her. She was still holding the heavy mug of coffee, which would probably still be hot enough to do some damage if she hurled it at him. He wasn't sure he'd put it past her.

"Hayley," he said. She said nothing, but still he saw the use of her name register; he never had before. "We're not the bad guys."

She studied him for a moment before saying, "Since my life is full of clichés lately, let me add another. If it walks like a duck and quacks like a duck…"

"If I'd had any other choice, you wouldn't be here."

He saw the skin around her eyes tighten, saw her lips part, then close again, as if on words she wasn't sure she should say. That smart—and sexy—mouth….

"Everything else is 'we,'" she said.

He had to give her points for picking up on that, he guessed. "Not groupthink. My decision."

"Because you're the boss."

"I am." He saw no point in denying the obvious.

"So you're the one I should blame for all this."

His mouth quirked. "That would be me."

She wasn't short on guts, Hayley Cole wasn't, he thought, using her full name in his mind for the first time. When they'd bought the place that was now a probably still-smoldering ruin, they had of course run full checks on all the neighbors. Rather, Charlie had; when you had one of the best on the job, it would be foolish not to use them. And when her mother had died eight months ago, it had turned up in one of Charlie's regular rechecks.

She gave a little shiver, and he wasn't sure if she was fighting to say something, or to stop herself. When she spoke, he wasn't sure if she'd won her battle or lost it.

"Why didn't you just kill me?"

This had gone far enough. Just the fact that he was enjoying this told him it had to stop.

"There's still time," he said, injecting what he hoped was the right balance of exasperation and threat into his voice. It seemed to work. At least she fell silent.

But somehow he doubted she would stay that way.

Chapter 15

Hayley, we're not the bad guys....

She shivered at the memory, wrapping her arms around herself. Scary part was she wasn't sure if the shiver was born in fear, or in the edgy awareness of Quinn that had begun to torment her. And the way her name had sounded on his lips.

She groaned inwardly at that thought. The very last thing she needed was to do something stupid. And she had a perfectly good explanation for why her pulse had gone into overdrive when he'd said her name in that deep, gravel-roughened voice of his. After all, it had been a very long time since she'd even thought about a man in her life. She'd met a few, but no one had sparked any interest. Taking care of her mother had sapped the energy out of her, and she'd assumed she was still in that numbed mental state.

Until this man did nothing more than say her name.

"Stop it," she ordered herself. "You're just off balance, that's all." She should think about what he said, not how he'd said it. And certainly not how he sounded when he said her name.

...we're not the bad guys.

But bad guys would say that anyway, wouldn't they? To lull her into cooperating? They'd say anything, tell her anything. They'd play good cop, bad cop, too, wouldn't they? To get her to confide in Liam, or maybe Teague, who had to be playing good cop? There was obviously no question who the bad cop was.

Although she had to admit, those moments in the kitchen had seemed...different somehow.

Yeah, because watching a tough guy cook turns you to jelly?

She was afraid it was true. Which was why she'd retreated to the loft, instead of staying down in the great room as she had taken to doing because it was more comfortable for reading. But now she needed to think, and think clearly. She needed to analyze and decide what she was going to do. Was she going to simply go along and hope it would end well, or fight back and try to make sure it did? Would it even make a difference?

She could be a model prisoner, and they still might kill her in the end, because she could identify them. And that thought rankled; she'd rather go down fighting, if she was going to die in the end anyway. At least it would probably be quick that way.

Obviously Quinn was in charge of the day-to-day operations. And his word was law; no matter which of the others she asked questions, the response would always be the same. "Sorry, can't talk. Quinn's orders." Well, Rafer omitted the sorry. The niceties didn't seem to be in his repertoire. But the result was the same. If she wanted information, she was going to have to get it out of the boss.

At least, she was pretty sure he was the boss. Except…

All of this seemed to revolve around Vicente, and she wondered again if perhaps her former neighbor—obviously he wouldn't be going back, since the house was in ruins—was their real leader. He could be coordinating everything, but since he was holed up in the bedroom all the time, she would never know. Maybe he was the big boss, and Quinn was just following his orders.

Her mind rejected the idea; Quinn had been deferential to the older man, but not in the way of employee to boss. More in the way you were with an important customer or client.

It hit her then. Quinn *had* been deferential to Vicente, and if her gut was right, that was something he didn't do lightly. So something about Vicente, who he was or why he was here, had earned Quinn's respect.

She knew by the way her mind kicked into gear, racing to turn over and inspect all the possibilities, that she was on the right track. This whole thing revolved around the man with the silver beard. She really was incidental, an archetypal case of being in the wrong place at the wrong time. And perhaps it was Vicente who was, by his order, keeping her safe. He'd seemed concerned, in those moments before Quinn had ordered him not to speak to her, that she'd gotten swept up in this.

But Quinn had ordered him. And he had meekly obeyed. Did that mean he wasn't the leader? Or simply that in this situation, Quinn knew best? Was that even possible, a leader who could admit somebody below him had a better idea?

Just about proves they're not government, she thought wryly.

She wrestled with it all for a very long time, and reached what she thought were the only possible conclusions.

One, they were in fact bad guys, in which case she was likely dead no matter what, and it could get very, very ugly.

Two, they were good guys with no plans to kill her, in which case it wouldn't matter all that much what she did or said. If she kept pushing she'd either get locked down or…she'd get some answers.

When she coupled those two options with the simple fact that it didn't seem to be in her to go quietly along, her course of action was clear.

She might be doomed, but she'd go down fighting.

Chapter 16

"Where's Vicente from? Originally, I mean."

Quinn kept chopping onion, ignoring her much as he would a gnat who was annoying but harmless. Although he would just swat away a gnat. And as much as he wanted her to go away, swatting just wasn't on the menu of options.

"I'd ask him, but of course he's not allowed to talk to me."

He was regretting offering to switch with Liam and make dinner; he'd been secretly flattered when the guy had picked up chicken on his supply run, bothered to buy ice to keep it cold all the way back, all in the hopes Quinn would make his spicy chicken with chilies fry-up. The dish was a favorite of the young Texan's, and normally Quinn didn't mind at all.

He only minded now because of that persistent gnat. This had been a very long four days, and if things didn't proceed as planned, if there were more delays, it was going to be very wearing.

"It's interesting. I've never been a pariah before."

I'm sure you haven't, thought Quinn.

She'd said it casually, with the sort of curious interest one might give…well, her dog, for one. Although Cutter went a bit beyond interesting. He'd never seen or even heard of a dog like this one. Liam had grown up in a family that bred dogs, and even he acknowledged Cutter was…different.

"Never seen a dog so smart, or who learned so fast. I mean, I had an old retriever that I used to joke could read my mind, but this dog…I'm not sure it's a joke."

Quinn knew the feeling. The second night they'd been here, he'd been ready to set out on his patrol of the perimeter and had realized he'd forgotten his trigger gloves. It was cold enough that he was about to go back to the cabin and get them when Cutter showed up at his side, as he had the night before.

Only this time, the dog had the forgotten pair of gloves held delicately in his mouth.

He glanced over to the doorway to the kitchen, where Cutter was sprawled, in the perfect position to trip up anybody trying to get in or out. But, Quinn noticed, he was angled so that he could see the front door, yet keep an eye on them in the kitchen. And he had to admit, the certainty that the dog was doing just that was an oddity.

"First time I've ever seen him really relax," he said.

Hayley's mouth twisted into a rather rueful smile. "At home he only does that when he's satisfied he's put everything to rights. Don't know what it means now."

As if on cue, the dog lifted his head to look directly at them both. And Quinn could have sworn the dog's expression was just that, satisfied, as he put his head back down and let out a sigh of relaxation.

Everything to rights? As in, he and Hayley, cornered in the same room?

He was not given to fanciful thoughts, and quashed that one immediately. It was the darn dog, he thought. He just didn't act like an ordinary dog.

"Where'd you find him?"

"I didn't. He found me."

Quinn paused in the act of slicing chilies. "What?"

She gave a half shrug. "He just turned up on my front porch one day. That collar, and the tag with his name. I tried to find his owner, ran ads and everything, figured the weird shape of that tag would be a giveaway, but I never got any answers. I even called the coast guard."

Quinn blinked. "What?"

"The coast guard. The name Cutter, and the tag looks sort of like a boat. So I thought maybe he belonged to somebody in the guard, maybe aboard a cutter. But no luck there, either."

"So you kept him."

She looked bemused, as he often felt lately. "I didn't seem to have much choice. After a couple of months, I couldn't imagine life without him. I...needed something then."

"Needed?"

"My mother had just died a couple of weeks before."

He stopped slicing and looked at her then.

"I was feeling pretty aimless, after two years of being focused completely on taking care of her."

He didn't even realize until he heard the faint tap of wood on wood that he'd set down the knife. An odd sort of ache was building inside him, and his hand was up and moving before he realized that he was about to reach out and cup her face. He yanked it back, even as he realized there was no way to hide the quick motion. He curled his fingers, digging his nails into his palm, using the pain as distraction.

Distraction from what would turn this whole thing to pure disaster.

Distraction from what he suddenly wanted so much he didn't trust himself not to take it.

He wanted to kiss her. Long and hard and wet and deep.

He grabbed the knife again even though his brain suggested it wasn't perhaps the best idea.

"Your choice," he said sharply, once he could remember what she'd said about taking care of her dying mother.

She blinked, drew back slightly. "It was. Of course it was. I loved her. But that didn't make it any easier."

Damn, he hadn't meant to say that.

"I just meant some people don't make that choice," he muttered, almost under his breath. He went back to slicing the last chili determinedly, wondering what the hell had gotten into him.

After a moment he heard her ask softly, "You?"

He didn't answer, hoping she'd just shut up and go away. He attacked the chicken with as much determination as if it had a knife of its own and was ready to fight back.

"Did you have brothers or sisters to do the job, is that why you didn't have to care?"

"Don't you have a book to finish reading?"

The words slipped sharply from him, violating the silent vow he'd just made not to get sucked into this. Cutter's head came up. Quinn thought the dog was reacting to his tone, but the animal was looking the other way.

"Sure. But since I have all the time in the world these days…"

She said it blithely, with a careless wave of her hand. As if this were just an ordinary conversation under ordinary circumstances.

"Nobody," he snapped, "has all the time in the world."

She flinched, although it was barely perceptible and she hid it well. If he wasn't so edgy, he'd admire her nerve. Again.

"Just wondering," she said in a credibly casual tone, "why some people abandon the ones they supposedly love."

The knife slipped, cut into the pad of his left thumb. He swore, grabbing a paper towel to apply pressure and stop the bleeding.

"I was ten," he said through gritted teeth. "If anything, it was the other way around."

He'd finally managed to silence her. He should be satisfied, but instead he was utterly, thoroughly disgusted with himself. Using the grim circumstances of his life to shut up a woman who got on his nerves was not his proudest moment.

"Get the hell out of here and go back to your kids' book," he said, and it was barely a step above a snarl. He was aware the leash was slipping on his temper. And so, apparently, was Cutter; the dog's head came up and he looked from Hayley to him with a new alertness.

"It's a kids' book, all right," she said, as if he'd said it wanting an explanation. "Full of abandonment and trials and unfairness, and eventual triumph. Perhaps that last one is why it's so enjoyable. You should try it."

"In case you haven't noticed, I have a knife in my hand."

"I noticed," she said. "I also noticed the only one bleeding at the moment is you."

He turned on her then. Stared her down with a look that had cowed armed men.

"Get. Out."

She hesitated for that fraction of a second that told him instead of instinctively running, she was actually considering what might happen if she didn't. Was she crazy? Or just too gutsy for her own good?

But then she turned and went, and he'd never been so glad to see the backside of anybody.

And all the ways that could be interpreted, fueled by appreciation for that fine backside, erupted in his imagination, and he forced himself back to shredding chicken with a ferocity that threatened to make his thumb start bleeding again.

Chapter 17

Hayley managed to control her shaking until she got out of the kitchen doorway. But then she ran smack into Rafer, back from his watch and standing just a couple of feet out of sight.

"Singed?" he asked, very quietly, as if he didn't want Quinn to hear.

Hayley glanced at the older man, saw a spark of something in those dark, haunted eyes that looked oddly like admiration. Or maybe it was just interest? Curiosity? That made a lot more sense.

"Maybe a little," she admitted.

"I gotta admire your nerve, lady. He's an intimidating guy, and not many men I know would stand up to him the way you just did, pushing like that."

"Might be good for him if they did."

She wasn't sure what had made her say that, or what had possessed her to speculate what might be good for the impossible man who had her so on edge. And to one of his own men.

"Maybe. Rattle his cage a little."

This support from such an unexpected quarter startled her. For a moment she just stared at this man who had been a quietly lethal—about that she had no doubts—presence since they'd arrived here.

"I'm not sure anyone could rattle that cage."

Rafer studied her for a long, silent moment. And finally the slightest hint of a smile curved his mouth. It was something she'd never seen before, and it struck her suddenly that, when his face wasn't grim or his eyes haunted, this was a handsome man.

"I don't know. I've known him since he was a kid, and I've never seen anybody get to him like that."

"Maybe he just doesn't like his prisoners talking back."

Rafer lifted a brow. "Prisoner?"

"What would you call it?"

"Nothing. Which is exactly what I'm going to say, as ordered. Because I want some of that fry-up of his before I head out to the perimeter."

"Too bad you can't hide from me, like Vicente."

"Be careful," came Quinn's voice from behind her, "or we'll reverse this and you can stay confined to the bedroom."

She froze. She refused to acknowledge the crazy place her mind had careened when she'd heard the word *bedroom*, even in this context, said to her by this man. Just as she refused to acknowledge the way her body tensed up in a hot, tight way any time she was close to him. She simply wouldn't, couldn't accept that she could be that stupid.

She spun around. "Why haven't you?"

"His choice."

"Why?"

"That's his business." He gestured to Rafer, a nod of his head toward the kitchen. "It's ready, and the skillet's hot. Turn the heat down after you get yours."

Rafer nodded and vanished quickly into the kitchen. Whether he was glad to escape or simply hungry for Quinn's concoction, she had no idea.

"So you've ordered all your men not to talk to me, too?"

"No."

"But he just said—"

"I've ordered them not to talk about this operation. You want to chat about the weather, wizards or anything else, have at it."

"How generous of you," she said, making no effort to rein in the sarcasm in her voice.

He studied her much as Rafer had. But for reasons she didn't want to analyze just now, it unsettled her much more.

"You just never quit, do you?"

Before she could answer, the outer door opened.

"Sorry," Liam called from the doorway. "Thought I'd see if I could borrow Cutter. I'm on my way to the south side now."

"Wait," Quinn ordered the other man. "I'll take it. Go eat."

Liam's face lit up. "Seriously?"

He didn't have to be told twice.

"Smells great," he said as he passed them. "Tastes better, huh?" he said to Hayley.

"I wouldn't know," she said, managing to tamp down the urge to sarcasm this time. It *did* smell good. Wonderful, in fact. Her stomach growled quietly on the thought.

Liam's gaze flicked from her to Quinn and back. He started to say something, then clearly thought better of it and darted into the kitchen.

"You're quite the host," she said when he was gone. "Cooking and all."

Quinn gave her a chilly look. "I'll cook for my men, my family and *invited* guests. Everybody else is on their own."

"Like I had any choice about being uninvited," she muttered.

"It is what it is," he said, sounding exasperated. "Can't you just make the best of it?"

"Make the best of it?" She stared at him. "I get kidnapped, dragged off to the back of beyond, you won't even give me a hint as to why—"

"I've told you it has nothing to do with you."

"I'm here, aren't I?" she retorted sharply. "So it has everything to do with me."

"So you're one of those women who thinks it's always all about her?"

"Oh, please, enough with the diversions," she said. "I know better than that, even if you don't."

If he was surprised that she didn't take the bait of his insult, he didn't show it. But then, until today he hadn't shown much of anything, emotion-wise at least.

I've known him since he was a kid, and I've never seen anybody get to him....

She wondered what exactly had gotten to him now; she'd asked questions before. And she'd pushed before, when he'd refused to answer those questions.

She wondered why he was so cool and remote in

the first place. She wondered, stupidly, what he'd been like as that kid.

And even more stupidly, perhaps unforgivably so, she wondered if he'd reacted this time because he was as edgily aware of her as she was of him.

Under normal circumstances, in the normal world, the thought might fascinate her, even thrill her a little, a man like Quinn unwillingly reacting to her.

In these circumstances, in this crazy situation, it should terrify her.

What she was actually feeling was an unsettling combination of all those emotions, leavened with a hearty dollop of fear brought on by the fact that she still had no idea who he was, what he was doing or what this was about.

Instead of thinking about whether Quinn was as aware of her as a woman as she was him as a man, she should be worried about staying alive. She should be worried about what was going on, about the story behind the man hidden behind that closed bedroom door. She should be worried about escaping all this somehow, no matter that she had no idea where she was except that it was a long way from any outpost of real civilization.

Instead she was letting herself be lulled, convinced they really weren't bad guys, lulled by the routine the days had fallen into, fascinated by Liam's seeming boy-next-door charm, by Teague's polite, military demeanor and his thoughtfulness in picking up things for Cutter on his supply run. She was even drawn, in a way, by Rafer's haunted, sometimes pained determination.

But mostly she was captivated by the cool efficiency and rigid control—most of the time—of their boss.

Not to mention that one glance from those eyes

made her heart pound. Yeah, she was the perfect prisoner, wasn't she? she thought, unleashing the full force of her sarcasm on herself. She'd never felt so tangled, so confused, so like she was going to fly apart at any moment. And Quinn walked away from her as if she didn't exist.

Without another word he grabbed up his jacket from the rack by the door, checked the weapon that he seemed to don as regularly and easily as other men put on shoes, and went outside. His absence didn't calm her much; how did she reconcile the man she kept telling herself she should be afraid of with the man who would not only cook for his men, but take the watch for one of them so he could eat?

A low whine came from Cutter as he stared after the man who had so taken his fancy. Yet he showed no sign of following, instead stayed close by her side as she walked over to the couch, as if he'd sensed her turmoil and decided his place was here this time.

As if, indeed, she thought as she sank down, feeling as weary as if she hadn't slept at all. She'd long ago given up trying to understand what uncanny instinct made the dog understand her mood so well. And she couldn't help feeling a twinge of satisfaction that the dog had chosen her over Quinn when she'd needed him to. Petty, perhaps, but there it was.

She threaded her fingers through the thick fur at his neck, trying to focus on the dog instead of the man who had just walked out, without much luck. She could read, but she who thought she could never get enough reading time was actually tired of it. She was used to doing, going, not sitting around all the time, and she was as antsy as Cutter got when his outside time was curtailed. Too bad it took more than throwing a stick to distract her.

It would, she thought glumly, take a lot more than that to get the man called Quinn out of her head.

Chapter 18

"What are you guys hiding from?"

Liam gave her a sideways look as he took a bite of Quinn's concoction. Cutter, still sticking with her for the moment, sat at her feet, but watched the young man with the food hopefully. Sometimes he was just pure dog, she thought.

"What makes you think we're hiding?" Liam said after he'd swallowed.

"You didn't come here for the fine beaches and tropical breezes."

The young man grinned. "It has its own appeals."

"Like what? Lack of neighbors? Isolation? Impossibility of escape?"

"All those," Liam agreed as if that last were a normal requisite one might ask of their real estate agent. "But it's also got wide-open spaces, peace, quiet and being able to actually see millions of stars at night."

It was the stars comment that got to her. Because it was one of the things she had missed most about being in the house she'd grown up in. When she'd moved, gone to work in the city, the stars had been lost, swallowed up by the constant glow of city lights.

"Are you from a place like this?" she asked, genuinely curious. "Or is it because you're not that you like it?"

He hesitated.

"I'm not asking you to tell me *where* here is," she said. "I know you won't. Quinn's made sure of that, hasn't he?"

Liam shrugged. "Quinn's a little short in the trust department. With reason."

"Who let him down?"

She immediately regretted letting the question slip out; Liam clammed up as quickly as…well, a clam. He handed the patient Cutter the last bit of chicken, made a lame excuse and escaped to those wide-open spaces outside.

That Quinn was a little short on trust was hardly a revelation, she thought. She wondered who or what made him that way. A friend? Colleague? A woman? Or was it some longer-ago betrayal? It seemed almost silly, a man as big, as strong as Quinn being tortured by some childhood memory, but she knew it could happen.

If anything it was the other way around.

What he'd said echoed in her head, just another part of the mystery that was Quinn.

She paced the great room, as she'd taken to doing, antsy for movement, exertion of some kind. Never setting foot outside at all was beginning to wear on her. She wasn't used to doing nothing, and she was finding long, lazy days weren't as appealing as they might sound.

Of course, long, lazy days because you were being held prisoner weren't exactly a vacation.

She heard voices on the porch, and instinctively walked that way. Liam she recognized. He must have stopped on the porch. But the other voice wasn't Quinn's. She felt a jab of disappointment that annoyed her. She had to stop this, get this stupid reaction every time she saw him or heard his voice under control.

It was Rafer who stepped inside, glanced at her and nodded, then headed for the kitchen for his own lunch. The limp was worse today, she noticed, and there had been a new tightness in his face. But he still moved quickly, even if he was in pain.

Still annoyed at herself, she retreated to the sitting area and took up her usual spot on the sofa. The book she'd been in the middle of sat on the coffee table and she picked it up, hoping the story would distract her from her inward irritation. At least it would keep her from feeling she had to make conversation with the closemouthed Rafer.

Cutter leaped up beside her. With his usual uncanny intuition, the dog seemed to know she needed his steadying presence at the moment.

After a couple of minutes Rafer appeared with a sandwich and a glass balanced in one hand. *Gotta keep that gun hand free in case the little woman jumps you,* she thought sourly. She knew it wasn't fair, really, they all did it so automatically she knew it probably had little to do with her. They'd been trained, well trained, and it was likely as second nature as waking at any sound in the night had become to her when she was taking care of her mother.

Rafer sat down on one of the chairs opposite the big coffee table and began to eat his lunch, rather methodically she thought. As if it were as impersonal as simply taking in fuel. Almost as if he were irritated at having to do it.

She tried to focus on her book; obviously the man was in no mood to talk. A few minutes later, after she'd heard the sound of the glass being set down on the table, Cutter slipped quietly off the couch. He made no sound on the rug, so after a moment she looked up to see where he'd gone.

To her surprise he was sitting at the gruff man's feet, watching as he rubbed at his left leg just above the knee. Was it pain that made him seem so prickly all the time? Pain that put that scowl on his face, that tightness around his mouth?

Cutter moved then, swiping his tongue over Rafer's left hand. The man's head jerked, startled, and he froze as he looked at the dog with a stunned expression.

With an audible sigh, Cutter leaned to rest his head against the spot Rafer had been rubbing, as if he could ease the pain. Hayley knew from personal experience that, with her at least, the dog had exactly that effect. It was no doubt simply distraction from the ache, but however it worked, she couldn't deny it did. But Rafer Crawford wasn't exactly the kind of guy she'd expect to believe that.

But even as she thought it, the man lifted a hand. Slowly he lifted one hand, and with a tremor Hayley was sure he'd have hidden if he realized she was watching, laid it on the dog's head. Cutter's tongue swept out again, laying a doggy kiss across the fingers of the hand that had been working the sore spot.

Rafer wore the strangest expression she thought she'd ever seen on a man. A confused mix of wonder, wariness and welcome. That he could feel such a tangle of emotions over a simple expression of aid and comfort from a dog spoke volumes about where this man lived in his head.

She quickly turned her eyes back to her book; the last thing she wanted was to get caught watching what somehow seemed a very private moment. A betrayal of emotions she was sure he'd rather keep hidden, at the least.

She sensed rather than saw him get up, heard him pick up the dishes. Only when he turned and began to walk toward the kitchen did she risk a look. After about three steps he slowed. Reached down to touch his leg. Then took three more steps.

He stopped. His head snapped around. For a long moment he stared at the dog, his brows furrowed.

Hayley went hastily back to her book, her question answered. She hadn't needed to see his face to know that the pain had eased, she'd known by the improvement of his limp. Cutter had worked his small miracle again.

Amazing how he always sensed who needed that particular kind of attention. When she got back home—if she *did* get back home—she was going to have to look into therapy-dog training. She might not be able to explain how he did it, but he had the knack for making anyone sick or injured feel better. She would do it, she thought, suddenly determined. And it wouldn't be some empty promise made to some higher power, to be forgotten once she was safe again. The dog had some sort of canine genius, and if it could really help people, it should be put to use.

The dog returned to his spot on the couch beside her. He curled up and rested his chin on her leg. She reached to scratch his right ear in that spot he loved. He sighed happily.

He even made her feel better about this situation, she thought. Or maybe just less alone. Less scared. Something. It was probably as simple as the desperate hope that the dog's uncanny judgment hadn't failed, that when he'd decided so instantly that he adored Quinn, it wasn't some aberration.

And again she was back to the same two basic conclusions. Either the dog was right, they weren't bad guys but, despite their actions, worthy of his help and in Quinn's case, adoration and respect. Or he was wrong, they were bad guys, and she wasn't going home. Ever.

Cutter would be fine either way, she thought. They'd found him useful, would probably take him with them when they were done here; she'd heard Liam and Teague both talking to Quinn about the feasibility of adding a dog to their team. Why not one who'd already proven himself as helpful? He'd need some training, probably—training that would be far different from the therapy-dog training she'd been thinking about.

She shivered slightly, despite the warmth of the room. Quietly, rationally considering what would happen after your own imminent demise did that to you, she guessed.

...we're not the bad guys.

"I hope you're right, furry one," she whispered to the dog.

Cutter lifted his head, and swept that soothing pink tongue over her fingers. She went back to her book, reassured.

She only wished she could hang on to that feeling the next time Quinn was the one who came through that door.

Chapter 19

The inactivity was making her twitchy, and Hayley was teetering on the edge of volunteering for kitchen duty. She supposed she should be thankful they hadn't assigned it to her, hadn't assumed she *should* do it because she was the sole woman.

Maybe that meant more than she'd realized. She'd been pushing back, slowly, against Quinn's order that she stick to the loft and the bathroom, and so far last night had been the only incident. She'd come back downstairs late, needing that bathroom. And had found Quinn and Vicente sitting at the small eating bar that separated the kitchen from the main room, talking. Intently. In Spanish.

He didn't even look at her, but held up a hand to stop Vicente, then switched to English and said, "Make it quick."

"It'll take what it takes," she snapped.

To her surprise, she thought she saw Vicente smile, albeit guardedly.

"Chica valiente," he said, so softly she barely heard. Not that it mattered, her Spanish was limited to the ever useful *"Habla Ingles?"*

Quinn had said something in return, and while she had no idea what it meant, there was no mistaking his wry, almost irritated tone.

She could have looked it up, she thought now, if she had her smartphone—assuming she could get a signal here—or if she had access to that laptop of theirs, but that was clearly out of the question. She shuddered to think what her email inbox must look like by now.

Which made her wonder anew what was going on in the world she'd left behind. Her kindly neighbor Mrs. Peters would wonder where she was, at least, but enough to report her missing? Probably not. Hayley had spoken to her, musing idly, about taking a trip, getting away for a while. It seemed inviting, a good way to decide what she wanted to do with the rest of her life, although she'd made no concrete plans. Mrs. Peters might well assume she had done just that, even though it would be very odd for Hayley to do so without letting her know.

She'd quit her job to take care of her mother, and thanks to the nice inheritance that was now hers, she didn't need to go back to work unless she wanted to— and frankly, she hadn't missed her work in the county clerk's office all that much anyway. But now there was no one to miss her when she didn't show up at an office or something.

Her best friend, Amy, would be getting worried, she knew. They spoke or emailed every couple of days, and had plans to get together at the end of the month when Amy had vacation coming from her job as a paralegal down in L.A. She'd be more likely to make a fuss, Hayley thought. And Amy was a force to be reckoned with, when she got motivated. She—

"Hayley?"

She snapped out of her reverie with a start as Liam said her name. She realized he'd been standing there for a moment, and was now looking at her curiously. No wonder, she'd been so lost in her own thoughts she hadn't even been aware he was there. At least not consciously; subconsciously she must have been, because she suddenly realized what he'd initially said to her.

"Outside?"

"Quinn thought you might be getting a little stir-crazy. So if you want to go for a walk, now's the time."

"This is Quinn's idea?"

She didn't know which astonished her more, that he'd agreed to this, or that he'd had the idea in the first place.

Liam chuckled. "I know he comes off as scary, but really, he's a good guy."

Hayley wanted to believe that. For her own sake. "Then why won't he talk to me?"

Liam's expression changed, his voice taking on a tone of almost-amazed amusement. "Now that's interesting. Teague thinks he's annoyed you're even here. Rafer thinks it's because you get to him, and he doesn't like that."

That answer set up an immediate battle in Hayley's mind. No matter how much her common sense, her logic, her sense of self-preservation told her the next question should be either "Why am I here?" or "Where *is* here?", the question she most wanted to ask was "What do you mean I get to him?"

Don't be an idiot female, she ordered herself.

"Which do you believe?"

"I have to choose?" Liam said, with an exaggerated look of dismay that would have amused her under any other circumstances.

"I'm not here by choice," she reminded him, rather sharply.

"I know. And I'm sorry about that. We all are. We know how scary it must be."

She thought of the team, of the four tough-looking, well-trained men. "Somehow I doubt that."

"No, really."

"Right. You know darn well any one of you would probably have escaped by now."

"Look, Hayley, we're not—" He stopped, clearly frustrated.

"The bad guys? So I've been told. Then why can't I get some simple answers?"

"Orders."

"Quinn's orders?"

"Yes."

"And Quinn's orders are sacrosanct, is that it?"

"Pretty much, yeah."

Liam didn't look the least bit discomfited at admitting it. Was his admiration that complete, that he wouldn't—or couldn't—ever question? Blind obedience?

"To just you, or—"

"To all of us. To anybody who works with him."

Which implied, she thought, that there were more than just these three men in that category. How many were there? And where were they?

"Why?" she asked bluntly.

Liam looked at her steadily for a long moment. It was hard to believe there was any ill intent behind those innocent-looking, soft brown eyes.

"Because he's the boss. He built this operation. Because he pays my salary, a good one. Because he gave me a chance at something better. But most of all, because he's earned it."

"You talk about him like he's some kind of—"

"Don't let her get to you, Liam."

Quinn's voice came from behind them; he'd come in so quietly neither of them had heard him. At least she hadn't. She wasn't sure Liam hadn't known it, and hence the high praise, intended to be overheard.

"Get back out there. Rafer saw a dust cloud in an odd place a minute ago. Nothing since, but I want the extra eyes out."

Liam nodded, but flicked a glance at her.

"I'll deal with this," Quinn said, and the younger man turned on his heel and exited like someone escaping a coming storm.

This? The word and his tone had hit a nerve already raw, depersonalizing her, sounded as if she were merely some bug to be swatted or, worse, dishes to be done.

"No, thanks," she said, rather fiercely. "I'd rather stay inside than go for a walk with *you.*"

"You're not going for any walk. You wasted your time asking questions you knew weren't going to get answered."

She hadn't realized how much she'd wanted to go out until he'd yanked the opportunity out from under her. "What?" she yelped. "It was only what, five minutes?"

"Better than nothing, which is what you have now."

"Don't treat me like some kid you have to teach a lesson to."

"Just a law of nature. Despite those who would like to deny it, actions have consequences."

"And reactions," Hayley muttered, wishing she was

the sort of woman to deliver a roundhouse slap to that hard-jawed face of his. But somehow she doubted that, even if she got her full strength behind it, it would have much effect.

"Equal and opposite?" he said, with that vague amusement that irked her.

"Opposite, anyway." She met his gaze, figuring she had nothing to lose. "What is it you're afraid will happen if you tell me the truth? It's not like I can run next door and tell someone."

"Not unless you're up to running sixty or so miles in this heat."

"Then what's the point of keeping me in the dark, if you're really not the bad guys?"

"It's for your own good."

Being treated like a child was one thing, being talked to like one on top of it was the last tug on Hayley's already stress-aggravated temper.

"And just what the hell makes you think you have any right to decide what's good for me?"

"I ended up with that right when you poked your nose where it didn't belong."

"I didn't poke my nose anywhere, my *dog* did! And you sure don't seem averse to letting *him* play your little game."

Quinn went very still. "This is no game," he said, his voice flat, and more grim than any she'd ever heard except for the doctor who'd told her her mother was dying.

"Isn't it? Isn't it all, with your helicopter and your guns, a big, deadly game?"

"Nothing involving guns is a game," Quinn said. "At least it shouldn't be."

The unexpected and uncharacteristic bitterness of

his last words surprised her. She wondered what he was thinking of, what had brought on the comment.

"Do you shoot?" he asked.

"I've shot skeet, a few times." Her mouth twisted. "Not handguns. My mom hated them."

"Hating guns isn't going to help you out here."

"I don't hate guns, they're only tools. My dad was a cop. They can save lives, fight evil. And take lives and perpetrate evil. So I just hate them in the wrong hands."

"Well, well. Something we can agree on." When she didn't speak his mouth quirked. "Obviously you don't think we're the right hands."

"How could I know?" she asked, not bothering to hide her sarcasm. "It's not like your name's all over that fancy helicopter."

"I object to that description," he said. "It's powerful, efficient, sleek and altogether cool, but fancy it's not."

Altogether cool...?

For a moment she just stared at him. He'd sounded like a boy with a new, heart's-desire toy. And for an instant, he looked like one, too.

"Whose is it?"

"Mine," he said with a satisfaction that matched that look.

"Yours? Not your boss's?"

"I don't have a boss. Well, except Charlie." His mouth quirked again, wryly this time. "We all answer to Charlie."

Instinctively, she nearly smiled at his tone. She caught herself in surprise. But she couldn't deny that at some time during this conversation that had started out so heated, something had changed. There was something so normal about his voice, his expression, now. Not a softening, she doubted if this man could ever be called anything remotely resembling soft. But a change nevertheless, a change that made him…less intimidating, less menacing somehow.

She was about to ask who Charlie was when he asked a question of his own.

"Your dad was a cop?"

She hesitated, wondering if she should have let that slip out. If she'd been thinking instead of angry, she might have considered if it was wise to let them know that before she came out with it. With any of the other guys, she probably would have; if they weren't good guys, then knowing she was in any way connected to a cop might tip them over into doing something about her.

But thinking seemed to fall by the wayside with this man. Besides, it wasn't as if she could unsay it.

"Yes," she said.

"Was, as in is no longer?"

"Was, as in killed in the line of duty when I was sixteen."

Something changed yet again in his face. The hard-edged planes, the strong jaw didn't shift, but his eyes widened just slightly, and his lips parted as if for breath, or words.

"I'm sorry," he said.

The words were simple, timeworn, and oft-heard, but never, she thought, had they sounded more sincere.

"Me, too," she said. "It's rough. Losing a parent so young."

She remembered again what he'd said, about being the one abandoned when he was ten. And she would swear there was a sad knowledge in his eyes, beyond the words that she'd heard so often they'd descended into platitude. Why could she suddenly read him so easily, when usually she found it impossible to even begin to guess what he was thinking? Was it because he was letting her see past the mask?

Or was this a new mask, donned to gain her confidence, her trust, and through that, her cooperation?

She didn't believe it. The remembered pain in his eyes was too clear, too real, too overwhelming. If that was faked, then she might as well give up and let them kill her, because she was too stupid to live.

"Quinn," she began, then stopped, in part because she'd never said it before and it felt strange, in part because she wasn't sure what she wanted to say anyway, and in part because of the way he went still when she said it.

She wondered if he would say her name back, but he didn't. He just looked at her. And it was with some certainty that she asked, "Who was it for you? Mom? Dad?"

"Both," he said, his voice so inflectionless she knew it was intentional, and she wondered what the neutrality cost him. When she'd thought about some childhood betrayal, she'd never thought of this.

Both his parents. At ten. That was more horrible than she could imagine. Losing her dad had been bad enough, but to lose both of them, at an even younger age—

Cutter's trumpeting bark from outside cut off her grim imaginings. Quinn's head snapped around.

"That's a warning bark," Hayley said, then felt silly for explaining the obvious.

Quinn was already crossing swiftly to the window. Hayley got there just in time to see Cutter streaking out of sight past the barn, head down, tail out straight; whoever it was was going to get a doggie greeting the polar opposite of what Quinn had gotten.

Quinn yanked the handheld radio from where it was clipped on his belt, forgoing the usual earwig since he was inside. "Report!"

"I heard, but the southeast perimeter's clear," Teague's voice came back.

"Half way around southwest, ditto so far." That was Liam, she recognized the trace of the drawl even over the radio.

"Rafer? I think the dog was headed your way."

"Hang on, heading for higher ground."

Quinn said nothing, but he didn't simply wait. He crossed to the gun rack on the far wall, unlocked it and took out a weapon that looked aggressive and menacing by its very design; unrelieved black like the helicopter, with an odd shape and all kinds of scopelike gear attached.

"Dog's cued on something to the northeast, I'm almost to where—"

Rafer's voice broke off, nearly stopping Hayley's heart. She'd come to like the guy, she realized.

"I've got incoming hostiles," Rafer's voice came over the small radio, so quietly that it made his words even more unsettling. "At least six on my front. Mile, mile and a half out. On foot, well armed."

For an instant Hayley just stood there, stunned. All of a sudden this was no longer an irritating and frightening puzzle. This was a war. A very small but very real war.

And they were under attack.

Chapter 20

Quinn snapped orders, not because his men didn't already know what to do, but to remind everybody where the friendlies would be. Each man had long ago scouted his sector and chosen his high ground; Teague in the dilapidated-looking windmill, Liam in the hayloft of the barn, with its panoramic view, and Rafer, as usual, in the farthest, most dangerous, most exposed spot, the single place that could really be called a hill in this mostly flat place, and the first line of defense. That the man was a sniper of the highest class made that line of defense more than formidable.

"I've got 'em. Still nearly a mile out," Teague said over the radio, and Quinn acknowledged, knowing from the background sounds that the man was getting into position already.

"Four more. Same distance."

Rafer's voice was, as always in these situations, deadly calm.

So ten men at least. "Any chance they're IBs, local hunters or hikers?"

Rafer didn't laugh at the idea they were innocent bystanders, but his answer was so swift he might as well have.

"Not unless they do a lot of hunting around here with high explosives. One guy's draped like a suicide bomber."

Quinn's jaw tightened at the familiar phrase. He calculated quickly. Each observation location had been fitted with a cache of handy weapons, including some explosives of their own. Not just out of expectation they'd have to use them, but because preparation was the best way to ensure they wouldn't.

Was there enough? He smiled inwardly; of course there was. Charlie would have seen to it. There'd be enough ordinance here to fend off a small army. Maybe even a big one.

Teague's voice crackled. "You want the chopper?"

"Not yet," Quinn said. "Until we see how they're armed. Don't want fly into an RPG or a Stinger or something."

The last time they'd run into a group like this, rocket-propelled grenades had not only been on the menu, but the surface-to-air missiles, as well. He had to keep the aircraft in reserve in case they had to fly Vicente out of here. Once he was safe, and only if all else failed, would the helicopter be outfitted with its nice little .50 caliber and used as a weapon. All they had to do was get it armed and airborne, and any remaining opposition could be cut to shreds.

But it was their job now to make sure it didn't come

to that. And their job alone; if the operation had been compromised, which seemed likely given how fast they'd been found again, they couldn't risk breaking silence to call in more backup. He'd been right to stay dark, but it gave him no satisfaction. What it gave him was another job to do; find the mole, as soon as this was over.

He was making his own preparations, slipping on a vest and filling the many pockets with various things. To he himself fell the task of being the last line of defense. He'd rather be out there, stopping this before it got started, but Vicente was still their top priority, and it had to stay that way.

Even if a smart-mouthed, quick-witted woman had complicated matters immeasurably.

"Who are they?" Hayley asked as he went back to the gun case and began to select other weapons, a luxury he might not have had if not for Cutter's early warning.

"That dog of yours," he said, "is a help. Nice to have warning."

"Yes. Who are they?"

"You said you went trap shooting. You any good?"

"Better than fair, not expert."

"That'll do," Quinn said, turning back to the rack of long guns, selecting one, a Mossberg 500. "It has the extended magazine, seven plus one." He handed it to her, with a box of shells. "Load it, and you can have it."

She took it without hesitation. He had to hope she'd shoot the same way if it came to that. She fed the shells in with only a slight clumsiness, as if she knew perfectly well what to do, but hadn't done it in a while. After a moment of assuring himself she really did know what she was doing, he went back to his own task.

He picked up two of the small grenades and slipped

them into the vest's large left pocket. And after a moment's hesitation, he picked up what looked like an industrial-strength stun gun. He turned to face her.

"You ever use one of these?"

She barely glanced at the electronic weapon before shaking her head.

"It's fairly basic," he said. "Make contact, push button."

She made no comment on the instruction. "Who are they?" she asked for a fourth time. And for a fourth time he ignored the question.

"The shotgun's a good weapon, but keep this handy just in case. If they get this far, my job is to protect Vicente. You'll be on your own."

If this announcement of her lack of importance in the overall scheme of things shocked or bothered her, it didn't show. He had to give her credit, she didn't rattle easy.

"Who are they?"

"They," he finally said, with no small amount of exasperation at her stubbornness, "are the bad guys you've been worried about."

All the while he was thinking. Two groups, one small, one larger. Where would the leader be? These were civilians, not military, so ordinary command structure didn't apply. It would depend on his orders and his ego, Quinn thought. If he was the type who needed that ego fed, he might be with the larger group, needing the feel of being in charge of more people.

If it were him, he'd be with the smaller, more maneuverable group. And that group would be made up of the best they had, be it shooters or bombers or hand-to-hand experts. The big group would, by its size, draw the most attention, allowing the smaller group to get closer.

He keyed the mic. "Anybody tell if they've got the head?"

"Got a guy gesturing a lot," Teague answered.

"Cool and quiet lot," Rafer said.

That decided Quinn. The guy doing all the waving likely thought of himself as the leader, maybe even had the title. But the other, smaller group could be the bigger threat; cool and quiet indicated experience, professionalism or training.

"Attack assessment?" he asked.

"Looks like straight ahead," Liam said.

"Ditto," Teague said. "They're making some effort to stay hidden, but I don't think they realize how far you can see out here."

City boys? Quinn wondered. "So we have two fronts confirmed?" he said into the handheld.

He got two responses in agreement, then a pause. He waited for the assessment that would mean the most.

"My gut says three."

The certainty in Rafer's voice came through the small speaker. And if Rafe was certain, Quinn knew better than to doubt him; the man's gut was as legendary as his sniper skills.

"Direction?"

"It was me, I'd come in over the mesa behind the house while we're fighting head-on."

Exactly what he'd do if he were trying to take this place. If it were true, they weren't dealing with complete amateurs.

"Want me to change position?" Liam asked; he was the only one who apparently had an empty field of fire in front of him.

Quinn turned to look at Hayley. "Can you set that dog to guarding something specific?"

She frowned. "Yes, but—"

"Hold your location, Liam, you've got the best view of the mesa from up there," Quinn said, ignoring whatever her "but" would have been. "Who's got the dog?"

"He just left me," Rafer said.

"Headed for me," Teague said. "I can see his tail."

"See if you can send him back here."

"And just how do I do that? You know what they say about giving somebody else's dog orders."

"Tell him to find Hayley," Quinn said.

"He'd probably have better luck," Hayley said, her tone sour, "if he told him to find Quinn."

Quinn flicked a glance at her. By her expression, he guessed that his amusement was beginning to irritate her.

"Jealous?"

"Just trying to figure out a usually reliable dog who's lost his ability to judge good character."

She had said the words before, but the heat in her voice was gone now. Quinn turned then, to face her straight on. She was looking up at him, her face so readable to him, the fear, the doubt, the annoyance, it was all there, so clearly. There was even hope there. It had to be hope that he hadn't lied when he'd told her they weren't the bad guys, he thought.

And underneath it all, buried by that tangle of emotions, was something else, something he'd been trying desperately not to acknowledge. Some hyperalertness in the way she looked at him, and in the way her gaze shifted over him in the quick, darting way of someone making sure they were really seeing what they thought they were seeing.

The same way he caught himself too often looking at her.

"He hasn't lost it," he said quietly.

For an instant she didn't react, and he wondered but didn't dare speculate where her mind had wandered. But then she clearly remembered her own words about Cutter's judgment. Her eyes widened slightly, the barest stretching of the muscles of expression.

And then the sound of racing paws sounded across the wooden porch. Cutter was here.

Quinn opened the door and let the dog in. For once the uncannily smart animal ignored him and went straight to Hayley. Teague had told him to find her, and find her he had. He sniffed her up and down, nudging her hand with his nose, not settling until she patted his head, assuring him she was fine. As if he'd understood, the moment she said the word "fine" the dog spun around to look at Quinn. Questioningly, for all the world like one of his team awaiting orders.

He was definitely going to have to think about adding a canine to this team. Although he wasn't sure dogs like Cutter came along often.

"Can you help me guard the back, boy?"

Quinn knew he wasn't imagining the change that came over the dog at the word *guard*. The tail-wagging stopped, the ears stopped swiveling and focused—if that was the word—on him. Every line of the dog's square, lithe body drew up, suddenly tensed and ready. His dark eyes were fastened on Quinn's face, and so intense that for a moment he understood how those hapless sheep felt.

And then, in the next moment, Cutter blew Quinn's expectations and everything he assumed about dogs in general to pieces. He pivoted on his hind paws and headed for the back of the cabin.

Quinn stared after him. That the dog understood

the word "guard" was no surprise, really. He supposed many dogs did. But "back"? How had he understood that?

His gaze flicked to Hayley. "How did he know that? How did he even know what I meant by 'the back'?"

"He knew."

"Obviously. But how did he know I didn't mean my back, or yours, or the back of just this room?"

"Because he's Cutter. He's not..." She hesitated, then continued. "He's not just a dog. Not an ordinary one, anyway. Sometimes I think he's a bit..."

Again she trailed off. Quinn knew he needed to get moving, but somehow this answer seemed crucial. "A bit what?" he prompted.

"Magical. Fey, at least."

The whimsy was unexpected, silly even, but she said it so hesitantly he knew she knew how it sounded.

And now was certainly not the time to have a discussion about potential supernatural qualities of a dog who was no doubt simply very, very smart.

"I've got range."

Rafer's voice crackled over the radio. Quinn thought quickly. If Rafer said he had range, that meant that group was down to two, maybe one as soon as he gave the order. The man simply didn't miss. Teague wasn't quite as good at that distance, but he could take out one for sure, maybe two of his larger group.

But once shots were fired, the force that was counting on surprise would know they were no surprise at all. So what would they do, learning they'd lost that advantage?

Depends on what that knowledge costs them, Quinn thought.

It was up to them to make that knowledge very, very expensive.

He headed for the back of the cabin.

Chapter 21

Hayley's heart was hammering in her chest, and she tried to breath deeper, slower. Her brain, however, wasn't racing. It was stuck in a silly, stupid rut as she watched man and dog meld into an efficient working team. As he always had with her, the dog seemed to respond not just to what Quinn said, but sometimes even before he said it. It was as if they'd been together for years.

Quinn stopped at the door of the bedroom, calling Vicente's name. And for only about the third time since they'd been here, Hayley saw her neighbor step out of the bedroom where he'd retreated for seemingly the duration.

"We have been found?" he asked.

"Looks that way." Then Quinn did something that once more shook her entire perception of everything that had happened; he handed the man one of the deadly looking pistols he held. "You know these men even better than I do. If they get this far, use it."

Vicente took it, handling it with familiarity, she noticed. "But…you will not let that happen?"

"If they get to you," Quinn said flatly, "I'll be dead."

Hayley's breath caught anew in her throat.

"And this will all have been for nothing," Vicente said sadly. "The murderers will go unpunished, and my head will make the journey back to my home, to be displayed on a post as a warning."

Hayley's breath caught. Murderers? The men after him were murderers? Quinn said nothing. Vicente glanced at her. She stared back. His head? As in, beheaded? She gave herself a mental shake, willing her brain to start functioning again.

"And an innocent woman will die, as well." Vicente was looking at Hayley with a sadness that made her feel, for a moment, bad for the man, even though it was obviously her own death he was prematurely regretting. Then the stark reality of it all began to set in, and fear kicked through her. She'd been better off, she thought, when her brain had been numb.

"I should have listened to you, written it all out," Vicente said.

The memory of what she'd overheard the other day flashed through her mind. She didn't know what Quinn had wanted Vicente to write out, but she knew now he'd wanted him to do it because he'd foreseen this possibility. Then the man had naturally been focused on his own well-being, but now he was obviously realizing Quinn may have been right.

She had the feeling Quinn was often right, at least about such things as this.

"Just keep the gun with you and ready."

The radio crackled. "They're closing in on my position," Teague said. "Less than a half mile now."

"Copy," Quinn snapped. "Hold for a couple more. Liam?"

"Thought I saw a bit of dust kicked up on top of the mesa, but there's a bit of wind, could be nothing."

"Assume it's not," Quinn ordered.

"Copy that."

Quinn turned back to Vicente. "If anybody gets through, it won't be many. Two, maybe three at most. I can promise you that."

"These are ruthless killers," Vicente warned. "Your men are that good?"

"They are," Quinn said.

He turned then, clearly intent on finishing his preparations. Cutter, obviously on high alert, paced near the back door while Quinn moved equipment from the weapons locker to various places in the cabin. It took her a moment to realize he was placing the items so they would be at hand if he had to retreat through the house from the back.

In a few moments he appeared to be satisfied, and headed toward the back of the house. And Cutter.

"What are you doing?" she asked as he reached for the lever-style handle on the door.

He glanced over his shoulder at her. "What I told Liam. Assuming that dust wasn't just the wind."

"You're not going out there?"

She hadn't meant to yelp, but it came out that way anyway. He just kept going.

"Let me amend that," she snapped. "You're not taking my dog out there."

He stopped. Turned. "What would Cutter do if someone threatened you?"

"He'd protect me, get between me and them," she admitted. She'd seen it, that day a drunk had stumbled out of the restaurant next to the post office right into her, and Cutter had done exactly that. That he had failed to get between her and Quinn was an anomaly she wasn't thinking about at the moment.

"That's what he's doing. Just a little earlier."

"But these men have guns."

"Yes. So do we."

She couldn't help glancing at Vicente; her quiet former neighbor hardly seemed like the gun-wielding type. Yet he was handling the weapon with an easy familiarity.

"Oh, he can shoot," Quinn said, with a grim undertone in his voice that hadn't been there before. "If they get in here, both of you get into the bedroom. Vicente, you know what to do."

The man nodded. Oddly, Hayley thought, he didn't look frightened, only regretful.

"What good will that do?" she asked.

"The room's armored, and there's a special lock."

Hayley barely had time to absorb that.

"Now or never!" Rafer's voice crackled over the radio.

"Time to start this party," Quinn said. The grimness, oddly, was gone from his voice. It took Hayley a moment to realize it had been replaced with…not excitement, or exhilaration, but some kind of adrenaline-pushed energy. Men at war, she thought inanely.

"Rafe, take out who you can. Other positions, hold and watch their reactions. When you see what they've got, what they do, respond appropriately."

Whatever appropriately means, Hayley thought, not able to think much past if they shoot, shoot back. Obviously the men knew, because no questions crackled back over the radio.

The reality of it just wouldn't sink in. That men were likely going to die here, in the next few minutes. Maybe even one of the men she'd come to know. Liam with his drawl, Teague with his charming smile, Rafer with his slower, more precious smile. Or even Quinn, standing as the last barrier between those men and what they wanted.

She shivered involuntarily. Not at the thought of Quinn going down, not any more than anyone else, anyway, she told herself. It was simply that the idea of gunfire tearing into this remote, isolated, extremely quiet place that had been her home for days now seemed utterly unimaginable, it was too—

As if her own thoughts had brought it on she heard three shots in succession. Big, loud shots. Then a rapid volley of several from two different directions, on top of each other so she couldn't tell what came from where.

"Three down, two terminally."

Rafer's voice was impossibly calm as it came through the small speaker. He'd taken out three of the four men who'd been approaching him, and announced it as calmly as he would say he'd picked up apples at the store. And she suddenly realized their job, those three men out there, was to whittle down the odds for Quinn. Her stomach knotted.

Another transmission came over the radio, Teague's voice, but Hayley missed what he said. Cutter's trumpeting, booming warning bark drowned it out. The dog was clawing at the back door, looking back at them, begging them to let him out.

They were coming.

"I'm counting on him to tell me exactly where they are. Then I'll send him back," Quinn said to her.

"But—"

"Don't argue. No time."

He started quickly down the hallway toward the dog. Hayley followed, unable to really think of doing anything else.

"But what—"

He cut her off again, this time with his hand on the dancingly eager Cutter's collar. "I'll look out for him as best I can. I don't think they'll do anything to him, since it's obvious we already know they're here."

"My question was what are *you* going to do?"

For a split second he gave her a startled look. "My job," he said simply.

And his job was to go out there alone, maybe die?

She walked to him, unable to stop herself. He was reaching for the handle of the back door. Cutter went still, his nose jammed up against where the door would open. Quinn elbowed the handle down and, oddly it seemed at that moment, she heard the small click as it opened. For an instant he looked at her.

"He'll be back shortly," he said. She wasn't at all sure the dog would desert him out there, even if ordered, but before she could speak he took her breath away yet again by pressing his lips to her forehead and adding softly, "Stay safe, Hayley."

Something in his voice made the words he'd said to Vicente flash through her mind.

If they get to you, I'll be dead....

And then they were gone.

Chapter 22

More gunfire came from the front, rapid fire that could be anyone, and the slower, inexorable crack that was Rafer's M24. But it sounded as though he'd shifted position, and Quinn smiled, the barest hint of a smile, in satisfaction. Rafer had taken care of his first group, and was now helping Teague whittle away at his, at a distance that would seem impossible to anyone who hadn't seen the Hathcock trophy at Camp Perry, where the name Rafer Crawford appeared three years in succession as the best marksman the marines had.

He was amazed that the dog wasn't going berserk, with all these hostile strangers approaching from all directions. Yet the dog seemed to understand that their mission was here, on the back side, in these few feet between the back of the cabin and the base of the bluff.

At one time it had been the perfect protection, a near-vertical, rocky, nearly impossible drop. But over the years parts of it had crumbled, slipping down and accu-mulating into a slightly milder slope at the bottom. As a result, the bottom section was easier to traverse. But it was also loose, and thus more treacherous underfoot. And for his purposes, also conveniently noisy; it was hard to travel more than a few yards without knocking something loose that rattled down the slope.

Cutter was trotting along the base of that toed-out slope, his head up, tail out straight, looking for all the world like a dog on a mission. Quinn watched as he himself worked his way slowly west.

Cutter stopped suddenly.

The slightest of breezes cooled his skin, and Quinn wondered what scents it had brought the alert animal. The dog took several steps up the crumbling slope, then stopped staring upward, stock-still. For the briefest sec-ond the dog's ears swiveled back, and Quinn guessed he was making sure the somewhat-slow-on-the-uptake human was properly reading his signals.

"I got you, boy," Quinn whispered as he edged qui-etly nearer. He wasn't sure just how keen the dog's hear-ing was, hadn't really said it expecting the dog to hear, but the ears swiveled back. And all the while his nose was working, his sides going in and out like a bellows, searching, sorting.

It wasn't the spot he'd expected. This was in plain view of the cabin, once they came over the edge.

"Wish you could tell me how many," he said as he got to the dog's position.

The dog's head moved back and forth, describing a short arc that, up top, would include a distance of per-haps ten feet. Oddly, it was similar to the hand signal they used to indicate the danger zone, the spread of the enemy, how much ground they needed to focus on. If it was one of his men, the movement would indicate a small team, two, maybe three.

But it wasn't. It was Cutter. A dog. But still, it seemed—

And it also seems you're going crazy, he told himself sternly. Trust the dog's nose and ears, but don't go making him any more than just a dog.

"Seven down."

Teague's voice came through the radio earwig he'd put in his ear the moment he'd stepped outside; no sense in letting the enemy overhear your every move, not to mention shouting your own position.

"Copy," he said quietly, knowing the hypersensitive mic would pick it up. Not as good as Cutter's ears, but close.

"In back?" Liam asked.

"Affirmative. Two, maybe three."

And that was based on the sound, or lack of, he told himself. Not a chance movement by a dog. A very, very smart dog, but still just a dog nevertheless.

"Copy."

There was no suggestion one of them come to help, nor did he expect—or want—it. The day he couldn't deal with a mere two or three hostiles, he should hang it up.

The day you can't handle a woman and a dog...

Teague's joke flashed through his head. He pushed the thought away, but not before he wondered if that day had come.

Cutter moved, three steps farther up the hill, every line of his body taut as he stared upward, at the lip of the bluff. Again Quinn thought that this wasn't the spot he would have chosen, were he the attacker. If it were him, he'd take the downward slope on the other side of the outcropping just ahead, because it offered a small amount of visual shelter from anyone watching from the cabin. But he also would have waited for nightfall. So did that mean they weren't as good as he was giving them credit for, or that they were impatient?

His mouth twisted. Maybe there were enough of them they weren't worried about stealth, which also meant they had that most dangerous of outlooks, that of "acceptable losses."

Or maybe he should quit trusting a dog quite so much, he thought wryly.

But Cutter had never let them down. Since he'd been here, he'd been tireless, and never given false warning. There was always some cause, if not armed men like today, then a hungry coyote or a venomous snake, or some other threat. He knew they all had come to trust the animal's sharper senses, that was only logical. It was interpreting his signals that was tricky. He was, after all, only a dog. Even if Hayley thought he might be a magical one.

He felt a split-second flash of longing, sadness for having lost the ability for whimsical thinking so very long ago. He quashed it with the ease of long years of practice; but Hayley's image remained. He should be thinking about the operation, the job at hand, and the goal that was so imperative. Hayley was secondary, he told himself. If it came to a choice between the two, his job was to keep Vicente safe and alive. Not Hayley.

Just formulating the thought made him recoil. And for the first time he admitted to himself how much she'd gotten to him. How much he admired her courage, never giving up in what had to be a terrifying situation for her, never backing down from him, when he'd tried so hard to intimidate her. And her smarts; after the initial shock, she'd never stopped thinking, planning, but she'd also never lost sight of reality. When the impossibility of escape had sunk in, she'd wisely abandoned the idea, and seemingly resigned herself to staying put. But still, she'd never stopped pushing, gnawing at him, poking him for answers he wouldn't give.

Cutter was still frozen, staring upward. Quinn studied the striking black-and-brown dog for a moment longer, thinking of another of Hayley's qualities: loyalty. She'd literally charged at armed men to retrieve this wayward pup. He was sure she saw nothing strange in that.

I'm responsible for him. He trusts me to take care of him. It's part of the deal.

Her words came back to him, her voice ringing in his head as if she were standing right here. That he remembered what she'd said, her voice, and her face so clearly, down to the last detail of how she'd raised her eyebrows in emphasis of what she thought the self-evidence of her declaration, rattled him. He was a trained observer, used to cataloging every detail that might be helpful, so it wasn't that.

It was that in her case, those details caused a ridiculous yet undeniable reaction in him.

And made him an idiot, he thought sharply, standing here mooning around when you've got an armed team about to descend. He had to decide, and now. This faction of the small force could crest the bluff at any moment.

Cutter was still intently focused upward in the same spot. He'd never wavered since that small breeze had brought him whatever scent had convinced him. Animals could triangulate much better than humans, he knew, with their moveable ears. But did that mean he should go against his own logic and training, which told him the spot to watch was on the other side of that outcropping?

He never was sure what made him decide. He only knew that when he moved, he was heading for that outcropping not to wait for an attack, but to use it for cover. If it could shelter men coming down the bluff, it could also hide him from men coming down somewhere else.

Like the spot Cutter insisted on.

For an instant the dog seemed ready to protest.

"It's all right, boy. I believe you," he whispered as he moved past the animal. "That's where they are. We'll turn it on them. Use the cover they should have used."

As if he'd understood every word, Cutter abandoned his post and followed. Trotting ahead until he was just past the outcropping, the dog angled up slightly and, amazingly, stopped in exactly the spot Quinn had chosen. He spun back and waited expectantly, now watching Quinn as intently as he had the top of the bluff.

Quinn shook his head wonderingly as he joined the dog. And when he turned and looked back, it suddenly hit him. From here, the profile of the slope was much clearer. And what it told him was worth volumes.

In the spot Cutter had warned him they were approaching, the slope was much gentler. More of the bluff had crumbled, making a wider toe, stretching up higher, enabling someone to come down at perhaps a forty-five-degree angle most of the way instead of sixty or seventy.

They'd chosen not the most covert way, the way most likely to guarantee surprise. They'd chosen the easiest way. Or at the least, the fastest way. And the choice told him what he needed to know.

He crouched out of sight behind the rocks, in a

curved space hollowed out by the wind over eons of time. It undercut the slope above, and eventually would crumble like the rest, but for now it was solid and holding.

Cutter pressed up against him, refocused upward now.

"You're something, you know that, dog?" he whispered.

The animal's dark eyes fastened on him for a moment, and just for a moment something seemed to stir there, some quick and ethereal connection between man and beast. And then Quinn nearly gaped as the dog's expressive face relaxed into what could only be described as a grin. A doggie grin, to be sure, but that didn't lessen the impact.

Quinn laughed inwardly at himself. He'd never been prone to fantasy. The gene, if he'd ever had it, had been knocked out of him at age ten by a fierce, bloody, evil reality, and it had never recovered.

But then, he'd never been prone to obsessing about a woman he barely knew, and that under the worst circumstances, either. For that matter, he'd never been prone to obsessing about any woman, even under the best circumstances. He—

Cutter nipped his hand.

He nearly jumped, and looked down at the dog, who was back focused upward. As if the nip had been a sharp reminder to pay attention.

One he'd needed, Quinn admitted ruefully. But how the hell had the dog known—

They were here. He heard the string of sounds as a small, dislodged rock tumbled down the slope. It was an ordinary sound, one you might not even connect to a presence, or even hear if you were inside the cabin. But Quinn knew what it meant.

"You'd better get back now," he told Cutter. "Go to Hayley."

The dog glanced at the cabin, as if he'd understood perfectly. But he never budged.

"Cutter, go. Find Hayley."

A low whine issued from the dog's throat, but still he didn't move. And then a rope unraveled down the bluff and they were out of time. Hayley was going to hate him if anything happened to that dog. He wasn't sure he wouldn't hate himself. Crazy how an animal and a stubborn, nervy woman had worked their way into being so damned important so damned fast.

With an effort larger than he'd been used to making for a long time, he made himself focus before he completely lost control of the situation. Still in the shelter of the rocky outcrop, he watched their approach.

The rope had large knots every few feet, so these were no experts. Quinn knew his best chance would be when they had both hands on the rope. Which they would, unless they had harnesses that would allow them to come down one-handed, but if they had those, there wouldn't be knots.

One man came over. His hesitation at the top told Quinn he was right about their unfamiliarity with the process. They may have found them, but they hadn't prepared in advance for the mission. Not the way he would have or Charlie would have. If it was Charlie, they'd have an elevator built by now.

He hoped he lived to thank their logistical genius once more for thinking of everything.

He hoped he lived to keep Vicente alive.

He hoped he lived to keep Hayley safe.

He wondered when he'd let the word *hope* back into his vocabulary.

Chapter 23

The shotgun felt familiar in her hands. It was a moment before she realized why her fingers were so tight around it, why her eyes were stinging. The feel of it brought her father so close, the memory of him hovering over her, directing her on how to track the hurtling piece of clay, when to fire, what she'd done wrong when she missed, or right when she hit.

She felt the urge to retreat, to go hide in that protected room now. She resisted it. Quinn was putting himself in mortal danger, putting himself between them and those dangerous men. It might well be his job, but that didn't negate the magnitude of what he was doing. So how could she simply retreat, when she was armed with a weapon she knew how to use and that was effective in a last-ditch fight, if it came to that?

She couldn't. She'd had more than enough of just sitting, waiting. She'd run through her store of patience and standing by. Instead she edged over to the small window Quinn had looked through before opening the back door. Startled, she jerked back, then looked again.

The window wasn't just glass, it was some sort of lens, like a wide angle or a fish eye, giving a much more expansive view of the area than you'd expect from such a small opening. She could see everything behind the cabin, from left to right, from the ground to a strip of sky above the top of the bluff. Whoever had outfitted this place, probably the Charlie she kept hearing about, was indeed the genius they proclaimed.

She spotted Cutter quickly, standing at the base of the bluff just before an odd vertical ridge of rock, staring upward. Quinn, for all his size, was harder to pick out in the slightly distorted image, because of the way his tan clothes blended against the matching backdrop and the fact that he was on just the other side of that vertical ridge.

Cutter moved then, over to where Quinn was, whether at a command or not she couldn't tell. She had little doubt the dog would follow a command from Quinn; he'd been astonishingly receptive to the man's every wish since he'd laid eyes on him. She didn't understand it. The dog was friendly enough with anyone he didn't take an instinctive dislike to, but he had, until now, obeyed only her. He might, occasionally, do something someone else asked, but it was usually something he wanted to do himself anyway. He'd fetch for Mrs. Peters's nephew for as long as the boy could throw, but he wouldn't do tricks for him.

But he would for Quinn. Somehow she was sure of that. The dog had just about taken out an ad declaring his devotion. And he had that annoying way of looking at her expectantly, as if wondering why she wasn't following suit, when it was so clear to him this was how it should be.

She shook her head sharply, telling herself to stop imagining a dog was thinking more than any dog thought, and pay attention. In the same moment, startling her, Cutter reached out and nipped at Quinn's hand.

Quinn jumped as if startled out a reverie. Which seemed impossible; the man never lost focus, any more than the dog did. He—

A movement from the top of the bluff interrupted her thought. Quinn's instincts had obviously been right. Her hands tightened around the shotgun. She resisted the urge to double-check the load; she knew the string of shells were there, she'd put them in herself. And she had another full load of shells in each pocket of the vest Quinn had given her to wear. If she needed more than that, she was going to die anyway.

"You should come back to the safe room."

Vicente's voice came from a few feet behind her. "Not yet," she said, not turning her face away from the slightly distorted view.

"But if they get past him—"

"I don't think they will."

"You have great faith."

She glanced at the man, realizing what he said was, at least in part, true. "In that, yes."

"But you do not trust him in other ways. In the ways a woman must trust her man."

Her man? Not likely. "Quinn," she said flatly, "is no woman's man."

"Not yet."

Vicente said it in a tone tinged with amusement and an odd sort of satisfaction. In a tone that irked her. The man seemed to realize it, because he smiled, a smile that matched the irritatingly amused voice.

"A woman needs a good man."

She turned her head to stare him down. "And what," she said, her voice as cool as she could make it, "makes you think he is one?"

"If you cannot tell that, then you are not as clever as I think you are. Perhaps not even as clever as you think you are."

A quick retort leaped to her lips, but a movement caught by the corner of her eye drew her sharply back to the window.

They were coming over the cliff.

In that instant, the last of her mind's stubborn resistance to this whole idea, the last of her normalcy bias, the idea that what was happening wasn't really happening, and that if she just waited, things would get back to normal, vanished.

It was happening. She was in a remote cabin with armed men attacking.

Knotted ropes unrolled down the bluff.

They were attacking *now.*

And she realized with a disgust aimed solely at herself that she'd been dwelling on the wrong questions all along. She shouldn't have been focused on who Quinn and his men were, or who the oncoming force was. She should have been pushing to learn who this man looking at her now was, because she realized now, too late, that that answer would hold all the others.

"This is my fault," he said, his tone regretful now. "But I assure you, I was attempting to do the right thing, the good thing."

It was too late to speculate what that would be, there

was only time now to react, to deal with the threat. And hope she was alive to unravel the truth afterward.

To hope that Quinn was alive, to find out the truth of who he was.

It was the last esoteric thought she had time for. A third rope followed the first two. Men came over the edge, heading down quickly, if without much grace. They were armed, heavily, weapons in holsters and shoved into belts and larger ones slung over their shoulders. Again her grip on the shotgun tightened and she wondered if she'd lost her touch, if she'd even be able to get off two or three shots as quickly as she used to.

Not to mention that while hitting a flying clay pigeon might be trickier than a man right in front of you, the mental aspect was something else again. Although she guessed the intellectual trappings would vanish when that man was coming at you with every intent to kill.

She heard two shots.

Two men fell the last twenty feet to the ground.

Cutter barked, a loud, thunderous bark, as if announcing the start of the battle.

The third man had let go and dropped, rolling and stumbling through the loose scrabble at the bottom of the slope. She watched what happened through the fish-eye seeming window, as if it were on a distorted-around-the-edges television screen. The third man fired a blast of automatic fire at Quinn's cover, bits of rock flying in all directions. Cutter barked, angrily. She could see him, at the foot of the wedge of rock that was giving Quinn cover.

Cutter. The dog didn't know what shooting meant, did he? He tended to face threats head-on, and had no idea about guns or bullets. He might run out into the line of fire, not realizing—

Even as she thought it, she saw Quinn reach out, lay a hand on the dog's neck, pulling him back to a safer position. For an instant, Quinn's head and neck were exposed, open for a shot, and Hayley's breath caught.

But apparently no one on the approaching force was quick enough to take advantage, and she breathed again as both man and dog were back in the semiprotected position.

He'd risked his life to pull Cutter back to relative safety.

In the instant that registered, three things happened. Cutter spun around to the east, behind them, barking furiously again. Quinn, busy with the man closing in, glanced over his shoulder. And Hayley saw another man, already on the ground and coming up on them from behind. Fast.

Cutter leaped into a run. Quinn whirled. The new threat fired a burst from the same kind of automatic weapon they all seemed to be carrying. But the man was distracted by the dog and the shot went wild. Cutter was on him, a furious whirl of fur and teeth and ferocity. Hayley held her breath yet again, waiting for Quinn to simply shoot, praying that he wouldn't hit the dog and not seeing how he couldn't.

But Quinn didn't shoot. He leaped, much like Cutter had, and the whirl of man and gun and dog seemed to engulf him, too.

Another shot rang out. From the direction of the original attack. She made her decision as quickly as it had all happened. She undid the lock and pushed down on the handle and swung open the door at the same time. She heard Vicente shout, but the words didn't register. She might have lost her edge as far as hitting a small, quick-moving target, but she could at least keep that other man pinned down.

Three quick blasts from the Mossberg did exactly that, stopped the man heading for the house while Quinn was fighting for his life, stopped him in his tracks. She heard a yell, thought she might actually have hit him with a pellet or two, although that hadn't really been her goal. She just wanted him to stay put and not shoot.

Her man edged forward. She waited until she could see his leg from the knee down, then sent a shell toward his foot. He jerked backward, swearing as the small storm of pebbles and dust exploded in front of him.

A quick look told her Quinn was back on his feet, standing over the man who had come down behind him. He glanced at her; if he was shocked at her intervention it didn't show. Nothing did. He was already moving. He looked at Cutter, said something, and the dog raced toward her. Quinn motioned at her to get back inside. He looked almost angry at her.

"You're welcome," she muttered, then grimaced at her own idiocy. She reached down to gratefully touch Cutter's warm fur, and receive a swipe of his tongue in return. At least she could get the dog inside and safe. Quinn had enough to think about, with the surviving men still armed and ready.

Or maybe not so ready; they were climbing back up the ropes, rather gracelessly. For a moment, they were wide-open targets, unable to shoot back with both hands on the ropes as they scrambled upward.

And then Quinn was there, beside her, lifting his rifle, but firing only one round as the survivors vanished over the top of the bluff.

"Gone," she said in relief.

"They'll be back," Quinn said, with a certainty that rattled her.

She watched, feeling rather numb, as Quinn called out to Vicente, who announced he was fine. Liam, Teague and Rafer checked in on the radio, advising the remnants of their own forces were also in retreat. And then he knelt beside Cutter, running his hands over the animal.

"You're okay?" he said, softly. "Good boy."

Cutter wriggled in the kind of adoration she'd only ever seen before directed at her. She stared at the dog, but once assured he was all right, she wasn't really seeing him.

A shiver went through her as Quinn left her side to check the men who were down. Now that the immediate threat was over and her adrenaline began to ebb, the reality of what had happened here struck hard. Men had died here. And Quinn, the man she'd almost convinced herself was sincere, was one of the good guys, had killed three of them practically right in front of her. One apparently with his bare hands, and without sustaining any more than a small cut on his cheek.

And yet all she could think of was the reason he'd had to do it that way, in a hand-to-hand battle that had been terrifying to watch.

He'd done it because he didn't want to shoot. And there was only one reason for that. He hadn't wanted to accidentally hit Cutter.

He'd risked serious injury, or even death—although Vicente was right, she had a great deal of faith in Quinn coming out on top in any battle—rather than risk the life of a dog that wasn't even his.

And that told her more about Quinn than all his sharp comments, strict orders, or cool glances altogether.

Chapter 24

"They will not give up," Vicente warned.

The quietly spoken words, full of conviction, made Hayley shiver.

"I know," Quinn agreed. "Rafer, long-range recon."

The man nodded without speaking, and quietly left the room, the lethal-looking sniper rifle still slung over his shoulder, and making his slight limp a very moot point.

In the lull after the fight, they'd all gathered in the cabin for this strategy meeting, which seemed to consist of Quinn snapping orders.

"Teague, check the bird, make sure it didn't sustain any damage." The former marine echoed Rafer's move and left without speaking. Quinn turned to Liam. "Get the package ready to fly."

He glanced at Vicente then, who looked grim but relieved. And apparently touched by none of the shock that was slowing her reactions, her movement, even her thinking. She shook her head sharply, trying to clear it.

"You ready to give that written statement?" Quinn asked.

Vicente sighed. "I am."

"Good. Liam, as soon as you're airborne, fire up that laptop of yours and take some dictation."

"My mom always said I'd make somebody a good secretary," the young man said with a grin.

Hayley couldn't believe he could be so lighthearted after what had just happened here. Again she shook her head, nothing was making sense, although everybody else was acting as if things were perfectly clear.

"We'll get you out of here safely, sir," Liam said to Vicente. "Trust us."

"You have proven yourself willing to die to protect me," Vicente said, his tone the only one matching how she was feeling inside. "I trust you."

Belatedly, it occurred to her to wonder what was going to happen to her, now. Would she be evacuated along with…whatever he was?

Protection.

Written statement.

If I do what you ask, they who want it will have no need of me.

Vicente's words rang in her head, and suddenly the answer seemed so clear she knew she should have seen it before.

They *were* protecting Vicente. Because of what he would say in that statement. The statement somebody very much wanted.

He was a witness. To something. Something big.

Her only excuse was that protected witnesses were not something she came across in her quiet life. And she would have also assumed protecting a witness was the government's job. But still, it all fit so perfectly she knew she should have seen it before. Long before.

And that it definitely and safely put Quinn and his team on the side of the angels didn't hurt any.

But why weren't those angels protecting their own?

She shook her head a third time, although she didn't expect it to do any more good than it had before.

"Adrenaline crash," Quinn said.

Hayley blinked. "What?"

"Adrenaline lets you function under stress, but it also depletes you. Drains you. That's why you're shaky, and your head feels fuzzy, like you haven't slept for a week."

That's exactly what it felt like, so she took his words seriously. She fastened her gaze on him. Saw he was looking at her steadily, as if assessing her. He'd done that before, in fact almost constantly, but there was something different about it now. Something different about the way he was looking at her, something different in his eyes.

Something softer.

"That was a nice bit of work you did out there, Hayley. Thank you."

An anger she couldn't quite explain sparked through her. "So that's what it takes to get you to treat me like a human being? Almost killing another human being? And watching you kill three, plus one with your bare hands?"

For a moment the room was so silent she could hear the ticking of the military-style, twenty-four-hour clock on the wall. Her angry words seemed to echo, bouncing around until they sounded harsh even to her. Hadn't she just decided he really was one of the good guys? And he had risked his life, gone up against seven men alone—well, he and Cutter—to do it. She might have helped, but not much.

And the fact that the goal had been to protect Vicente didn't change the fact that he'd saved her, too. He had put himself in the line of fire with full intent and knowledge, and here she was, snapping at him.

"The crash also saps your governors," he said quietly. "makes you lash out, do and say things you wouldn't if you weren't so drained."

She was feeling like an idiot now. "But you're completely calm."

"I've learned to control it, over the years. The adrenaline surge, and the crash." He very nearly smiled at her. She was almost glad he'd stopped himself. She wasn't sure she could withstand that. Instead he quietly restated what'd he'd said before.

"You did good out there. You shouldn't have done it, mind you, and I should be chewing you out for stepping outside when I told you to stay safe, but once you did, you did good."

She stared at him. "Well, if that isn't the most backhanded, double-sided, damned-with-faint-praise compliment I've ever heard."

The smile came then, leaving Hayley breathless, and with the unmistakable impression that she'd played right into his hands.

"Now that's the Hayley we've come to know and love," Liam quipped.

She realized suddenly that the jitters had stopped. The trembling she'd noticed, like shivers from a nonexistent cold, had ebbed. And she knew with a sudden certainty that had been Quinn's aim. He'd gently jabbed at her to get her to think about something other than what she'd just witnessed.

And she also noticed that at Liam's words, Quinn's expression had changed again, softened even more. It was an infinitesimal shift around his eyes and mouth, but it had happened. Either he wasn't hiding as well, or she was learning to read him. She wasn't sure how to feel about either option.

"Bird's good, boss."

Teague's voice crackled over the radio. Quinn spoke into the mic on his shirt collar. "Give it another twenty, to full dark, then fire her up."

"Copy."

Full dark. She'd been so wrapped up in what had happened she hadn't even realized how close they were to darkness.

"That's how much time you have," Quinn said to Vicente, who merely nodded and turned to walk back to the bedroom, Liam on his heels.

He shifted his attention back to Hayley. "You, too."

"Good thing I have nothing to pack," she said, thankful she'd kept up on the laundry, alternating her own clothes with the sweats and T-shirt from the cabin's stock. She was in her own now, so she didn't even have to change.

Once more he stood there, assessing her. She held his gaze, glad her voice had been relatively steady.

And then, slowly, Quinn smiled at her. And unlike the first time, there was no ulterior motive, no jab to jolt her out of the shivering aftermath of the adrenaline rush. Just a genuine smile.

"You'll do, Hayley Cole. You'll do."

For an instant she thought she should be offended; who was he to make that judgment? But reality forestalled her; he was the man who obviously knew what they were facing and how to deal with it.

Belatedly it struck her just how ruthless the men after Vicente must be. They were willing to kill four men, an innocent bystander and a dog to get to him. And sacrifice several of their own to do it.

And Quinn was convinced they hadn't quit, they'd merely retreated to regroup for another attack. He hadn't been wrong yet.

It was the fastest twenty minutes of her life. In the moment she realized the light had faded, she heard the distinctive sound of the helicopter's engine starting up. Moments later Vicente and Liam emerged from the back of the cabin, Liam with the older man's duffel over his shoulder.

"I'll get the go bags," Quinn said. "You—" He stopped suddenly, one hand snapping to his ear, indicating he was listening. Liam obviously heard the same thing, because instantly he began to hustle Vicente toward the door.

"Get back here, Rafer. The bird's live." Quinn turned to her. "Let's go. They're on the move. We've got only minutes."

She didn't waste time arguing, not after what she'd seen today. "Cutter," she called, sharply enough that the dog, who had been pacing restlessly, knew she meant business. He was at her heels in seconds.

By the time she got outside, Quinn at her elbow, Cutter sticking close, Vicente and Liam were already aboard. Hayley's heart leaped when she saw a figure approaching from the west, but calmed again when she recognized Rafer's slightly impaired but seemingly unslowed run. By the time Quinn had helped her and Cutter aboard, he was there.

Rafer glanced inside the helicopter, lingering for a

moment on Teague, at the controls. Then he looked back at Quinn.

"Why'd you call me back?"

"Get on board."

Rafer shook his head. "You know we're pushing the limit as it is."

"Get on board."

"We'll never make it with all of us."

"I know. Get on board."

"Somebody needs to lay down cover—"

"I know. Get on board."

"Boss—"

"Do it. My decision."

As Rafer complied with obvious reluctance, Quinn shifted his own gaze to Teague and raised his voice to be heard. "Head north until you're over the horizon. Then get the package—and the civilian—to location Z. Do what you have to do. Once you're clear, contact Charlie. No reason not to now, they've already found us."

Teague nodded. She was obviously the civilian, she guessed, but location Z? Hayley's mouth quirked; that was a corny name if ever she'd heard one. She was a little surprised she could even muster that much reaction, after everything—

It hit her then.

We'll never make it with all of us.

Somebody needs to lay down cover—

I know.

Rafer's argument suddenly made sense. Quinn was going to stay behind. He'd ordered Teague to take off, and leave him behind. *Lay down cover.* He was going to stall them, hold them off until they were clear.

"Quinn, no!"

The words broke from her involuntarily. Quinn's gaze shifted. And he gave her that smile again, that smile that changed everything.

"Stay safe, Hayley."

As he said those words to her for the second time, she wondered for an instant if that was what he always said when he headed into a situation he didn't expect to come out of.

It was crazy. He knew that, he had to know that, it would be just him against all the men who were left. He was good, she couldn't doubt that after what she'd seen, but they'd be looking for blood, revenge. They'd already proved they were ruthless. She had no doubts anymore that Vicente's story of his head making the trip home without him was nothing less than the truth.

But Quinn was going to make sure they got away safely.

No matter the cost.

Even if it was his life.

Chapter 25

The rotors began to turn as Teague focused on preparing for takeoff. In desperation Hayley looked at Rafer, who was seated in the copilot's seat now. He returned her gaze, letting the full knowledge of what was happening show in his eyes.

"He'd have my head if I didn't follow his orders."

"So instead they get his?"

Rafer looked surprised, then bemusement spread across his usually expressionless face. Followed by an unexpected smile she didn't understand.

Her head snapped back to Quinn, who was loading Vicente's duffel behind the second seat. Before she could speak he stepped back and reached for the helicopter's door as the pitch of the engine changed, escalated to full power, making any further conversation impossible.

Teague made the final adjustments she now recognized. She could still see Quinn through the narrowing gap as the door began to slide shut.

Cutter gave a sharp yelp. He was looking at Quinn as well, and apparently realizing the object of his adoration was not coming with them.

The dog exploded into frenzied motion, startling Hayley and breaking free. He leaped to the ground beside Quinn. He looked back at Hayley, barking urgently, audible even above the helicopter's engine. Instinctively, without thought, as had become habit, she moved to retrieve her dog.

The door nearly caught her as it slid shut. She hastily stepped down to the skid, and the door latched behind her. She gasped as she saw the gap between the helicopter's skid and the ground, realized they were already lifting off.

She had no choice, she was already in motion and knew she would fall if she tried to stop. Better to jump, and have some control.

It was only a three-foot drop, but it seemed like more when she hit ground. She wobbled for a moment as one foot hit a rock and slid, but then Quinn was there, his strong arm steadying her even as he swore, words she hadn't heard since the time her father had found her hiding in Toby Baxter's tree house, hours after a fight with her mother. He'd been terrified for her; Quinn, she was sure, was just angry.

He made a circular hand gesture toward the helicopter. It didn't take much to guess what it meant; keep going. Hayley had never thought she'd be sorry to see the last of that black helicopter, but the reality of the situation began to sink in as the aircraft lifted out of reach.

She didn't have time to dwell on feelings of abandonment. In the moment that Quinn grabbed her arm and starting pulling her back toward the house, she heard odd popping sounds. She thought something had gone wrong with the helicopter, but it continued to rise, began to assume the angle she knew now meant they were about to start making speed.

Quinn whipped up the rifle he held. Fired bursts of automatic fire to the west. She barely stifled a startled yelp at the sound. The helicopter kept rising. Quinn pushed her to the ground behind him. He went into a crouch, rifle still up. Little puffs of dust and pebbles kicked up from the dirt within inches of them.

Gunshots. What she had heard before were gunshots, she finally realized. They were back.

Quinn sent out another spray of fire, apparently knowing where the shots were coming from. Cutter stood beside him, barking angrily, as if he understood the threat. Who knows, Hayley thought numbly, maybe the uncannily smart dog had learned the danger of gunfire during that last heated battle.

Quinn grabbed something out of his vest. He rose slightly. Her mind screamed "No, they'll see you!" in the instant before his arm came back and he threw. Cutter jumped forward a little, wire-drawn and frighteningly intent. She grabbed the dog's collar. She didn't think even the sometimes amazingly strong Cutter could drag her deadweight with him. Not that that would stop him from trying.

The explosion was deafening, even to ears still ringing from the sound of gunfire. The grenades, she thought, a little numbly, also belatedly realizing they had probably known exactly where he was from his return fire anyway.

Quinn fired again and again, and she couldn't even see who he was shooting at. But obviously he could, and since the helicopter seemed safely out of range now, he had clearly succeeded with his goal of covering their escape.

He threw another grenade.

And then she had no time to think at all; Quinn had her running. Another grenade exploded. She felt the shock through the ground, swore she could feel it rock the very air around her. But they kept going, so fast all she could think about was staying on her feet as he charted a dodging, crooked, crazy path back toward the cabin.

Then they were inside, and Quinn slammed and secured the door behind them. She wasn't sure what good it would do stopping bullets, but she hadn't known about the armored bedroom, either.

Quinn whirled on her.

"Not many people do something that stupid and survive," he snapped.

"I know," she admitted, and saw the surprise in his eyes at the ease of her capitulation. "But it was too late to stop. And I couldn't just leave him."

Quinn glanced at Cutter. The dog looked from him back to her, and Hayley could have sworn there was a look of approval—even satisfaction—in his eyes.

"I can see why sheep obey him," she murmured.

"Are you saying he made you do it, or that you're a sheep?" Quinn asked. She wished there had been a bit more humor in the question.

"Maybe both," she said, suddenly weary.

For a moment Quinn said nothing. When he did speak, his conciliatory tone—and his words—surprised her. "He does have a way."

"Yes. Yes, he does. And a powerful will."

"Must be how it works. The sheep."

She didn't know if it was supposed to be another jab at her, but she felt the need to explain. "He does do it with people, too. I don't know how, he just communicates."

Quinn nodded. "I've seen it."

She felt a little relieved, his anger seemed to have ebbed.

"I could do without the smugness, though," Quinn said.

Hayley's gaze shot to his face; had that been a joke? But he was looking at the dog, a wry expression on his face. Could he really see it? Usually it was only she who read such human emotions into Cutter's expressions, and she kept the notion to herself.

"He does seem a bit full of himself," she said carefully.

"He looks," Quinn said drily, "like a guy whose plan has come together."

Hayley's eyes widened. She never would have expected something so...fanciful from the cool, commanding and undeniably deadly man before her.

"Make yourself useful, dog," he said to Cutter. "Let me know if they decide to make another run. Guard," he added, making a sweeping gesture around the cabin.

The dog gave a low, whuffing sound, she supposed the canine equivalent of "Yes, sir," and trotted off toward the front door and the single window. He began to pace, stopping now and then with his head cocked, clearly listening, or with his nose up, sniffing deeply.

"I swear, sometimes I think he's..." Quinn's words trailed off.

"Me, too," Hayley agreed. "Sometimes I really wonder. And then he chews up a shoe, or digs a huge hole in the yard, or brings me a dead rat, and I realize he's just a dog again."

"At least he'll be a help." Just like that, that softer Quinn vanished, and the professional was back. And none too happy with her.

"Unlike me?"

He looked at her then. "You held them off with that shotgun, even if you did miss."

"I didn't miss. I wasn't aiming *at* them."

Quinn drew back slightly. "Are you saying you could have hit them, but you didn't?"

"I didn't want to kill anybody—"

"There is a time for mercy," Quinn said, his voice suddenly like ice. "When the men trying to kill *you* don't know the meaning of the word is not it."

He didn't point out that her qualms had left them with more men to deal with now, and for that she was grateful.

"You'd better believe this now, Hayley. Those men out there are beyond ruthless. They are the kind of men who kill for revenge, to make a point, to teach a lesson and simply because they enjoy it. And your innocence will not protect you. You are in their way, and that's all it takes."

"But so many of them have died—"

"They're as ruthless with their own as they are their enemies. They'll keep coming to the last man. My team will come back with help, but until then we're on our own. And we, in case you hadn't noticed, are pinned down here."

She felt shaken, but she couldn't deny the truth of what he'd said, she'd seen it for herself. She drew in a deep, steadying breath, and let it out in a quick gust. She walked to table where she'd dropped the shotgun when she'd come back inside. She picked up the powerful, reliable weapon and methodically reloaded it.

Then she turned to face Quinn.

"What else can I do?" she asked, working to keep her voice calm, although inside she was scared to death.

He looked at her, assessingly. His gaze flicked to the shotgun, then back to her face. He gave her a short, sharp nod of approval, and she was stunned at how good it made her feel.

"We may need to retreat to the armored room. Move any food that doesn't require cooking in there. There's also a cache of freeze-dried food in the closet."

She nodded. "What about water?"

"There's a tap in there. And bottles we filled when we first got here."

"Somebody thought of everything," she said.

"Charlie," he said, already moving before she began to walk toward the kitchen. He was rechecking all the places where he'd left weapons earlier. Then he started carrying what was left in the weapons locker into the bedroom.

By the time she was done, the locker was mostly empty, everything that wasn't out and within reach of various parts of the room was moved into the safe room.

Including all but one of the boxes of shells for her shotgun.

"What if I need more?" she asked, eying the box.

"If you need more than that," he said, "you'll be heading in there." He gestured toward the bedroom. "Shotgun's best at shorter range. If they get close, your job is to just keep them back until you can get into that room and lock it."

"You say that like I'll be alone."

Even as she spoke she already knew the answer. He'd given it to Vicente, barely an hour ago.

If they get to you, I'll be dead.

Chapter 26

She was holding up remarkably well, considering.

Quinn made another circuit, checking the carefully placed windows. As with everything else here at this site and all their others, Charlie had sited them personally, at the best possible observation points. And before long Vicente would be tucked away at their most impenetrable and unassailable stronghold, one rarely used for various reasons, but in this case he'd not hesitated to give the order.

One of those reasons was at this moment in the kitchen, and his nose had just told him why; the enticing aroma of fresh coffee had wafted his way.

Good thinking, he told her silently. But then he'd come to know she was good at that. She never stopped thinking.

Except for that moment when she'd come after her blessed dog. Again. He'd intended for her—and Cutter, for that matter—to be out of here and safe before the next attack.

And yet he, the cool, unemotional pragmatist, understood. And that surprised him. But Cutter was an amazing dog. Like now, for instance; instead of being at Quinn's heels, he was on the opposite side of the cabin, obviously alert and on guard, nose twitching, ears swiveling. And every time Quinn moved to another viewing post, Cutter moved in turn, so at least two sides of the cabin were always covered.

In other words, Quinn thought in amazement, the dog was doing exactly what he would have ordered one of his men to do. Oh, he wouldn't have picked those particular places, but the animal apparently knew what spots gave him the best audio or olfactory reception. Amazing indeed.

Hayley approached him with a mug of hot coffee.

"Thanks for thinking of this," he said, accepting it and taking a sip. It was exactly as he liked it. Obviously she'd seen him do it enough times to get it just right.

"Don't know if there'll be a chance later," she said.

Her voice was low, quiet, and he didn't miss the undercurrent of strain. He would have been amazed if she was calm, indeed would have assumed she didn't understand the severity of their situation. But she obviously did.

"They'll be coming back soon," he said between sips.

"Why didn't they just keep coming now?"

"We were in the open, now we're not. Their first plan of attack here didn't work, now they need a new one. And it's getting dark."

"You think they won't come in the dark?"

"No idea. Depends how desperate they are."

He took another gulp of coffee then set the mug

down. There was no point in sugarcoating this for her. And it seemed she was able to handle reality better than most in her position would be, so he gave it to her.

"If they have enough ammo, they may just open fire and try to tear the place down with bullets. If that happens, you run for the bedroom."

"And leave you out here to do…what?"

"My job."

"I thought your job just left on that helicopter."

Like I said, she never stops thinking, Quinn thought wryly.

"And you should have, too."

"I don't think we have the time to waste going over that again."

He couldn't stop his mouth from quirking upward. "Point taken," he said.

He glanced at the items he'd selected from the weapons locker. As soon as it was fully dark, he'd go out and set some booby traps. There were some land mines which, if put in the right place, could give the illusion of an entire minefield. Trip wires, portable laser beams that sent up a shrieking alarm, he had many options.

And he might be using them all tonight.

"Who are you? Who's Vicente, really?"

He hesitated. Her chin came up. She stared him down in a way few men had the nerve to do.

"If I'm going to die out here because of all this," she said, "I damned well want to know why."

"You're not going to—"

"You can't guarantee that. They found us here, didn't they?"

She had a point, and one he couldn't deny. A couple of points, actually.

He chose to give her the answer that would come out eventually anyway.

"Vicente Reynosa is going to be the prize witness in hearings about a drug cartel that's murdered hundreds, maybe thousands of people along the Mexican border. Including nearly two dozen American citizens."

Her eyes widened. "The man they've been talking about on the news?"

He should have guessed she'd probably heard the blaring news reports about the investigation. Hard to miss, given the fury over how long, and how many deaths it had taken to get the bureaucracy moving. Vicente was the only person they'd found willing to give evidence against the huge, well-armed and utterly ruthless cartel.

"He's…a drug dealer?" She sounded astonished.

"Not really. He was coerced. Forced to cooperate with the drug lord. They hold his family. His wife, three children and his sister. They've already tortured and brutally murdered his only son."

He saw the expressions cross her face, and found them as readable as if she'd spoken every stage, from shock, to the realization that her neighbor was in fact a hero of sorts, to anger.

"Those bastards," she exclaimed.

"Exactly."

"And good for Vicente. No wonder you respect him."

"Yes. He's a brave man."

"What about his family, when he testifies?"

"We're working on that." He gave her a sideways look. "If it makes you feel any better, the guy I killed with my bare hands, as you said? He was the one who tortured and murdered Vicente's son."

He saw something spark in her green eyes, a flash of

satisfaction that warmed him. It was a moment before she said, "Which brings me back to my other question."

No, she never stopped. He let out a compressed breath.

"Hayley," he began.

"Are you government agents?"

"No."

"But I thought that's who protected witnesses."

"Normally, it is."

"But?"

He opened his mouth to say something diverting, one of the usual answers given to anyone who got too curious. But what she'd said before stopped him cold.

If I'm going to die out here because of all this, I damned well want to know why.

It was a very grim, very real possibility. When he coupled that with how she'd handled all this, keeping what had to be extraordinary fear under control, and dragging up enough courage to not only confront him at every turn, snipe at him, argue with him, but when the chips were down to take a shotgun and hold armed men at bay to help him—better that she'd eliminated them, but even what she'd done had been incredibly brave and unexpected, and had probably been what had allowed him to escape that fracas without even a scratch.

"Vicente asked for us," he finally said.

That seemed to surprise her. "He did? Why?"

Quinn's mouth quirked. "He apparently lost his trust in the government of his own country long ago, and now he's lost trust in ours, as well. He knows where the cartel got many of their weapons."

"So he doesn't trust either to protect him?"

"No."

"So you are a private operation."

"Yes. Very private."

"Contracted by the government?"

"No. They called us in this time, at Vicente's demand, but we've never worked for them."

"But…how did he even know you existed?"

"We retrieved an American citizen and her daughter last year, out from under his particular drug lord's nose."

"Did the government call you in then, too?"

He grimaced. "No. And they weren't too happy when her husband did."

"You'd think they'd take all the help they could get."

"They have a tendency to be very territorial. And to think they do things best."

"Right," Hayley said, with a grimace that nearly matched his own. Then she looked about to ask another question, hesitated and asked something else. "So that's why Vicente trusted you? Because he knew you got that woman and her daughter out?"

Quinn nodded. "One of law enforcement's main focuses is their legal case, and convictions. They're spread thin that way."

"And you're different."

He nodded. "We focus on only one thing. Keeping our target alive."

She was quiet for a moment, and he could almost hear her mind working, absorbing, processing. He jumped at the chance to stop talking and start doing; he'd told her enough, and more than he ever told most people not directly involved in a case.

But then, right now she was about as involved as anybody could get. And now that Vicente's safety was out of his hands, her safety, as an innocent bystander, became paramount.

He went to work, preparing his booby traps and early-warning devices for deployment as soon as he had full cover of darkness. He's have to work fast, just in case they were also waiting for dark to attack. He'd like to think they were a bit cowed, and would take longer to regroup, but he couldn't assume that.

Hayley stood quietly, in fact handing him things as he worked. He noticed that after the first mine he didn't have to ask, she knew exactly what to give him when. If she'd been an applicant, he'd have given her a serious look, just based on how she'd handled all this.

"There are only two of us," Haley said finally. "One really. I won't be much help."

"You just keep yourself safe, let me worry about them."

"But there are more of them."

"And a lot fewer of them than they started with," he said with no small amount of satisfaction. "There's maybe five left. So odds are about even."

"Five to one is even?"

"Close enough," he said as he carefully adjusted the sensitivity of the trigger.

"Do you even know the meaning of the word 'outnumbered'?"

He glanced at her then. He hadn't realized it until that moment, but the adrenaline was building again as he dealt with the familiar weapons. These were mostly defensive, but setting them was going to be tricky, and risky.

"Nah," he said, with a grin he couldn't hold back. "Must have missed class that day."

The look she gave him made him feel an odd sort of warmth, a sensation he didn't have time to analyze just now. Because a glance outside told him it was dark enough, and he wanted these set as soon as possible.

"Hey, dog." He said it in the exact same tone he'd been using in the conversation, no louder, with no different inflection. Yet Cutter, who had been patrolling the back of the cabin, spun instantly and trotted over to them. Yes, this was one smart, smart dog.

The animal looked up at him expectantly.

"Wanna come out and be my early-warning system again?"

The dog had been alert before, but now his head came up even more sharply, and he made that same sort of sound Quinn had heard before, a low, whuffing growl that sounded for all the world like spoken assent.

"Back," Quinn said, watching the dog. The animal spun on his right hind leg and headed for the back door.

"Testing him?"

"If I was, he passed." He started to go after the dog.

"Quinn?"

He stopped.

"Stay safe."

The use of his own words was too pointed not to be intentional.

"Both of you," she added.

Quinn couldn't stop himself; he kissed her. A brief, barely there brush of his lips, but this time it was her tempting mouth, not the relative safety of her forehead. He yanked back at the spark that seemed to leap, made himself turn away.

But she didn't protest him taking the dog this time. Telling her the truth—well, most of it anyway—had been the right thing to do, if gaining her cooperation had been the goal.

As he stepped outside, he was still trying to convince himself that that was his only goal. That telling her the truth had had nothing to do with not liking her suspecting he was one of the bad guys. Nothing to do with wanting her to keep looking at him the way she had when she'd told him to stay safe.

Nothing at all.

Chapter 27

It was official, Hayley thought. The boys have bonded, and she was the odd one out.

When Cutter had first dropped into her life, she'd researched the breed most knowledgeable folks told her he looked like. Intensity, a proclivity for mischief if left too long to his own devices, and the need for a job to do were high on the list. She thought she'd dealt with him fairly well; while there had been some minor incidents of doggy-style waywardness, for the most part Cutter's manners were impeccable. For a dog, anyway.

But the animal also seemed to have a madcap sense of humor, and seemed inordinately pleased whenever he made her laugh. Like the time he'd come out of her closet wearing a knit hat at a rakish angle, or—

She stopped her own thoughts as she realized she was dwelling on memories and silly things to avoid thinking about the kiss. It had been short, a mere touch of his lips on hers, but it might as well have been a marathon liplock the way her body responded. Waves of heat and sensation had swept through her, all out of proportion to the brief contact.

She thought for a moment that it was his reluctance—for he had obviously been just that—that had caused the untoward conflagration in her. Wouldn't any woman thrill to the idea of a man like Quinn driven to kiss her against his own will?

Any woman, she thought, *would thrill to the idea of Quinn kissing her, period.*

But not every woman's life was in danger, and that's what she should be thinking about, she told herself sternly. She should be thinking about what was going on in the here and now. About the fact that they could be under fire at any moment. She'd finally gotten some answers out of Quinn, but they hadn't made her feel any better. Worse, if anything. And not just because what he'd told her was grim, frightening.

Because now she was wondering if he'd finally answered her because they were likely to die here.

There's just no pleasing you, is there? she told herself sharply. It didn't help.

How on earth had she, boring, simple Hayley Cole, ended up in this mess? And no matter how she turned it over in her mind, she couldn't see herself doing anything differently than she had, couldn't see herself not going after her dog, and abandoning him to his fate when he'd dashed toward that helicopter.

But she was honest enough to realize that if she had done just that, they would likely both be safe at home right now. Quinn would probably have just ignored the dog, the helicopter would have lifted off with the intended passengers only and she would have always wondered about that strange, unmarked aircraft. From the safety of her home, with her beloved dog at her feet.

Of course, if the house had still blown up, things might have changed. She would have had to tell authorities what she'd seen then, and she'd have ended up mixed up in all this anyway, albeit from a much safer place. She would have—

A memory suddenly shot through her mind, of the first day here, when she'd peered over the loft railing at Liam's laptop screen. Only this time it wasn't the image of the inferno that had been Vicente's home that struck her, it was the two words she'd been able to hear from her vantage point.

Explosion.

Leak.

He hadn't meant the explosion had been caused by some sort of gas leak.

Her thoughts were tumbling now, faster and faster.

He'd meant the house had been blown up because there was an information leak. And it had to be that same leak that had allowed the men outside to find them in this remote, isolated place that should have been safe.

If all the people who worked for Quinn were like the three she'd met, it was hard to believe the leak could be one of his own. In fact, she didn't believe it; those men were utterly loyal to him, and there was no reason to think he didn't inspire the same feeling in others.

It's what he inspires in you that you should be worried about.

That little voice had been nagging at her lately, and it was getting harder and harder to shut it off. And no amount of telling herself she was suffering from some variation of Stockholm syndrome had seemed to help.

And now that she knew the truth about Vicente,

knew that Quinn and his crew were indeed on the side of the angels…well, she didn't know what now. And there wasn't time to figure it out.

She made herself walk around the cabin, checking every stash of weapons Quinn had left. It took her a moment to realize that he'd placed things so that no matter where you were or in what room, there was a weapon within easy reach. You'd never have to move more than five feet. And while easily accessible, some were also hidden, so that if you knew they were there you could get them without being noticed. The smaller handgun between the chair cushions, the deadly look-ing grenade dropped into a coffee mug, indiscernible unless you were on top of it.

She'd seen him move the sofa away from the wall then put it back, so went to look there. A large, lethal-looking knife was pinned between the back of the sofa and the wall, hilt protruding upward, and hidden by an extra pillow that looked as if it had just been put there to get it out of the way.

She spun around at the sound of Cutter's nails—she really needed to trim those, it had been on her list to do that next morning—on the floor, headed her way. Quinn was behind him, his hands empty now, his traps obviously set.

His gaze flicked from the pillow she'd just put back in place to her face. "What are you doing?"

"Believe me, if I was going to try and slit your throat, I would have done it long before now."

To her amazement, he grinned, a lopsided, heart-stealing grin like the one that had flashed when he'd cracked that joke about missing the lesson about being outnumbered. And her pulse reacted in the same way; it leaped and began to race.

The atmosphere between them changed with an almost audible snap. Became charged, heated. She lowered her eyes, but she could feel him still looking at her, could feel his gaze on her as if it were a physical thing. They were alone here now, except for Cutter, who seemed delighted to have finally gotten exactly that result.

To cover her own reaction, she hastily spoke.

"Why aren't they gone, if it's Vicente they want?"

The question had occurred to her as she was checking the various weapons. She realized it was probably wishful thinking, that they might abandon this fight to go after the man they really wanted, but it did seem a logical question to her.

"Because they don't know where he's going. Yet."

Quinn added the final word with a bite of anger; Hayley didn't envy the person who was the leak, when Quinn finally found him. And find him he would, she had no doubt of that, if for no other reason than she knew he would never give up until he did.

"But if you have a leak, they will know soon, won't they?"

He'd been loading up more explosives and trip wires into a pack, but at her words his gaze shot back to her face. "You really don't miss much, do you?"

"Happens when I figure my life depends on knowing what's going on," she said, managing to keep the sarcasm in her tone to a minimum.

To her surprise, he grinned again. Rather lopsided, but still pulse-speeding.

"You've got a knack for this, you know?"

Hayley frowned. Why was he being so nice, so normal? All of a sudden he was talking, saying nice things to her.

"Come on, Cutter dog," he said, and headed for the front door this time. He reached out and hit the light switch by the door, plunging the room into a darkness only eased by a little overflow from the kitchen. This way he wouldn't be silhouetted in the doorway, she realized, a too-tempting target for the men no doubt planning their next attack.

"Stay inside," Quinn said. And then they were gone again, man and dog. Leaving behind the woman who had just figured out the answer to her own question.

They were still here because they had an easier, faster way to find out where the man who could destroy them had been taken. They had, almost at their fingertips and certainly outnumbered, the man who had sent him there.

They were staying to get Quinn.

Chapter 28

She watched as Quinn slipped off the now-empty vest; he'd gotten done what he'd gone out there to do.

"So if you aren't some kind of paramilitary outfit, what are you?"

Quinn gave her a sideways glance, showing he'd heard the fourth question she'd shot at him in the same number of minutes, but again, he didn't answer.

He was cooking, quickly, in the manner of someone who doubted they'd have time later but knew they needed the fuel. He'd resorted to eggs, and tossed some other things into a big scramble in a skillet. Every now and then he'd toss a chunk of the ham he'd efficiently diced to Cutter, who caught it with ease and whuffed his thanks. When it was done, he scooped up half of it onto a plate and held it out to her.

"You should eat now."

The unspoken "because you may not get the chance

later" registered, but she didn't say anything. She was too busy staring at him; he'd wrapped his share of the results in a flour tortilla, like a burrito.

"There are few foods that can't be wrapped in a tortilla," he said when he saw her look. "Less messy and more portable than a sandwich, same effect. And no dishes."

She could see his point. "Where'd you learn that?"

"My ex."

"Your ex?" she said, startled both at that bit of information, and that he'd revealed it. He seemed almost startled himself, and seemed to try to cover it with a joke.

"Hard to believe some woman actually married me, isn't it?"

The grin flashed again, and any hope she might not react so strongly to it vanished as her pulse leaped yet again. Damn the man. Never mind all the guns and grenades, that grin was his most lethal weapon. To her, anyway.

Which made her realize rather ruefully the problem wasn't him, but her.

"It's not hard to believe," she said. "Just hard to believe you ever left this job of yours long enough to marry some woman."

He seemed to hesitate, then gave a half shrug. "I didn't," he said, his voice oddly soft. "That was the problem."

So he was a workaholic? It didn't surprise her. But somehow this seemed a little different. Being fiercely dedicated to keeping someone like Vicente safe seemed different from being addicted to spreadsheets or the next microchip. But she supposed the end result was the same if you were the wife who barely saw her husband.

"So she left you? Because of your work?"

He grimaced. "Let's just say she didn't share my dedication." His tone held the finality of a man through discussing a subject he hadn't wanted to let come up in the first place. So much for the personal revelations, Hayley thought, although she longed to ask more, much more. She wanted to know who this man was, why he got under her skin so easily.

She finally took her first bite of the concoction on the plate, and was pleasantly surprised. It didn't just taste like the individual ingredients he'd mixed. Somehow the combination was savory and appetizing in a new way.

Handy guy to have around, she thought, her mouth quirking. Flies helicopters, shoots straight, good with explosives, cool under fire and he can cook, too.

"When will they attack again?"

"If they haven't already, I'm guessing they'll wait until the dead hours."

"Charming phrase."

"It's just what we call the time when most people are the most deeply asleep. Varies with the person, but two in the morning to about four or five is optimum."

"For them, you mean."

"Yes. So you should get some rest now."

"Me? Seems you should be the one resting."

"I'll be fine."

"I don't want fine. You're the one between us and them. I'd prefer well rested and ready, thank you."

He drew back sharply, his eyes widening. And then, to her shock, he laughed. It was a gravelly sort of laugh, rough, as if it didn't escape very often, and no one seemed more surprised than he did at the sound of it.

"That," he said, "was a very concise assessment."

"And true. Isn't it?"

"You're not helpless."

"I know."

"Question is, could you take that kill shot if you had to?"

"I...don't know."

"What if they hurt him?" he asked, gesturing at Cutter.

"Yes." It came out strongly, certainly. And then, without thinking, she added, "Or you."

Again surprise flashed across his face. "Me?"

"Is no one allowed to want to protect you? Is it always the other way around?"

"I don't need protecting. That's my job."

"It always comes back to that, then? Are you that wrapped up in being the big strong man, the protector, that you can't accept it from someone else?"

He took the last bite of his tortilla, ignoring her now.

"Is that also why your wife left?"

He quickly washed the skillet he'd used. Silently.

Driven by some need she didn't quite understand to break through this man's formidable defenses, Hayley pressed on. She seemed to irritate him easily enough, but now she'd gotten a laugh out of him, and she wanted more. She wanted more laughing, more smiles, that rare and precious grin. She wanted to know who he really was, why he was who he was, what had brought him here, not just to this place but to this work. She wanted to know now what drove him so hard, wanted to know if he ever stopped, what would make him stop.

She wanted his whole damned life history, inside and out, and the fact that she wanted all that so much she'd practically forgotten about the men outside and the dire situation they were in was not lost on her.

"Or could she not handle what kind of work you do?

Is that the real reason she left, she couldn't deal with a man who has to arm himself to go to work?"

He put the skillet away and finally turned to look at her. "Speaking from experience?"

"It nearly split up my parents, yes," she said. "My mother had a hard time with realizing every time she sent him out the door he might not come back."

"It's a hazard of the job."

"And yours?"

"We're not talking about mine."

"I am."

"Then stop." He finished clearing the kitchen, leaving her to deal with her own plate and fork.

"Quinn—"

"Will you just leave it?"

"I can't."

He let out a compressed breath. Started to walk past her.

"I need to know."

He stopped. In front of her. Practically on top of her.

"We could die here. I need to know who you are, why you are—"

His mouth came down on hers, cutting her off. Shock immobilized her. Then, as if every nerve in her body had been jolted into awareness, heat flooded her. For an instant it seemed as if he were as stunned as she at the unexpected and sudden conflagration. But then he moved, encircling her with his arms, pressing her against him as he deepened the kiss.

Her every nerve was sizzling. She couldn't feel her knees anymore, and her arms felt heavy, weak. But it didn't matter, none of it mattered, not as long as he was there, holding her, she wouldn't fall, he wouldn't let her. All that mattered was his mouth, coaxing, probing, tasting.

It was going through her in pulses now, that heat, that surging, delicious heat, like nothing she'd ever known. Some tiny part of her brain tried to insist it was because it had been so long, but she knew it wasn't that, knew it had never been like this in her life because she'd never kissed a man like Quinn before.

No, not that, she thought as, after what seemed an eternity, he at last pulled away. Not a man *like* Quinn. Because there was no other man like Quinn, there was only Quinn.

For a moment she wished could be endless he just stood there, staring down at her. He looked as stunned as she felt. He started to speak, then stopped, as if he were rattled. He shook his head as if to clear it, and she felt a jolt of reassurance; he was feeling it, too, this huge, powerful thing that had swamped her. It wasn't one-way.

And it seemed vitally important that it not be one-way.

"Quinn," she whispered, a little startled at the low, husky sound of it.

He drew back, shook his head again, sharply this time. For a moment his fingers tightened on her shoulders. She held her breath, thinking he might pull her close for another melting kiss, then another, and—

He pushed her back. Gently but definitely.

"You—" He had to stop to clear his throat, which ameliorated the pushing away a little. He reached for a small automatic handgun from the table. "Your time would be better spent learning to handle this than asking questions I'm not going to answer."

She clung to that break in his voice, that moment

when he hadn't quite been the tough, cool, unflappable Quinn. But his words were too flat, too grim to deny. The realization that she might really be in the midst of a pitched gun battle soon was beyond chilling, it sent icy tendrils curling through her, draining the wonderful heat he'd kindled.

She fought for calm, fought not to give in to the simple plea for another kiss that kept trying to rise to her lips. What was she, some weak-willed wimp of a woman, so immobilized by a man's kiss that she couldn't even think?

Yes, she admitted wryly, at this moment, she was.

She drew herself up, sucked in some air. She reached out and took the weapon from him, careful not to become a complete cliché and run her fingers over his hand. It was heavier than she'd expected, and she had to exert more effort to lift it. Then she made herself speak in a level, composed voice.

"Then teach me," she said.

For a moment he just looked at her, oddly, as if he was somehow proud of her. It warmed her even though she wasn't sure what exactly he would be proud of. Or how she'd gotten to where it mattered so much to her.

The only thing she was sure of was that kiss. And that, for now, she had to forget it. It had probably been a fluke anyway, born of adrenaline and too long alone.

And with that unsatisfying explanation, she was able to turn her mind to the matter at hand. Learning to shoot a handgun.

Learning to, if necessary, kill.

Chapter 29

Hayley was, Quinn thought, a lot tougher than she looked. She might seem quiet, even reserved at times, but there was a lot of fire behind that calm facade. And courage, but he'd known that all along. True, life would be easier now if she'd taken down a couple of those guys out back, but she'd held them until he took care of his own, and by then they'd thought better of their plan and scrambled back up the bluff rather than face the gutsy woman with the shotgun any longer.

And now she had set about learning the small handgun he'd given her with a fierce intensity that told him she understood what they faced. And he realized that while she might be a brand-new amateur with the Kimber, her nerve wouldn't fail, and that was more than half the battle.

She would do what she had to do. Which cut the odds against them suddenly in half.

Yes, a lot of fire....

He shook his head sharply, then again, wondering what the hell had gotten into him. The moment his mouth had touched hers he knew what had been a strategic decision had been a very, very bad one.

Quinn.

The husky whisper echoed in his mind as if the slight breeze was carrying it in an endless loop.

He'd heard his name whispered before. He'd heard it spoken, yelled, screamed. Heard it said neutrally, heard it in friendship, laughter, or anger and panic.

He'd never heard it said in a way that sent a shiver down his spine. Or made a rush of heat follow that path. Or made him wonder if his knees were going to hold out.

He steadied himself, and it was enough of an effort that it irritated him all over again.

She'd stripped, reassembled and dry-fired the weapon repeatedly, until he was sure she had it down. But nothing could prepare her for the recoil, the noise, the actual act of shooting except doing it. He figured they could spare one magazine of ammo, no more. He had to hope she was as quick at learning the actual shooting as she had been everything else. He didn't need her to be a sharpshooter, he just needed her to get close.

"Cutter?"

The dog, who had been snoozing comfortably on the couch, apparently satisfied they didn't need his supervision for this, came alert instantly. Before Quinn could say another word, Cutter was off the couch and at his side, looking up expectantly.

"Let's go do a little recon," he said, and heard the little whuffing sound he'd learned was assent. The dog couldn't possibly understand "recon," tempting though it was to think the clever guy understood perfectly, but Quinn guessed the "Let's go," was pretty clear.

"Where are you two going?"

"To pick out a firing range," Quinn said.

"But…won't that draw their attention?"

"Honey, we've got their attention, I promise you." He'd drawled it out like a joke, he'd meant it as a joke, there was no reason for her to flush as if he'd meant the endearment in the usual way. Because he hadn't. The fact that it wasn't a word he usually used even as a joke didn't change that.

"I'm actually going to go out and shoot this now?" she asked, gesturing with the pistol, carefully keeping her finger off the trigger and safely resting on the trigger guard, as he'd instructed.

"Nothing can replace actually putting rounds through it," he said. "Besides, it'll throw them off guard. Make them wonder."

She got there quickly. "You mean they'll wonder what we're shooting at?"

"Or who? If we're lucky, maybe they'll wonder if they aren't alone out here."

"Then why don't we—I—just step out and start firing?"

"I'd rather direct their curiosity somewhere else."

She looked thoughtful, then barely a second later said, "Because if they're having to watch two places, their attention will be divided."

Yes, she was quick all right.

They were maybe a couple of hundred yards from the cabin, a midnight trip that made the one that had started this whole thing seem like a stroll down a peaceful city sidewalk. The moon was full, and her nerves were screaming that they were lit up like a stage. Not only was it unfamiliar ground, but Hayley knew they were out there, watching. A fact that was pounded home when, after setting Cutter to watch their backs, Quinn told her in a harsh, low voice that she had nine minutes to get minimally familiar with firing the weapon, no more.

"A minute for them to react, five for them to figure out where they think we are, and three for them to decide what to do. If they're still where I think they are, it'll take them ten minutes to work their way over here. I want us back inside long before that."

He'd made her trade her white blouse for a dark sweatshirt, and used what looked like electrician's tape to cover her white sneakers. And he hadn't helped her over the rough ground, and she didn't know whether to be offended at his lack of assistance, or flattered that he'd been confident she could do it herself.

She'd finally decided he had enough to think about without having some needy female on his hands. But thinking about his hands immediately set her to thinking about his mouth, and there was nothing to be gained on that track except shaky hands and too-quick breathing at the memory of that unexpected, fire-inducing kiss.

She steadied herself, focusing on the target he'd laid out for her. He'd marked the side of the bluff itself with some kind of paint he'd taken from the locker, paint that put off a slight glow. The target was under an overhang that looked as if it could go at any second, which made her question the wisdom of the location, but then again, if the bluff did collapse, it would cover the target and any evidence of what they'd been doing. Better the bad guys think they were facing two expert marksmen, not one and a brand newbie.

She wasn't sure what good the target was going to do though; in the darkness of the overhang she could see the faintly glowing outline, but how on earth would she know if she was even close to hitting it?

Quinn answered the question for her as he took out what looked like a short, clunky telescope and focused it on the target. Night vision? She barely had time to wonder before he told her to fire three rounds in succession.

The moment she fired the first shot, Hayley realized three things. The kick wasn't quite as bad as she'd expected, the noise was much worse and Quinn had, not surprisingly, picked the perfect place.

Perfect because, the way the sound echoed around under the lip of this part of the bluff, she guessed from distance you'd have no idea how many shots or shooters there really were.

"You're up and to the left. Try and compensate, but don't overdo it. Three more."

She shifted her aim level and right, tried again.

"Better. Empty it."

When she was done, they headed back at a crouching run. Cutter was out in front of them, pausing for a second or two to test the breeze before glancing back at them and starting out again, as if to make sure they'd read his all clear and were still with him. If she hadn't been looking for him, hadn't been able to spot the gleam of his dark eyes and the slightly lighter fur on his legs and lower body, the nearly black dog would have been invisible.

"You," Quinn said to Cutter when they were safely back inside, "are damned near as good as anybody I've worked with. Better than some, back in the day."

He accompanied the praise with a thorough scratch of the dog's ears. The usually cool Cutter practically wiggled with delight, managing to look smugly proud at the same time.

"How much does he understand?" Quinn asked.

Hayley smiled, despite the fact that she was in the most ominous position of her life. "I know he understands a lot. He's got an amazingly large vocabulary, for a dog. Sometimes he seems to understand context, too. Like when the wind blew my side door shut, locking my house keys inside. Now, he knows the car keys, he brings them to me, because he gets to go for a ride. But the house keys are on a different ring. I sent him through the doggy door for the car keys, because then I could unlock the car and use the garage opener. He came back with the house keys."

Quinn looked startled. He gave Cutter an assessing look, as if his opinion was shifting yet again.

"In the beginning," Hayley said, "on our vet's recommendation, I took him to obedience school. Not because he needed it, more of a bonding thing. What a waste."

"He didn't learn?"

"He didn't have to. He blew through everything in the first day, then sat there looking at me like 'Now can we go do something interesting?' The trainer asked me to bring him back so she could test him."

"Test him?"

Hayley nodded. "She started out with colors and shapes. Blue cube, red ball, yellow triangle. He got the right one every time. Then she went to a red one of each, told him what shape to get. Every time."

"Is that…unusual?"

"A bit. But then she got into trickier stuff. She'd hide stuff from him. A lot of dogs can't make the jump, for instance, that the ball you just had in your hand is now behind the chair, even if they saw you put it there. They just know it's gone. Cutter got it out of a closed box."

"Smart dog, all right."

Quinn gave the dog another sideways look as she went on. "But then it got really interesting. She showed him a picture of a rag doll. He went and got it out of a pile of toys. Same thing with a plastic bird, and a small basket, so she was pretty sure he hadn't seen any of them before."

"Hayley?"

"What?"

"Stop pacing."

She hadn't even realized she had been. Talking about Cutter, and the trainer's amazement at his intelligence, had distracted her from her worry, but her subconscious apparently hadn't forgotten that there were armed men out there waiting for their moment to strike. She wondered if that was why Quinn had let her ramble on like that.

"Sorry," she muttered, and stopped midstride. But as if her body had to do something, she felt the faintest of tremors start.

"Why don't you sit down?"

She did, mainly because she was afraid the trembling would get worse and she might simply fall down.

"Why now?" she said. "I was fine when we were outside, when we were most likely to get shot at, but now I fall apart?"

"It's natural," Quinn said with a shrug. He gave Cutter a last pat and walked over to her. He seemed even taller, towering as he stood next to the sofa. And then he sat down next to her, something he'd never done before.

Quinn looked at Cutter, who had quietly padded

across the room to sit at their feet and look at them with benevolent pleasure.

"No idea where he came from?"

"Another planet is my best guess."

Quinn's gaze shot back to her. After a split second that crooked grin flashed across his face. "Now that wouldn't surprise me."

Almost involuntarily she smiled back. She had, she realized, stopped trembling. In fact, she'd felt better, calmer, since the moment he'd sat down beside her. She told herself it was simply that he was, still, distracting her from the threat outside.

Oh, he's distracting you, all right.

And what better way to spend what could be her last hours than distracted by a man like this one?

An odd sensation flooded her then, not unlike the adrenaline that had coursed through her when she'd been outside, firing that pistol at the target she could barely see. It was a sort of recklessness she'd rarely felt in her life. She wanted to know.

She needed to know.

She *had* to know.

"Quinn?"

"What?"

It took a very deep breath to steady her enough to say the words.

"Kiss me again."

For a split second he looked startled. "I'm not sure that would be a good idea."

"I don't care."

"Hayley—"

"I know you just kissed me before to stop me asking questions. Should I start asking again?"

His mouth quirked at that. But he reached out,

cupped her face in his hands. She made herself fight the urge to lower her eyes, to look away. He was so damned intense, it was more difficult than she ever would have imagined simply to meet his gaze.

She was trembling again. But this time it had nothing to do with fear.

Chapter 30

Every instinct he had in him was screaming at him not to do it. He'd learned to trust those instincts, and more than once they had saved his life, or other lives.

Now, he wasn't fighting them.

He was ignoring them.

Because he wanted, more than he could remember ever wanting anything, to do exactly what Hayley had asked. Even knowing her simple, stunning request was born out of fear, the fear they might not survive this. He knew they had a good chance, with a certainty born of his faith in his own skills, his experience and what he knew of the disorganization of their enemy. They might run a tight ship in their criminal enterprise, but there were too many big egos for them to make an efficient fighting team.

But even knowing what was driving her didn't slow his response to her simple yet shattering request. Be-

cause he wanted to kiss her, to sample that hot, hon-
eyed sweetness again. He wanted the taste of her, the
feel of her.

Taking advantage of her fears, of the situation, would
be wrong. Unethical. She wasn't a client, so he wasn't
bound by those rules, but she wasn't here willingly,
either. She was trapped in a situation not of her own
making, thanks to his having to make a snap decision
to protect the operation.

He still wanted to kiss her. He wanted the rush of
sensation that had rippled through him, seductive, ad-
dictive. He wanted to hear her say his name again, in
that husky, stunned voice that sent delicious shivers
racing through him like nothing in his life ever had.

Truth be told, he wanted a lot more than just a kiss.
But reality was, and there wasn't going to be time for
anything else.

But he would take time for this, and damn the consequences.

The tiny gasp that broke from her in the instant his
lips touched hers destroyed his last reservations with a
power much stronger than the faint sound warranted.

It was as hot, as fierce, as consuming as he'd remembered. And suddenly he knew why she'd asked for this.
And he understood.

Then the feel of her mouth seemed to destroy his ca-
pacity for thought. He asked for more, his tongue flick-
ing over her lips. They parted, just slightly, allowing
him to probe, to taste. She was as sweet, as tempting as
before, only this time his goal wasn't to quiet her questions, it was to drink all of what he'd only sipped before.

He was barely aware of what he was doing to add
to the fire, stroking, caressing, knew only that the taut
yet soft feel of her drew his hands onward. She moved,

not to pull away but to press closer. He held her there, marveling that he'd never really noticed how incredible that womanly curve was, from hip to waist, how perfectly made for his hands.

Her fingers tightened on his shoulders, then slid down his back, leaving trails of fire behind them. And suddenly any thought that he was in control of this vanished. He'd never known anything like it, and he wasn't sure it could be controlled. He wasn't sure he wanted to control it.

And that alone should have scared the hell out of him, he who had spent his adult life and half his childhood trying to do just that, control every circumstance. But it didn't scare him, he was too revved up, too pumped to allow fear to take hold. More than he'd ever been in any battle, anywhere.

And then her tongue began its own hesitant exploration and his muscles clenched in response, so fiercely he was vaguely surprised his bones didn't snap. His body was on full alert, ready to discard reality and take what it wanted. It was a feeling he'd never experienced before, a consuming, fiery need he wouldn't have believed existed if he weren't being swallowed up by it himself.

He felt an odd sensation at his waist, realized her hands had slid downward and were tugging at his shirt. Just that knowledge threatened to destroy the last little bit of his control. As if her actions invited his, he slid his hands up beneath the soft sweatshirt, savoring the silken skin, feeling the slight ridges of her ribs. He reached the curve of her breasts, felt the soft flesh round into his palms. He groaned, unable to stop the escape of the harsh, almost helpless sound.

Cutter barked. Quietly. It sounded odd, almost reluctant, as if he didn't want to interrupt them with that reality.

Reality.

A tiny part of his trained mind that was still functioning sent up a warning, a warning he'd ignored until now.

With a tremendous effort he broke the kiss. Hayley's small sound of protest sent shivers through him, and nearly sent him straight back to her sweet, soft mouth.

But Cutter barked again, still sounding reluctant, yet more definite this time.

Quinn looked at the dog. If it was possible for a dog to look apologetic, this one was doing it. The moment he saw Quinn looking at him, the animal trotted across to the front corner of the cabin, then looked back.

As clearly as if he'd spoken, Quinn understood the dog's message.

They're coming.

Reality slammed back into him like an iceberg, and that lovely, burgeoning heat vanished.

"It's them, isn't it?" she asked, her eyes starting to refocus, but still touched with the remnants of that exploding heat.

He nodded. He sat up, ordering a body resistant to the abrupt cessation of the most pleasure it had ever known, to stand down. There was a battle coming, and he couldn't let this, whatever the hell it was, cloud his thinking.

Nor could he resist reaching out and lifting her chin with a gentle finger.

"Hayley."

It was a voice he'd never heard from himself, a voice full of longing, need and promises he'd never made before.

She met his gaze, steadily, and he could almost see her gathering herself to deal with what was coming. Admiration spiked through him. Yes, she would do, he thought.

"It wasn't a fluke, Hayley."

Surprise flashed in her eyes, confirming his guess that this was what had been behind her request. Not that it changed anything. He spared a split second for regret, knowing full well that when this was over she'd likely want to walk away and never think of this, and that he would have to let her.

But first, he had to keep her alive to do it.

She'd been wobbly at first, as if Quinn's strength-sapping kiss had somehow liquefied her bones. But Cutter, now that he'd interrupted them, was indicating they had little time before the enemy was upon them, pacing anxiously by the door, growling, casting impatient glances at Quinn.

But she was steadier now. Something about the act of picking up a handgun you actually expected to have to use did that, she guessed.

Quinn had given her a holster that clipped onto the waistband of her jeans, and she slipped the small semiautomatic into it. She slipped on the vest he'd given her as well, then took up the shotgun.

When she was done, he was already at the door. He'd suited up quickly, wearing his own vest of a different kind, loaded with weaponry and ammo. Cutter was dancing at his feet in his eagerness to get at it. Two of a kind, she thought, her throat tight.

"This could get nasty," he said. "Maybe you should get in the bedroom now and—"

"Don't even think about it."

She said it with more bravado than she was really feeling, and was surprised it sounded so steady and determined. But the upward quirk at the corner of Quinn's mouth was reward enough for much more than a declaration of a strength she wasn't sure she really possessed.

"Hang on to him." He gestured at Cutter. "I need to get to the windmill."

"You've witnessed how well that works when he's determined," she pointed out. "Why the windmill?"

"High ground. And as clever as he is, I doubt he can climb that narrow ladder."

"I'll try."

"Lock up after me."

She nodded.

He reached for the door. For an instant he paused, looking back at her. Their gazes locked, and something deep and primal and undeniable leaped between them, as if the connection were a living, breathing thing.

He moved as if he were going to kiss her again, and Hayley's pulse leaped. At the last second he stopped himself.

"Later," he muttered. It seemed he said it as much to that vivid connection as to her.

And then he was gone into the night.

Chapter 31

Cutter lasted until the first explosion.

It was distant, probably one of the mines Quinn had set, but the dog didn't care. He clawed at the door his idol had left through, clawed at the knob, trying to turn it with his paws. He whined, so loudly and insistently it tore at her. She went to try to calm him, but he spun away from her. From a yard away he stared at her, then the door, intensity radiating from him.

I have to go, I need to help him.

Hayley shook her head sharply. If the situation weren't so dire, she'd laugh at herself for putting human thoughts into a dog's head, even if that look in his eyes was more commanding than she'd ever seen in some humans, let alone an animal. No wonder sheep did what he wanted; it was all she could do not to herself, not to just open the door and let him out there.

Another explosion—was it closer, or was that her

imagination?—sounded. Still Cutter stood there, silently demanding she let him out into the melee.

Quinn would understand, she thought. Whatever code he lived by, it didn't include staying behind while others fought. Apparently Cutter lived by the same code. And at this moment it didn't even seem ridiculous to think that a dog had a code.

A third explosion. Definitely closer. And this time it was followed by the sound of gunfire. Not the rapid automatic-spray technique of their attackers, just steady, single shots fired with calm purpose. Rafer Crawford might be the team sniper, but Quinn was no slouch.

She heard several shots before the automatic return fire started. Bursts of it, fired by men whose strength came from firepower instead of skill. The steady, calm response of Quinn's shots continued; obviously he wasn't rattled by the attack.

Cutter, on the other hand, was about to claw his way through the door. She crouched beside the frantic dog.

"I know you want out there, but it's too dangerous, you need to stay here, where it's safe."

The dog gave her a swipe of his tongue over her cheek, as if in appreciation for the sentiment, but went right back to clawing at the door.

The next explosion was much, much closer. It had to be, it was so much louder. Cutter barked, a booming, angry sound. He looked at her, again with that demanding expression in those expressive eyes.

Out of nowhere a thought hit her. That explosion. Had it been louder because it was closer?

Or louder because it wasn't a mine, muffled by the earth around it?

She ran to the window. The now-familiar tableau was painted an eerie silver by the moonlight. She could just see the edge of the windmill, the high ground Quinn had headed for. And several feet off the ground, smoke curled out from one of the vertical legs. Even as she looked, something flew through the air and hit the leg. Another explosion, bright yellow flames a shocking burst of color in the silver light. More smoke and some debris burst from the base of the tower.

Explosives. The man draped like a suicide bomber.

They were trying to take it down. Apparently unable to get any closer because of Quinn's deadly accurate aim, they were trying to take it down with explosives, lobbed from a safe distance. She couldn't see them, both because they were far enough away and they were out of the field of vision of the small window.

If they managed to collapse that leg, the whole thing would go. With Quinn in it.

The sound of Cutter running spun her around. The dog was headed toward the back door. She called to him, but he kept going. Much as he had that night this had all began.

She watched in shock as the dog reached the door, reared up on his hind legs and batted at the lever-style handle with his front paws. She started toward him, but before she got there he had gotten enough pressure on the handle to release the lock. The crazy dog had opened the door.

"Cutter, no!"

His dark head turned, and he gave her a look she could only describe as apologetic. And then he was gone, racing into the fray with all the determination of the man he was following.

For an instant she just stood there, staring at the empty place where the dog had been. The sounds of more gunfire and another explosion echoed from the bluff just outside the now-open back door. If that door hadn't had that lever-style handle, Cutter would still be safely inside. She should have known the too-clever dog would figure out that he could open it if he just got his paws in the right place. And she had inadvertently aided his escape by not immediately throwing the dead bolt on that door.

She didn't do it now. Anybody who came through that door who wasn't Quinn or Cutter she was going to shoot, she thought with determination. She darted to the small, lens-style window. Cutter was racing down the open space at the foot of the bluff in an odd, zigzagging pattern it took her a moment to figure out. When she did, her breath caught; he was dodging the mines Quinn had buried. As if he not only knew the threat they posed, but remembered where each and every one was.

To her surprise he headed, not toward the windmill and Quinn, but to the south. He skidded to a halt just past the outcropping of rock that had sheltered Quinn and him before. He crouched there, looking ready to pounce, his gaze and that powerful nose pointed upward.

Her fingers tightened around the shotgun still in her hand. Quinn could handle himself, as she'd seen. He was a dangerous man, a formidable opponent. And he was armed and ready, trained to fight against just such an enemy as this. She knew that as surely as she knew his eyes were blue, even if she didn't know where he'd gotten that training.

Cutter, on the other hand, was a dog. An impossibly smart, clever and resourceful dog, but still, just a dog. Something she had to force herself to remember at times like this, when he seemed to exhibit an intelligence far beyond ordinary canine capabilities.

The tumble of a rock down the bluff, just a few feet away, brought her out of the reverie she could ill afford. Her gaze shot upward, just in time to see a rope coming over the lip of the bluff to the south. And she realized with a shiver that Cutter hadn't headed for Quinn because he knew they were closer than that.

They weren't just trying to take down Quinn's tower. They were coming after her.

Chapter 32

They would kill Cutter. Because he would try to stop them. She had no doubts about that. Just as she no longer had any doubts about the nature of this enemy. The story Quinn had told her had made it clear they were merciless, and would do anything to get what they wanted.

And what they wanted was in Quinn's head. Anything or anyone else was just in the way.

But she wasn't in the way. She was here, and if she'd been thinking clearly enough, Cutter still would be, too. So why were they coming after her? Why bother, when she was so obviously harmless?

They'd been hurt, badly, by Quinn and his men in their first attack. They had to know it would take everything they had left to get to him. For all the good it would do, he would never tell them a thing. She knew that down to her bones, although it made her shudder inwardly to think of what they might do to him to try to get him to talk. What they might use on him to—

It hit her then. They wanted her, to use on him. They might not know what she was to him—couldn't know, since she herself didn't—but they did have the measure of the man. And somehow they knew he was the kind of man who would never allow an innocent to be hurt if he could stop it.

They wanted her for leverage.

For an instant she felt a flash of relief at the realization that for that, they'd need her alive. In the next instant, self-disgust filled her. Had she always been such a coward? Quinn had risked his life to keep Vicente safe, and now was risking it for her; she had belatedly realized he wasn't in that tower just for the high ground, but to lead them away from her.

Cutter barked, and she heard a shot. Close. Too close.

She grabbed up an extra box of shotgun shells and shoved them into the one empty vest pocket that remained. She yanked the door handle until it unlatched. She kicked the door open, simultaneously putting both hands back on the shotgun, ready to fire.

Cutter had dug in, literally, behind and below the outcropping. Amazingly, he was in a place where the angle made it impossible for anybody from above to get a clear shot at him. Did he somehow sense that?

This was not the time to dwell on the wonders of this particular canine mind. She could see the tracks Cutter had left in the dry dirt, thrown into stark relief by the moonlight. It didn't really matter whether he knew where the mines were, or maybe smelled them, he'd gotten through and therefore his was the path she should follow.

Assuming the mines just weren't set so that his slighter weight wouldn't trigger them....

She shook off the thought. It didn't matter. She'd had enough of this, enough of being a helpless pawn in all this.

"God made man, Sam Colt made them equal." She tightened her grip on the shotgun as she whispered Quinn's words. "Or in this case, Mr. Mossberg."

She made her way through Quinn's minefield safely, thanks to Cutter trailblazing the way. The dog's ears swiveled, and she knew he heard her coming. But he never looked away from the vertical outcropping, as if he expected someone to pop out any second.

And if he did, she thought, he probably had very good reason. This was Cutter, after all.

She thought quickly. The back of the cabin and thus her position was also out of the range of vision of anyone on the other side of the rocks. Here in the shadows no way they could see her, even with moonlight pouring down, without sticking their head out. Out into her line of fire.

And if they were looking somewhere else....

"A little noise would be good, dog," she whispered, wishing the dog would bark again from his protected spot, draw their attention.

She knew he couldn't have heard her, but in that moment Cutter let out a trumpeting volley of barking like she'd never heard from the dog before. If she hadn't been so focused, she would have been staring at him in surprise.

A head and shoulders popped up like a tin target in a county fair shooting gallery. Hayley had always been good at those. And her eyes were completely adjusted to the silver light now. The man aimed a handgun in Cutter's direction. She snapped the shotgun to her shoulder and fired in one smooth, easy motion. A satisfying yelp echoed off the back of the cabin. The next thing she saw was a pair of feet in ridiculously shined boots and a set of back pockets over a skinny backside as her target tried to scramble back. She peppered the backside just because, and heard a string of curses that she was guessing called into question her parentage and her occupation.

Much easier than skeet, really, she thought, barely suppressing a grin. "Shoot at my dog, will you," she muttered.

Cutter was quiet now, and back to looking up. The rope over the lip of the bluff moved slightly, and Hayley lifted the shotgun once more. She'd lose efficiency at that distance, and she'd have to compensate for shooting at such a sharp angle, but she could still make anyone who looked over in response to the injured man's yells very sorry.

Someone did, a round-faced man who looked as if this was the last place he wanted to be. She reinforced the feeling with two quick shots that took the edge of the bluff almost out from under him, and she hoped from his yell, had put his right arm out of action.

Her breath caught in her throat when Cutter suddenly burst from his cover and headed back toward her. He paused for barely a second, just long enough for her to run a hand over his head, and for him to give her a wet-nosed nudge. And then he was moving again, heading around the corner of the cabin.

Heading for Quinn.

She glanced back, but there was no more sound of movement except for the first man crawling painfully away, scuffing his shiny shoes in his effort to move with shotgun pellets in his backside. And then a volley of gunfire, so many shots in succession she couldn't count them, came from the direction Cutter had gone.

She swiftly replaced the fired shells. Then she followed her dog.

The moment she rounded the corner of the house, she saw Quinn had a problem; the wooden leg of the windmill was burning, and the flames were climbing the rickety-looking structure at an alarming rate. She guessed the thing was reinforced, as was everything around here, but that didn't mean the smoke alone couldn't kill him.

Cutter apparently sensed the danger as well, because once again he ran a crazy, zigzag pattern across the open space to get to Quinn.

A shot rang out from somewhere near the barn. Cutter yelped and went down.

Hayley screamed.

Cutter struggled to get up, drawing another shot. This time she saw where it came from. It was the human-size door in the big sliding barn door nearest her. In the crouching kind of run she'd seen Quinn use, she made it to the old, rusted-out tractor. She braced herself against the rotted seat. Gauged the angle from there to where Cutter lay, figured he had to be on the side to her right. She fired three rounds in rapid succession, spacing them from knee height to head height on that side. The spread of shot was a good seven feet by three.

For an instant she held her breath. She heard what sounded like a piece of metal hit the ground, followed by a faint thud. Just the sound she'd have expected from a dropped weapon and a wounded man falling. Maybe dead, she wasn't sure she cared, not looking over at where Cutter lay, helpless, maybe dying....

She took a step toward her dog. A loud pinging sound echoed from the tractor. A bullet; somebody had obviously spotted her. Not surprising after all the noise she'd made.

But she had to get to Cutter. He wasn't dead, he just needed help, he couldn't be dead, not Cutter. He was too alive, too vital, too clever.

The moment she moved again another shot hit the tractor, this time shearing off a piece of metal that sliced at her cheek. She was effectively pinned down.

"Cutter!" she screamed, watching, telling herself she really had seen the dog move in response.

And then, out of the swirling smoke of the burning tower, came Quinn. He dropped the last ten feet as if it were nothing. He crouched, spun to his left. Fired several rounds at the far side of the barn, where the shots at her had come from. In the same smooth motion he grabbed something from his vest pocket and straightened, then lobbed it with amazing accuracy toward the same spot.

The explosion made her jump, even though she'd known it was coming. That corner of the barn blew inward, fire and smoke billowing.

And Quinn ran straight for Cutter. She heard more shots, from farther out, someone who must have been clear of the barn. Quinn jerked once, but kept going. In seconds he had scooped up the dog from the dirt.

He was helpless now, Hayley realized, with his arms full of dog. And, she saw with a sick feeling, he was hurt himself; a dark stream was flowing rapidly from his left shoulder. She had to cover their retreat. She stepped out from behind the tractor, firing toward the corner of the barn to where those last rounds had come from. Quinn passed her, Cutter cradled in his arms.

She kept firing, with each shot taking a step backward, toward the cabin. She emptied the shotgun, took the chance to swiftly reload three more shells, then fired again, although now it was for show and noise more than effectiveness at this distance.

"Get inside!"

She heard Quinn's yell, but her blood was up and she wasn't quite through with the pigs who had hurt her dog. She fired her last two shells. Then she heard the rapid, steady fire of a big rifle, coming from behind her, and knew Quinn was back in the fight. Only then did she do as he'd ordered.

"About time," Quinn said.

She was about to snap at him when she realized the words hadn't been directed at her. Then she heard a new, glorious sound. A helicopter. If not the same one, then a twin, shiny, black, unmarked and lethal looking.

And this one was wearing teeth, large-caliber rounds chewing up all in its path.

And in the distance, a faint line of light marked the coming of sunrise.

It was over.

Chapter 33

"Take it easy with him! He's been as much a part of this fight as any of us."

Hayley heard Quinn's order, snapped across the room from where Rafer, who had led the new team in, was applying a tidy field dressing on his upper left arm. She wanted to go to him, to embarrass him in front of everyone with a huge hug for those words, but she couldn't and wouldn't move until she knew Cutter was going to be all right. She petted him steadily in reassurance.

"Yes, sir," Teague said as he ran his hands over the dog lying on the couch where Quinn had put him when they'd staggered inside just as the cavalry had arrived. "I've stood enough guard shifts with him to know he's one of us."

Surprisingly, Quinn's wound filled her with an entirely different emotion; he'd gotten it saving her dog, he'd risked his life—and taken a bullet—doing it. But he'd kept coming, never wavering, his goal the dog, and getting him out of the line of fire. Any lingering doubts she had about the man had vanished with that act.

She waited, her thoughts so occupied by the two injured males in the room that she was only barely aware of the change in atmosphere, the new quiet and calm that had settled in. It truly was over. And so quickly she was still a little stunned; the ubiquitous and all-knowing Charlie had apparently had backup on standby from the moment they'd gone dark.

"I think he'll be okay," Teague said as he cleaned the ugly-looking furrow, while Cutter bore it stoically, as if he understood that despite the pain Teague was helping him. "It looks like it's as much a graze as anything to me. There'll be a vet standing by when we land."

"Thanks, Teague," she said.

"Thank Quinn, he ordered it."

She sucked in a breath as Rafer came up behind her shoulder. "He stays cool, uninvolved because he has to," he said to her softly, and she knew he wasn't talking about Teague. "If he gave his heart to every case, it would kill him. It's not that he doesn't care, he cares too much."

She looked sideways at the lean, rangy sniper. "I see that now."

"Problem is, he's forgotten how to let himself off the leash. Maybe you could teach him that."

Before she could think of a thing to say to that, the man had turned and gone.

Once Teague was done, Cutter began to gingerly get to his feet. Hayley tried to coax him to lie back down, but Quinn was there now, on his own feet, and stopped her.

"Best to let him, if he can."

Slowly she stood up, and watched as Quinn, now in a one-sleeved shirt and a tightly bandaged arm that matched Cutter's side, crouched down to the dog's level, laid a hand on his head and looked him straight in the eyes.

"You're a good man, Cutter Cole."

The whimsy of him giving the dog her last name made her smile. It seemed to please Cutter inordinately; his thick plume of a tail began to wag.

"My two wounded warriors," she said softly, barely aware of saying it aloud.

Quinn straightened, looked at her. She braced, waiting for him to chew her out for leaving the cabin. And then it hit her. It really was over. She was no longer an unintended hostage.

"Yes," she said abruptly. "I came outside."

"You did," Quinn said, without heat.

"You're not my father, to order me. Or my husband, to suggest. Or even my boyfriend, to request."

"I could work on that," he said, his voice still startlingly mild. "Except for the father part, of course."

She gaped at him. He looked suddenly unsettled, as if he hadn't meant to say that.

"You did what you thought you had to," he said, briskly now. "And as it turned out, it was a good thing you did. I didn't think they had enough men left to come at us effectively from two flanks."

Mollified, even pleased, she said, "There were only the two in back."

"And you took out one and sent the other scrambling."

"Cutter showed me where they were."

Quinn glanced down and smiled. The dog was sitting now, dead center between them, looking from one to the other as each spoke. "Good man," he said again, and the dog gave him his best doggy grin. Quinn laughed. And again it transformed his face. It took her a moment to think of something safe to say.

"Vicente is safe?" she asked.

"He is. As is his family. We pulled them out three hours ago."

"Good. He's a brave man."

"Yes."

"As are you."

"I have a good team."

"Not one of whom was here when you risked your life to save Cutter."

"He'd earned it. I meant what I said, he was as much a part of this fight as we were."

"But he's still just a dog."

"I'm no more sure of that than you are."

She blinked; she hadn't expected that.

"We're ready, sir," Teague said.

This time when she boarded the sleek, black helicopter, Hayley did it willingly. And this time, she was the one on the floor with Cutter, while Quinn sat and watched them both.

They lifted off into the dawn sky.

"Who are you? Will you tell me now?"

"Hayley—"

"I think we've earned that, Cutter and I."

He studied her for a long, silent moment. They were in an office on the top floor of an unmarked, three-story building in a clearing hidden by a thick forest of evergreens. It felt more like home to her than the barren, rolling land they'd left, but the presence of an apparent office building out in this rural area, with a helipad and a large warehouse the only other structures, seemed odd.

Quinn turned to Rafer and Teague, who seemed to be carefully not looking at them. "Rafe, let Charlie know what needs to be replaced and fixed at the cabin. Teague, go lock down the chopper."

The two men exchanged a look Hayley thought a little pointed, but they left without comment. Liam, Teague had told her, was closeted with Vicente, still taking down the details of his long, bloody story.

Quinn turned back to her. He gestured at the couch on the far wall, a resigned expression on his face.

She wondered why it was so hard, now that it was over, to just explain. But she sat, ready to settle in for a long story, if that's what it was. Cutter was safely in the care of a kind-eyed vet who had gone all soft at the dog's story; Hayley had trusted him instantly. And had smiled inwardly at the way Quinn had automatically leaned down and lifted the dog gently onto the examining table, and more at how he'd stroked the dog's head and assured him that he'd be okay, and that they'd be back to pick him up in a few hours.

For an instant she'd even thought the dog had pulled back a little, as if he wanted to look at the two of them together. Then he made a whuffing sound that she'd swear held a note of satisfaction, and lay down to await the vet's ministrations.

Normally, Hayley would have stayed at the vet's, but she had too many questions that demanded answers, and she wasn't about to let Quinn out of her sight until she had them. Now, he sat down beside her.

"Who are you?" she asked again when he didn't speak.

"We're a private foundation. We work on referral only."

She'd meant who was he, personally, but she figured they'd get there, and she wanted to know this, too. She wanted to know everything. And she was past worrying about what that meant.

"Protecting witnesses?"

"Not usually. This was a special case, because Vicente insisted on us. Mostly it's other things."

"Like the kidnap victim you saved."

"That was actually unusual, too, but yes."

"What else?"

He let out a compressed breath. "We take on jobs nobody else will. For people who have nowhere else to turn, or who have been let down by the people supposedly there to help."

"Like the police?"

"Sometimes…although it's usually not the cops, but the brass who have things mucked up. Or some politician who's decided what's politically expedient. And we're strictly domestic, unless a case has elements elsewhere, like the kidnapping that brought us to Vicente's attention."

"What about the military?"

"That's a pool we don't swim in. We don't do military-contract work, if that's what you're asking."

"But you're all ex-military?"

"No. Liam, for example, isn't. It's not a requirement."

"What is?"

"That you be the best at what you do."

"This team of yours here—"

"Is one of three security teams we can field. We also have a tech team, a couple of investigative teams, a transportation team and a couple of others."

Her idea of the size of this operation suddenly shifted. "That's a lot."

"We started out small, but the demand grew."

"These…private cases?"

"We tend to call them lost causes," he said.

She liked that idea. "Who runs this foundation? Who started it?"

"My…family. What's left of it."

"Quinn?"

"What?"

"Just start at the beginning. Please."

"I'm not sure where that is." He ran a hand through tousled hair. "We formed the foundation four years ago. But I guess we really started in 1988."

"What happened in 1988?"

He looked at her then, and she had the oddest feeling he was watching for her reaction to what he was about to say.

"Lockerbie."

Her breath caught. "The bombing?" She'd only been a small child when it had happened, but even so she remembered her parents' horror, the nightmare photographs she'd seen since.

He nodded. "My parents were on that plane."

I was ten…. She just stared at him as his words echoed in her head. Memories swirled, including the later, hideous findings that it was likely some of the passengers had survived the explosion and died on impact. What could she possibly say in response to such horror?

"I knew I had to become a soldier, to fight back."

"And you did. Marines, like Teague and Rafer?"

He smiled. "No, but I like them anyway. Second Ranger Battalion."

That didn't surprise her; she'd already seen he was a well-trained warrior. "But you left?"

"I quit," he said, his voice so grim it sent a chill through her, "the day they let that son of a bitch go."

"The bomber," she breathed, remembering all the controversy a few years ago about backroom deals, talk of a compassionate release for a dying man with mere months to live, who was alive and apparently quite well years later. "You must have been outraged."

"Beyond. I knew I'd never again really trust the men in charge after that. The injustice destroyed my faith."

Hayley drew back slightly. "That's it, isn't it? That's what you're doing."

"What?" he asked, and again she had that feeling he was testing her somehow, waiting for her answer.

"Injustice. That's why the 'lost causes.' You're doing what should be done but isn't."

He smiled then, so warmly she wondered that she could ever have thought him cold. She felt as if she'd done something wonderful, and she didn't even know what.

"We work for people in the right, who haven't been able to get help anywhere else. Or who can't afford to fight any longer."

The simple words tugged at something deep inside her, reminded her of what it felt like to have a sense of purpose, something she'd lost in her life when her mother died. Something she had missed, without realizing that's what she was missing.

"You mean...you do it for nothing?" she asked.

"The Foxworth Foundation is self-supporting, yes."

"How?" She gestured in the general direction of the building that now housed the sleek black helicopter that had started it all. "This can't be cheap."

"We started out with quite a bit of money from our folks, and we have a genius at investment at the financial helm, somebody who keeps it growing and makes the occasional figurative killing."

"Sounds like a good person to have around."

"She is."

"She?"

"My sister."

She blinked. "Your sister?"

"She was fourteen when they died. We went to live with our only living relative. Mom's brother. We had money our parents had left us, so we weren't a burden, but Uncle Paul wasn't a kid kind of guy. He tried, but it was mostly my sister who raised me."

"Obviously she did a fine job."

He blinked. "I… You…"

For the first time he looked utterly flummoxed, and Hayley took no small pleasure in that.

A sharp knock on the door interrupted her enjoyment.

"All locked down here, sir. Charlie wants reports ASAP, of course, and asked if it was you who needed the vet."

Teague said it with a grin, Quinn reacted with a grimace. "Tell Charlie I appreciate the concern. The reports'll get there when they get there. You guys are clear."

Teague looked from Quinn to Hayley and back. He looked as if he were trying to hide another grin. "What about Hayley?"

"I'll get her home."

"And are you going to—"

"Just leave me a vehicle," Quinn said, an edge creeping into his voice. "Go home. Get some rest. You've all earned it."

When they'd gone, Hayley made no move to get up. Quinn looked at her warily, as if aware he'd dodged the real intent of her first question.

"Where's home for you?" she asked.

"At the moment, St. Louis."

"That's a ways."

"It's central. When we started, we needed that. But now we've got setups like this here—" he gestured around them "—and in three other regions, too. So we can respond more quickly. We'll be putting team leaders in all of them."

She noticed he'd responded with an answer about his work, not his life away from work. If there was such a thing.

"Is that where your sister lives, too, St. Louis?"

"Yes. She's happy there."

"But you're not?"

He shrugged. "I'm more of a cool-weather guy. Humidity kills."

She smiled. "You'd like it here then. Most of the time."

"I do like it here. I was here when the call came in for Vicente."

It felt odd to her, that he had been here in her neck of the woods and she hadn't known. He commanded so much space, it almost seemed to her she would have somehow sensed his presence.

Her mind was racing, absorbing and underneath it all ran a relieved delight, not just that he wasn't the bad guy she'd feared that night, but that he was one of the very good guys, doing work she could respect and admire. Perhaps on some level she'd known it all along.

Why else would she have had the nerve to get in his face all the time?

Which was a good thing, since the vivid, unquenchable memory of his kiss had surged into her mind with undeniable force.

"Quinn," she said, then stopped, uncertain what to say.

She saw by the change in his expression that he'd read her easily.

"Hayley, I'm sorry you got sucked into this. I know now we can trust you to not say anything until the hearings are over and Vicente is safe in his new life."

"Of course," she said, "but that's not—"

"Someone will let you know when that is, in case you miss the news."

She didn't bother to ask how they'd find her number, knowing they probably already had it. "All right, but—"

"You know it was he who insisted you have the run of the cabin, while he stayed hidden. He felt responsible for you getting sucked up into this."

"I know he's a good man. But it's you I—"

"Let's pick up Cutter and get you both back home."

He moved as if he were going to stand up and leave right now.

"Just like that? It's over?" She sucked in a breath and made herself say the one thing she knew he was trying not to hear. "What happened between us—"

"Is impossible, Hayley." The only thing that kept her from being furious was the genuine regret in his voice. "You were caught up in a nightmare situation, you handled it incredibly well, now it's time to go home."

She ignored the compliment. "Why is it impossible?"

"Because it wasn't real, not really. You were scared, in danger, that does strange things to your psyche."

"So I just imagined that meltdown that happens when we kiss?"

His eyes closed. She saw his lips part as he drew in a deep breath. She relished every sign that he wasn't as cool and calm as he tried to appear. Not about this.

"No," he said softly, in the tone of a man who wished he could say otherwise. He could have lied, Hayley thought, but he didn't. Her pulse kicked up another notch.

He opened his eyes and met her gaze. "My life is crazy. I'm always going from place to place. Most times it's routine, but sometimes it's like this was, dangerous. It's not a life anybody would want to share." He shook his head slowly, lowered his gaze, rubbed at his forehead as if weariness was finally catching up with him. "I've tried. It just doesn't work."

"I'm sure it would be difficult. It would take the right person. Somebody who understood why it has to be the way it is."

"I won't ask any woman to put up with it. Not again. And I can't stop doing it."

"No!" It broke from her so loudly it startled even her. "No," she repeated, more normally. "You're doing a great thing, you can't stop."

"Easy to say when you haven't had to live with it. It's time for you to get back to your life."

"I had no life," she said, not realizing until the words came out how true they were. "I was treading water, floundering, since my mom died. Going through the motions. No job to go back to, no work that interested me."

"Applying for a job with us?"

"Would you give me one?"

He grimaced. "I think that might complicate things even more."

"You mean...because of this?"

She leaned in, before he had a chance to pull back, and kissed him. For an instant he stiffened, but so quickly it soothed her nerves and calmed her uncertainty, he responded, making a low sound that thrilled her as his hands came up to her shoulders and pulled her close. The fire that had only been banked flared up fiercer than ever, and this time Hayley let it burn, in fact stoked it as best she knew how, not caring if she looked foolish or inexperienced, risking it all on the certainty that what she was feeling had to be mutual.

Quinn slid back on the sofa, pulling her on top of him. She went, eagerly, kissing him harder, deeper, loving every groan she ripped from him, every tightening of his fingers on her, every arching move of his aroused body against her that proved she was right.

When at last she pulled back he was gasping.

"That," she said unsteadily, "is something else I didn't have in my life. Have never had. Because it's something rare, special."

"I know," he said, looking a little shell-shocked. "I wish—"

"Don't wish. You of all people should know that's for kids."

Something odd flashed in his eyes then. "Yes, I do know."

"Then you should also know this—us—is too special to walk away from."

"I never said I wanted to walk away." He tightened his arms around her. "God, who the hell would want to walk away from *this?*"

"Then don't."

"But—"

"You need to just listen. I want purpose in my life. I lost that for a while, but I've found it again now. I need that kind of goal, to do the right thing. The kind of thing that used to be the rule, not the exception."

His eyes had widened slightly, and he opened his mouth as if to speak. She put a finger on his lips, hushing him.

"You said I was strong, that I handled this better than you ever would have expected. I can handle what you sometimes have to do. I would love to help you in your work. But I need you more. If I can't have both, and I have to choose, I choose you."

"Ah, God, Hayley, you're killing me."

"Don't walk away from this. From us. You're not asking me to put up with it. I'm volunteering."

He reached up and smoothed back a strand of her hair. His mouth quirked. "I meant that literally. If you don't move I may never be able to…show you how much what you said means to me."

She realized suddenly her leg was pressing rather definitely against a very rigid and highly sensitive part of him. She nearly jumped, but he seemed to sense it and grabbed her in time to stop the sudden move that might have made things worse.

"Easy. I have plans for that later."

She was so embarrassed it took her a moment to process the change in him. She lifted her head to look at him, saw in those blue eyes that seemed so readable now the truth of what had just happened. Quinn had given up fighting her.

"Just like that, you surrender?" She wasn't quite sure she believed it, and it echoed in her voice.

"Maybe my heart wasn't really in the fight," he said. "Maybe I wanted to surrender all along."

Hayley's heart began to pound, so hard she marveled he couldn't hear it.

"You're the most amazing woman I've ever met, Hayley Cole. And you're right. What happens between us is too rare to turn my back on. And maybe…maybe you *can* deal with it."

"I dealt with it when I had no idea what the heck was going on. Imagine what I could do if I knew the plan."

That won a smile from him, and Hayley felt it was no small victory.

And then he was kissing her, and all thoughts of plans vanished, leaving only victory and surrender, and the sweetness of sharing both equally.

They were late picking up Cutter, but the dog didn't seem to mind at all.

Quinn woke with the pleasant knowledge that his arm was merely tender, not aching, and the far beyond merely pleasant knowledge that Hayley was curled up against him. The room was pleasantly cool, and the predawn air held the promise of the impending winter. He'd been happy to find she liked to sleep as he did, warm and snug in a cold room.

Oh, and naked. There was that, too. She'd told him she'd had to resort to pajamas when she'd been running to check on her mother at all hours, but now she seemed to have forgotten where she'd put them, and he wasn't about to complain.

He'd never known such unending sweetness. Whether he woke her in the night, hot and needy, or even better, she woke him in the same condition, or they came together in the daylight, in the morning in her big shower, the afternoon on the big couch or the evening in her bed, it was hotter and more imperative than anything he'd ever known, or even known was possible.

He even liked the cuddling afterward. Of course, that'd she'd told him to think of it as foreplay for the next time helped, he thought now with a grin into the faint light of dawn.

"Going to do something with that, or waste it?"

Her sleepy voice was accompanied by a delicious wiggle of her hips against flesh that had been well aware of her closeness long before he'd actually awakened.

"Got any suggestions?" he whispered against her hair.

"I'll think of something."

He laughed, and pulled her closer. And then, so easily, so perfectly, he was sliding into her. A groan of pleasure rippled up from deep in his chest, and he marveled again how it always seemed new, fierce, intense. Deeper, long slow strokes, until she went wild beneath him, driving him wild in turn, until the moment when she cried out his name and sent him spiraling out of control with the clenching of her body.

Much later, when he normally would have been back to sleep, he instead was thinking of the day to come. It had been a quiet, healing, lovely week, enough to tell him that he should seriously consider this as his permanent location. He'd even managed to, temporarily, put the mole out of his mind. But this afternoon he was taking her to St. Louis, to see the headquarters of the foundation. Cutter, back to himself now, feisty and energetic, would be staying with Mrs. Peters and her son for a few days, although Quinn had the idea he'd better start looking into crates for transporting the dog wherever they were going. He wouldn't mind having the dog along on a lot of operations; he'd more than proved his usefulness.

As had Hayley. When the chips were down, she'd come through beautifully. For the first time he was entertaining the idea that maybe he could have it all. That maybe she was right, that in the past, he'd just never found the right person.

He couldn't be sure it would really work, not until they tried. But try they would. Because he did know, deep in his gut, that if it couldn't work with Hayley, it would never work with anyone.

Well, Hayley and Cutter.

Just the thought of the dog made him smile; it seemed to Quinn that Cutter thought he himself had brought them all together on purpose.

And who knows, maybe he had.

Hayley sat up, shoving her hair back, yawning before saying, "Quinn?"

Her voice never failed to make him smile, just because. He lay there and just looked at her, letting it flow over him, that sense of peace he'd never found anywhere else.

"What?"

"Who's Charlie?"

He laughed; she'd repeated the question almost daily since they'd been here.

He answered as he always did.

"You'll see."

And she would. Today. The first day of a future that seemed brighter than anything but her smile.

* * * * *

IF YOU ENJOYED THIS BOOK
WE THINK YOU WILL ALSO LOVE

LOVE INSPIRED SUSPENSE
INSPIRATIONAL ROMANCE

Courage. Danger. Faith.

Find strength and determination in stories
of faith and love in the face of danger.

6 NEW BOOKS AVAILABLE EVERY MONTH!

LISXSERIES2020

SPECIAL EXCERPT FROM

LOVE INSPIRED SUSPENSE
INSPIRATIONAL ROMANCE

*A K-9 officer and a forensics specialist must work
together to solve a murder and stay alive.*

Read on for a sneak preview of
Scene of the Crime *by Sharon Dunn,*
*the next book in the True Blue K-9 Unit: Brooklyn series
available September 2020 from Love Inspired Suspense.*

Brooklyn K-9 Unit Officer Jackson Davison caught
movement out of the corner of his eye: a face in the
trees fading out of view. His heart beat a little faster.
Was someone watching him? The hairs on the back
of Jackson's neck stood at attention as a light breeze
brushed his face. Even as he studied the foliage, he felt
the weight of a gaze on him. The sound of Smokey's
barking brought his mission back into focus.

When he caught up with his partner, the dog was
sitting. The signal that he'd found something. "Good
boy." Jackson tossed out the toy he carried on his belt for
Smokey to play with, his reward for doing his job. The
dog whipped the toy back and forth in his mouth.

"Drop," Jackson said. He picked up the toy and patted
Smokey on the head. "Sit. Stay."

The body, partially covered by branches, was clothed
in neutral colors and would not be easy to spot unless you
were looking for it.

He keyed his radio. "Officer Davison here. I've got a body in Prospect Park. Male Caucasian under the age of forty, about two hundred yards in, just southwest of the Brooklyn Botanic Garden."

Dispatch responded, "Ten-four. Help is on the way."

He studied the trees just in time to catch the face again, barely visible, like a fading mist. He was being watched. "Did you see something?" Jackson shouted. "Did you call this in?"

The person turned and ran, disappearing into the thick brush.

Jackson took off in the direction the runner had gone. As his feet pounded the hard earth, another thought occurred to him. Was this the person who had shot the man in the chest? Sometimes criminals hung around to witness the police response to their handiwork.

His attention was drawn to a garbage can just as an object hit the back of his head with intense force. Pain radiated from the base of his skull. He crumpled to the ground and his world went black.

Don't miss
Scene of the Crime *by Sharon Dunn,*
available wherever Love Inspired Suspense books
and ebooks are sold.

LoveInspired.com

Copyright © 2020 by Harlequin Books S.A.

LISEXP0820

**IF YOU ENJOYED THIS BOOK
WE THINK YOU WILL ALSO LOVE**

HARLEQUIN
INTRIGUE

Seek thrills. Solve crimes. Justice served.

Dive into action-packed stories that will keep you
on the edge of your seat. Solve the crime
and deliver justice at all costs.

6 NEW BOOKS AVAILABLE EVERY MONTH!

HIXSERIES2020

HARLEQUIN

Heartfelt or suspenseful, inspiring or passionate, Harlequin has your happily-ever-after.

With new books published every month, you are sure to find the satisfying escape you know you deserve.

SIGN UP FOR THE HARLEQUIN NEWSLETTER

Be the first to hear about great new reads and exciting offers!

Harlequin.com/newsletters